FALLOUT

BY
TETSUO TAKASHIMA

VERTICAL.

Published by Vertical, Inc., New York

Originally published in Japanese as *Merutodaun* by Kodansha, 2003, and reissued in paperback in 2008.

This is a work of fiction.

ISBN 978-1-934287-15-6

Manufactured in the United States of America

First Edition

Vertical, Inc.
451 Park Avenue South, 7th Floor
New York, NY 10016
www.vertical-inc.com

Table of Contents

Chapter 1
The Letter

November 200X
Barton, California
Ten past noon

Kenji Brian, Associate Editor-in-Chief of *The Daily Californian,* walked across his office and collapsed into his chair. The old wound in his right leg was aching again, so much so that it had been a bother to even get out of bed in the morning. It was more reliable than TV weather reports. Glancing outside, he saw the cars splashing through puddles. It had been raining since early morning—a rarity for California. Californian rain is a thousand times more depressing than rain anywhere else.

"Ken, there's a letter for you. First Class," hollered Susan Miller as she walked into Editorial, a steaming cup of coffee in her hand.

"Yeah, I know."

He'd just come back from interviewing the mayor about the Christmas decorations that were set to go up in three weeks in front of city hall. Normally, the Christmas tree had been a regular ten-foot-high fir with the usual lights, but this year, the mayor had decided the tree was to be cut into the shape of an elephant. This was probably due to the fact that the mayor was a Republican and had the upcoming presidential election in mind. Of course, the Democrats were opposed. Elephants were Republican. Word on the street said the next election was going to be a two-man race between a rattlesnake and a mongoose anyway.

Sitting up and reaching over for the envelope on his desk, Ken noticed there was no return address, just a postmark for San Diego. He opened it and pulled out a single piece of paper with a design on it. A geometric pattern with a religious sensibility. At least, that's what first came to mind. It was a near-circular polygon comprised of fine lines that were symmetrical across both axes. Yet it was a diagram of something. A stamp in the top-right corner said "SS1."

There was no title, the expected indication of scale, or any description of the material. It was just a complex jumble of finely drawn lines which made the diagram seem all the more mysterious. Ken didn't care for anonymous letters. After all, if someone can't step out into the light, what right do they have to say anything? He knew that was a biased way of thinking. But what could he do? That's just the way he felt.

He stared for a while at the diagram. The assemblage of lines clawed at his mind and tugged at his nerves.

The phone rang. As he reached out to pick it up, another hand beat him to it.

"There's been an accident on Mountain Street, at the freeway exit. A tanker burst through a guardrail and smashed into someone's house. Slipped from the rain. It's full of gas and it's in danger of exploding," Bob Campbell, a reporter colleague, explained quickly as he exchanged a look with Ken.

Ken slipped the diagram back in the envelope, tossed it in the tray with the other mail, pulled out his camera and checked it for film. He stood up just as Bob replaced the receiver. For the rest of the day, he hung around the giant metal caterpillar with its head buried in someone's living room, but thankfully the tanker never exploded.

The next day, the news began with a bank robbery in San Francisco by three men who shot and killed two people at the scene. Intel had the robbers escaping in the direction of Barton. The police had set up a checkpoint where the freeway entered the city, with freeway patrol and San Francisco police inspecting cars. For two days, Ken and his colleagues took turns shadowing the operation. On the third day the men were apprehended in a topless bar in New York, and the dragnet was ended. All in all, it had been an unusually eventful week.

President Jefferson is in attendance at the senate committee... Large-scale protest march planned in Washington, D.C.... Until just a month ago the government was planning to thoroughly revise plans to expand the military, yet all of a sudden... Senior Policy Advisor Frank Curley, a moderate, has had a heavy influence on the president... wielded major clout regarding next-generation stealth fighters...

The image on the screen switched to a view of the National Mall in Washington, D.C., commonly called "The Mall."

Advisor Curley's body was found slumped on a bench... that he had been shot in the chest at close range... D.C. police are investigating both lines, homicide and suicide... President Jefferson has expressed his special concern...

The television in the corner of the room was spitting out news bulletins about how a top aide to the president had been found dead from a bullet wound to the chest on a bench near the National Museum of Natural History. The incident, over which the District was in a tizzy, could have a considerable impact on the White House's deliberations over plans for next-gen stealth bombers.

Was it homicide or suicide? The incident capturing attention across the country had occurred far away on the opposite coast of the continent. The realization that *The Daily Californian* was never going to be digging into the story brought a pang of desolation to Ken's heart. He sat up and faced his computer.

Ken Brian, 42 years old. At 5'11" he was tall for a Japanese American. The stubble that covered a third of his face added a touch of maturity to his otherwise boyish face, and the occasional lonesome look and devil-may-care attitude added an air of mystery. The off-balance vibe often drew people's attention, and airport security never failed to give him a thorough body check.

After an hour spent glued to the display, he closed the file. He'd completed his column for the Sunday paper. He reached for the stack of letters to the editor in his tray. In the middle was that envelope.

In the anonymous envelope was the paper with a diagram. It was a beautiful geometric pattern with a number of complex elements laid out in point symmetry framed by a dodecagon. Ken recalled it from several days ago. After gazing at the paper for a while he turned it over. There was a website address alongside a seven-digit combination of numbers and letters.

He reached for his keyboard, but then stopped. Something went off in his subconscious. He didn't want to believe in premonitions, but such inklings certainly had been there when he thought back after significant events. It was similar to the way the felt the instant he reached for a glass full of amber liquid while sitting at a bar. Something welled up from deep in his soul—a kind of anxiety, compounded by a temptation that surpassed it. It was that odd force that had caused Ken's fingers to hesitate. He looked at the diagram once more and set it down on the fax machine. Ken was about to push the SEND button, but stopped again. That force again. He decided to scan it to his computer and send it by email.

He picked up the phone and dialed.

"University of California, Lawrence Livermore National Laboratory," said a voice in a curt, metallic tone. It was Albert, who worked in the same lab as Yamada. Ken had met Albert a couple of times and remembered his frameless glasses and neurotic appearance. Both Yamada and Albert were doctors of science who'd obtained their degrees from one of the nation's best-known institutes of technology. Five minutes and a number of transfers to other extensions later, Yamada finally picked up.

"So, how's Ann?" Yamada always asked after Ken's partner.

"She's back at her parents' place in Salt Lake City."

They exchanged news for a few minutes. The two of them had been roommates for a year at a college on the East Coast over ten years ago. Yamada had been an exchange student from Japan, but the two of them had a lot more in common than just Japanese ancestry. Ken had spent four years in that town before returning to Barton. Then two years later, Yamada finished his master's degree and joined the atomic energy research lab in California.

"So what can I do to help you?" Even after fifteen years in the U.S., Yamada's English was still a little awkward and peppered with stiff, hackneyed expressions that sounded like they'd been lifted straight out of a grammar book.

"There's something I want you to investigate."

"Can it not be handled by your paper?"

"Well, first I want to find out if it's something the paper *can* handle."

"Send me a fax."

"I just sent it by email."

"Is it something you want to keep from other's eyes?"

"Take a look at the file."

Ken heard a chair moving, the phone receiver being set down on a desktop, the tapping of keys, then quiet. The silence dragged on.

"What is this diagram?"

"That's my line." Another silence followed. "Would you know?"

"I'll call you later." Yamada hung up.

Ken propped his feet onto the desk and looked around. Editorial was on the second floor of a shabby old building. All the reporters were out and only the two student part-timers were left in the office.

The Daily Californian had a circulation of 42,000, made up of readers across California, but concentrated around Barton. The paper had been in business for over twenty years reporting on crimes, industries, personages and traditions in and around Barton. It also provided a forum where locals could exchange ideas and featured coverage with a regional emphasis. Although nobody ever talked openly about it, everyone in the office knew this humble regional paper's survival and steady circulation were the fruits of Editor-in-Chief Charles Brown's efforts. With his sober approach, he'd managed to secure a steady subscriber base by holding back the owner, Steve Austin, who tended to be reckless and had a love for all things flashy.

The antique clock on the wall showed two o'clock. Someone or other should be returning soon. Ken looked at the diagram once more before putting it back in the envelope.

The helicopter shot up rapidly. Horrid clangs of machine gun bullets strafing against the fuselage mixed with the roar of the rotor. Without thinking, he tried to get up and let it pass, but his body didn't respond. Vibrations coupled with the sounds, growing louder and creeping closer.

By the time he realized the noise was his phone, it had already been ringing for a while. He was cold, damp from icy sweat.

After calling Yamada the day before, Ken had finished his article about the city hall Christmas decorations. The mayor had caved in to the citizens' fierce protests and switched from an elephant to a dolphin and its calf. Ken had left the office and stopped off for a drink at a bar. He ended up closing the bar at 2:00 a.m. Or at least he assumed as much, since he couldn't remember anything after the first hour.

Typical. He checked his clothes for damage and his body for cuts and bruises; since he'd woken up in a bed, he concluded that he must have sat there drinking quietly until closing. Every December, Japanese Americans became the enemy of patriots all around the country. The ghost of Pearl Harbor still wandered this country. Ken fumbled for the receiver, dropping it.

"Are you still sleeping or still drinking?" came Yamada's voice from the phone as Ken managed to scoop the receiver up to his ear.

Ken bit back an impulse to curse at his aching leg and craned his neck to read the clock. 9:00 a.m.

"I'm coming over," Yamada said, his voice suddenly a whisper.

"Can't we discuss it over the phone?"

"No. Especially as I am a foreigner in this country."

"What do you mean?"

"Just what I said." It was the first time Yamada had spoken so bluntly.

"I've got to do an interview at a nursing home this morning. The grandmas are going on hunger strike until they get free condoms."

"It will take me until noon to get there. I'll call you when I arrive. Keep your cell phone on."

Ken crawled back under the covers. That very moment, the shrill alarm stabbed his brain. He hurled the clock to the opposite end of his bed and pulled the covers back over his head.

The atomic lab was about an hour away from Barton by car, but knowing Yamada it would take two. He never went over the speed limit and slowed down whenever he saw a stoplight in the distance, which always made Ken want to slam his foot on the gas for him.

At ten to noon, Ken's phone rang as he drank a beer and carried out the interview at the nursing home. Quickly wrapping up the interview, he headed for the cafeteria where they'd agreed to meet. Yamada was sitting toward the back, waving. He wore a navy sweater and a tie. His black-rimmed glasses were settled on his overly serious face and he had an I'm-going-to-memorize-all-the-data-in-the-world look about him. His hairline had receded and his broad forehead reflected the light, making him look more like an accountant for some mob outfit rather than the scientist he was. To his side was a bright red down jacket—a present from Ken and Ann last Christmas.

Ken took the seat in front of Yamada and covered his mouth to stifle a burp. Yamada frowned.

"Do I smell?"

"I thought a liquor bottle had walked over."

"You Japanese have a way with words."

Yamada shrugged. *You're Japanese, too,* he probably wanted to say, but Ken had never considered himself Japanese. He didn't know what it meant to feel Japanese in the first place.

"It's been three months. Last time I saw you, we'd paid a visit to

Disneyland together," said Ken. "For Christmas why don't you, Ann and I go to Palm Springs—"

"About that diagram…" Yamada interrupted, leaning forward. He looked nervous. A waitress appeared at the table, and Yamada straightened up and ordered another coffee. After confirming that the waitress was gone, Yamada put a sheet of paper on the table. It was a printout of the diagram Ken had sent Yamada the day before. Ken reached for it but Yamada stopped his hand.

"Where did you get this?"

"It was sent to the paper, addressed to me. First Class. It was postmarked San Diego."

Yamada cast his gaze down, deep in thought.

"What is it? A blueprint of a bread machine? A UFO?"

"It's a nuclear bomb." Yamada raised his eyes to meet Ken's.

"A nuclear bomb?" Ken parroted.

"Yes, a nuclear bomb. What's more, it's not the conventional atomic or hydrogen bomb. It seems to be a new type."

"You showed it to someone?"

"To Albert, in my lab. He was at Oak Ridge until two years ago. He was involved in researching high-power lasers and had access to the military's confidential documents. He was surprised to see this diagram. Apparently it's categorized as top secret. Top top-secret." He pointed to the stamp that said "SS1" on the edge of the diagram.

"Are you sure?"

"That's why I came all the way here." Yamada sat back in his seat and shook his head slowly a few times.

"I didn't know there were any secrets left for nuclear bombs."

Yamada looked at Ken and sighed.

"I thought all you needed was enriched uranium or plutonium."

"If that was true, all countries would have nuclear weapons. It's true that the basic idea is introduced even in high school textbooks. Or you can buy *The Los Alamos Primer* outlining the mathematical basics of atomic bombs for $2.60 at the Atomic Energy Commission. Or for $4 you can buy *The Los Alamos Project* at the Technology Administration in the Department of Commerce. Both outline the technological issues faced by scientists at the initial stages of atomic bomb production. Forty years ago, spies from around the world were trying to get their hands on this information, sometimes in exchange for their lives. Now it's cheaper and easier to get than a comic book. Still, there is no limit to technological know-how."

"So what should I do with it?"

"Tear it up and burn it. Erase it from your memory." Yamada fixed Ken with a steady gaze. Ken had never seen him with such serious eyes.

The coffee arrived and Ken took a flask of whiskey from his coat pocket and poured a little into the coffee. The smell of alcohol filled the air and a middle-aged woman sitting nearby scowled at them. Yamada sighed. Ken ignored this and downed half his coffee at once. The warmth of the coffee and a heat of another kind, several times stronger, slowly spread across his body.

The two sat chatting for about an hour. When Yamada got up to leave, he looked into Ken's eyes.

"Throw it away, immediately," he said in a low voice, shredding the paper and stuffing it into Ken's breast pocket. Then he tapped Ken's coat pocket. "Here, too."

When Ken returned to the office, Susan was the only one left, minding the phone.

"You've been drinking." Susan waved her hand in front of her nose with a look of boredom.

"Yeah. Coffee."

"You'll get a taste of Charlie's shoe leather if he finds out." She frowned at him, took out her compact and carefully fixed her lipstick. She stood up, handbag in hand, and said, "Watch the phones for me."

"Going on a date?"

"Silly. Work, of course."

"Be back by late afternoon."

When Ken sat at his desk by the window, he felt all his strength draining from him. He propped up his feet and looked out onto the street. People and cars were coming and going; a typical provincial West Coast winter scene. He felt a tar-like stickiness spread through his body. It was a sensation that had been growing lately. He knew the cause. He took the flask from his pocket and poured the contents down his throat.

At first he'd had strict rules for himself. Never carry around a pocket-sized flask, no day drinking, no drinking at work. The only rule that had narrowly survived was the one about not drinking in the office when others were around, and he wasn't sure how long he could make that one last. It was just like Ann had said: there was someone else inside of him.

Ken pulled out the envelope from his desk and took out the diagram, stared at it for a while and flipped it over. He ran his eyes over the URL and password. He turned to his computer and switched it on, then typed the URL into his browser. A website appeared in the window. Clicking to one of the pages, Ken carefully typed in the password. The screen blinked and fine dots of lights appeared. The salutations from a long letter addressed to him came onto the screen.

Mr. Kenji Brian,

Thank you.

I believe you are aware that an article entitled "The Secret of Hydrogen Bomb Production" was supposed to be published three months ago in the August edition of Knowledgment. *The article was written by a freelance journalist who based his article on government records publicly available at the Los Alamos National Laboratory library. Right before publication, however, the Department of Justice ordered the article suspended.*

Following this incident there was expected to be a trial concerning the freedom of the press and protection of confidential government information, but the publisher withdrew its charges at the last minute. Half a year ago, a similar incident happened with The Daily Washington *in our capital. There must have been unfathomably strong political pressure and bargaining behind both these incidents.*

Ken read through the letter. Unconsciously, he'd cast his flask aside as he devoured the words on the screen. Each electronically displayed word wriggled its way into his brain cells as if trying to recover something buried so deep he'd nearly forgotten it. He felt the core of his body heating up. It was like that something called spirit that had snapped in him at some point.

After finishing my master's degree in physics at the University of California in 1940 I moved to Maryland State University and continued my research in nuclear physics. Collegiate-level nuclear physics research at the time was on a scale so small it would be hard to imagine in the present day. Atomic power itself hadn't even been properly defined and everything was still vague and theoretical. For someone like me, who specialized in carrying out experiments, experience and funding were hard to come by. You could say it was an extremely unfortunate time to be in the field. However, it was then that I had the biggest break in my life.

I was able to participate in the Manhattan Project launched in 1942. This was the A-bomb production scheme ordered by President Roosevelt on the advice of Dr. Einstein, who was concerned about the German development of an atomic bomb. The president allocated two billion dollars for the project, established the Los Alamos National Laboratory as the core and two large factories in Tennessee and Washington State and procured 540,000 staff members. Distinguished scientists were gathered, not just from the U.S. but also the U.K. and Canada, to work at a lab in the middle of a desert in New Mexico. Einstein, Szilárd and Wigner, who had escaped from Germany, were also involved. The project was undertaken in near-airtight secrecy.

We young scientists, told only that it was a top-secret project to save the world from the advancing Nazis, were brought in with only the clothes on our backs. We went for months without being able to contact our families. The laboratory was surrounded by dozens of miles of barbed wire, and guards with German Shepherds patrolled the grounds. The road leading to the laboratory had many checkpoints, and even we scientists had to go through heavy security clearance to get inside.

As scientists, we quickly realized what it was that we were researching, though nobody ever put it into words. That was because the lab was paradise for a scientist. We had virtually unlimited funding, the very best equipment and, above all, direct contact with the best brains in the world and the opportunity to learn from them. For the fearless young scientist, everything about the laboratory gave the sense of having powers that surpassed even God Himself. We gave everything we had to the research. Perhaps we were overconfident; it was as if we'd trampled over God and sold our soul to the Devil. And in the end, we built a weapon from hell.

Ken finished reading the letter and settled his chin on his folded hands to think. He reread the last words on the monitor.

I pray that you will find my life of some interest. I will be waiting to hear from you.

> *Yours sincerely,*
> *Dr. James Williams*

At long last, Ken lifted his head slowly, reached for the phone and dialed the number on the back of the diagram.

A calm voice stated, "This is Naval Medical Center San Diego."

The next afternoon, Ken was on an airplane headed for San Diego. He took out from his pocket the letter he'd printed out the night before and absently scanned his eyes across the words. He'd read it many times already, but the vivid message still struck something in his soul.

Dr. James Williams' email. The excitement he'd felt when he first read it hadn't dissipated. He didn't hesitate to ask for a day off as soon as the editor-in-chief, Charles Brown, returned to the office. He drove to San Francisco airport that morning with a fire in his heart he hadn't felt in years. After a two-hour wait, he boarded a plane. By past four in the afternoon, Ken was standing in front of the medical center.

The chalk-white five-story building was situated in the outskirts of San Diego on a small hill overlooking the ocean. Simple, elegant and clean, it was far from Ken's memories of the Marine Corps and his image of a military hospital. The hospital Ken had been committed to in Haiti had had the latest equipment, but it was still clearly nothing more than a field hospital. Its compounds, roasted by an island sun and surrounded by tropical plants, were full of soldiers who'd had their legs and arms torn off, internal organs ruptured or psyches damaged. It was a place smothered by the sticky smell of death and blood and Ken had spent three long months there.

In October 1983, President Reagan had sent 2,000 marines to Grenada, a Caribbean island with a population of 110,000. The purpose had been to protect a thousand or so Americans living in Grenada, given that an anti-American coup d'etat had erupted. The marines were told the operation would involve little danger, but Ken's rescue helicopter had been attacked over the capital, St. George's, and forced into an emergency landing in the middle of enemy territory. Over the next few days, the Americans toppled the pro-Soviet military regime and declared the mission over but had suffered more than a few casualties.

The hospital for sick and wounded soldiers in Washington where Ken was sent after Haiti was even worse. Dozens of beds were lined up, enveloping madness in silence. The smell of excrement and disinfectant. Apathy and despair. Wheelchairs and crutches made dry, scraping sounds as patients moved about. The place was completely devoid of hope.

Ken had spent half a year there before returning to his hometown of Barton. But what had the conflict been for? After that mission, other Latin American countries became increasingly wary of the threat of U.S. intervention in their affairs, and many began gathering votes to pass a bill through an emergency session of the U.N. Security Council to call for the immediate cessation of armed intervention. The U.S., however, used its veto power and maintained a hardline stance.

Wounded veteran. Half the joint in Ken's right leg was made of a special plastic prosthetic. The only lasting effect was that he dragged his foot slightly. The damage to his mind was orders of magnitude greater. Further…

When he recovered, Ken returned to his university on the East Coast and graduated in two years. After living on the East Coast for a while, he moved back to Barton and got a job at the newspaper. Back then he was still trying to find some ray of hope for his future, but within a few years he'd become a full-blown alcoholic. He'd managed to keep working mostly due to inertia, but he'd never felt anything resembling hope. At least, not until several hours ago when he'd read the letter from Dr. Williams.

As he stood outside the hotel-like hospital, he took the whiskey flask from his pocket. He was about to twist off the cap, but stopped. He hesitated for a moment, then put the flask back in his pocket. His heart was pounding. He took a deep breath and moved towards the sliding doors.

The spacious lobby didn't smack of a hospital, either. A high ceiling, evenly positioned sofas and chairs, ornamental plants. Everything was lovely and in perfect functional harmony. Only the nurse in a white uniform pushing a wheelchair reminded Ken that the lobby, reminiscent of a hotel, indeed belonged to a hospital. He walked up to the front desk and asked for Dr. Williams.

"Do you have an appointment?" the thirtyish man sitting upright at the desk asked politely.

"Please tell him that Kenji Brian from *The Daily Californian* is here."

The man turned to his computer and pressed some keys. "Mr. Kenji Brian," he said without looking away from the screen. "I have a message here requesting that I call his room. Hold on a moment please." He picked up the phone and exchanged a few words. "Room 567, last one on the fifth floor. Please use the elevators over there," he said, indicating the other side of the lobby with his eyes.

A wide and bright hallway stretched out before Ken as he stepped out of the elevator. When he reached the door, he stopped, took a deep breath, then knocked. No response.

"Come in," came a monotonous voice just as he was raising his fist to knock again.

Ken opened the door and squinted into the dim space. Thick curtains were drawn over the windows, and the illumination from behind him just barely lighted the interior. After a moment, his eyes adjusted to find a room fifteen feet wide and long with a bed and a TV. There was a desk by the window with a computer on it, and Ken could make out the faint hum of an air conditioner.

"Do you mind flipping the switch on the wall?" said a husky old voice.

Ken flipped the switch, bathing the room in bright light. An old man in a wheelchair sat looking at Ken.

"Dr. James Williams…" said Ken in a low voice.

The old man kept his eyes on Ken and nodded quietly. There was yellow sleep in the corner of his eyes, he was holding a portable oxygen mask and on the pillar behind his wheelchair hung an IV bag.

"Please sit down." Williams indicated the chair by the desk with his eyes and Ken pulled the chair over and sat down.

He looked again at Williams. The broad-shouldered old man in a yellow yarn hat who returned his gaze had a pointy nose, thin lips and largish ears. A rough sharpness stood out as if his face was a thin layer of meat pressed onto the skull. His exposed skin was dry and looked like it had thin brown paper pasted onto it. Ken couldn't discern the finer points of the man's expression, but he could sense both the loneliness and the obstinate willpower of an old man.

"Sorry for my appearance. The anti-cancer drugs and radiation therapy haven't been kind to me." The old man took off his yarn hat, showing the same flat, blotchy skin that marked his face. For an instant, Williams' image wavered in Ken's mind, strangely vivid, as if he was seeing a man with all his internal organs exposed.

"So I got your letter and the diagram," said Ken.

Williams' oxygen mask was shaking in his trembling hands. "And, what do you make of it?" His face contorted and his body doubled over as he gave a pinched, rasping breath. Ken stood up to help, but Williams lifted his hand to stop him. He brought the mask back to his mouth and took several deep breaths of oxygen. Once his breathing stabilized he looked up towards Ken, mask still on his face.

"I should have come sooner," Ken apologized.

"I was about to give up if I hadn't heard from you by tomorrow." Williams looked relieved.

"I'm terribly sorry. I've been snowed under. We get a lot of letters every day at the newspaper. It takes some courage to glean the truths and to decide whether or not to share them with the public."

"And what do you think about mine?"

"I believe it is true and I've decided it should be communicated to our readers. That's why I'm here. I would like to publish your life story in the form of a serialized memoir."

Williams closed his eyes quietly and didn't move for a while. Long moments passed. He finally stood up, straining the IV, which pulled out of his arm. Ken rushed over to help, but the man ignored him and instead stepped toward the window. Clutching at the curtains, he opened them to let in the southern California sunshine, bright and strong. Ken squinted. The shining ocean stretched out in the distance.

Toy-like ships were floating in San Diego bay. The old man's face was flushed and tears were glimmering in his deep-set eyes. Something hot seemed to flood Ken. Williams tottered, but again he refused Ken's help, with a shake of his head.

"My feelings are as I wrote in the letter," the old man said, his voice faltering. He took several deep breaths, regaining control of his breathing. When he spoke again, his voice was quiet. "The fire of my life is about to burn out now. It would be a lie if I said I have nothing to regret. Watching that all-too-bright ocean while waiting here to die, at times I almost went crazy, wondering what the purpose of my life had been…"

Ken traced the old man's profile with his gaze. Williams' parched, blotched skin suggested that there was no hope of ever healing.

"Why did you send that diagram to me? Why not someone else?"

The old man slowly turned towards Ken. "I read your report on Native Americans."

"I wrote that fully three years ago."

Ken had published a series called "The Dying Americans" once a week for three months. It was a report based on two years' research of Native Americans in California and its environs. It had been nothing glamorous, but it gave Ken the sense of writing a real article for the first time since joining the newspaper. The series was halted, however, because the owner, Steve Austin, preferred not to irritate conservatives. Perhaps that was one of the things that had driven Ken deeper into the bottle.

"I think it was about six months ago. My legs still worked well enough to get me around, and I was looking at Barton's newspapers at the public library when I happened to read it. I lived in Barton until high school. I consider it my heart's home." The old man gently closed his eyes as though trying to retrieve something from memory. "I was deeply moved by that report. I've read several histories of America written from a Native American standpoint, but yours was different from any of them. It overflowed with a bigger anger, something like the perspective of the discriminated. 'The Last Americans' and 'The Great Earth' were also good. Americans should remember their roots, regain the humility of our ancestors who crossed the ocean, landing on this land for the first time, and give thanks to God."

"I was just writing the truth."

"Sometimes that can be difficult. Your report conveyed a suffering that goes beyond the simple truth."

"Maybe I was able to write it because I'm Japanese American."

The term that he'd obsessed over and rarely uttered sounded nearly natural.

"Well, I'm Jewish." Williams looked at Ken with a burning intensity in his eyes, then turned away to the view outside the window. The sun hung above the horizon and the blood-red ocean glinted. It reminded Ken of the sun in Grenada. Blood-soaked, he'd watched the sunset cast its red light over the Caribbean islands from a stiff stretcher inside the rescue helicopter. In his fading consciousness, the red color had filled his vision. He was twenty-one at the time. He wondered what he had been thinking about at that moment. Had he thought about his comrades who had died, or about himself having faced death?

Williams moved over to the desk as if he'd just remembered something. "This is what I wrote during the last year about myself and the research I did throughout my career. Use it as you see fit." He pulled a thick envelope from the drawer and handed it to Ken, who hesitated to receive it.

"You don't know anything about me," said Ken, looking at the old man. "I was in rehab for two months. Alcohol. I just got out a month and a half ago. I was in there before that for a couple of months about a year and a half ago as well. My body and mind are—"

"I'm interested in the journalist who wrote that reportage. And you are that person."

Journalist. The ring seeped deep into Ken's mind. How many years had it been since he'd felt that word with any sincerity?

"I came to believe that the journalist who wrote that was an honest man with strong convictions. That's why I sent you the blueprint and wrote you the letter," the old man repeated, softly placing the envelope in Ken's hands.

"I want to help," Ken said, squeezing the old man's hand. Its palm was dry and devoid of muscle. It was like touching bone. Ken held this hand that lacked the strength to grip as if he were cradling the man's heart.

Suddenly, the door opened and a cheerful voice piped up, "Okay, doctor, it's time to take your temperature. Do you want to go pee first?"

Ken turned around to find a young nurse standing in the doorway with a look of shock on her face.

"Sorry, I didn't realize you had a visitor." She stared at Ken without moving for a few seconds before recovering her liveliness. This nurse was like a bouncing rubber ball. "I'm Emmy. Emmy Jones," she said, flashing Ken a smile, lowering the bed and signaling for Williams to lie down.

"Isn't this hat nice? It was a present from me," she said, fussing over Williams like he was a child.

"Yes. Yellow cap. That's my password." Williams followed the nurse's instructions and lay down. She placed a thermometer in his mouth and took his pulse, chattering cheerfully all the while. Ken remained by the window, watching them. A short lock of blond hair peeked out from the side of Emmy's nurse's cap.

"I'm sorry, but visiting hours are over. The doctor will be here in ten minutes," she said, glancing at her watch.

Williams was quiet and his eyes were closed, with what seemed to be a tear running from the corner of one eye. Ken bid Williams goodbye and left the room with Emmy.

"I've never seen him look so cheerful. Everyone calls him Dr. Cool," explained Emmy as they walked toward the elevator.

"How does he spend his time?"

"He either sits still with the curtains drawn or is at his computer writing something. Other than that, he just lies on his side with his eyes shut. Sometimes you wonder if he's dead. I hear he was a great scientist, but I just feel sorry for him."

"Why?"

"Well, he's been with us nearly a year, but you're his first visitor."

When they reached the lobby on the first floor, Emmy waved goodbye and started walking away. Then she stopped in her steps, turned and came back.

"I think it was about a week ago. In the late afternoon, I went to take his temperature and pulse. He was crying, looking at the ocean. He kept on crying while I took his temperature, and there seemed to be nothing

I could say to cheer him up. So in the end, I let him be and went home. But when I returned the next morning, he hadn't budged and was still crying. I couldn't believe tears could last that long. I got worried and called a doctor, but by the time we arrived he was back in bed with his eyes closed. The doctor lost confidence in me, you know. In any case, he's truly a sad old man. So please come visit sometimes, okay?" And with that Emmy turned and hurried off to the nurse's station.

Ken stayed in a motel near the airport that night. Train whistles sounded in the distance. In the wee hours, a young Mexican couple next door started screaming at each other.

Lying in bed, Ken thought about Williams and the article to be written. He felt his pulse quicken. Wanting to leave a mark on the world was something that Ken could strongly identify with. The image of the lonesome old man staring into the sunset stuck in his mind.

His throat was parched, but it wasn't whiskey it was aching for. He got up and held his mouth to the faucet to gulp down the gushing water.

As daylight came he fell asleep for just a couple of hours. He caught the first flight to San Francisco and was in Barton before noon.

When he returned to the office he suggested an editorial meeting to Charlie, who countered with a suspicious look, raising his brows. It was the first time Ken had asked for a meeting. They convened a little after six, just after the morning edition's articles had been submitted. Editorial included Charlie, the editor-in-chief; Ken, who doubled as associate editor-in-chief and reporter; and Jimmy, Bob and Susan, staff writers. There were also four editorial assistants.

They all took their seats in the conference room while Susan switched off the air conditioning and opened the window. The daytime heat had vanished without a trace, and a breeze from the ocean brought in a refreshing coolness. For the past few days it had been almost like summer around noon. Bob mumbled to himself about what a crazy winter it was.

"If this diagram is the real deal and contains real nuclear secrets, then the government isn't going to just keep quiet. They'll take measures, not just against the writer but our paper. Having said that, I think it's something we have a duty to publish." Ken stood in front of the group and explained the gist of the diagram and the letter.

"Have you been imbibing again? It's interesting, but it's not something we should be discussing over drinks," said Susan, nonchalantly checking her nail polish. No one seemed to be on board.

"So exactly how does society benefit by us publishing this?" asked

Jimmy Tokida in a shrill voice. "I don't think there's anything here that our readers need to know."

Everyone's eyes turned to Jimmy. He was 32 years old. It was rare for this third-generation Japanese American to speak up in any meeting. Usually he'd just sit there, his small body hunched over, nodding along with spaced-out eyes. But today was different. He stared at Ken and his high-pitched voice cracked, perhaps with agitation.

"In our society, there's no such thing as a truth that no one needs to know. This is not the Soviet Union twenty years ago or China. It's not Iraq or North Korea. It's the United States of America. We have an obligation to publish this essay to support freedom of thought, and of speech."

"As the press, we have a duty to publish responsibly, too. What's the point of publishing a blueprint for a nuclear bomb?"

"This was supposed to be a top government secret, but already it's been leaked to several people. So it's not a secret anymore. The government is merely trying to restrict our freedom of speech by saying it's classified. I believe we need to expose that fact."

"I disagree," said Jimmy. "Treating plans for a nuclear bomb so lightly is the real problem." Jimmy was being unusually persistent. His typically mild-mannered and unexpressive eyes were red with excitement and his voice trembled. His distinctly Japanese round face was slightly flushed. Somehow this made Ken feel intense irritation and frustration.

"It seems I've erred." Ken stood up, looking at all the reporters in turn. "I should have introduced this letter first. It contains not only the author's name, but details of his position as well. I think you'll all understand the impact it would have if it was made public." He slowly sat down and retrieved the letter from the envelope.

Someone was tapping a pencil, and the sound felt incredibly loud. Ken started reading the letter that took up three A4-size pages.

July 16, 1945
The sun had yet to appear over the horizon, but the desolate rocks of the desert already absorbed the rays of morning and shone faintly red. We were at Campaña Hill, twenty miles from Ground Zero, where the atomic bomb had been set, waiting for a certain moment. The atomic bomb installed on a 100-foot steel tower was just a dot in the desert.

It was two minutes to detonation. A siren echoed and the countdown began. The leaders who executed the largest project in history, M Project commanding general Major General Groves, Dr. Oppenheimer, Professor Fermi and others, and the rest of us put on the navy-blue sunglasses we'd prepared.

5:30 a.m. We all shuddered in anticipation of a great atomic explosion, the first in the history of mankind. It was truly the dawn of a new era. I know all too well that it's arrogant to use such an expression, but I'll never forget that excitement.

A fireball one mile across was climbing slowly, powerfully, up to a height of 40,000 feet. This was, beyond a doubt, the defining moment in which man had broken through the order of the atom. The sun quietly appeared over the horizon as if to bless this giant ball of flame. To me, it looked like two creations, one by the hand of God and one by the hands of man, had united to ascend the heavens.

Four years after that, in 1949, the Soviet Union also had a successful atomic test. We'd stepped into God's realm and never thought to stop. We poured all our efforts into creating a hydrogen bomb that could destroy the whole earth and turn it into a planet of death. In 1952, we at last succeeded in an experiment at Enewetak, a solitary isle in the South Pacific. The next year the Soviet Union followed suit. Fortunately, I must say, if this old man's soul were to know any solace, these nuclear weapons were used only in Hiroshima and Nagasaki. Those two detonations caused us to realize that the weapons held a power too great for mankind.

But think about the foolish race between the champions of the Eastern and the Western blocs that followed. Armed diplomacy was conducted in the name of peace through nuclear deterrence, the world at the mercy of superpowers, or rather their handfuls of people in power. It finally came to an end when the Soviet Union fell and the world took its first steps towards nuclear arms reduction.

From now on, nuclear weapons will slowly be dismantled and eventually disappear. I am relieved, but I also feel a despondency bordering on despair. What was the point of my eighty-odd years of life? For what purpose had I continued the research? These are the questions I now pose to myself.

Here Ken deeply exhaled. The room was as still as death. The room echoed with Ken's voice as he continued to read the letter.

A year ago, I was diagnosed at a naval hospital with a fatal illness and was told that I had a year to live. I don't hold my life dear. If anything, when considering the hundreds of thousands of lives I helped steal and the everlasting *terror our work introduced to all of mankind, my life is worthless.*

As I stand here staring at death's shadow and look back on my life, I wonder whether we scientists did the right thing. As a human, as a resident of Mother Earth, I cannot say that we did. Under the guise of national interest and security, we scientists had become drunk on intellectual stimulation and treated the number dead as simply data relating to the weapons. Were we secretly satisfied with its magnitude? Secretly proud when we saw the world shriveling back in fear of our foolish nuclear power? Such doubts constantly tug at my heart.

As I lie on my deathbed, I feel I have a duty. The M Project and all the research that followed was conducted under the utmost secrecy, and most of the discoveries have been kept sealed tight. Ever since learning I had a year left to live, I've spent all my time organizing the information I've stored in my head over dozens of years and the few documents I could lay my hands on over the years. Then finally, a few days ago, I finished writing a paper and a record of my life. I believe they will solve more mysteries about the nuclear project than what Knowledgment *had planned.*

There is no doubt that giving these documents to an outsider is a major betrayal of my country, but my conscience pains me when I think that these secrets will die with me, buried under the veil of government confidentiality. I believe it is my final task and duty to provide true knowledge about nuclear weapons so that our citizens themselves can decide our direction for the future.

If you contact me, I will provide the paper and the record to you. It is up to you to decide how to handle them. Whatever happens, I am not likely to leave this bed again. Please do what you think best with the paper and record.

Dr. James Williams

Ken gently set the letter on the table. Nobody was tapping a pencil anymore. Everyone exhaled, and their breaths seemed to flow in one direction.

Susan's voice broke the silence. "I see why it was too heavy to take sober." When Bob glared at her, she returned his look with a shrug, fished out a cigarette and put it in her mouth.

"I'm still not satisfied," said Jimmy, rising. Everyone turned to look at him. "I mean, why disclose it now? It's meaningless."

"It was sent to us. That's why we make it public. It's our responsibility. What's the problem?"

"Making it public," Jimmy spat back, unable to control his agitation which turned his ruddy face pale. "There are things the world needs and others it doesn't, so—"

"Do you have proof to back this stuff up?" Charlie asked, cutting Jimmy off and fixing his sleepy eyes on Ken. His nickname in the office was "Charlie Boots" because his peeling leather boots looked like they were part of his body.

"This diagram is the proof. According to an ex-Oak Ridge National Laboratory scientist it's top secret." Ken planted his hands on the table and looked around at Jimmy and the other reporters as if to intimidate them. "It'll draw a reaction, that's for sure. Some will laud us, others will lambast us. But just as readers have the right to know, we have the responsibility to report."

"The First Amendment," said Susan, holding the unlit cigarette that was still in her mouth.

"Regardless of possible government opposition, we should publish this. I also want to introduce our readers to the author's life journey," declared Ken with determination.

"Looks like we've got the next Pulitzer Prize winner here," teased Susan, clapping her hands slowly. Bob poked her with his pen and told her to shut up.

After the meeting, Jimmy sidled over to Ken. "Could I look at Dr. Williams' letter again?"

Ken handed it over without a word and Jimmy read it with eyes more serious than Ken had ever seen on him.

Two mornings later, across papers all over the country, the headlines danced:

Daily Californian Publishing Nuclear Bomb Secrets?

DOJ vs. Freedom of Speech Battle Inevitable

Conflicted Nuclear Scientist Reveals Hidden Los Alamos

"The man on the bench was sitting with his head hanging. His arms were crossed in front of his stomach, and he was slumped over, his eyes shut, like someone who'd fallen asleep in front of the TV."

"You didn't think he was dead?"

"No. I didn't take much notice, I just passed by. He only caught my attention because he was still there when I came back on my way home. I walked over and asked if everything was all right, but he didn't respond in any way whatsoever. I thought he was asleep. I ought to have just gone on my way, but I saw that he wasn't wearing any shoes. I thought he must have passed out drunk and someone had stolen them. That's when I shook him by the shoulder."

"Didn't you notice the blood? There was so much. The front of his jacket was soaked through."

"It was dark, and his arms were laid across his stomach. I pushed back his forehead to try and see his face. Suddenly he toppled over, and I realized he was dead."

"And that was 5:03 in the morning."

"I looked at my watch right away. Right when I figured I'd need to tell a cop, I saw a police car, so I yelled for help."

"Did you hear any noises? Voices? Arguing? A gunshot?"

"No, nothing."

Warren stopped typing and rested his hands.

He was trying to give a feel of the scene, but it ended up sounding like a novel. He was trying to recreate the statement of the first witness as shown to him by John Morse, his friend at the MPDC. It had been made clear that he shouldn't take notes; Warren was working from his memory of the document on the table in the interrogation room. He had padded the account in a way that wouldn't elicit objections, but it was still accurate. In the end, though, it wasn't appropriate in a newspaper article.

3:10 p.m.

The editorial department of the *Washington Post* headquarters was abuzz. The vast floor was filled with all kinds of noise: keyboards tapping, phone conversations, printers, the CNN broadcaster's rapid-fire delivery of the news from a television in the corner.

Warren McCarthy, age 34, a reporter with *The Washington Post*'s political desk, had spent his seven years at the paper covering the White House and Capitol Hill. He'd watched the center of American politics, in other words, the core around which the whole world spun. His delicate, nervous face made him seem like he was still in his twenties. He was 5'8" and weighed just 135 pounds, and he always wore a dark jacket and jeans. Once, when he walked through a college campus with his wife, Cathy, he was mistaken for a student, which really pissed her off. He was mild-mannered and could be indecisive, but he sometimes surprised those who knew him with bold articles. He was born in Dazey, North

Carolina, a small town with a population of just 30,000 in the southern part of the state.

He graduated from Harvard Business School and spent the next four years working in a bank in New York. All that time, he couldn't shake his desire to be a newspaper reporter and ended up going back to school to study journalism before graduating and joining *The Washington Post.* He got married and had one child but was living alone at the moment.

Biting back a yawn, he returned to his screen. The night before, he'd returned from Georgetown to his downtown apartment and collapsed into bed at two in the morning. Cathy had asked him to babysit their only child Teddy, who was five years old, so he was at her place until a little past 1:00 a.m. He'd only been supposed to look after Teddy from six to nine, but Cathy couldn't get away from work for four hours more.

He put Teddy to bed and was dozing off on the couch when she found him and woke him up. The mere thought of asking if he could stay the night annoyed him so much that he just left.

It had been six months since Cathy moved out. He'd agreed to pay a thousand dollars a month for child support, and in exchange she'd agreed to let him spend Saturday afternoons with Teddy. But recently, she'd been calling to get him to babysit twice a week when work kept her until late. Last night, too, he picked Teddy up from kindergarten, brought him to Cathy's house, fed and bathed him and put him to bed and waited for her to return.

...the issue in California regarding secrets of nuclear bomb production... President Jefferson has called it lamentable... will strongly object to The Daily Californian *through the Justice and Energy Departments... The Iraqi and North Korean governments, expressing their support for the paper, will...*

The CNN anchor's voice droned on.

Warren settled his feet on the desk and pulled out his lunch of coffee and donuts. The Mickey Mouse clock sitting next to the computer on his desk showed a little past 3:10. He had bought it for Teddy as a Christmas present to give him in a month, but a female colleague had pestered him so much that he'd ended up unwrapping it to show her and had been using it ever since. He shifted his attention to the notepaper tacked to the board in front of his desk.

MR. CURLEY CALLED. WILL CALL BACK TOMORROW 5:20

"Curley? Frank Curley, the advisor to the president?" he asked his female colleague who'd taken the call. She was still new, having been hired just half a year ago.

"I don't know. It was a middle-aged man, and his tone was refined and calm."

"Anything else?"

"He seemed disappointed to learn you were out. He asked when you'd return so I told him you didn't plan to come back until today."

"Why didn't you give him my cell number?"

"I offered to get in touch with you but he said he'd call again tomorrow and hung up."

That day, Warren had been out at a press conference held by Senator Northrop, a Republican who wielded a great deal of influence over next year's defense budget, which was currently under deliberations. President Jefferson was coming around on next-gen stealth bombers, the issue that had roiled the White House until just a few weeks ago, and was moving toward a cabinet decision in their favor.

Plans to develop B3A bomber planes equipped with the latest cutting-edge technology had been indefinitely postponed under the last president, mainly because it would cost 5.4 billion dollars—2.3 billion for R&D and the rest on the actual production of eleven planes over two years. The prevailing view was that even if the plan was approved, it would undergo some drastic cutting. While the B2A in use had a maximum speed of Mach 0.65, a flight duration of 11,000 miles and a takeoff weight of 170 tons, the next-gen bomber aimed to improve those numbers by 1.2, 1.4 and 1.5 times respectively. Its stealth capabilities would receive even greater emphasis. If B3A planes were deployed, their range would increase America's military might by leaps and bounds.

Even if the White House approved the plan, however, its passing through Congress was considered unlikely. Capitol Hill was geared toward rebuilding a teetering economy.

Warren had gone straight from the press conference to Teddy's kindergarten. He saw the memo the next morning. The man never called back. Twelve hours after his phone call, he was found dead with a bullet hole in his chest. If the Curley in question was Frank Curley, that is.

Warren unglued his eyes from the memo and reached over to grab a printout.

The article headlined "Presidential Advisor Frank Curley's Mysterious

Death" featured the case that was dominating conversations across the capital.

Five days ago, a 45-year-old male jogging by the National Museum of Natural History at the Mall found a dead man seated on a bench. This would not have been a particularly unusual incident for Washington, D.C., except that the dead man was President Richard Jefferson's Senior Policy Advisor.

The estimated time of death was 3:00 a.m. The media couldn't keep quiet about the corpse of a powerful White House official discovered in the early morning on a bench on the Mall. To make matters worse, police found heroin in his coat pocket and in his bloodstream. Was it homicide or suicide? It was an indecent death either way. Various bits of info circulated among the police and the press.

At first, D.C. police investigated both possibilities, suicide and homicide, but now they were leaning towards the former, mainly due to the gunpowder residue found on the deceased's hand. Maybe he'd cracked under the pressure of his job and turned to drugs and, in the midst of a hallucination, shot himself in the chest. Yet, when the corpse was discovered, the gun that would have been used was nowhere to be found, and the deceased's wallet, watch, briefcase and shoes were also missing, so the view that it was a mugging gone wrong was still strong.

Whether it was murder or suicide, Advisor Curley's name had been dragged through the mud. It was an unseemly death for a high-ranking government official. Yet doubts nagged at Warren. He didn't have a clear reason, just a hunch. No, in fact, he had a reason. As far as Warren knew, Curley had been a good husband and father. Why would such a man… It just didn't make sense.

"They still going on about that guy?"

Warren's boss, Elmore Anderson, was towering over him. He was about to turn forty-eight next February and had a vitality and strong will that was surprising considering his lean 5"11", 135-pound frame. The five-year-old rumors that he'd make editor-in-chief were still just that only because the current chief was, in his own as well as others' estimation, sharp as a tack.

"Eddie Curley, Benton Curley, George Curley… Look at this phone book. How many Curleys do you think there are in this country? There's got to be more than a page's worth."

"Well, this Curley didn't call back this morning. Why do you think that is?"

"Maybe he lost your number, lost interest in talking to you. Maybe whatever problem he had was resolved. There are any number of reasons."

"Or maybe he couldn't get to a phone because he had a bullet in his heart. A perfectly good reason."

"Then go find proof. Back it up. Reporters research the facts and ask tough questions. Don't try to be Sherlock Holmes. Evidence before speculation. And don't you even think about trying to find the culprit."

"It's not as if I was a staunch supporter of Frank Curley or anything."

"Then leave it to the police. Your primary job is to find what the administration and the police have to say and to convey it in an accurate and timely manner to our readers. Or is there something about this case that's bothering you?'

"If I remember correctly, your take was suicide."

"Ruin caused by derangement."

"But suicide just doesn't feel right. Here's this guy, a 42-year-old policy advisor to the president who graduated top of his class at Harvard. He was also a lawyer admitted to the New York bar and had tenure at Princeton, where his progressive views made him popular with the students. On top of that, he wrote two books that are being used as textbooks. He met the First Lady at a charity fundraiser and was recruited to the president's campaign to be the brains behind his foreign policy platform. He stayed on as White House staff and was the aide that the president trusted above all others in his inner circle. Adding up his book royalties, lecture fees, and manuscript fees, he must have been earning over 400,000 dollars a year. After leaving the White House he would be guaranteed to make at least a million a year. Beautiful wife, lovely daughter. They just bought a house last year. Why would such a man want to shoot himself in the chest at three in the morning in the Mall? And how come nobody heard a shot?" gushed Warren in one long torrent.

Anderson gave him a long, hard look, then smiled. "People are like that. All kinds of skeletons in their closets. Not getting blood all over his bed sheets at home was the one kindness he did his family."

"Suicide at the Mall by an important administration official in the middle of the night. Heroin in his pocket. Loads of heroin in his blood as well. It's too perfect. If it were me, I would at least throw away the heroin before pulling the trigger. For the family's sake. Besides, where's the gun?"

"Maybe he needed the drug as a crutch in order to pull the trigger. In a nutshell he was out of his mind, high as a kite. Someone came along and took the gun along with his wallet and briefcase. Plenty of people around there who'd have no qualms robbing a corpse."

"Now who's speculating? You didn't witness that. What about the heroin left in his pocket? And why not take his wedding band?"

"Not enough time to rifle through his pockets. Not enough guts to pull a ring off a dead man's finger."

"But whoever it was had the leisure and courage to take off the man's shoes," Warren murmured. "Come on, there's just too many loose ends to consider this a case-closed suicide."

"That's the way these things are. You button your shirt wrong and things start falling like dominoes. Misfortune and happenstance conspire quite naturally. Curley's mistake was that he started using heroin."

"He's not the type to use heroin. I'm certain of that." Warren's voice had grown louder, but he couldn't find the words to press on.

"Seems to me like there's something personal about this for you," said Anderson, looking over Warren's shoulder at the picture of him with Cathy and Teddy, all lined up and smiling in front of a lake somewhere.

"What I can't stand is that everyone's sensationalizing this just because he was on the White House staff. This guy was a lovable, decent father but he's getting treated like some filthy junkie who went on the prowl late at night for a woman or a boy. Imagine how his wife and daughter must feel. For the family, it's nothing but a media mugging."

"Then follow the kid's line. Curley's daughter goes to the same kindergarten as Teddy, right?" Anderson gazed at Warren, who couldn't help but look away.

"I don't want to use the kid."

"You're not 'using' her. Think of it as embracing an opportunity."

"This has nothing to do with the kid."

Anderson sighed with a fed-up look on his face. "Well, then, think of a better way."

Warren nodded yes.

"In no way is it true that Frank Curley had important documents on him and that they were stolen. That was the White House's official line, right?"

"Well, that's what they say, but who knows," doubted Warren.

"And the capable, fastidious advisor was working on what at the time?"

"He was a senior policy advisor. He was responsible for comprehensive foreign policy including economic and military matters for North Korea and the Middle East, including Iraq. A little while back he was also involved in Russian policy. Basically, he was the point man for all foreign policy. He was probably far more capable than the chief of staff, Simon Schmidt. More recently, a lot of his work was for the presidential reelection committee. He'd been meeting frequently with Democratic Party and corporate executives. All the president's important staff members are on the reelection committee because they know the election next year is going to be tough. For a senior advisor to die now must be quite damaging for the president."

The former governor of California, Donald Rosenberg, had already expressed his decision to run as a challenger for the Democratic ticket. It looked like it was going to be a tight race if Rosenberg managed to maintain his current level of support.

"Are you kidding? This is a huge upset. The Democratic nominee could end up being Rosenberg instead. That's how badly this whole thing reeks of scandal. The Rosenberg camp is already painting Curley's death with the darkest shades they can. If you die the way he did, of course, it doesn't take much to trump up a scandal," Anderson said coolly, setting down a newspaper on the desk. "By the way," he continued, "can you look into this thing with *The Daily Californian*? It's nothing particularly new, but something about it bothers me. I'd like us to get their back if we can."

"A Nuclear Scientist's Confession," read the headline splashed across the paper. The article took up half the front page.

"It's a local paper on the West Coast," Anderson noted.

Dr. J. W. joined the Manhattan Project in 1942 and spent the following 60 years as a nuclear scientist developing atomic and hydrogen bombs for the United States of America. At present due to a fatal illness...

Warren picked up the paper and scanned the article.

Starting next week we will be introducing the materials and memoir that were sent to us.

"How sentimental. A blueprint for a nuclear bomb in this day and age? I can't understand why the government would get so upset," Warren said, looking up form the paper.

"Well, it's not just that. It's about freedom of the press. The First Amendment. We're *The Washington Post*. We can't not lend our support."

He was referring to the Watergate scandal. In 1972, five men were caught sneaking into Democratic Party headquarters, located in the Watergate office complex. Thanks to tenacious investigative reporting on the part of two young journalists with *The Washington Post*—Bob Woodward and Carl Bernstein—the full scope of what had appeared to be a simple break-in was uncovered, and the case developed into a major scandal embroiling the White House. In the end, the President of the United States of America was forced to resign. It was an example of the victory of mass media, which had proclaimed freedom of the press and locked horns with high officials from all quarters of the federal government including the president himself.

Anderson took a manuscript from his pocket and handed it to Warren to read.

The issue on the West Coast is similar to that faced by The Washington Post *in 1972—a case of the mass media vs. the administration. The press versus the government. Today,* The Washington Post *urges* The Daily Californian *to stand up to any and all pressure.*

"This is our stance. We'll publish it under my name."

"I hear all the major newspapers in the country got a press release from these guys," said Warren. Anderson nodded. "They're aiming for media attention. It's a great story for a regional paper."

"Perhaps. But we should still back it."

"You want me to just follow it up?"

"You seem uninterested."

"It's just, my hands are full with the Curley case." Warren put the newspaper on the desk. The headline, "A Nuclear Scientist's Confession," seemed divorced from reality and to be nothing more than local-paper sentimentalism. Or maybe there was something about the provincial town of Barton.

"About Curley, can't you check his phone records?" Anderson reprised, his eyes on the note on the board.

"Well, I know the call was placed from a cell phone. I tried my luck with the phone company, but of course they wouldn't tell me anything, since this country places a premium on privacy. I'll have to find another route."

"If it really was Frank Curley, what would he have wanted with you?"

"I have no idea. I met him a few times at preschool events."

"I see," Anderson nodded. "Well, we'll get nothing from talking here. If I were you I would start by following every step the man took that day. Find out why he was there at that time."

I'm already on it, Warren wanted to say, but instead swallowed his words. He was on it but hadn't found anything relevant. Curley's trail seemed to go cold after he left the White House at 11:10 p.m. that night.

"There's a press conference at the White House scheduled at three," Warren said, getting to his feet and glancing at his watch.

The Washington Post was founded in 1877. Its circulation of 800,000 ranked seventh in the nation, but it was no ordinary regional newspaper, its robust influence making it a rival of *The New York Times*. Over 90 percent of government officials—including congressmen and the president—were subscribers. The paper was particularly noteworthy for its political section, owing to its advantageous location. Quoted often by other media, it wielded influence not only across the U.S. but the world.

November in D.C. was when autumn ended in a hurry and winter crept in. This year, in particular, snow was forecast from the beginning of December. People walked briskly down the street with their collars held together and their backs hunched over.

The White House was just a third of a mile south of the *Washington Post* headquarters. Warren rushed to the conference room in the West Wing. The main functions of the White House including the president's office were concentrated in this area, which broadcast America's intentions to the fifty states and beyond.

The press room was already full of reporters, but Warren wormed his way up front to near the podium, which bore the presidential eagle emblem. Behind it on the wall hung the Stars and Stripes.

"Quite a turnout. There must be more than a hundred people," murmured a female journalist to her colleague in the row in front of Warren.

"We swarm to juicy gossip like bees attacking a blooming flower and sucking it dry."

"Finally we get Clinton-grade smut amidst all the boring political shit. Everyone's chomping at the bit. I'd be curious even if it wasn't my job."

"The elite falling from grace. The whole country's watching. TV ratings are rising across the board."

For each paper represented in the room, there was someone from the city desk as well as the political desk. There were also a bunch of unfamiliar faces—perhaps tabloid or television reporters.

The conference began half an hour late. When the chief spokesman, Stock Gerald, appeared along with ten other members of the staff, murmurs arose and a couple of dozen flashes started going off. Usually, conferences like these were given by someone a little lower down the pecking order, so the decision seemed to reflect how nervous the White House was feeling about the incident. Gerald merely covered the same information the police were giving out, stating that the case was still under investigation but that the chances of it being a suicide due to a nervous breakdown brought on by overwork were relatively high. A press conference seemed like a lot of ado just to trot that out; that itself was unusual. Gerald scanned the reporters as sociably as always, but something about him was awkward and tense. It was no surprise. As a spokesman for the president, he was used to announcing the views of the U.S. government to nation and world alike from that podium. It was the first time he had ever given the kind of briefing that a press officer for the police was wont to deliver.

"Since this incident is so irregular, we wouldn't normally accept questions—" Before Gerald could finish, murmurs of protest arose from his audience.

A nearby aide rushed to clarify, "We're not saying we won't be accepting questions. Simply that we'll be limiting it to ten minutes."

"Ridiculous!" rang out a voice from the back. "This may have been a murder!"

"Nine minutes remaining," the aide responded mechanically. They clearly had a game plan.

"What does the president think about Advisor Curley's death?" asked a young journalist in the front row without waiting to be called on. The din in the room instantly died down as all eyes turned towards Gerald.

"The president has already expressed his deep concern," replied Gerald dryly and looked around the room to prompt the next question.

"I'm not talking about that bureaucratic statement. I mean on a personal level," continued the young journalist. "Curley and the president were close. As friends, as tennis partners."

"Well, at first, he did seem to be in deep shock, but presidents do not have the luxury of extended mourning. Especially now, when there's a long list of issues that need to be dealt with. The president is currently meeting with the Russian Ambassador to consider the Iraq situation and to review the nuclear arsenal." Gerald glanced at his watch.

"Will there be problems with establishing policy in the near future? As senior policy advisor, Frank Curley was a central figure in the White House."

"Fortunately we have a lot of good people on staff. Already, Thomas Fried has taken over his post."

"Even if it was suicide, what does the White House have to say on why he was where he was at that time?" asked a female journalist.

"That is a personal matter. There will be no comments whatsoever on that point. Now, if there are no further questions—"

"What was Advisor Curley working on at the White House before his death?" interrupted Warren.

"We have no comments to make about his work at the White House."

"Advisor Curley was also heavily involved in the presidential reelection committee. Won't this situation necessitate a drastic revision in your plans?"

"No comment."

"You have no comment on anything."

"I wouldn't go that far. What I can answer I will answer with sincerity. Naturally, I cannot disclose state secrets or anything regarding the next presidential election." The chief spokesman gave an elaborately calculated smile.

"That doesn't sound like anyone's definition of sincerity."

Other journalists piped up in support.

"So is the White House view that it was, as some say, an unpremeditated suicide caused by a drug hallucination?"

"You seem to forget who you're addressing. We're not the police. Please direct such questions to the appropriate authorities," the spokesman neatly parried.

"Isn't it possible that top-secret documents may have been in the briefcase that was stolen from Curley?"

"As we announced right after the incident, that is not a concern. All White House staff are expressly forbidden from removing official documents. And we don't even know if he had a briefcase."

"So Frank Curley—"

An aide stepped forward and showed Gerald the time. This bit of performance, too, had probably been worked out in advance.

"We're out of time. I'm afraid that was the last question." Gerald closed his file and stepped away from the podium as the journalists raised a ruckus.

"I heard Curley had a major clash of opinion with the president recently. Is it true that Curley was thinking of resigning or was about to be relieved?" shouted Warren from his seat.

All the clamor halted as all eyes turned to Warren. Gerald's feet stopped dead in their tracks, and he turned around. Gone was his friendly smile, replaced now by a stern, defiant expression.

"Who told you that?"

"A little bird."

"Groundless rumors will not only hurt individuals but can plunge an administration into crisis. I urge you to exercise discretion." Gerald slowly looked over the journalists. "There is no such fact. We always act in solidarity. Otherwise…" Gerald said, thrusting his finger at Warren, "we cannot protect the office of the president of the United States." With that, Gerald turned his back to the reporters. Shouts of protest rang out, but this time Gerald didn't turn back and walked out of the room.

"Where did you hear that? That's the first I've heard of it."

"Don't you mean Chief of Staff Schmidt? I can understand it happening between him and the president." A crowd had formed around Warren.

"I was just fishing. There's no ground." Warren looked around and shrugged.

"Just another *Washington Post* bluff?" said one of the reporters.

"In D.C., scoops aren't dug up but concocted, eh?" said another.

The journalists took shots at him as they slowly shuffled out of the room.

Warren felt a tap on his shoulder from behind. "The White House is hiding something. They didn't look amused." It was a friend of Warren's from *The New York Times*.

"Nah, they're just being cautious. I expect them to be a little shell-shocked by this incident. Nobody knows what might come out next."

"Or they just don't want to be in a tough spot in the campaign. As it is, the next-gen stealth plans are likely to be squashed, so they don't want us digging into Curley's private life. The public is fed up with scandals of that ilk, yet they can't get enough. Those guys don't want the dignity of government to be defined further down."

"You think Curley was really a degenerate?"

"He was in a strange place at a strange time. Makes you wonder why. It's not about whether it was suicide or murder. He was there for a reason. A hookup, with a woman or even a boy, or drugs. What else could it be? If he wasn't the White House's senior policy advisor it wouldn't even make the news. People would just think some lecherous perv partied a little too hard."

"You don't think it's possible someone might have plotted to murder him?"

"Did you switch to the city desk? If you have, you're investigating in the wrong place. Some homeless guy has his shoes, bag and wallet. The guy's probably shitting his pants just about now, having found out who he's stolen from," the reported said as if the matter was already settled.

A tall African-American man was standing by the door and looking towards Warren. It was John Morse. Warren tried to wave and call out, but the detective joined the crowd and disappeared. Warren rushed out of the White House.

When he got out onto the street, he found John waiting for him. The 37-year-old D.C. detective was the only cop Warren trusted.

Seven years ago, on the day after moving to the city, Warren's car had been stolen. At the time John was with the traffic division and ran around the city the whole day for Warren, who was at a loss, and found his car right as it was about to be disassembled for its parts. What surprised Warren even more was that he refused the five twenty-dollar bills he offered. He never forgot the look in John's eyes that day, and the two met up at least twice a week since then. A year after their first encounter, John realized his long-standing dream of joining the homicide division.

John was wearing a neatly tailored suit with a black coat and polished Italian shoes. His attire always made Warren want to ask how much the cops in this town were paid.

"So how come you're here? You're not assigned to the case, are you?" asked Warren.

"I got special permission. It isn't often that I get to attend a White House press conference," John replied. He leaned closer to Warren. "What was your source for that last question?"

"I've confessed that it was just a rumor."

"So it was a charade? No wonder people hate the *Post*," John spat, pulling away. He sighed. "I thought journalists were supposed to be bright. Is that just a lie or a hoax? Or is it a legend handed down from the Ice Age? So where were all the incisive questions? It was like an elementary school debate in there."

"No matter what we asked, they'd have responded in the same way. From the outset the White House had no intention of answering anything. It was to parry our questions and to keep mum that they sent out Spokesman Gerald himself."

A car stopped on the other side of the street and a middle-aged couple emerged. They started taking pictures with the White House in the background, and John nonchalantly moved to turn his back to them.

"Let's go somewhere. I don't want to stand around talking."

"What, is this a problem? Can't a homicide cop and a *Washington Post* journalist be having a chat in front of the White House?"

"Don't ask if you already know the answer." John started walking. They went downtown and entered their usual cafeteria, taking the booth at the back.

"So how's the investigation going?"

"No investigation, not squat. A guy high on drugs was killed at the Mall in the middle of the night. Or a drug addict had a bad trip and lost a fight with a gun. What else could it have been?"

"Well, the gun was never found. Neither was his wallet or bag. Not even his shoes."

"So what? Listen to me," John said as he leaned in close. "Some thug killed him and took it. Or some random homeless guy rolled his corpse. Whether it was suicide or murder it doesn't make much of a difference. Tomorrow, the day after, a week later or a month later, some thug or a homeless guy brought in for larceny or extortion might fess up to this. Even if it was murder, they'll only get tried for second degree. If the perp is mentally ill or a drug addict, even that will be a long shot. Whatever the truth is, the fact remains that Frank Curley is dead and his wife and child will never be in his arms again," pressed John breathlessly, then leaned back.

"But they'll have closure."

"Is that so important?"

"For some people. It can help people put it behind them and start anew."

"Why are you so concerned about this case? Curley got what he had coming. He ignored the rules of this city. He chose to be in the wrong place at the wrong time."

"His daughter and Teddy—"

"Look, it wasn't just the heroin in his pocket," John interrupted. "There was a flyer for an S&M club, too. The hidden life of the elite advisor. He was no different from you and me. Just another guy. He should have known not to be out there at that time of night. Even with a gun he had to be either overconfident about his gunmanship or completely out of his mind."

"He was neither. He was a gentleman, a Harvard graduate without a mean bone in his body." Warren recalled a mild-faced middle-aged man linking arms with his wife and holding hands with his daughter.

"Did he have any enemies? Inside and outside the White House?"

"There must have been more than a few. He was known as a rare no-bullshit guy. Guess that's how he became a presidential aide. To have many enemies in politics just means you've arrived."

"Even big shots don't always resist impulses or avoid the lure of suicide."

"Loitering around a park in the middle of the night doesn't mean he was gay."

"I don't know if he ran that way, but I did hear he had a parade of mistresses like he was in a contest with some of our past presidents."

"Who told you that?"

"Someone from the White House. But that's probably just a rumor, too. Once these things start coming out they're impossible to control. It's all unofficial and won't make it into the report."

Warren stared off silently.

"You don't seem satisfied. What's bugging you? You know assumptions are dangerous. I suggest you go home, take a shower and think it over. This case isn't too complicated." John peered into Warren's face with a puzzled look.

"But he wasn't that kind of person. A family man with a beautiful wife and a lovely daughter."

"You'd met him?"

"Several times."

"That's news to me." John's expression had changed.

"His daughter and Teddy go to the same preschool."

"Why didn't you say so?" John glared at Warren. "Now I see why you're taking his side."

The two of them sat there without a word, thinking.

"Okay," said Warren, "let's take a look at what we've got. The estimated time of death was three in the morning. He was found at 5:03 a.m., which means he was there on the bench for two hours. No witnesses during that time."

"Or there were, but they didn't report it. In any case, someone took the gun, his bag, wallet, watch and shoes. Probably a homeless guy or some thug."

"And not even a patrol passed by?"

"One did at around three, but there was nothing out of order."

"And how about the first witness?"

"He was jogging. Chris Horne. 46 years old, Caucasian. He's a dishwasher at a restaurant downtown."

"Why was he jogging at five in the morning?"

"The restaurant closed at two. He had a drink with his buddies and went home at three. Apparently it's his custom to take a breather and then go running. Says he likes the dark D.C. before the sun rises. I don't understand the Italians. He has a record so I looked into it."

"A record?"

"Small-time thief. Purse snatcher, too. But..." John thought for a moment. "The shoes as well as the briefcase, wallet and watch were missing."

"What kind of shoes?"

"A four-hundred-dollar pair, Italian. Birthday present from his wife. Gone. That's why the force can't declare it a suicide. But cases of aggravated theft usually don't get around to a guy's shoes. His wallet and watch were taken, yet he still had his wedding band. You go so far as to kill a man but leave the ring? It's all weird."

"Would they usually take it?"

"Depends on the criminal. Young ones just take the cash and cards. Desperate ones will even take belts and coats. But almost never the shoes. Used shoes don't amount to much cash. That's why it's not a robbery gone wrong. It's suicide."

"How about his coat? He was wearing one, right?"

"Only amateurs steal coats. Clothes are easy to track down. In this case there would have been a hole in the chest and blood all over it. I guess for the shoes, it's possible the thief just wanted them for himself."

"The heroin found in his pocket was left unstolen."

"The punk thief was a coward. The coat was soaked in blood. Would you wanna stick your hand in there?"

"The ring was left on his hand."

"Pang of conscience. Didn't want to swipe the man clean."

"What about his cell phone?"

"He didn't have one on him. Probably ditched it on the way. No calls have been made from it since then. That's the extent of what I know."

"Can't you get a hold of the records I asked for? It must be easy for you to request it from the phone company."

"You mean regarding a call from his phone at 5:20. Having released the full records to the police, they are unable to respond to any individual inquiries. That was the carrier's response."

"To a city detective?"

John nodded.

"Can you check the records at the station? I want to know if that was actually Frank Curley."

"I don't know where they are."

"And you call yourself a cop?"

"We're known for our superior teamwork."

Warren glanced at his watch and stood up. "I gotta go."

"You have something?"

"Yeah, I'm going back to the office to write up an article about that press conference. Then I'm babysitting Teddy."

"You still separated, right?"

"From Cathy, yeah."

Leaving John speechless, Warren strode out of the cafeteria.

The road spread out gently, quiet. The European-style houses flanking the wide road gave the neighborhood a sense of history. Georgetown, situated northwest of D.C., still retained an old-city feel. Warren parked on a corner and walked into a house. Only six months ago he'd lived here with his family.

"You're half an hour late. I'm in a hurry," said Cathy with a stern expression.

Warren sat on the couch in the living room and Teddy climbed onto his lap.

"Can you hand me my scarf there?"

With Teddy in his arms, Warren reached for the scarf and handed it to Cathy. She was 35 years old, a mathematician with a degree from M.I.T. She wore her chestnut brown hair short enough to show her red star-shaped earrings. They were the ones Warren had bought for her the year after he'd graduated from college and started working for the bank. It had been his first present to her. Rings, watches, necklaces, earrings… Whenever he came over to babysit she'd always be wearing a present from him. He couldn't tell if she was doing it intentionally or if he was just reading too much into it and she was just being insensitive. It was probably the latter.

Or maybe it was her way of conveying some message. He wanted badly to get back together with her. He'd tried to raise the subject with her countless times, but she'd always wriggled out of it. By now he'd firmly decided not to be the one to bring it up.

Cathy was currently doing research on codes at a mathematical strategy lab at Georgetown University. She'd had an offer to teach at Cal Tech, but at the time she'd had to turn it down because of Warren's job. They'd reached that decision together, but Warren felt guilty nonetheless.

"Can you make it back by nine today?"

"I'll try. There is a chance I'll be a little later."

"I have work too, you know." Warren carried Teddy in his arms and followed Cathy around the house.

"I had to leave work to pick up Teddy and feed him, before going back to work."

"You could work from home," said Warren, and immediately regretted it. They'd recently gotten into an argument when he had said something about mathematicians only needing a pen and paper for their work.

"Do you think I can do 1.2 trillion calculations in a second? Think about the capacity of your own brain. You can hardly remember your cell phone number!" she'd snapped at him with a terrible glare. She needed a supercomputer for her current work. "If anyone's work can be done from home, it's yours. All you do is stir people up with empty stories anyway." Such arguments always dissolved into ad hominem attacks.

Cathy had fallen silent then as they both looked at each other.

Just as Warren had sensed real danger, Cathy had asked for a divorce. Once Cathy called him a low-life muckraker, he'd felt ready to agree to a separation. Until then he had thought that they should stay together until Teddy could understand them both, but it made him realize that they were tired out and could use some time apart. Warren was the one who had left the house.

"Look, I know it's important to tell the world about corruption and crime," said Cathy as she walked through the house. "I'm just saying it's also important to look after Teddy."

"The newspaper's about more than that."

"Okay, so it's the guardian angel of freedom of speech, the citizen's spokesman, society's pilot. An outlaw of sorts that can't be bothered with good manners. A big-eared donkey that sniffs around others' misfortunes. I don't care how you describe it, but Teddy is your child. His security comes first." Moving from the bathroom to the bedroom, Cathy gathered little items and threw them in her bag.

"And your work is so important? I agree, computers made the world a more convenient place to live. But that's not all. Computers are good enough as they are now. What's the point of doing more calculations?" Cathy's work involved creating codes for online trading. She had tried to explain her work to him a number of times, but Warren hadn't been able to follow a word of what she was saying.

"I have no desire to argue about that with you."

"Me neither."

"Just put Teddy to bed at nine, please."

"That's ten minutes before I go to bed."

"Last time he was up until ten. He was talking about the nightly news and some stupid commentary. You know, the one that starts at ten."

Warren ignored her accusation. "Should I take Teddy to preschool tomorrow morning?"

Cathy stopped in her tracks. "What are you trying to get at? Have you done something wrong?"

"Cool it with the accusations. I just thought it would be nice to take him there. I used to all the time."

"I don't remember that. You used to complain about it for half a day before going, even on mornings when I'd come back from an all-nighter at the lab." She walked toward the door, pulling her coat on. Then she stopped and turned around. "It's Cindy, isn't it?"

"What's Cindy?"

"Cindy Curley. Frank Curley's daughter. You want to talk to Patty about her husband, don't you? Patty, that's Cindy's mom, Patricia Curley, wife to Advisor Curley."

"You know them personally? Then…"

"No," she said firmly, raising a hand to stop him speaking another word.

"I just want to see how they're getting on."

"How can you say such a thing? You want to ask a widow how she feels about losing her husband? What do you think she's going to say? 'Yeah, life's just dandy right now'? How he died doesn't matter to the family. Now they have to keep on going, just the two of them. Is that what *The Washington Post* has become? Nothing more than a gossip rag?"

"Look, asking around is just part of the job. It's necessary to keep our stupid readers happy."

"That's why I say you've changed. Besides, ever since the incident she hasn't come to preschool."

"So you don't want us to meet?"

"Exactly. Besides, she can't leave the house at all. The crazed media has her house surrounded. The world is overflowing with vultures like yourself."

"I haven't been to her house even once."

"I don't have time for this. My answer is no. I'll take Teddy to preschool." With that, she rushed out, glancing at her watch.

Warren let Teddy watch television while they ate the frozen pizza he'd brought and the spaghetti Cathy had left on the kitchen table.

"Daddy, do you want to see Cindy?" asked Teddy, his eyes never moving from the television.

"You know her?"

"She's my friend. I see her at the park often, too. We play together."

"Do you want to go somewhere on Saturday?"

"The zoo would be nice."

"Daddy wants to go somewhere where Cindy might come. You want to see her too, right?" Warren sat next to Teddy. Stuffed puppets were dancing on TV. He took out *The Daily Californian*. It had a 4-inch square diagram with thin lines and details too fine to make out, enhancing the mystery. Once the series starts next week there will be a larger picture with explanations, it promised. The journalist's name looked to be Japanese American. His enthusiasm was clearly on display in the article.

Warren felt tired as soon as he started to read.

"Okay, it's time to take a bath and go to bed." He stood up and looked at the clock. It was 7:40.

"But it's not eight yet."

"You can read the clock?"

Just a week ago Teddy couldn't tell the difference between the short and long hand.

"Mommy taught me."

"That clock is slow."

"Mommy always says don't be fooled by daddy."

"Every clock in the world is slow. Only daddy's watch is correct."

"I set it to the TV this morning."

"I'll give you a clock for your Christmas present. With Mickey Mouse on it."

"I already have one. Mommy bought it for my birthday. Didn't you see it by my bed?"

"I'm sorry. I hadn't forgotten…" Warren held Teddy close. Last week was his birthday. It had completely slipped his mind.

"Can you read me a story?"

"I'll do anything," said Warren, and Teddy skipped off up the stairs to get his pajamas.

Cathy returned at a little past 1:00 a.m., checking on Teddy then taking a carton of milk from the fridge and downing it in one. Warren stood behind her and watched.

"Don't start in on me again. I'm exhausted. And I'm on Patricia's side," she said, raising her right hand to stop him from talking.

"I was wondering if I should hug you," he retorted.

"Don't. I'm tired as an old rag." She turned towards the bathroom. Reaching around her body from behind, he tried to stop her. As he did, he felt her soft breast in his palm. It was a sensation he had forgotten, or rather, that he'd tried to forget.

"Stop it. You're not going to fool me like that. I'm not as dumb as I was ten years ago," said Cathy, brushing away his hands. She closed the bathroom door, and soon the shower came on.

"Do you think Frank Curley was the type of man the media says he was?" shouted Warren through the door. The shower grew louder. "I know you can hear me. Answer me."

"You'll wake Teddy!" Cathy yelled.

"Look, you've seen them together. You saw him give that speech about childrearing at the parents' gathering last summer. You were impressed. They attended the fall potluck party, too. I had three servings of his homemade potato salad." Warren waited for a response, but only heard the splashes of water. "I just can't believe he's a hypocrite. I think he was a good father and a good husband. At least, a lot better than me."

"So you think it's odd that he would commit suicide at such a place and time when he made good potato salad?"

"People have all sorts of issues that others can't understand. But if I were going to commit suicide… There would be a reason that you, at least, might understand, though maybe not the whole world. I just want to know what that was.

"Besides…" he paused. "I would never have done it like that. For my family's sake." The sound of the shower became softer. "The thing is," he said, "I got a phone call from Frank the day before he died."

The shower stopped.

"I was out. There was a memo for me the next day, but I didn't think it was *that* Curley."

"Are you saying he called you knowing you were a journalist at the *Post*?"

"Why else would he call? He did know me personally, as Teddy's father."

Silence. Warren slowly opened the door and put his head through the crack. On the other side of the steam-tinted glass door he could see Cathy's clouded outline. She was bending slightly forward. He could make out her breasts, her long arms and legs, her narrow hips and heavy buttocks. She'd put on a little weight, but it was the first time in six months that he'd seen her naked. In the past he'd held that body and caressed it. And she'd responded. His heart pounded and he tightened his grip on the doorknob.

"Don't come in," echoed Cathy's icy voice. "The day after tomorrow the preschool's going on a trip to the Smithsonian. I heard Cindy was really looking forward to it. She wants to become an archaeologist, though her dad apparently wanted to steer her toward science. Teddy was worried whether she'd come." She turned the shower back on.

"I'm leaving. There's leftover pizza in the fridge."

As Warren stepped out of the house, the cold November air seeped into his body, making him pull his collar tight to his neck and hurry to his car.

Chapter 2
Developments

"I'm opposed." Steve Austin turned his eyes away from the diagram on the wall. "We should just burn it and flush the ashes down the toilet."

He had brownish blond hair, smooth, fair skin and a prominent nose—a textbook example of a haughty WASP. His husky voice added roughness to his otherwise elegant appearance. He was a successful local entrepreneur who owned two supermarkets, two real estate agencies and one trucking company in addition to *The Daily Californian*. Austin stared down at the two men sitting at a wooden table that was covered in cigarette burns.

The 30-feet square room they were in had originally been used as documents storage, but now it was the usual place for unofficial editorial meetings. It had a large table in the center, a scattering of mismatched chairs and a sofa partially bleached by the sun. Two of the walls had bookshelves that reached all the way to the ceiling, their rusted shelves bearing piles of dusty files. On the wall by the door shone the diagram, blurred in the light.

Ken, Charlie and Steve had been sitting here for over an hour discussing the slide projected on the wall.

"But we've already announced that the series will start next week," lamented Charlie, sounding fed-up.

"Why didn't you consult me first?"

"We've never had to consult you before for a series. I thought you didn't have time for that."

Everyone at *The Daily Californian* knew Austin didn't read his own paper. The only printed words his eyes ever glanced upon were contracts and stock reports. He'd learned about the article in question during his stay at a hotel in Los Angeles for a real estate deal. He'd rushed back after a friend happened to mention hearing about the government making a lot of noise over one of his paper's articles.

"Look," said Ken, absorbing Austin's thorny look. "I'll shoulder full responsibility." He knew what made this man two years his senior tick. Austin put the profitability of his company before anything—anything except his personal stakes, of course.

"This isn't the kind of problem that can be solved by you turning in a resignation. We're talking about defying a direct order from the Department of Justice. Do you understand what that means?"

"I do understand," answered Ken flatly. "But we haven't received any orders to stop the presses. The series hasn't even started, after all."

"My lawyer said it's only a matter of time. I'm having an accountant sizing up the worst-case-scenario damages."

Charlie stared at the table and shook his head in disbelief. Ken glanced at Charlie. Trouble. That was what this skinny, overextended man had avoided most of all. He'd just turned fifty-five the previous week and he'd told everyone on his birthday how he thanked God for a calm life in a quiet town.

"How about this? We'll say you never knew about it. You can blame it on the associate editor-in-chief, who just went crazy!" offered Ken, his eyes fixed firmly on Austin.

"The lawyer says we'll be taken to court if you keep this up," stated Austin, glaring at Ken and Charlie.

"I'm prepared for that."

"Think about the current state of the world. The Soviet Union has long since fallen along with Communism, and now even Russia might join NATO. Iran, Iraq and North Korea out in the boondocks are so fragile a strong wind could topple them. Who wants to hear this kind of nonsense in this day and age?"

"I want to tell the world about the author's life. I want people to know of the existence of this unknown scientist and his struggles."

"I hear you, but the readers won't take it that way. Other media outlets will sensationalize it. As the lawyer says this threatens U.S. national security, aids nuclear arms proliferation and puts nuke-making capability into the hands of terrorists everywhere at a time when the mainstream in

Congress is trying to cut down on defense spending. In this environment not even the president's next-generation stealth bomber plans can get passed. This whole thing could turn into a crisis for all things nuclear, including power plants. Really, there couldn't be a worse thing for us to do. This is too big for a regional newspaper with a circulation of just 42,000," spewed Austin. He sounded like he'd done more homework than usual, though it was unclear how much of it he really understood. The lawyer must have had his way with him.

"This will not affect you," said Ken, his voice tinged with anger. He knew Austin all too well—how he let subordinates take the lead before removing himself to a place of safety. Then, when things seemed to be going smoothly, out he stepped into the limelight. No way would the ambitious man miss an opportunity to take the credit for this as well when the time was right.

"Fine." Austin looked away from Ken and moved slowly away from the table, fixing his tie. "So you say you think we need to increase the print run by 58,000 copies?"

"That's right."

"42,000 plus 58,000. That's 100,000 copies. For us, it'll be a gamble. We'll need to maintain that momentum." Austin was obviously saying this with their local rival, *The Barton Journal*, in mind—a newspaper with a 50-year history and a circulation of 240,000, definitely the top dog in the area and with close relationships with *The Los Angeles Times* and *The New York Times*, too. They easily overshadowed *The Daily Californian*. Recently, Austin was interested in increasing sales of his newspaper without a care about appearances so he could use it as a stepping-stone into politics in the future.

"I'll call the printers myself."

"Thank you."

"By the way, do you know Donald Fraser?" Austin asked, changing his tone of voice.

"The head of the environmentalist group, Green Earth?"

"He's had a few run-ins with the government. I've contacted him. Might do you some good to have a chat with him, just in case. We do, after all, donate $10,000 every year to his group," Austin mumbled and turned his gaze back to the diagram on the wall. "Do you plan to use this as well?"

"Yeah."

"It looks more like some sort of mystical pattern than a blueprint for a nuclear bomb. Like the things in Tibet."

"A mandala? I'd have to agree with you there," Charlie reluctantly spoke again.

"How have you been holding up?" Austin asked, as he took in Ken's appearance.

"Winter's not so easy on me," responded Ken, tapping his leg, even though he knew that wasn't what Austin was asking.

"Well, hang in there." Raising his hand, Steve Austin hurriedly left the room.

Ken sat there in silence for a while, listening to the departing footsteps. Was he doing the right thing? A sting of anxiety crossed his mind. It resembled that heavy feeling he had during his stint in the military when, rifle at the ready, he had to enter a house thought to be abandoned but from which some sound had come. His hand checked for the whiskey flask in his jacket. He ached to pour its contents down his throat, but he was able to check himself.

"How's Dr. Williams?" Charlie had been watching Ken without a word until his question broke the silence.

"He's well. Since I told him the articles will be published, his appetite's returned and he can sleep at night. He told me so by email."

The projector started to make a racket. Ken switched it off and stood up. He walked over to the window and looked down on the shining main street.

He had a momentary spell of vertigo.

Californian winter. The sun was all too bright, the sky emerald blue, green grass lined both sides of the road and everyone walking along seemed terribly shiny.

The next night Ken, Charlie and Jimmy headed to San Francisco. They were to meet a man with influence across the West Coast on all matters relating to the environment and the fight against nuclear power. The headquarters of the environmental protection organization Green Earth was located on a small hill overlooking the San Francisco bay. It could pass for a regular house, except for the large parabolic antenna for satellite communications mounted in the backyard and facing the sea.

As soon as they entered the door they were surrounded by hustle and bustle—people talking, phones ringing, the sound of tapping on keyboards. Inside the spacious living room were three rows of desks with about thirty people moving about. A third of them looked as if they might be students, while the rest were a mixture of men and women of different ages and styles of clothing.

On the tables by the wall sat nearly ten computers, several printers and phones and fax machines. This must be where they sent out directives and information and received correspondence from branch offices and kindred organizations around the world. Green Earth supporters the world over sent in info 24 hours a day.

They were ushered into an adjacent room. As soon as the door was closed they were met with oddly complete silence. The room was soundproofed. It was empty except for a table and chairs and the faint but unique smell of pipe tobacco in the air.

"I wouldn't be surprised if they kicked us out. What's Fraser thinking?" whispered Jimmy as he clutched his blue rucksack to his chest. "They're anti-nuclear power and weapons after all."

"Austin told us to come here. He must've put us through," replied Charlie bluntly.

"The only thing on Austin's mind is how much he gives to this organization," remarked Ken, studying a picture on the wall of a seagull covered in oil. Next to that was a photo of a rusted Soviet nuclear submarine.

After waiting ten minutes, the rear door opened and a man walked in. He had a face that was familiar to them from newspaper articles, magazine covers and television programs. He was the head of Green Earth, Donald Fraser.

Fraser was a tall, thin, 53-year-old gentleman with long, graying hair. He had a gentle aura about him that could easily have belonged to an artist. His smart fashion sense coupled with his vigorous anti-establishment movement and, recently, his criticism of nuclear power garnered support from a broad range of people. He drew admiration particularly from young men and women due to his charismatic nature.

Jimmy, Ken and Charlie rose to greet him. Fraser dropped his gaze to Ken's feet and offered his hand. It was a tepid handshake with a rather weak grip.

"Please…" Fraser politely indicated the chairs. "Have a seat."

Five years earlier, Green Earth had been established by a San Francisco housewife for the purpose of protecting the California coast after she'd seen a sea lion covered in oil thanks to a tanker accident. Intellectuals in the area flocked to the group and it soon grew into a large environmentalist organization. Three years ago, when Fraser became the head of the outfit, they expanded exponentially through collaboration with environmentalist and antiwar groups across the country. They'd become a nationwide organization, with offices along the West Coast and all over the United States as well as in major cities around the world. At this point they had political clout.

Most of the time, they followed the proper channels in court and the media with their protests, but occasionally they opted for more headline-grabbing actions. It was Fraser who had called in a hundred oil trucks to park outside the Capitol in D.C. to protest the war in Iraq. Another time they'd protested against a proposed nuclear power plant on the Snake River in Idaho and invited Native Americans to join in, which led to intervention by the National Guard. They continued to be persistent in their anti-nuclear power stance.

"Steve told me you were coming," said Fraser with a gentle smile. He was wearing a white turtleneck sweater and neatly creased slacks. His fearless tanned face and slender body made him look closer to forty than fifty.

Charlie laid out the email from Dr. Williams in front of Fraser. The name and other identifying parts were blacked out. Fraser spent nearly ten minutes reading it, then he seemed to be lost in thought with his eyes still stuck on the printout.

"So what do you want from me?" He slowly looked up at the trio.

"We plan to publish his memoir and we're expecting quite a response based on previous instances. Some will be supportive, some not. So we wanted to hear your advice on how to handle it, from your perspective as a leader of the anti-nuclear movement," explained Charlie. Austin should have already filled him in on the details.

"What kind of article will it be?"

"I'll let its writer explain," Charlie said, giving the floor to Ken.

"I'll refer to the author of this information as Dr. J.W.," said Ken, hurriedly gathering his concentration. "As I mentioned in the article a couple of days ago, the series will take the form of a kind of memoir. A scientist's school years, his time as a researcher with the Manhattan Project and at a military facility in the postwar nuclear development era. It'll trace the changes in his thinking as the world underwent a transformation. I plan to add commentary on world affairs during each time period along with his research documents. I want to relate the spiritual pilgrimage of a scientist. He spent his whole life in the bosom of a state secret called nuclear development. In other words, his life was veiled by government-imposed confidentiality so he was never free to publish his theses or step into the spotlight. I want to shine a light on his life. Of course, I realize that the research data and content we will be printing might touch upon state secrets, but I plan to handle it as carefully as possible," Ken said quickly. His forehead gleamed with sweat.

"I'm all in favor of publishing it. Our country has too many secrets regarding the military and its nuclear policies, even though this country is supposed to the leading democracy. Things should be more open, even with regards to military matters."

"What we're really worried about is the government's reaction. Our paper is small, with a circulation of only 42,000. If the government comes down on us... Well, let's just say it'd be more than our lawyer could handle," said Charlie, wiping his forehead with his hand.

Fraser looked at them. "Do you know *The Albuquerque Tribune?*"

"Of course." Ken nodded.

The *Tribune* was a New Mexico newspaper with a circulation of 35,000. A female reporter working there published an article accusing the government of running a covert experiment between 1945 and 1947 where plutonium was injected into eighteen patients with terminal cancer. Furthermore, she'd been able to find out the names of five of the patients from the code numbers used in the experiment. Her article sparked a media frenzy that led to major national newspapers and TV outlets running the story. The media hunted down and brought to light a number of other top-secret government-sanctioned radiation experiments performed on humans. This in turn forced the Energy Department to release piles of previously classified documents and even confront the issue of compensation. The journalist responsible for breaking the original story was awarded the Pulitzer Prize in 1994.

"We'll do all we can within our power," offered Fraser, lighting his pipe. The room turned fragrant with smoke that tickled their nostrils.

Ken watched in silence. He felt something was out of place in this man with his constant smile, but he couldn't put his finger on it.

"By the way, do you mind if I photocopy the diagrams and manuscript? I'd like to check its authenticity using my own sources."

"Please do."

Fraser gathered the documents and went into the back room, from which emanated sounds of keyboards being tapped, ringing phones, people talking and at times female laughter. Now it was silent again.

Jimmy was ceaselessly shaking his head and sighing.

"All public campaigns need momentum. Good momentum can

brush aside a few contradictions and inconsistencies," Fraser said gently as he showed them to the front door. He raised his pipe as if to say farewell.

The lights of San Francisco twinkled like stardust. Far in the distance to their left, a string of taillights could be seen crossing the Golden Gate Bridge. It was a rare fog-free night. A cold sea breeze blew past.

Green Earth immediately handed over a copy of the paper titled "The Secret of Nuclear Bomb Production" to a nuclear physicist at the University of California. By the next afternoon, they were met with a surprisingly excited response.

It was a paper in two parts, the first being "The Basic Theory of the Nuclear Bomb" and the second "The Production of the Nuclear Bomb." It contained the blueprints for a cylindrical multi-section implosion-style hydrogen bomb developed in the nineties at the earliest as well as detailed data from experiments.

On the first Sunday in December, the series hit the newsstands. It ran as a special feature entitled "A Scientist's Confession" with the subhead "The Secret of Nuclear Bomb Production" and included the memoir of Dr. James Williams. The article began with the diagram he'd first sent to Ken.

Half the front page concentrated on Dr. J.W.'s university years and covered in a rather dramatic fashion how the memoir had come to fall into the hands of the newspaper. It was to be a series with five installments, with the final one running on December 23rd.

As Ken entered the editorial room, Austin came shuffling over with a contorted look on his face, probably from suppressing a smile.

"You did it!"

Austin offered his hand and Ken shook it.

"I just got an order for another 100 copies. They're coming here to pick them up."

"Two hundred more over here. We only have a thousand left."

Susan, Bob and four temp staffers were overwhelmed with phone calls.

"I'm having an extra 3,000 copies printed right now. They should be here in about half an hour."

"I've never heard of a newspaper issue going into a second print run. I hope I'm just having a nightmare," said Susan, her voice dripping with irony, in reply to Austin.

"We have a responsibility to get this significant article out to as many people as possible. That's why we're printing more."

"If you smell profit, go after it with all you've got. Whatta lesson," whispered one of the temps.

"I guess this means we can all look forward to a fat bonus. You want us to really enjoy Christmas break, eh, Austin?" Bob yelled out to Austin's back.

The response to the story had been greater and speedier than any of them had expected. The phones at the office started ringing early in the morning and the fax machine kept spitting out sheets. They were ringing with orders, with more streaming in via the internet. By the afternoon, everyone was running around the office like some kids at an amusement park. Over three thousand comments were up on the website.

As time wore on, peace gradually returned to the editorial department, which had looked like a war zone. By evening, the phone rang only a hundredth as often as it had earlier in the day.

With Charlie's permission, Ken left the office early. A cold winter wind had been blowing at last for the past two days. Ken held his collar tight to his skin as he walked along. They had made it over the first hurdle, he told himself, but for some reason he was increasingly depressed. Instead of satisfaction, he felt emptiness. When he got home he slipped straight into bed. His cold sheets chilled his spirits further.

Next morning, Ken was surprised to read the front-page of *The New York Times*:

PRESS CHALLENGE AGAINST DOJ—WEST COAST PAPER RE-VEALS SECRET BEHIND MAKING OF NUKES
      The Daily Californian *in Barton, California plans to publish in a five-part series excerpts of a paper on nuclear bomb production by a Manhattan Project scientist along with his memoirs…*

The article was quite detailed. *The Los Angeles Times* and *The Washington Post* also gave the story wide coverage with headlines like "Why Now? Nuclear Secrets Revealed," "Los Alamos, Exposed" and "How Far Will Gov't Intervene?" The angle varied, but each paper included the diagram.

The nation's most influential newspapers, with readers across the country, had devoted ample space to a regional paper's special feature.

The issue of proliferation to non-nuclear powers and the production of bombs by terrorist groups... Doubts about the conscience of a newspaper that publishes such a provocative article when Iraq and North Korea are suspected of having nuclear ambitions... The IAEA has completed another swift inspection of North Korea's nuclear capabilities... Nations grappling with the nuclear issue can't hide their befuddlement...

While few in number, articles criticizing the series did appear. On the whole, however, the national media cited *Knowledgment* and *The Daily Washington* and called it a brave move by a regional paper when others had caved to government pressure to halt their dissemination of nuclear development details and secrets. They called on *The Daily Californian* to withstand expected government pressure for the sake of the free press and free speech and continue to publish the series. These articles emphasized that the demise of the Eastern bloc had allowed the construction of a new peace and insisted that terrorism was a completely separate issue. They also pointed out that the structures of atomic and hydrogen bombs were no longer a secret anyway.

From that instant, all eyes were on *The Daily Californian*. Members of the press inundated the editorial department and their office was in a state of chaos.

The twelve phones rang nonstop and the newspaper received thousands of letters a day with orders for future issues carrying the series. At first, the reporters and temp staff were excited, but by the end of the day, they'd taken all the office's phones off the hooks and given up opening letters. Available staff were brought in from printing and general affairs to help sort things through, but they weren't able to keep up. Austin called in five student part-time workers from his supermarket to help out.

The senders ranged from a university newspaper editor who asked for 100 copies of issues with the series, individuals seeking copies, unknown organizations and research institutions. There were a fair amount of orders from overseas. As expected, there were some letters filled with criticism for publishing the series and some threats.

The next day the news hit the international press. It was covered heavily in Europe and Asia. South Korea, with the current state of the North on its mind, condemned the series in no uncertain terms. Israel, wary of its Islamic neighbors obtaining nuclear capabilities, requested the U.S. government to shut down the series immediately. Over all, it seemed that countries with nuclear weapons were against publication while those without nukes were supportive.

That day, Ken returned home and called Dr. Williams. "Did you read it?"

"Yes," a weak voice replied.

"Your memoirs are getting picked up by newspapers around the country. *The Washington Post, New York Times, Los Angeles Times…*"

"I'm so very grateful to you. At last my life has taken form. Light shines on my life, kept in the dark for so long. Now I can die contented."

"Hey, it's not over yet. This is just the beginning."

Even after Ken replaced the receiver, he stared at it for a while. The old man's weak voice echoed in his ear. He switched on the TV.

Senior Policy Advisor Curley was found mysteriously dead in a section of the Mall in the middle of the night… The investigation has reached a standstill… The White House has released an unusual statement asking for this case to be solved summarily…

Ken turned the sound off and just sat there watching a proud image of the Capitol. He tried to move and cried out. A sharp and sudden pain shot through his knee and spread across his leg and entire body. He lightly massaged his knee. Tomorrow was going to be a cold day.

At 5:45 a.m., he was woken by the phone. It was still dark out his window. He reached out from under the blanket to pick up the phone and the cold air latched onto his arm and chilled his entire body.

"Come to the office, now." Charlie's hoarse voice pierced his eardrum. He was still apparently at home, as Ken could hear his wife calling out that his coffee was ready.

When Ken reached the office, Susan and Jimmy were already there as well as a suited Austin who was pacing around the center of the room with a frown on his face.

"As we expected, the Pentagon and the Department of Energy have sent orders through the Justice Department to suspend the series," said Charlie, almost to himself as he slouched in his chair with his eyes closed.

"That indeed was expected," said Jimmy, indifferently. "Why are you panicking?"

"Now that it's actually happening, I feel terrible. Like we're doing something wrong," Susan sighed.

"And why not? We are," Jimmy muttered.

At 6:20, Bob came running in. He looked around, as if he wanted to make excuses, but no one gave him any attention so he went silently to his seat.

Austin read aloud from a document in his hand. "'The article published in your paper accurately describes seven important classified facts relating to nuclear arms production. This endangers national security, thwarts our efforts to halt nuclear proliferation and violates laws concerning nuclear energy. We are deeply concerned that the remaining installments will also contain top-secret information.' This was faxed to my home from a Congressman I know, and apparently the official version will be delivered to this office later today."

"There's no point in getting all worked up over it now. Just like Jimmy said, we anticipated this. What happened to your lawyer?" asked Ken.

"He's in Vegas. Work or vacation, I don't know. He's already packing and sweating bullets. I called him and woke him up," Austin replied, looking displeased. "I certainly hope you guys have a plan."

Charlie, who until that moment had been keeping quiet, took a manuscript from his pocket and placed it on the table. "As is clear from the precedence of a newspaper and a magazine publishing details on the structures of nuclear weapons, the information is already in the hands of a portion of the population. Forcible suspension of this series in order to try and pull the wool over the eyes of the public would be a severe violation of the freedom of press. That's the gist of it."

"And you really think that'll be enough to make the government back off?"

"I don't, but offering a rebuttal in our own paper, that's something in our power to do. We still have most of the national media on our side. There's no need to fret."

"Well, I'm going to discuss this with my lawyer. Don't do anything until I give word. I don't want this trouble with the government to escalate." Austin wiped the sweat off his forehead. "The legal counsel will be here by this afternoon. I expect you to let him read every article before it goes to print," he said and left the room.

"I feel a tingling in my body," Susan said.

"You should see a doctor. Try a neurologist. My stomach hurts. If this goes to court and we lose, we're all getting hauled off to jail. I'm sick just thinking of it. And just in time for Christmas, too," Bob said, glancing at Susan.

"Well, we only have ourselves to blame," accused Jimmy.

"Whose side are you on, anyway?" Bob glared at Jimmy.

"We don't know whether this will go to court, so for now let's leave all the legal matters up to the owner and his lawyer and just focus on our own jobs," said Charlie, unusually superior-like.

"So when did you write that editorial?"

"The night we decided to run with the series." Charlie stood up. "It's still a little early, so use this time to make up for all your slacking off." Charlie let out a loud yawn and went into his office.

Just as Austin had foretold, a message from the government arrived at 1 p.m. demanding that they suspend the series. Charlie had Bob deliver it to the lawyer's office. Charlie's editorial went to press without waiting for the lawyer's response.

From the next day *The Daily Californian* faced challenges that it had never known: government vs. press.

The Washington Post ran a pointed commentary on how the press should handle matters of national security, citing the Watergate scandal as an example. They also featured an article on the UN-resolution-backed nuclear inspections by the IAEA of Iran, Iraq and North Korea.

The *Los Angeles Times* ran a special on nuclear power, including the problems with recertification of the Diablo Canyon Power Plant that had become an issue in southern California.

"54.2 percent in favor, 38.5 percent against. 7.3 percent undecided. Those are the results of the survey carried out by the *Los Angeles Times*," said Bob with a serious look on his face. "At least half of Americans support our series. I think those are pretty amazing results." Susan nodded in agreement, her somber expression uncharacteristically non-ironic.

Jimmy interjected with a typically negative thought. "Immediately after 9/11, the majority of people in the U.S. supported retaliation. It was only when things had started to calm down a little that other opinions started to be heard. Right now, everyone's all worked up about all this."

Like mother whales looking after their young, all the major papers came out in seemingly coordinated support of a small-town newspaper with a circulation of 42,000. Rather than the newly in-session Congress, all eyes in the country were on Barton. Every day, the town's facilities and university lecture halls were used for debates and gatherings. The journalists at *The Daily Californian* were run off their feet. A large number of universities and other organizations came out in support of *The Daily Californian* whose pages became synonymous with the voice of Barton. That voice grew louder and spread farther thanks to amplification through various groups and mass media outlets. It all happened at a much faster pace and larger scale than they'd ever expected.

...dispute over the death of Curley, the senior policy advisor, on the 24th of November... Chief Carlock from the D.C. Police Department held a press conference and the suicide theory is gaining traction... President Jefferson still remains silent... Chief Spokesman Gerald held an unprecedented press conference... Various camps are refusing to budge in the lead-up to the next presidential election...

The dry voice of CNN's anchor came from a corner of the editorial office.

This string of White House scandals will heavily affect the next-gen stealth bomber proposal to come to the floor in Congress early next week... Congress has pushed back, members from both parties calling for a fuller accounting... But the president has expressed his strong will to push the plan through...

The female newscaster with salient features reported in closing that the president would most likely acknowledge the hawkish elements within the White House and send the stealth bomber plan to the House of Representatives. She commented, in something of an assertion, that the proposed budget was dead on arrival as the public was in favor of prioritizing economic growth over military expansion.

The people of this nation strongly wish to shake off the after-effects of 9/11, the world is on the path to arms reduction and the U.S. is headed towards drastically cutting down on its defense spending.

The news then proceeded to report that the federal deficit surpassed 3.4 trillion dollars and accrued interest of nearly 300 billion dollars each year, swallowing up a little over 42 percent of the country's tax revenues.

Ken looked out of the third-floor window of the waiting room. He could see a group holding placards, surrounded by onlookers and journalists. The throng undulated as a whole. The shouts of the protesters sounded like a dull roar.

It was 10 a.m. Excitement spilled out of the first-floor lecture hall in the Sociology Department at the University of California Barton campus. Green Earth had scheduled a debate coinciding with the release of the second installment in *The Daily Californian*'s series. Responding to the call, a large number of civic organizations had added their names to the list of participants, including the California Anti-Nuclear Alliance, the Anti-Nuclear Arms Proliferation Alliance, the Anti-Nuclear Citizens' Coalition, The Group to Protect Freedom of Speech and of the Press, as well as parents' organizations, such as Protect the Forests—Conscientious Citizens Group and Protect Our Children's Future. They were also expecting a large press turnout.

Charlie was set to deliver a progress report to the audience, while Ken was to talk about the forthcoming articles in the series. But staring at the protesters outside for half an hour now, Ken couldn't help but feel as if something was wrong. He hadn't set out to do anything like this. It was a feeling that he'd harbored ever since Dr. Williams' email initiated a ground swell that trapped both him and his paper. A wave was pushing them in a totally different direction from what his heart had desired.

"It's amazing," remarked Bob as he practically jumped into the room. "There's still an hour to go and already it's packed. There are people sitting in the hallway. It looks like there might be over 5,000 people attending."

"It's because of all the publicity. It's certainly put our paper on the map," Susan, who was standing next to Ken and staring out at the protesters, turned to say. A glimmer of giddiness showed through her sarcastic tone.

"It's not about how many people show up," Jimmy said from the corner of the room where he sat looking over the lecture summaries each group had submitted. "It's about what gets discussed. To look outside it seems more like some progressive mass festival. Take a look at the placards and flyers. Protecting nature, additives in food, genetic manipulation and engineering, cloning, abortion… They're all just here to promote their own causes, when what matters right now is J.W.'s memoirs." He seemed downright grim.

Susan scowled. "Jimmy, what's gotten into you lately? Can't you just be happy? Look at that crowd! There are reporters from *The New York Times* and *The Washington Post*, too. We're nationally famous."

"So do we want to write or be the subject of news articles?"

"How about both?"

Hearing this exchange, Ken pulled up a chair and sat down. He felt sluggish. His entire body was fatigued. Listening to Jimmy made him feel even more exhausted until he barely wanted to stand up. His knee ached as soon as he sat down. He pressed down on the joint with his fingers. By now he could tell where bone ended and plastic began.

Suddenly a voice boomed across the room, "So how's it going? Are you prepared?" It was Steve Austin, standing in the doorway, looking even sharper than usual in what looked like an expensive brown suit, gleaming shoes and a crimson necktie. All eyes turned to him.

"Yes, Miss Havisham," whispered Susan.

"Let's just hope he doesn't get too excited too quick, if you know what I mean," giggled Bob.

"Nothing to prepare. I'm just here to do what I do," replied Ken without getting up from his chair.

"We need this to be a success, no matter what," said Austin with a slightly concerned look at Ken's unaffected reply. "Reporters from *The Barton Journal* are here. I saw the owner's face, too."

Susan arched her eyebrows.

"Well, we're simply going to tell the truth. A paper was sent to us, we felt it had value as an article, so we published it. That's the duty of the press."

Austin clasped his hands behind his back and sauntered over to Ken with his chin in the air. "Yes, that's the best way. The masses bear grudges against the system and favor the underdog. If we come across like we have an agenda then they'll hate us, but they'll be on our side as long as we stay within limits. Beyond that, the media will have our back."

"Please don't look at it like that," challenged Susan. "We want to consider this issue with our readers, as one."

"Let's hope we can." Austin relaxed the muscles in his handsome face and smiled.

The discussion began with an explication of the paper by a young lecturer in physics at U.C. Berkeley. He clearly wanted to impress his audience and sounded somewhat overdramatic, a picture of awkward youth. He used technical terms with abandon, and his numerous diagrams, charts and graphs were largely unintelligible to the participants. Nucleus, neutron, collision cross-section, uranium, plutonium, nuclear bomb... Words with distinct rings were hurled mercilessly at the audience, and the hall became suffused with a scent of evil that melted and stirred the heart toward danger.

The leaders of each organization took the stand one after another. The air in the hall was full to bursting with roiling enthusiasm.

The final session was a roundtable on state confidentiality and concluded with the ratification of a statement protesting the government and military's penchant for secrecy. It was as if a massive flow were swelling up right there in that spacious, unadorned lecture hall; a tide picking up everything in its path and sweeping it along. Ken stood there, watching the flow with a cold objectivity.

Any public campaign needs momentum. Good momentum can brush aside a few contradictions and inconsistencies. Fraser's words rose up in Ken's mind.

"Then all that remains is the energy of a crazed mob," Ken mumbled under his breath.

The applause and cheers of over 5,000 people hit Ken like a roaring wave.

Lemmings. Members of the rodent family. Reproducing in the wilderness until there are hundreds of thousands of them, they migrate en masse. They breach the borders of the wild, run through towns, over mountain ranges, swallowing everything in their path. Eventually they reach the ocean, but they don't stop running, rushing right over cliffs until the surface of the sea is covered with their little corpses. Nobody can stop them. Ken wondered if he, too, was being pulled along by some unseen hand. Were they just racing towards the ocean, too?

The next day, Ken and Jimmy drove north along the coast, the Pacific sparkling in the sun stretching out on their left. Half an hour outside of San Francisco, a peninsula came into view in the distance to their left. There were gray buildings near the tip, and a cooling tower shaped like a silk hat could be seen through the haze. It was the Bridal Peninsula Nuclear Power Plant.

Today they'd been invited to an anti-nuclear power demonstration there and Ken was expected to give a short speech.

The ocean side of the power plant was exposed hard rock. The contrast between the rough seaside rock surface and the large gray concrete building struck an odd chord.

Over 3,000 citizens had gathered for the protest.

"Not another Three Mile! Not another Chernobyl!"

"You are not welcome!"

"Stop what you're doing, before you turn the Earth to ash!"

"No more nuclear bombs! No more nuclear power!"

Colorful placards peppered a section of the sloping hill in front of the power plant. The wind occasionally carried the voices of the protesters shouting in unison.

City of Parramatta Council
Parramatta Library

Customer ID: W0459905X

Title: Fallout
ID: P1017290t
Due: 30/5/2019,23:59

Total items: 1
09/05/2019 13:03
Checked out: 1

Visit us online at
www.parracity.nsw.gov.au/library

"I think nuclear power and nuclear bombs are two very different things," Jimmy said, looking at the demonstrators.

"From their point of view it's all the same nuclear power. Radiation kills, no matter where it comes from."

"But war and peace, creation and destruction, ought to be complete opposites."

A few dozen armed security guards were lined up along the inside of the plant's fence with blank looks on their faces. The press flanked the protesters with their TV vans and cameramen. Behind them were five police cars and twenty or so officers standing around looking bored.

Ken and Jimmy stood in front of the van in the center of it all. Beside them, the head of the California Anti-Nuclear Alliance, the sponsoring organization, was addressing the crowd with a megaphone, his distorted voice flowing all around Ken. Ken turned to look behind, past the barbed-wire fence that surrounded the power plant to where he could see the smooth curve of the cooling tower and the edifice that housed the reactor. Its calm, cool appearance belied the enormous energy that was harnessed inside.

"Nuclear power, environmental destruction, energy resources—I believe if they are managed right, nuclear power plants are a clean way to produce energy with no carbon footprint. But we do, of course, have to consider the issue of nuclear waste." Jimmy leaned forward and whispered to Ken.

"Then can you talk instead?"

"No, I'm a major coward. I'm trembling already," he said, shaking his body hyperbolically, eyes swimming.

The gathered people applauded. The organizer looked at Ken, who winked at Jimmy and walked up to the microphone. Ken repeated the story he had already told many times. While speaking, he sensed something odd and looked around. He felt he was being subjected to a special kind of gaze; someone was watching him.

Surrounded by female students passionately chanting, "No to nuclear power! Destroy all nuclear weapons!" he felt like he'd been left behind. *What am I doing here in the midst of all these protesters anyway? Was this what I wanted?* He was parched, and his heart palpitated as if his body were accruing heat. He glanced toward the ocean to where windsurfers were gliding smoothly with sails in primary colors. A trickle of cold sweat ran down his spine. He took several deep breaths and split off.

"What's Dr. James Williams like anyway?" asked Jimmy. "You met him, right?"

"He's an intelligent, solitary old man. Why?"

"Just interested. I wonder what a person who's dedicated his whole life to developing nuclear weapons is like." Jimmy shifted his gaze from Ken to the ocean. Ken studied his profile, the already pale skin looking even more fair lately, and discerned the trace of a dark shadow, hitherto absent, on Jimmy's gentle, effeminate face.

Ken suddenly doubled over, forcing back a retch. He hurriedly left the crowd.

"You look sick," Jimmy, who followed him, said peering into his face with worry.

"I'm fine. Nothing to worry about," assuaged Ken, wiping the sweat off his forehead while holding down his nausea. How many days was it since he quit drinking? He'd started counting, but given up. He'd been down this road before, so he knew that it didn't matter even if he didn't have a drop for a hundred days. If he took a drink on the hundred and first day, he'd be right back where he started. Finally conscious the next day, his body would be craving alcohol even more than before.

Jimmy held out an icy root beer and Ken took it and downed it in one.

An hour later, the two of them were driving south on the freeway.

"Next destination is a San Francisco radio station."

"So we're celebrities now."

"Susan even went on local TV today."

"So that's why. I nearly jumped when I saw her this morning. She looked like her makeup was applied with a palette knife. Like she mistook herself for an actress."

"Don't tell me, tell her."

"I told you, I'm a coward."

The afternoon interview took place at a local radio station outside of San Francisco. It was a panel discussion with a sociologist, a scientist and citizens and the main theme was the limit of free speech regarding matters on national security.

"There is no security for the nation, let alone the citizenry, in a society where speech is controlled. It only safeguards the establishment and doesn't deliver genuine safety for the people. Look at Iran, Iraq and North Korea. It leads to autocracy. We have to seek as much information as possible." Ken felt a sense of hollowness as he spoke, the words flowing to others, disconnected from his will. Wasn't getting a lonely scientist's life sinking into the recesses of history known by the world all he'd wanted to accomplish?

Jimmy kept his mouth shut wherever they went. He simply gave the shortest answer possible to all questions. It was as if by refusing to talk, he was maintaining his will.

Warren was woken by the phone. It was Chief Anderson, who sounded like he was in the car on his way to work.

"There was a call from the office. Go to the Crystal Hotel downtown immediately. They found the body of a young girl, stabbed to death," Anderson's hurried speech passed through Warren's still half-asleep brain.

"I'm with the political desk. Why don't you rouse someone on the city desk from his slumber instead? This doesn't concern me unless the body was found in the White House."

"She was with Frank Curley on the night of the twenty-third."

Warren jumped out of bed.

"I don't know the details, but get down there. Meet up with the guy from the city desk. I'll be in the office so report back when you can."

Warren placed the receiver back and ran to the bathroom. He took a shower with the cold water tap on full-blast. The icy water hitting his body woke him up.

He got into his car and checked the time. It was 8:07. It could take forever if he got caught in rush hour. He exited the car and ran toward the avenue. Would he get to the subway stop first or see a cab he could hail? As the subway entrance came into view, a taxi drove by. He stopped it and got in.

Once he approached downtown, the traffic started to clog up the roads just as he had expected, so he got out of the taxi and ran. The Crystal Hotel was a seedy place on the outskirts of downtown.

When he arrived, there were a few police cars parked in front and men in uniform rushing in and out the entrance. Yellow police tape hung in front of the crowd, telling them to keep out. Warren took out his press badge and hung it around his neck. A few television stations were already there with heavily made-up female reporters and crew members with cameras on their shoulders. The ones trying to push past the police were from newspapers. It was impossible to get in. He looked around for the city desk reporter but couldn't find him.

"How was it established at this late date that the girl was with Advisor Curley?" Warren asked an officer standing near the tape. A twenty-something reporter standing next to them hurriedly took out a notepad and studied the police officer, who shifted his weight and looked slightly upward trying not to meet their eyes.

"The customer in the next room complained that something smelled, so the old man at the front desk went to see. No one answered, so he used the master key to enter and found a naked girl tied to the bed, her blood flown out of her heart," a man in worker's overalls butted in from behind. The cop retained a blank expression but strained his ears. It was possible this was news to him, too.

"And her relationship with Advisor Curley?"

"They found his wallet."

"What was in it?"

"How would I know?"

The worker looked at Warren suspiciously, but caught sight of his press badge and nodded to himself in understanding. Warren gave up questioning the man and went looking for John, who was bound to be there with the MPDC homicide division.

The door of a van parked next to a police car opened and a man in plain clothes stepped out. Warren didn't recognize him. He wore a tailored jacket that closely fitted his slender figure and gave him a look of authority.

"The Chief will hold a press conference at the MPDC Headquarters in two hours," he yelled to the gathered press. "The details will be announced then, so we would like to ask the media to leave the premises now."

All the press members voiced protest, but the man started making his way back to the van expressionly. A crewman aiming a television camera moved forward, trying to get this figure on film, but an officer raised his hand to block the lens.

"Who is that guy?" snapped one of the reporters.

"Ask for an introduction. In writing. Standing around here for hours won't get you anything," the police officer who had silently blocked their way spoke for the first time.

"The media is completely shut out," Warren told Anderson over the phone. "They've sealed off a half-block, and I can't even get close to the hotel. But there'll be a press conference at Police HQ."

"We were notified of the press conference here, too. Go directly there, will you?"

"Do we know anything about the girl?"

"Nothing. Just that Frank Curley was with her the night he killed himself. They've promised to tell everything in the press conference. Goldman and others from the city desk have already headed over."

Warren hung up and looked for John again, but it was impossible. He left the crowd and headed toward police headquarters.

By the time Warren got there, the area was overflowing with the press. A huge throng clogged the entryway. Usually press conferences were held in front of the building, but apparently a meeting room had been prepared for today.

"Entry limited to two people per organization," shouted a uniformed press officer as he checked IDs. It would be impossible for him to keep track unless he had some kind of super memory. At the least, Warren noticed four *Washington Post* reporters and photographers there.

He entered the meeting room and looked for Goldman. Someone was waving in his direction from the second row. It was Goldman. He'd been told for his part that Warren would come.

Warren moved through the crowd and sat next to him.

"The crime scene is blocked off for a 30-yard radius. Police everywhere. There's more to this than just the murder of some girl," Warren whispered.

"It's a murder involving the White House. I mean, an advisor to the president stripped a girl, tied her to a bed and stabbed her to death. It would damage the president, too," Goldman whispered back into Warren's ear.

"Are the police saying it was definitely Advisor Curley?"

"His wallet was left on the table. The contents were all there—money, credit cards, driver's license, and White House ID."

"It's too perfect."

"100 percent perfect."

"In this type of incident the perp…" Warren was in mid-sentence when Police Chief Sam Carlock walked in and the bustle died in an instant.

"Today at 06:05, the body of a young female was found in room 352 of the Crystal Hotel. Her identity is unknown. She's Caucasian, 15 or 16 years old. A wallet was found at the scene belonging to Frank Curley, who committed suicide by handgun at the Mall on the twenty-fourth," read Carlock from his memo, disinterestedly.

"Did Advisor Curley murder her?"

Carlock glared in the direction of the voice. "That is under investigation. No comment."

"Can you tell us the state of the victim when found?"

"She was naked. Her hands and feet were tied to the bedposts with rope. Her mouth was stuffed with underwear and duct-taped shut."

"Cause of death?"

"She was stabbed in the chest with a sharp blade. Elsewhere too her body was covered with wounds. Details will be announced once we have the results of the autopsy." Carlock looked menacingly around the room.

"It's been six days since Curley's death. Why wasn't she discovered sooner?"

"The room was paid up for ten days. The cold had slowed the decay of the body, so the corpse was only discovered today."

"Was there evidence of sexual activity?"

Carlock looked at the reporter who'd asked this as if to say, *Don't ask such a stupid question.* "There'll be an announcement after the autopsy. That is all we know at this time." He stood up.

"You know nothing, then."

"Are there pictures?"

"Will the White House be investigated?"

"Sounds like the work of a total psycho. No wonder he committed suicide."

"Answer us, dammit."

As the press cried out, Carlock kept his eyes fixed forward and walked past them in silence.

"Things might take an unexpected turn," Goldman whispered into Warren's ear.

"They're just reinforcing what was already reported. It just switched from Curley shooting himself up with heroin before shooting himself to him killing himself in remorse over shooting himself up with heroin and raping and murdering a young girl. Curley's abnormality has been perfected."

"Damage to the White House image is unavoidable. There was a pervert on the staff, in the innermost circle."

"It's too perfect. Everything is too put together, don't you think?"

"That's the way it is with crimes of the elite. Once they go off track they can't stop. The rest is a dash to the end."

"I have an errand to run," said Warren, standing up. "Go back without me."

He was swept along by the crowd out of the room. He stopped in a corner of the hallway and dialed John's number on his cell phone. John's phone rang for a while with no hint of anyone picking up. Suddenly it was cut off. John must have seen a reporter's name and rejected the call. Warren clicked his tongue and returned his cell phone to his pocket. He left the MPDC HQ and raced to the office.

Later that afternoon, Anderson visited Warren with a memo. "The autopsy results, released by the police five minutes ago."

Warren grabbed at it and looked it over. "This is basically the same info they gave us at the press conference."

"That's what Goldman and the others said. You can tell the police are on their toes, though. They even faxed this to us."

"Of course. The White House is tangled up in all this."

"I guess this sinks any apologetics for Curley."

"The only evidence of Curley's presence in that room is the wallet. The person who stole it could have left it there."

"The money and credit cards were still in it. That would only be the case if he left it himself."

"If he was guilty he wouldn't be dumb enough to leave it."

"He was in a rush. One minute he's having fun with the girl, the next he's gone too far and killed her. He wandered over to the park, got a hold of himself and realized the gravity of the situation. It was too much so he killed himself. These privileged guys are like that. Mystery solved."

"Up until now, heroin was the reason he shot himself. Not that I ever really believed he would be the sort to even carry a gun."

"Believe what you want," shrugged Anderson, and walked out.

It was after 8 p.m. by the time Warren managed to get in touch with John. The detective didn't want to meet up, but Warren finally got him to agree to see him at the cafeteria downtown. Warren was there for ten minutes before John, surveilling their surroundings, walked in.

He sat down without removing his coat and ordered a coffee.

"Even in winter, if a body is left for a week it starts to decay. The customer in the next room complained. The girl had countless wounds all over her body. No foreign bodily fluids were left behind. But there was a tear in her genitals. She was raped, and the guy used a condom," John started in a low voice.

"Would a rapist bother with a condom?"

"Maybe he was concerned with disease. He's got a wife. The elite are such paragons of restraint, unlike me."

"Look, he committed suicide a few hours later. He didn't have to worry about that," Warren said, loudly enough for the customers around them to turn and stare.

"Don't raise your voice. At that point he hadn't meant to kill himself," muttered John, ducking his head down. "The girl was a horrible sight. Hand and feet tied to the bedposts… I only saw the pictures, but still. If I were the girl's father, I'd kill the guy without any hesitation, in the cruelest way possible," fumed John, leaning toward Warren.

"The only evidence that Curley did such an evil thing is the wallet left behind."

"What else do you need?"

Warren searched for words. "How about fingerprints?"

"None."

"Then someone else may have left it there."

"Who? For what purpose? Be specific."

Warren lifted his coffee and took a sip. The lukewarm liquid flowed down his throat. "How about his briefcase?"

"We haven't found it. Someone must have taken it after he committed suicide."

"You mean he left his wallet, took just his briefcase and headed toward the park? That's one idiotic senior advisor. We couldn't have expected much for the future of the United States with guys like that in the White House."

"Face it. There was a side of Frank Curley you didn't know about."

"My boss' words exactly."

John took a piece of paper out of his pocket and slid it onto the table. "These are Curley's cell phone records."

Warren jumped at the sheet, running his eyes over the times and phone numbers. "17:20. This is it. This is *The Washington Post*'s main number. No mistake. Curley did call me."

"Maybe he wanted to ask you to babysit his daughter? You are a pro after all."

"Spare the jokes at a time like this. When was the last call? Exactly at 11 p.m. To somewhere within the city."

"I don't know. I haven't heard anything. I don't want to get involved any more than this. It was tough getting my hands on these records," said John, glancing around. "And don't come to the police station from now on, and don't call me, either."

"What's the problem?"

"First of all, I'm not on the Curley case so I don't know anything. But I have friends, you know. They're usually good guys, but they're also very simple-minded. I'm sure you understand."

"Go ahead and spit it out. It's not like you to be so coy."

"We received direct orders to watch our interaction with the media. That's how nervous this case makes everyone."

"I'll be careful."

"That's not enough. I need your word."

"Yes, sir." Warren raised his right hand.

"You will call my cell phone or home phone, and that only in an emergency. Promise me."

Warren nodded wordlessly. John pushed the check over to him before getting up.

That night, Warren didn't get home until after midnight. He sat on the sofa and gazed at a stain on the ceiling. He was overcome by a desire to hear Cathy's voice. He knew she'd still be awake, but as soon as he reached for the phone he stopped himself. Maybe he'd try after this case was closed, once more…

After taking a hot shower, he crawled into bed. He was exhausted but couldn't fall asleep as his mind was still buzzing with the girl's autopsy results and John's words. In the middle of it all was Curley.

Just after 3:00 a.m. he switched on his computer and checked his email. There was a message from Chief Anderson. He'd attached the reactions from major newspapers to *The Daily Californian*'s series. It was basically an order for him to follow the coverage.

By the time he'd gone back to bed it was past 5:00 a.m.

Out of nowhere, a dark hand reached out and wrapped its fingers around his throat. He tried to escape, but his body refused to move. He knew it was all a dream, but still he couldn't wake up.

It was always like this.

In the distance, he heard the phone ringing. Warren summoned all his concentration and reach out for the phone.

"Daddy, were you awake?" It was Teddy.

"What is it?" Warren groaned.

"Mommy told me to call you."

Warren lifted his head to look at the clock. It was 7:30. He'd only slept for about two hours. "Give the phone to your mother," he said in a raspy voice.

"She said to say no. Daddy, take me to preschool. Then we're going to the Smithsonian."

"Please, Teddy. Get your mother on the phone."

"Mommy's still sleeping. Daddy, you wanted to meet Cindy's mommy, didn't you? She's coming to the Smithsonian today. Mommy called her."

"I'll be there in thirty minutes. Get ready and wait for me."

Warren jumped out of bed. His whole body had that particular lack-of-sleep sluggishness. His conscious mind was dragged forward from the depth of his brain as he splashed his face with cold water.

It was before eight. The roads were crowded. Nevertheless, it only took a little longer than usual to reach Georgetown. Teddy was sitting on the steps in front of the house with a lunch box in his hands. It was a twenty-minute drive from Cathy's house to the preschool. No sooner had Teddy got in when Warren's cell phone started ringing.

"Don't talk to Mrs. Curley in front of anybody, and tell her who you are first. Not that you're Teddy's father, the other thing. You understand? Don't screw it up," warned Cathy. "She's a mother and a wife who lost the love of her life in the most horrible way. Don't you forget that." She hung up before Warren could even think to reply.

Warren waited at the preschool for more than an hour. Most of the adults were mothers, and as for men, there were a few grandfathers. Warren looked for Mrs. Curley but couldn't find her. He didn't imagine Cathy would lie, so perhaps they were joining the group later. The adults made carpooling arrangements for the Smithsonian outing. Warren rounded up the three other kids who'd been assigned to his car.

The Smithsonian was having a preschooler day and more than a hundred children and caregivers were there. While the children were in the museum, the parents would wait in the lobby.

Warren set about looking for Mrs. Curley. There was a woman sitting on a bench at the edge of the lobby wearing dark sunglasses, a gray coat and a black turtleneck. She had elegant features. There could be no mistake. Tearing himself away from a middle-aged man who started speaking to him, Warren approached her.

"Mrs. Curley?"

"Are you with the press?" she replied, giving him a frightened glance. The media circus must have taken its toll on her since the incident.

"I'm with *The Washington Post*, but I'm not here for work. I'm Theodore McCarthy's father," said Warren, nodding in Teddy's direction.

"We've met at preschool functions a few times. I'm here with him today."

"So you're Cathy's husband."

"I'm a reporter in the culture section. Family columns, novels and movie reviews. I'm not on the city desk."

He'd lied again.

A hint of relief appeared in her eyes.

"I'm sorry, is Cathy…"

"We're separated. She couldn't get off work today, so I brought Teddy."

"Cathy…seems happy," she let drop, smiling sadly.

"Your husband must have been… I mean, look at the world today. Ah, damn it. Work habit, sorry."

"It's okay. The newspapers and television have said all kinds of things, but he was the perfect husband and father."

"I believe you. The media likes to sensationalize things. They especially like gossip stories."

"But…" she faltered. "What's being said… It's all wrong. He never went around at night. Never. He got in trouble once in New York and… He'd never go near a park at night since then."

She stiffened briefly and looked down at her shoes. Warren didn't know what to do, desperately trying to remember what Cathy had told him.

"And he always called me before coming home. That night, he called to say he was on his way…"

"From a White House phone?"

"No, personal calls are only for emergencies. It leaves a record. He used his cell phone."

Warren gave a number. Her expression clouded.

"That's my number. Did Cathy tell you?"

"No, the records of your husband's cell phone had a line for eleven sharp. It was his last call. I found out through my work."

Warren looked over to the exhibit hall, where Teddy was peering into a glass case with a girl, their heads side by side.

"Did your husband bring work home?"

"Only since about half a month ago. He hadn't in the past. His policy was to not bring work home."

Warren remembered how an unassuming Frank Curley had brought homemade potato salad to a gathering. That night, Cathy had chided him. *All you're good for is slicing pizza!*

"He'd bring home a briefcase full of documents, then stay in the study until late."

"So he had a briefcase with him," Warren blurted out without thinking.

"You're..." A look of fear washed across her face.

"I'm on your husband's side. To tell the truth," he said in a formal manner, "Advisor Curley called me. It was the afternoon before his death. At 5:20 p.m. I wasn't there so he left me a message."

Mrs. Curley's expression went rigid. "What did it say?"

"Just that he would call again. But that was the night..." Warren trailed off. He didn't quite know how to proceed. "Anyway, he was planning to get in touch with me." Warren took out the copy of the phone records he'd obtained from John. "This is the main number for the *Post*. And at 11:00 p.m., this is the call he made to you. That's the last call. Something happened to him after calling you."

"But the police said..."

"Did you trust him?"

"Yes. Completely." She stared into Warren's eyes.

"Is there anything you can think of? Work, private life, anything."

"No. Our family was happy. At least, our daughter and I were. He never spoke about his work at home."

"Daddy," a voice called. Warren turned to see Teddy standing with a fair, lovely girl who was several inches taller than him. Probably Cindy. She took after her mother more than her father. The teacher in charge stood near the entrance, signaling for the kids to gather around.

"We're heading home now. She's taking time off preschool," said Mrs. Curley, getting to her feet.

Warren drove the same group of kids back to preschool.

"Teddy," he called out as his little boy walked away from the car, "Cindy's a cute girl."

"I'm going to protect her. From the bad guys," Teddy nodded, then went running off to his classroom.

"But she looks like no pushover," Warren muttered to himself and headed to his office.

That day there were no new developments with regard to the girl's murder. All the newspapers had written it up as though Frank Curley had raped and killed the girl.

Warren hesitated, then dialed a cell phone number. "John?"

"I told you not to call me at the station," said John, trying to keep his voice down.

"I thought your cell phone was okay. What, do I need to check where you are before calling?"

"What do you want?"

"You knew whose number Curley called last, didn't you?"

"Yeah… So?"

"So the police know Curley left the White House and planned to go straight home."

"Washington nightlife is inviting. He changed his mind."

"He wasn't as unhappy as you are. He had a loving family waiting at home."

"How many times do I need to tell you, this is not my case."

"Tell me what you guys know about the girl's murder."

There was a pause, as if John had moved somewhere else.

"Yes, I understand. I'll get back to you on that."

After that awkwardly polite response, the line went dead. Warren gazed at the phone on his desk. What could have awaited Curley on his way home after he'd made his call? Ten minutes later, the phone finally rang.

"That room was reserved by a man on the twenty-third. Ten nights were paid up front. The front desk thought it odd but left him alone," John started in before Warren could utter a word.

"And that man was Curley?"

"The front desk doesn't look at faces. That way if something goes south they can claim ignorance. That's how that whole hotel is set up. You reporters should know how those places work."

"Did anyone see the girl?"

"No one can recall. That kind of hotel tolerates all kinds of goings-on. The man had left a ten-dollar tip. That's the only reason anyone remembered."

"Anything left behind?"

"Not even a fingerprint. A few strands of hair on the girl's body, though. They're running a DNA check as we speak."

"But would a murderer who leaves no fingerprints leave hair?"

"It's not necessarily Curley. The DNA is still being processed."

"So the only evidence that points to Curley is his wallet?"

"Must've been too engrossed in torturing then stabbing the girl to death."

"What was the weapon?"

"A sharp tool with at least an eight-inch blade. Probably a knife. But it hasn't been located. Same as the gun. Someone must have taken it."

"That's just your imagination."

"There was heroin in her blood. They probably got high together, started getting into a little S&M, then that got out of hand and the next thing he knows, she's dead. He freaks out, leaves the hotel in a hurry and goes to the park. The rest, as they say, is history." John's tone was matter of fact.

"Why do you keep jumping to conclusions?"

"Why do you keep covering for him?"

"I'm not. I just want to know the truth."

"The truth may be the last thing his family needs."

"I'm very much aware of that," Warren said, chewing each word.

"Then stop asking questions."

"What was in Curley's briefcase?"

"I told you, there's no briefcase."

"But there was one. He was on his way home from the White House. Apparently he always carried a briefcase."

"We looked. We haven't found one." John's voice sounded increasingly irritated.

"I saw Mrs. Curley today. According to her he always carried a briefcase. He was a very cautious man, apparently. She said he'd never go to such a place at such a time alone."

John didn't react.

"Are you listening?"

"I'm thinking about what could have happened."

"So why isn't anyone asking questions about the briefcase?"

"We have. The area was searched thoroughly. But it wasn't found. We asked the wife, too. She said he carried a good leather one. According to the White House…" John stopped, mid-sentence.

"What is it?"

John gave no response. After a pause came the sounds of running water and a door shutting.

"You're in the can?"

"They're prohibited from taking sensitive documents out. They say Curley wasn't handling any classified information," John continued.

"You believe such an obvious lie? He was an advisor to the president for policy. As far as I know he was the president's most trusted aide. He was swimming in classified information."

"I can't say. That's the government's line."

"What was Curley working on for the past two weeks, anyway? Whatever it was it kept him at the office until close to midnight and had him holed up in his study even after getting home."

"Hey, go ask at the White House yourself. 'Hi, Mr. President, I'm a big fan and I'm definitely going to vote for you next year. By the way, why don't you tell me what your friend Advisor Curley was doing sitting in the park at three in the morning?'"

Warren could practically see John pulling faces. Ignoring that, he asked, "What about that first witness?"

"Give me a break. I told you about it before and even showed you the investigation write-up."

"Any chance he's involved?"

"He hailed a police car right after finding him."

"How do you know?"

"Another patrol saw him running near a subway entrance. The call came right after that. He wasn't holding any shoes or briefcase."

"You said he was Italian?"

"Going the racism route?"

"Curley was wearing Italian shoes."

Warren heard John sigh. "And his watch was made in Japan."

"Give me his address."

"Why are you so hung up on this case?"

"I told you, I just want the truth."

"You already know the truth."

"I think it's no more than fiction. There's nothing decisive. Even I could have planted that wallet."

"I'll only say it once." Warren heard the sound of pages being flipped, then an address and phone number.

"You aren't my best friend for nothing," the reporter said and was about to hang up, but the detective's voice pierced his ear.

"Guess who had Curley's phone records?"

"Stop with the act. If I had that fertile an imagination, I'd be with the force."

"The FBI. It's going to be a joint operation from here on, with them leading. In other words, the White House wants to know every move we make."

"Are you gonna let the Feds do with you as they please?" provoked

Warren, immediately wishing he hadn't.

John's face floated before his eyes. Warren knew exactly how much John longed to join the bureau, and also how it was still a far-off dream. Skills aside, FBI investigators were an elite corps answering directly to the federal government.

"My bad."

"Anyway, I have nothing to do with this case," John said in a low voice, hanging up just a moment later.

Warren lowered the receiver and remembered the suited man who'd stepped out of the van parked by the Crystal Hotel. That van… The faces of Mrs. Curley and Cindy came to Warren's mind and then faded.

The next day Warren woke up at two in the morning. He'd gone to bed at eleven so he'd only gotten three hours of sleep.

As he stepped outside, the cold air seeped into his bones. He hurried over to the car. The engine groaned a few times before starting. He stopped off to pick up a coffee and a burger at a drive-through.

He parked twenty yards from the National Museum of Natural History in the Mall, from where he could easily see the bench. The digital clock on his dashboard showed 3:00 a.m. He turned off the engine and the car filled with coldness. He cupped the coffee in both hands and sipped, but it was already lukewarm.

A quiet, winter park stretched out before him. Indeed, no one could be seen walking around here at this hour. He wrapped his face with his scarf, leaving a narrow gap for his eyes. He buried himself deep in the seat and looked ahead. The bench was located toward the middle—on it Curley had been found with a bullet through his chest. Although Warren had heard it had been an instantaneous death, it was a lonely way to go whether it was murder or suicide.

When the clock showed 3:10, Warren heard footsteps approaching in the distance. In his rear-view mirror, he saw a jogger move into a patch of street light and head towards him.

He slid lower in his seat. He wouldn't be visible unless someone were to stop and peer inside the car. If anyone did see him, they'd probably just assume he'd passed out drunk.

The man passed by his car and headed toward Union Station. Warren sat up and watched the man's back. The man maintained a good pace. When he passed the park Warren thought he saw him glance at the bench. According to the guy's statement he had gone to Union Station then returned to the park where he found Curley's body.

Warren started his car. The frozen engine coughed for a few seconds, then turned over. He passed the man, headed toward Union Station, parked again two hundred yards from the entrance and took out a pair of binoculars. From here, the station looked little more than a shadow in front of the sleeping city. The man appeared and entered the station. Warren thought he caught sight of another person, but he wasn't sure. After ten minutes or so, the jogger exited the station and headed back toward the Mall.

Warren drove downtown, coming to a stop in front of an old apartment building. The lamps wanly illuminated the night of a city in early winter. The street was quiet and devoid of people. Warren buried himself in his seat as he had done earlier. The jogger appeared in his rear-view mirror, ran past his car and entered the building, breathing hard. Warren glanced at the clock. It was 4:30. Soon he saw a light go on. The jogger's apartment.

Glancing at the clock once more, Warren started the car again. He needed sleep before his body broke down, though he doubted he'd be able to get much rest at all.

Chapter 3
Ripples

The car sped along a road forty miles south of Barton. Half an hour out of the suburbs, the rolling hills stretched out on both sides and the white road looked like a chalk line. Ken took a turn, leaving the freeway for a road along the coast. After driving another five minutes east, a line of gray buildings came into view, like tips of horsetail grass sticking out in a field.

The Lawrence Livermore National Laboratory. The arcing building in the middle housed the nuclear reactor, flanked by the box-like control tower, the research building and the turbine set against the navy blue of the Pacific.

The digital clock on the dash showed eight minutes to ten, meaning he was right on time. He could almost picture the surprise on Yamada's face.

A long metal bar as thick as his arm blocked the entrance. When Ken pulled up near the security checkpoint, an armed guard in a gray uniform peered in. Ken gave him Dr. Seiichi Yamada's name. The guard made a call, then the steel gates opened. Ken had heard that some of the guards at the checkpoint were armed with automatic rifles and that the site's alarm linked directly to the police.

Ken passed through and drove at a pace a jogger could best in the direction the guard had indicated to him. Not another soul could be seen anywhere. A nine-foot-high barbed wire fence surrounded the laboratory, and craggy hills stretched beyond the fence to the ocean.

Yamada was waving his hand in the parking lot of the research build-ing. Ken got out of the car and Yamada ran over with a friendly smile.

"So, you're off the booze today, are you?"

"Yamada, you're a truly excellent scientist. You can smell sobriety?"

"You arrived on time and your eyes aren't red." Yamada, who was dressed in an oil-stained lab coat, laughed out loud joyously. The kind-ness of this man who shared his heritage made a strong impression on Ken.

"When's Ann coming home?"

"I don't know," answered Ken, curtly.

"How is she—"

"Let's get moving," Ken cut Yamada short with a push of his shoul-der. The man's smile was replaced by a stern expression.

Together, they entered the cramped lobby of the research building. Yamada led Ken to a scale model of the laboratory in a plastic case.

"There are 150 researchers and an equal number of auxiliaries work-ing here. We have one Nobel Prize winner and countless potential laure-ates, including myself."

"If you ever win it, I'll throw you a party. In return, I want an exclu-sive interview."

"There are three research buildings surrounding an experimental pressurized water reactor with a thermal output of 270,000 kilowatts. We do basic research on nuclear matter, reactor fuel and reactor materials. As a university-affiliated research institute, it's among the largest in the world. Seventy percent of our budget comes from the national and state governments, and we have major ties to the military."

"The military?"

"The Pentagon outsources a lot of research to us. Nuclear subma-rines, nuclear aircraft carriers, they all house reactors and are powered by atomic energy. Universities often have links to the military in this coun-try. Not like in Japan, where that would be a scandal. Shall we start the tour in the control room?" said Yamada as he led the way.

The empty hallway was bright and clean, and red, blue, yellow and white lines ran along the floor. "Each colored line has a different destina-tion," explained Yamada, as their footsteps echoed loudly.

Ken had been to visit Yamada several times before, but this was the farthest he'd ever gone inside the building. He'd always been offered a tour by Yamada, but every time he had declined. Ken preferred not to get involved in anything beyond his own sphere, and the nuclear issue was decidedly out of bounds. This time, however, Ken had asked for a tour.

"The yellow line leads to the main control room." They rounded three corners and entered a small room at the end of the hall. Yamada handed Ken a white helmet from the wall, explaining it was a regulation, before putting one on himself. The two of them then took an elevator in the back of the small room to the third floor.

A narrow, long hallway stretched out ahead of them. One wall was a glass window with a brightly lit space beyond it.

"This is the main control room," Yamada said directly into Ken's ear as the latter stared inside.

Light blue control panels lined three walls and in the center were three displays six feet wide and three feet high. Around the displays were a few hundred gauges and lamps. There was also a line of PCs and os-cilloscopes, a few thousand cables leading out of the control panels and a printer continuously spewing out data. On the display panels on the oscilloscopes fluctuated shiny waving lines.

Three rows of table-like control panels were lined up in the center of the room and over ten men in uniforms were busy moving among them. The large display in the front control panel showed the pressure vessel in the heart of the containment vessel. The eerie, silver-white special-alloy cylinder looked somehow like a tombstone.

"Everything in the reactor is controlled here."

"They look busy," said Ken, peering down with his forehead against the glass.

"Sixteen universities and research institutions around the country use it. There are no Saturdays and Sundays while experiments are in prog-ress, and they are 24 hours a day. Today they're running tests on refrac-tory lining."

Ken shrugged silently. In high school he'd been crazy about cars, but this was different. In a car's engine there were pistons and cylinders and plugs—things that combined and began moving before your eyes. An obvious object. But in this modern space, there was nothing he could readily identify. Everything was moving out there, yet controlled and operated here. To Ken, it made the whole system seem as slippery as an abstract painting. They returned to the empty hallway.

"Big science," said Yamada, turning to Ken. "Science changes in na-ture with scientific development. We need huge accelerators for nuclear physics, high-speed calculators for quantum mechanics. Science has left the hands of the individual and entered the realm of institutions and funds. The age of Edisons and Einsteins is over. Massive infusions of money and manpower drive things. Science is now a political and group affair." Yamada's high-pitched voice bounced off the concrete walls. Ken thought about the Manhattan Project, as described in Dr. Williams' manuscript.

"These are the times we live in. Personally, I think that's sad," concluded Yamada. Ken, who stood a whole head taller than him, looked at his profile. Behind his thick glasses shone the same black eyes as Ken. It was only his receding hairline and wrinkly forehead that made this otherwise baby-faced Japanese look believable as a scientist.

They made their way to Yamada's office. The wall across the door had a large window and against it were two desks with computers and numerous data sheets chock full of numbers scattered about. A bookcase covered half of the back wall, bursting with books and files tagged with handwritten labels.

"Albert is running an experiment, so he won't be back tonight," said Yamada, studying the timetable on the wall and pulling up Albert's chair for Ken. Yamada opened his desk drawer and pulled out a thick paper bag.

"The materials and diagrams are all very interesting."

"And they're top secret?"

"Something like that. They span a variety of topics, from fission to fusion bombs. It's certainly not the sort of thing the government or military would happily divulge. Albert thought so, too."

Ken let out a sigh. He felt something in the corner of his heart get up and listlessly disappear. What had he been hoping to hear?

Yamada pulled out a sheet from the diagram and laid it out before him. "Albert said these are used in large strategic nukes like ICBMs," Yamada said, retrieving a candy from his desktop and popping it into his mouth. He offered one, but Ken declined. They were sent from Japan and contained some kind of sour plum that had an odd flavor.

Yamada took out a booklet and opened it to a bookmarked page. "There are two types of nuclear bombs, one of which is the fission bomb where heavy elements like uranium-235 or plutonium-239 are bombarded with neutrons to release a blast of energy. The other is the hydrogen bomb, which uses an opposing principle—nuclear fusion—involving a thermonuclear process that uses isotopes of hydrogen, the lightest of the elements."

Yamada pointed at the periodic table of elements tacked on the wall.

Ken recalled memorizing the table in his high school days, although he couldn't say he'd ever understood it.

"For hydrogen bombs, you need to create a high temperature to initiate a fusion reaction, which is achieved via nuclear explosion. The heat must reach at least ten million degrees and the higher the temperature, the better the reaction rate. The theoretical hydrogen bomb in the paper you sent me has a very interesting structure with regard to this point." He took a blank piece of paper and began drawing a diagram. "Atomic bombs are set at two opposite ends of a cylindrical capsule. The hydrogen-bomb fuels lithium-6 deuteride and tritiated lithium are in the middle. When the atomic bombs are set off, they create heat and shockwaves. In addition to generating a high-temperature environment, the shockwaves compress the hydrogen-bomb fuel and increase the reaction probability. The shockwaves from each end clash at the center, further raising the temperature." Yamada looked to see if Ken was following.

"So what does that mean? Give me the bottom line," asked Ken.

"This cylindrical capsule represents an original twist that increases the concentration of energy at the very first stage of the explosion. With this method, the rate of reaction would go as high as 80 to 90 percent. The birth of a truly powerful hydrogen bomb."

Ken stared at the diagram. From the complexly intertwined lines, he felt intense flames flare up that melded all.

"The paper even touches on laws of scaling that determine the size of the nuclear explosion and on the timing from the atomic detonation to the ignition of the hydrogen bomb. That is to say, it's peppered with top-secret information."

"So in practical terms, would a non-nuclear country or a group of terrorists be able to build an atomic bomb or hydrogen bomb using this?"

Yamada placed the copy on his desk, took off his glasses and pressed his eyelids for a moment. "Well, the theory is relatively straightforward, but actually building one is difficult. You'd need technicians with high-level expertise and skills in engineering, mechanics, physics, electronics, chemistry... You'd also need a vast amount of money and time, and materials that aren't easy to come by."

"What's your point?"

"You need brains and equipment to make a nuclear bomb, plus all kinds of knowledge and technical skills of an advanced level. The materials need to be of a very high grade, too. You need to have experience and proper equipment to handle radioactive materials. That's not all. The accompanying equipment is highly specialized, too. And just making a bomb isn't enough. You have to know how to transport it and have it detonate properly. The list goes on."

"But what if it was a government, or some government-level organization?"

"It would be possible. Quite possible. But most importantly," Yamada focused on Ken as he spoke, "how would they get their hands on the materials? A fission bomb needs either uranium or plutonium. Uranium, for example, was what comprised the bomb that was dropped on Hiroshima. When uranium is mined, however, it is actually a mixture of uranium-235, which is fissile, and uranium-238, which is fissionable but not fissile. The irksome fact is that natural uranium contains just 0.7 percent of fissile uranium-235. The remaining 99.3 percent is useless uranium-238. For nuclear reactors, you can use the natural uranium as fuel or enrich it so that the uranium-235 concentration is just 3 to 5 percent. But that stuff isn't good enough for a nuclear bomb. For that you need uranium-235 at almost 100 percent concentration, and the technology needed to concentrate it poses the challenge."

Yamada turned to a few sheets of illustrations on the wall. It was of the nuclear power and fuel reprocessing plant currently planned for development in Texas.

"The Nagasaki bomb used plutonium. Plutonium doesn't exist in nature. It's created when uranium-238 absorbs neutrons and emits beta rays. You need an accelerator to make it. The thing is, spent nuclear fuel from a reactor contains a percent each of unused uranium-235 and newly created plutonium. By collecting these materials, you have the materials needed for an atomic bomb. This is called reprocessing, which also requires high-level technology. The problems for countries wanting to make nuclear bombs concern ways to obtain enriched uranium-235 and plutonium."

"How about Japan?" Ken asked with a straight face.

Yamada blinked a few times and looked away.

"You always ask awkward questions." He threw another candy in his mouth and chewed on it noisily. "Nuclear power is the science with the strongest ties to politics. You know about the three non-nuclear principles of Japan?"

Ken shook his head.

"Japan's basic policy is to not make, possess or allow entry of nuclear weapons. Nuclear power development is conducted independently, democratically and openly. While no one can research nuclear bombs directly, Japan has succeeded in creating enriched uranium. They have a wealth of experience in handling nuclear materials, and I'm sure you're familiar with their electronics prowess."

"So they can make one."

"I'm not in a position to state that. But currently the U.S., Russia, the U.K., France, China, India and Pakistan possess nuclear arms, and even North Korea is openly declaring that they have them, too. Do you think Japanese technology is behind the tech of those countries? Besides…" added Yamada, "Japan needs nuclear technology. It's an energy issue. For a country with limited natural resources, it's essential know-how. However, the technology for atomic energy will always be inextricably linked with that for nuclear arms. Even this lab—"

Yamada stopped short, shutting his mouth.

"Six weeks," he resumed after a moment. "Two weeks for basic calculations and design, two weeks to gather the materials and the last two weeks to construct it. Even faster if they need to hurry."

"Just from this paper?"

"Well, they'd certainly consult it. The basic parts could be used as is, but it's not a be-all and end-all." Yamada straightened his posture. "Let me tell you another interesting fact. There's a large volume of radioactive isotopes stored at this research facility at all times. Some were bought for experimental purposes, some were manufactured here. Furthermore, we hold a large amount of highly enriched uranium for the government and the private sector. Of course, exactly how much is a secret."

"So you act as a depository for radioactive materials."

"That's right. You saw the security." Yamada nodded emphatically, looking straight at Ken. "Some curious guy actually calculated the damage that would be caused if this place were destroyed somehow. Since it simply involves calculating the amount of nuclear material that would disperse into the air, it's not that hard. According to this person, with the help of the sea breeze all of California would be contaminated in one day, and half of Nevada and Arizona in a matter of two or three days. Like a dirty bomb."

"A terrorist suicide attack using an airplane…"

Yamada nodded slightly. "The reactor would be able to withstand the impact of a small aircraft, but we don't know what the effect would be of a jumbo jet crash with a tank full of fuel. Whether it could survive that… Moreover, if the storage facility or fuel reprocessing plant were attacked, they wouldn't stand a chance."

"And this lab doubles as a storage facility."

"Of course, the public doesn't know about that little bit of math. Every researcher at this facility does, though." Yamada sounded like he was joking, but his eyes were very serious.

"Don't tell me—" Ken swallowed his words. He was about to ask whether plutonium was stored there, too. They sat in silence, thinking back on the damage on 9/11. Over 3,000 people lost their lives in attacks that damaged two complexes that symbolized the U.S. To think of what would happen if terrorists aimed not for office buildings but a nuclear research facility…

"Of course, a more effective way to destroy the place would be to pull the control rods in the reactor or to shut down the cooling system. Both can be done at the push of a button. We have redundant safety systems in place, but for anyone who's mastered them, it wouldn't be difficult. If the reactor ran wild, this building would be as good as nothing. The reactor would melt down, effectively becoming a type of nuclear bomb."

"China Syndrome."

"Yes. The idea that the melting reactor could burn through bedrock and reach China on the other side of Earth. Of course that's just nonsense that ignores the law of gravity completely."

Scientific curiosity. The words from Dr. Williams' email came to Ken's mind, entwining themselves with images of a deep red fireball bursting out of the reactor, melting California, America and finally the whole world.

"Meltdown…" Ken mumbled to himself.

The collar of Yamada's white shirt peeked out from under his oil-blotched uniform. He had the same black hair and eyes as Ken, plus a slightly balding head and broad forehead marked with creases. Behind thick glasses his eyes always seemed to be focused on something. He looked so full of confidence.

"It's time," said Ken as he slipped the copied diagram back in the envelope and stood.

"But…" Yamada looked up at Ken, hesitated for a while and opened his mouth again. "This paper is too well done. It's sensational, but there are many unclear points as well."

"It's enough for me."

"Do you really have to continue publishing it?"

"We can't stop now," said Ken, as he strode toward the door.

"It's just too bad that this has to be made public in this way. We should have been the ones to write it. It was our responsibility, as scientists."

"Well, the guy who wrote it, he's a scientist, too," said Ken, turning to face him before the door.

"I guess you're right," nodded Yamada.

As Yamada and Ken neared the lobby, Yamada slowed his pace by a row of sun-bleached photographs in frames along the hallway. They showed ten or so young men with short-cropped hair and wide slacks. Yamada stopped in front of one photo. The brick building in the background looked familiar. A metal plate on the frame read "Class of 1940: Physics Majors." Yamada pointed at a tall youth with sunken cheeks and thin lips that were shut tight, but whose sharp eyes hinted at mirth. His entire body seemed to exude willfulness and a seriousness beyond his years.

"Dr. James Williams," Ken mumbled without thinking.

"The author of the paper. A Japanese-American journalist named Jimmy came along to ask about him. Jimmy Tokida, I think."

"Jimmy did? He's a reporter at my paper."

"He was in the archives for five hours. He made copies of the list of Williams' papers and everything he could find from Williams' student years. Not that anything of significance is stored here. He seemed to be looking at other research institutions and universities, too. There was a search record left on the computer," Yamada said, facing Ken. "I saw him standing here at around six in the afternoon. I passed again at eight and he was still here. For more than two hours he was in a staring contest with one guy in the photo." Yamada looked at the photo figure of Dr. Williams. "It wasn't an ordinary gaze," he said, pulling up the corners of his eyes with his fingertips.

"He's against publishing the paper," Ken said, still looking at the photo. He thought back to the face of the old man he'd met in that dark hospital room in San Diego. Ken couldn't make the connection between the coolly smiling young man in the picture in front of him and the sallow-skinned old man in a wheelchair. The unease that always lurked in the back of his mind bubbled up. The anxiety made him feel like he was being pulled down into a bottomless pit. Gravity yanked at his right leg. He crouched down, clutching at it. Yamada looked on with a worried expression.

That night, Ken and Jimmy headed for San Francisco to meet Donald Fraser. It had been arranged after Steve received a call after five requesting a meeting. Charlie was at the lawyer's to discuss strategies for opposing the Department of Justice's orders to suspend the series, as the government was said to be taking some sort of action within the next few days.

"Have a seat," Fraser politely offered, just as he'd done the first time they'd met. "Tough work, isn't it, activism?" he asked with a soft smile.

"Sure..." replied Ken vaguely.

"I imagine your life has undergone something of a change lately. Conventions and meetings day after day, prying interviews, requests to supply manuscripts for free, people dropping in unannounced, endless phone calls and letters—plenty of which are very unpleasant... Of course, if you ignore them, they'll call you rude or insincere. You get put on a government blacklist and branded an enemy by organizations with an opposing goal..." Fraser carried on, his voice getting a little louder. "It's really not worth it, you know."

"What can I say, somebody's got to do it," said Ken, looking down as he snubbed Fraser's words. He was unsure what to make of the man.

"Be that as it may," said Frazier in a different tone, "I asked for you to come because I want us to be clear on where each of us stands and how we're going to proceed."

Ken knit his brow and looked up, not understanding what Fraser meant.

"We're not your enemy. You should know that by what's already transpired. What we're dealing with has the potential of becoming much bigger. In fact, it's already an issue at the national level. If you continue to refuse to comply with the government's orders, you'll doubtless be dragged before a court. But we want you to proceed without cowering away."

"That's our plan." Ken's expression asked, *Why are we discussing this so late in the game?* Fraser quietly took in his look.

"I'm relieved. That's what I hoped you'd say. We'd like to expand this issue a little more. But when push comes to shove, things get tough. The media will be content just to fan the whole thing then drop it and move on. They're so irresponsible. Er, sorry, I know that's your business."

"Are you saying you'll help us?"

"If necessary. You see, our group has lawyers who specialize in these kinds of issues. Myself being one of them." Fraser leaned back in his chair and leisurely crossed his legs. "We actually hope this will end in court.

If that happens, not only will our country's nuclear power policy come under question, but the extent of governmental secrecy as well. This may cause a lot of problems for you, however."

"We're not afraid of anything."

"That is encouraging," said Fraser, fixing his eyes on Ken.

Ken glanced away. He sensed cold thorns behind those kind eyes.

"But it's easier said than done. You're prudent and have good instincts. You probably noticed, but I've watched you at a number of gatherings."

"At work, I'm known to be as dull as a donkey," said Ken, thinking back on how he felt he was being watched at a gathering. So he had been watched.

"You don't scare easily. And you're honest. But that's not enough. You're a novice. You have the will and passion, but you really don't know how to go about all this."

"I know. But we've come this far. All we can do is move forward."

"Social movements are not games," said Fraser, his usual smile disappearing and his voice getting louder. "You need technique. That's why I want to help."

Ken stayed silent. Within Fraser's gentle way of speaking was a pushiness he hadn't sensed before.

"Nothing ostentatious. We'd just be giving advice."

"Please do. As long as it's just advice."

Fraser nodded with a confident smile. "The last installment is going out on the day before Christmas Eve. I wouldn't call that a smart move," said Fraser, his voice moderated once again. "Christmas, then New Year's is just around the corner. How many people do you think will continue thinking about this worrisome problem into the holidays? For 99 percent of the population, Christmas presents and vacations are more important than the nuclear issue."

"Well…" said Ken, lost for words. "We didn't expect such a response. And the schedule is already laid out…"

"I'm not criticizing you, but the timing isn't good. After finishing the series we need to do something. Something big," Fraser said, taking a pipe from his breast pocket and lighting it. "How about running a feature on the nuclear problem for your first issue next year? It doesn't have to be anything splashy. A summary of the series along with an interview will do. We'll organize a venue. How does that sound for a segue into next year?"

"Okay. I'll discuss it with Charlie."

"By the way, how is Dr. James Williams?"

Ken and Jimmy looked at Fraser as he stood up and slowly strolled around the room.

"Where did you get that name?"

"This is what I called experience and technique. It wasn't difficult to track down the author from the email you first showed me. Specialists can get a good idea of the author's name from the manuscript alone. All you need to know is that it's widely known among us."

"I hope we can trust you not to disclose it."

"Of course. If found guilty of violating nuclear energy laws, the author will face up to ten years in prison and a 10,000-dollar fine. I don't think he'd survive that kind of ordeal. He's just a sad old man in a yellow hat."

A thin smile swept across Fraser's face. Ken quietly looked away. The unpleasantness was of a kind that waded unbidden into one's heart.

"How many copies are you planning to print for the next issue with the series?"

"A hundred and fifty thousand. So far we've had 30,000 requests through the mail. There were too many phone calls and emails to manage."

"You should print at least 300,000."

Jimmy sighed. "That's impossible. Our regular circulation is 42,000. The printing department hated us just for requesting 100,000. Even if we were to run our printers for 24 hours straight, we still wouldn't make it."

"No, it has to be 300,000. I want to send it to Washington, to every member of Congress. And to everyone of influence across the country. I'll get my people to help," Frazer insisted.

"What can't be done can't be done. Our office printer is maxed out at 100,000."

Fraser nodded, and thought quietly for a moment. "I'll take care of it. I'll talk to Steve about it." He went to the adjacent room where he argued into the phone, returning quickly.

"*The Barton Journal* has agreed to print the remaining 200,000."

Ken and Jimmy reflexively exchanged glances. They were seeing what this man of gracious appearance and demeanor was capable of.

"Can I ask you something?" said Jimmy, suddenly breaking his silence. "Why are you so interested in the paper? You're against nuclear power, so why would you support publicizing instructions on how to make a nuclear bomb?"

"You don't seem to have a clear grasp of what you're doing," said Fraser in a strong tone as he turned a piercing gaze on Jimmy. "We don't support anti-establishmentarianism for its own sake. We only decided to support its publication after a thorough discussion. For us it isn't about freedom of the press or of speech, as the mass media—yourselves included—say it is. Nor is it about the salvation of a man's soul. We decided that citizens need to know about nukes because it would aid the anti-nuclear movement."

"Why? It seems pointless to me," retorted Jimmy.

"You know about Three Mile Island. We were faced with a worst-case scenario among reactor accidents, namely fuel damage. The NRC stated fifty percent of the fuel rods had been damaged."

"It was just a step before meltdown," Jimmy said. Fraser nodded.

"But did the power company or government make the truth public? It was blamed on operator error and labeled a man-made disaster. According to a survey conducted after the accident, 60 percent of residents in the area were willing to have the power plant resume operations, when highly radioactive water remains in the containment vessel even after more than two decades. Chernobyl was even more tragic. Even though there was a decisive technological defect in the control rods, all the blame was shoved onto the operating staff. To this day, there are over ten reactors of the same design in operation in Russia despite IAEA warnings. How ignorant is that?"

"That has to do with politics."

"Everyone uses that as an excuse. We cannot move forward that way. If we tackle the issue head-on, the technology will eventually advance and provide a solution. What's necessary is to enlighten the public."

"That's a different matter." Jimmy had turned pale and his voice trembled.

"It's very much the same. Atomic energy is not an illusion, nor something only those with high-level technical educations can comprehend. My area of expertise is law, but I'm endowed with enough knowledge not to be fibbed by a power company's PR officer."

"But what we need—" Ken grabbed Jimmy's arm to stop him. There was no point in arguing further.

"I do think your publishing the paper is problematic on several fronts, but the fact remains that it has sparked the interest of the people. We need to expand and deepen their interest. That's what social movements are about." Fraser took a deep draw on his pipe, filling the air with swirls of fragrant smoke. Ken felt the aroma to be somehow out of place.

Ken and Jimmy left after an hour. The city at night felt wintry and lonely. Jimmy drove in silence, his expression hidden by the darkness. Turning on the car radio filled the interior with "Jingles Bells." A news broadcast came on after the song ended.

The government has agreed to provide emergency assistance of 1.2 billion dollars to Afghanistan and Iraq... A drastic reduction in the military budget appears to be inevitable... Key player Senator Northrop, pushing back against fellow Republicans who favor increased defense spending... President Jefferson, despite expressing an intent to withdraw the next-generation stealth plan... Congress remains largely opposed to the bill...

The two of them thought on Fraser's parting words:

"The government is not stupid. They'll push when they need to, and pull when necessary. They know a tiny leak can turn into a big problem. Our guess is that they'll soon rescind the order to suspend the series. What concerns us comes after that. The general public is quick to heat up and just as quick to cool down. But I want to build on the momentum that is there."

San Francisco was covered by a thick layer of fog, punctured occasionally by blurred Christmas lights.

Jimmy was driving at half the speed limit. "Donald Fraser. That man's eerie. I can't tell what he's thinking," he sighed, breaking the silence. His face still looked pale in the street lights.

"He's managing that large organization. Plus he got our rival paper to take action with just a phone call. His influence must be considerable."

Ken thought of Fraser's eyes on him. He'd seen them in the past, too. He tried to remember where, but a dull pain sprang up in the back of his head and soon spread to the rest of his body. Jimmy fell silent, lips tightly sealed as he stared ahead into the darkness. Ken could see a newfound determination in his eyes.

By the time they reached Barton it was already after ten. Jimmy went into the office to work, so Ken parted with him to grab a hamburger and a cup of coffee at a nearby restaurant for a late dinner. For the first time in a while, he went to a bar.

"Ah, the famous Ken Brian!" shouted the large African-American bartender as he placed a napkin down in front of Ken. "The man who's single-handedly taking on the United States government!"

Everyone in the bar turned around, but the attention of the room soon returned to the football game on television.

"Just a beer, thanks," said Ken, as the bartender was about to pour his usual glass of whiskey.

"What's up? You sick or something?" the black man asked with an odd look on his face as he set a beer in front of Ken.

"Just falling apart."

"I already knew that." He shrugged and turned to some other customers.

Ken stared at the beer for a while, then downed it, paid, left the bar and went back to his apartment. The sink was full of dirty dishes, the bedroom was strewn with worn clothes, and the scent of heavy dampness had long since replaced the scent of Ann. She'd be back for Christmas, so he'd need to get everything cleaned up and deodorized soon. Right now he didn't have the strength. He fell into bed without undressing and slipped in between the cold covers. A thick, moist darkness enveloped him.

The roar of the freeway sounded like a rumbling of the earth. Why did he feel so depressed? What Jimmy once said came to mind: *We need to write articles based on our conscience.* A feeling similar to cowardice pierced his body. No, it was a more instinctive revulsion.

He remembered how Fraser's eyes had seemed to bore deep into his brain. A deep, black, foggy anxiety was submerged in the core of his heart. The more he struggled to break away, the further it seeped through his body.

He sat up in bed and opened his eyes. He desperately tried to snatch at the black shadow sinking into the darkness. His body was dead tired and his head was confused, but he wasn't sleepy. His mind drifted in the darkness. He wanted to hold Ann's warm and soft body.

He went to the kitchen and returned with a carton of beer. He knew beer wouldn't get him drunk, but it helped defuse his feelings.

"Do you really want kids?" Ann had asked him.

Four years had passed since they'd moved in together, but Ken couldn't answer the question. He didn't understand his own feelings. It was an issue he needed to deal with at some point. They'd both been avoiding it.

"Let's adopt. I don't care what race. Asian, white, black. I can love the child as my own. We can raise a child together. That would be a wonderful thing."

"Are you okay with that? Don't you want to raise your own child? A child who shares your blood. You're totally capable."

It was Ann's turn to not have an answer. A few years passed without a decision. A year prior, they had gone to a clinic. Six months later Ann got pregnant by artificial insemination. That was also about the time that Ann had learned that her mother had cancer. One life ending as a new life began. It proved to be a real hang-up for her.

Ken kept on drinking until morning, watching television with the sound off. He dozed as the sky outside the curtains grew light.

He was in total darkness. Not a single thread of light. His body was soaked in sticky liquid. He was struggling to get out.

Stop it! Ann's voice echoed. He looked around, trying to locate the voice. *How horrible!* The voice seemed to be coming from inside his body.

I'm drunk, he told himself. He applied the full force of his will to pull himself out of the light sleep. His body was soaked in cold sweat and he smelled bad. Dragging his aching leg to the bathroom, he turned on the shower full-blast and let the scalding water strike his skin.

The Washington Post. Office of the Editor-in-Chief.

Warren and Anderson were looking at Bill Whitney, the EIC, who was sitting at the desk with his feet up. He rubbed his chin with his left hand as he read the manuscript he held in his right. The title was "The Enigma of a White House Aide's Demise." The subhead ran "Early-Winter Calamity in the District: the Mysterious Death of the Policy Advisor to the President" and was followed by a decidedly objective rundown on the passing of Senior Policy Advisor Frank Curley.

The missing gun, briefcase, shoes and watch. The gruesome murder of a girl in a downtown hotel room. The wallet found there. The article pointed out that as the still-missing briefcase proved, the initial investigation by the police had been inadequate. Why wasn't the corpse of the woman discovered sooner? Why was the hotel room devoid of Curley's fingerprints? Why hadn't the gun surfaced? Why didn't anyone hear a gunshot? Why... There were too many questions.

The article finished up by describing Curley as an honest, decent family man. The last part was somewhat subjective, but the general brunt was to bring into doubt the manner in which the case had been reported so far.

It was supposed to fill a sixth of the front page with Warren's byline.

"No. This reads like a gossip piece out of a third-rate rag. It reeks of emotion. This isn't an issue that can be cleared up with a sob story," criticized Whitney in a low, resonant voice as he looked up at Warren from under his brow.

He was only 5'3", but his presence was overwhelming if you stood close to him. He'd been the editor-in-chief at *The Washington Post* for nearly ten years. His smallish head was packed with the complete history of the past three presidents and the history of the world as seen from Washington, D.C.

"It covers inconsistencies and questionable parts in the investigation. The real point I want to make is how dangerous sensationalized, baseless blame is," Warren argued.

"An emotional take is what's dangerous. Curley was a nice guy, therefore he wouldn't use heroin. He'd never, ever rape a girl. Are those truths that will persuade our readers?"

"Just because he was a senior advisor, it doesn't mean we should ignore what kind of person he was and write sensational articles. He's got rights, and a family, too."

"Are you trying to say you don't believe Curley committed suicide?"

"I'm saying this case is full of holes, and the cops aren't even trying to conduct a proper investigation."

"Don't you think it's too sloppy to be a murder?"

"Watergate all started with an article about a poorly executed break-in. In the end it brought down a president."

The editor-in-chief raised his eyebrows slightly but looked back at the manuscript, then set it down. Anderson nodded.

"It's impossible. There's too much conjecture. Especially the latter half."

"The articles in the other papers offer nothing but conjecture, too."

"Conjectures based on time, place, occasion and other hard facts that make them very convincing. Time and place are everything in this kind of case. And if the main character's an exceptional big shot? The rest is like a novel. The article will stand up and walk on its own. The readers will fill in the details in their minds the way they want to. The article supplies the situation and the setting and gives the readers' mind a little nudge."

"I thought *The Washington Post* didn't write articles based on just that."

"No, indeed. Our reporters have the pride and passion to write articles grounded in conviction."

"That's what I believe, too," said Warren, picking up his manuscript from Whitney's desk.

"Get people to give you facts. Take good notes. If you can get it on tape they can't wriggle out of it later. Line up truths. Then let the readers make of it what they will from there." Whitney's words were delivered in a tone meant to light a fire under Warren.

Warren and Anderson walked out of Whitney's office.

"So who, exactly, am I supposed to interview?" complained Warren on the way back to his desk. "What should I do, ask for an exclusive with the president?"

"I wouldn't be opposed to one, but you'll have to set it up yourself."

"On it, boss. Give me his direct number, will you?"

"Look," said Anderson, wearily. "How long have you been a journalist? Have you talked to the first witness?"

"Met him three times. First time was a group interview at the crime scene, then there was that interview at the Police HQ. The cops seemed hell-bent on not having him interviewed one on one."

"And the third time?"

"I only saw him," said Warren, keeping mum about checking in on the man's jogging and following him back to an apartment just that morning.

"You didn't speak to him?"

"The place wasn't right. Nor the time."

"Address?"

"Northeast, downtown. On the east side of Dupont Circle."

"So it's within reasonable jogging distance of the Mall."

"Nearly two miles. Jogging distance for him, perhaps. Not for me."

"It's been ten days since he found the body. He's probably itching to get the truth off his chest. Even if someone was on his back before, he'd love to think that the heat's off by now."

"I agree with you there."

"Go meet him and see what you can get. It's the only way your article will ever see the light of day," said Anderson, throwing a glance at the manuscript then walking away in the direction of his room. Warren left the building.

For now, just one fact to contradict the current press coverage would do. It could be a simple technicality, something to even hint that Curley was neither a perv who offed himself out of self-hatred nor a heroin addict. A new current running in a different direction could cause a land-slide. Public opinion was like that. But in order for it to happen…

Warren called John and asked to meet up at a cafeteria near the police station. Initially, John was reluctant, but once Warren threatened to come and visit him at the station he quickly changed his tune.

"I'm going to talk to the witness."

John glared at him with his typical sour look. "Don't you dare!" he said in a wrung-out voice, leaning in close as usual. Everything this man did looked staged. "There are lines you shouldn't cross. And when you do, things get dangerous, no matter who you're dealing with."

"What are you so worked up about? It's just a pervert's suicide, right?"

"That's right. But too many people tend to get the wrong idea."

"Like people in the White House?"

"Don't underestimate them. Real crooks don't always go around flashing guns and knives. The ones wearing suits that cost thousands of dollars with their hair all neat and nicely parted and smelling of lotion are the ones you need to watch out for. Those are the types that can commit crimes and think that they've done nothing wrong. That's why they're scary. They get carried away and things escalate. They think the true villains are anyone who dares to get in their way. They think it's for the good of the country and the people to rub you out. And these guys have the means."

"Tell me something I don't know."

"You don't know the half of it. You think these people are just like you, suited up with their feet on their desks. That they'd never do anything outrageous. Sure, they can't do their own dirty work, they don't have the balls for it. But there are plenty of people in this city who'd gladly stab their own brother in the guts for a hundred bucks. That's America for you. That's Washington, D.C., home to the U.S. government," John spouted, glaring at Warren.

"Apparently, Curley was a unique presence in the White House. You've got your doves, the ones who oppose military expansion, like Secretary of State Robin Dayton and Vice President Gerard Hopkins. Then you've got your hawks who support military expansion like Chief of Staff Simon Schmidt and Secretary of Defense Stewart Jones. The White House staff is divided between the two sides. The president's role actually has been to moderate between the factions. He's indecisive, you see. That isn't good when you're POTUS."

"Stop this."

"Curley was more a dove than a hawk but wasn't aggressive about it. He was taking a cautious stance on the new defense plans. He had a special friendship with the president as well, at a personal level. And now he's dead."

"What do you want?" John's voice showed his irritation. "Just drop this case."

"Then what will happen to Curley's child, his wife?"

"They'll grow stronger."

Warren stood up and told John to follow him. John obeyed. The two went into the bathroom.

"Lend me your gun."

John looked at Warren suspiciously. Warren extended his hand toward John's belt. John slapped it away, glaring, but relented, pulled out his firearm and made to remove its magazine. Warren quickly snatched it and pointed the gun at his own head.

"Don't move! It's loaded," hissed John, his face twitching.

Warren's finger was already on the trigger. Just as he moved his thumb to cock the gun, John's hand grabbed it, lever and all.

"You wanna die?" John's voice trembled, still gripping the gun.

The bathroom door opened and a fat middle-aged man walked in. After seeing two men looking pale while wrestling over a gun, he quickly exited.

"If I was going to commit suicide, I'd shoot myself in the head. A shot to the chest doesn't guarantee death."

"All depends on how you shoot. And that's moot for an accidental discharge," John said in a husky voice as he peeled the gun from Warren's hand.

"Curley called me before he died. I feel responsible."

"That's not all, is it?" John carefully placed the gun back in its holster with a look of relief on his face.

"It's about saving a man's honor."

"That's not going to keep anyone fed."

"It can nourish the soul."

"Curley's widow must be a looker."

"It's not like that," said Warren, sternly. John raised his eyebrows and shrugged. The images of Cindy and Mrs. Curley flickered in the back of Warren's mind. If Cathy and Teddy were to suffer the same...

"Look, I plan to meet the first witness, Chris Horne."

"You shouldn't. He's very hard to deal with."

"So I hear."

John sighed. "He's a bit weak upstairs. Anyone who jogs before sunrise around the Mall has to be," he said, pointing to his head. "Don't go to his house. You never know what might happen if you're alone with him. And don't argue with whatever he says. He's the type who could get out of control if he loses his temper." He pulled a paper towel from the dispenser on the wall before scribbling something on it and pushing it into Warren's breast pocket. "This is where he drinks. He's there every night he has off. And he has tonight off."

"I owe you one."

"Fine, then just wait ten minutes after I leave before you walk out. I can't have people thinking we had a lover's quarrel," he muttered and left.

Warren returned to the office and took care of the work that had piled up. After night had fallen, he drove to a place on the outskirts of downtown to the address scrawled on the paper towel.

As he entered, his vision blurred. Cigarette smoke drifted about like fog. Noise and the smell of nicotine. Warren made a face and held his breath. Indeed, no decent person would want to soak up this environment; the clientele had to have special genes. He looked around for Horne but couldn't find him. Under the dim light everyone looked the same.

Warren called over the bartender and put a twenty on the counter. "Chris Horne. An Italian fellow who likes to jog early in the morning."

"He's over there," whispered the muscular bartender. Warren looked in the direction where the bartender pointed to where a stout man was drinking alone. He looked quite different from the time he was out jogging, but it was definitely Chris Horne. Warren pushed the twenty toward the bartender and, glass in hand, planted himself next to Horne. The man looked at him and made an ugly face, but quickly recovered and returned to his drink.

"I want to ask you something."

"You don't look like a cop. Newspaper reporter, or some other media?"

"Newspaper."

"I want to drink alone. Leave me alone."

"Very sorry to disturb you, but I feel much worse for Curley."

"There's nothing left to say. I told the cops everything I know. The only thing you'll get outta me is a belch." He burped out loud, tinting the air with a sour alcoholic odor that made Warren turn away.

"Why's everyone so interested in that guy, anyway?"

"Has someone else been asking you questions?"

"After the cops interrogated me, you media types came at me every day. Everyone from nightly news TV reporters to gossip rags. But nobody's bothered me these past few days. Not since that girl was found in the hotel."

"I'll be the last one, so can you tell me everything you know? Whatever you've got," said Warren, carefully laying three twenty-dollar bills out on the table. Horne was facing straight ahead but his eyes were trained on the table. "Maybe there's something new, something you forgot to mention to the police, perhaps?"

"No way. I saw the body for less than five minutes. Then the police quizzed me about it for ten hours."

"I heard you found him when you were jogging." Warren downed half his beer at once, ignoring Horne's protests.

Horne looked at Warren. "I told this story dozens of times. I'm sick of it. You've seen the papers and TV, right? They're even saying I said things I didn't."

"You jog at five in the morning?"

"I work until two, okay. I go home and eat, take a breather, then I go jogging. I can't sleep otherwise. The cops seemed to get it."

"Everyone just wants to get over this."

"I do, too."

"You've got nice shoes," said Warren, glancing toward the floor. "Hey, what time is it?" Warren grabbed Horne's wrist, but there was no watch.

"I left my watch at home. I only wear it when I run so I can time myself."

"But you weren't wearing one that night."

"Knock it off."

Horne stood up. His right palm was shaking slightly, and Warren saw a bizarre glimmer in his eye. As John said, maybe he really was dangerous.

"I don't want trouble. Especially not here," said Horne in a low voice. The bartender walked over and glanced at them in turn. He looked like he was ready to smack Warren at the drop of a hat.

"We're not arguing," assured Warren, glancing at Horne for him to back him up. Horne nodded and the bartender walked back over to the other end, turning around a few times.

"Listen. I'm not a cop. Anyone would want a pair of nice shoes. A watch, too. He sure doesn't need 'em anymore. But mucking around with an investigation would be a serious crime, especially in a case like this."

"Just because he was an presidential aide?"

"I have a son. He's five years old. Adorable, and such a kind boy. I'd do anything for him. Now he has a girlfriend. She's a very nice girl, too."

"So what's your point? I hate kids."

"She's the daughter of Frank Curley."

Horne's body twitched.

"She's suffered terrible misfortune. For the rest of her life, she has to live with the fact that her father died like that. Same goes for her mother, who married a heroin-addicted girl-killer. All the newspapers call him a pervert. How would you feel?"

"The watch and shoes are really that important?"

"I just want to learn the truth, and I think you want to tell me the truth. Don't you think there's a pretty big difference between killing yourself and getting killed?"

Warren stared at Horne, who quickly looked away.

"You were locked up for two years for petty theft. Sorry, I did some homework."

Horne was lost in thought.

"I understand you have your problems. If my theory is wrong, you can get up and leave the bar. If I'm right, I'll leave."

Horne nodded slightly.

"You jog at three in the morning, right after getting home from the restaurant. That morning, you passed by the National Museum of Natural History at 3:10. There was nothing there. You continued on to Union Station. You met someone there, as always. Am I right?"

Warren peered at Horne, who immediately downed the contents of his glass.

"Then you ran back to the Mall on your way home. But when you passed the National Museum of Natural History you saw someone on the bench. You walked up to him. That was Frank Curley. And he was already dead, right?"

Horne kept his eyes on his glass.

"You've got some business instincts, so your eyes notice some things up for grabs. His shoes, watch. His shoes were very nice. Italian-made. The size was about right for you, too. You were reluctant about the ring. You're not such a bad guy, after all. Don't want to do anything that'll get you cursed. But you looked through his pockets before that. You didn't find a wallet but found something else. Am I right?"

"What do you mean?" Horne gasped.

"Heroin. You went back to the station with his shoes, his watch and the heroin. Perhaps to hide them in a locker or to sell to someone. Anyway, you went back to the station and had to pass by the National Museum of Natural History once again. This time you ran into a cruiser and thought it would be suspicious of you not to report it. That's how the time of your statement wasn't until after 5 a.m., well past the time you'd normally be back at the apartment."

More than half of this was speculation, but still Horne kept quiet.

"Did you take the gun, too?"

"There wasn't one. I didn't take the briefcase or wallet either. I was surprised to hear they found heroin. I don't think there were two bags. I searched twice. I wouldn't have missed it."

"You didn't see anyone else? A car parked nearby?"

"I run so early in the morning because no one's round. I hate people. A few cars would be parked but I never pay much attention. You're not going to report me to the police, are you?"

"We journalists have a real bothersome moral code. We look after our sources. Don't worry."

Horne slipped off the stool. "Please give these back. You know the family, don't you?" he said, taking off the shoes and shoving them towards Warren. "I don't have the watch anymore. I had a friend in New York sell it. I was… I always wanted some Italian shoes."

"You know, you can get some pretty good ones out of China now. How are you going to get home?"

"I'll reap what I sowed. I stole a dead man's shoes. I went back because I meant to take his wedding band."

Warren placed another twenty on the table.

By the time Warren reached his apartment it was already after midnight. He placed the shoes on the table and stared at them, the soft leather polished to a sheen so brilliant he could almost see his reflection. They spoke of the gift-giver's good taste. For a moment he hesitated, then he picked up the phone and dialed John's number.

"Your theory was half right and half wrong," he said as soon as John picked up.

"What do you mean?" came a sleepy voice on the other end. Warren proceeded to tell him all about his encounter with Horne.

"Whoever killed Curley carried his body to the bench and sat it there to make it look like a suicide. Suddenly Horne came along, so they quickly hid. They must have panicked when Horne took the shoes, watch and heroin. They replaced just the heroin with what they had on hand. They probably didn't have the right size shoes. In the meantime Horne came back. With a police car, at that."

"Why did Horne go back to the station? He could have just gone home."

"He understands quite well that it's too dangerous to keep heroin at his place. That's probably why he runs to the station every night. No one goes jogging at three in the morning to stay fit. He meets someone at the station."

"A drug dealer?"

"I don't know. I'm not a cop."

"How about the gun? Did Horne take it?"

"Horne must have showed up before they could plant the gun. It would be bizarre if a guy didn't have shoes but had a gun in hand. The perps probably had to make a quick change of plans with this unexpected interruption."

"Horne, that bastard. But nobody's going to believe you. Horne can just deny it, especially with heroin being involved."

"It's obvious Curley was killed. It wasn't a suicide."

"But why?" John was wide awake now, just as Warren started getting a headache. He was feeling most in need of sleep.

"Let's think about this in depth tomorrow." Every time he moved, fatigue spread to his whole body.

"Wait, this is of utmost importance," said John, who sounded like he was getting out of bed rather than setting down the receiver. "I'm coming right over. Put some coffee on, strong enough to put hair on your chest!" With that last near-shout, the line went idle.

Warren gazed at the shoes on the table for a while before getting to his feet as if to shake clear of everything. He went to the kitchen, filled the kettle with water and set it on the stove. Twenty minutes later, the doorbell rang. Warren looked through the eyehole and saw John in a jersey and coat, hugging himself and stomping his feet with cold.

"Damn Horne, lying to us D.C. cops," John spat out as he stepped in.

Warren brought two mugs with piping hot coffee and handed one to John.

"The brass wants to file it away as a suicide, right? The suicide of a degenerate at that."

"You don't say. It's like they're afraid of something jumping out at them if they poked around too much."

"Or is there pressure from somewhere?" Warren followed up.

"We're dealing with a presidential aide. The White House can't but enter the picture if the investigation gets too thorough."

"Who's your source?"

"Your favorite, speculation." John slurped his coffee. "Not impossible. D.C.'s got the FBI, CIA, the military. There are enough people and organizations who could cause trouble here to make you belch. One man's life isn't worth shit to them."

"Hardly the words of a cop, but I think you're right."

"Curley left the White House around eleven, right after calling his wife. This much was confirmed by our people in a statement from a White House security guard. We've also checked the security video."

"Was he carrying a briefcase?"

"According to the guys who saw the video, yes. The White House security guard made a statement to that effect, too. His wife also said he left the house with a briefcase."

There were security guards with metal detectors at the White House staff entrance and everyone was checked thoroughly. There was also a video camera recording the time staff came and went.

"So should we talk to the security guards too?" John suggested.

"I'll do it. I'm sure they're already sick of cops."

"You're probably right. I'll get the number for you."

John talked with him for about an hour, then left.

The next morning, Warren found an email from John once he arrived at the office. It was the phone number of a White House security guard who'd been on duty the night Curley was murdered. Warren called and got a groggy voice on the other side.

"Sorry, were you asleep?"

"I was on the night shift until this morning. I went to bed only an hour ago," answered a displeased voice, which abruptly changed its tune when Warren introduced himself as a journalist with *The Washington Post.* "You won't print my name?" it desired to know.

"If you want to be anonymous, then I promise you will be. Our sources are our life's blood."

"I'm a security guard. I'm sure you understand."

"I understand completely. I've interviewed many people in similar positions."

"I read the *Post*. I hope you dog them about this. The White House is full of arrogant bastards who don't amount to much."

"You're a member of the White House staff too, aren't you?"

"I don't think the higher-ups see me that way. I'm just a security guard."

"I wanted to ask you about Advisor Curley."

"I figured. The police have asked a lot of questions already. Apparently, for now, I'm the last person who saw Advisor Curley alive," a rather buoyant voice declared.

"Was it ten minutes after eleven when Advisor Curley left the White House?"

"No mistake there. I remember thinking it was fifty minutes until the date changed. I thought he must've been really busy to work so late."

"How did he seem?"

"Same as always. Wearing a frown, raising his right hand slightly as he exited. I always thought he might be a difficult person, but I suppose that was just the way he greeted people. Thinking back now, maybe he was a polite and kind man. Either he was really unlucky or people are not always who they seem to be. But hearing about the incident and what they're saying about him… I just feel sorry for him."

"How about his briefcase?"

"The police asked the same question. He held it to his chest, as always."

"Anything out of the ordinary?"

"Not really. Thinking about it now, he looked like he was thinking hard about something."

"Who is it?" a woman's hoarse voice interrupted. Warren could sense the guard quickly covering the receiver with his hand.

"Well, thank you for your time. If you remember anything else, please contact me anytime." Warren gave his phone number and hung up.

He tried to imagine Curley, back slightly hunched, clutching his briefcase as he stepped out of the White House. According to the police report, Curley then headed downtown, went into a hotel with a girl, then shot himself in the chest four hours later.

Warren shook his head to clear it of the image.

Chapter 4
Rescindment

Two days after Ken saw Fraser, the Department of Justice rescinded the suspension order on the grounds that the incident's enlargement had already disseminated the contents of the paper to such an extent that the directive was effectively pointless. It was a bit of an anti-climax.

Our guess is that they'll soon rescind the order to suspend the series. Ken could almost hear Fraser's voice.

Alongside news of the in-session Congress, the media gave the rescindment wide coverage: "Gov't Kneels Before Public Opinion—Nuclear Bomb Secrets To Be Fully Revealed," "Freedom of Speech Rules Day: Truth Will Be Exposed," and "Biggest Press Victory Since Watergate."

Smiles could be seen all over the offices of *The Daily Californian*, except on Jimmy, who looked as sullen as always and kept quiet.

What remained was a final debate in two days to be attended by more than twenty groups of both supporters and the opposition as well as the media. Originally, the purpose of the debate had been to adopt a declaration against the government's suspension order, but that was now moot.

Ken sat in the deserted editorial department. Most of the reporters were out chasing up new stories, and the sole part-time student still on hand had gone out to grab a bite to eat, leaving Ken in charge of manning the phones. The trouble was over, and everything seemed to be running smoothly. Yet Ken's heart was still clouded. The only thing that could stop the articles from running now would be the outbreak of WWIII, a large-scale terrorist attack on Barton or a major earthquake in California. But what next? Ken decided to stop thinking about it. He told himself that they had overcome the biggest obstacle at hand.

He lifted the phone and dialed Jimmy's cell. He couldn't forget Jimmy's face when they received the news of the rescindment. He needed to discuss tonight's radio show with him, but all he got was an automated recording of a female voice saying he was either out of range or his phone was switched off—the same as when he'd tried thirty minutes ago.

He walked to the window and gazed out absently. All the shops along the street were sparkling with Christmas decorations and he could hear Christmas songs playing. The sun was setting and the electric illuminations on the trees lining the street and the lighted-up church blinkered to life.

"The Pulitzer Prize is in the bag!" Ken turned around to see Susan standing there, smiling. "You look dog tired," she continued as she leaned on the windowsill next to Ken. She placed her hand with its bright red manicured nails on his shoulder, touching the muscles in his neck.

"Everybody's tired," said Ken, still gazing out the window.

"Someone's not in a great mood."

"Everyone else is in too good a mood."

"You haven't been drinking much lately, have you?"

"You'd love to get me drinking again, wouldn't you?"

"You're more yourself that way."

Ken laughed faintly. They watched the street in silence. People walked by wrapped in coats, their backs hunched over. Now that it was December, winter had arrived with a vengeance, making those summery days just a couple of weeks ago little more than a dream.

"It's almost over," Ken mumbled.

"I disagree. It's just gone beyond our control." Susan also sounded down. Perhaps she felt something, too. "I have trouble sleeping. I wake up in the middle of the night from bad dreams. Sometimes I wonder if we've made a big mistake. It's taken on a life of its own. No stopping it now. This thing was just too big for us all in all."

Ken thought she might be right, but he did his best to push the thought away. "Have you got a fever? This is unlike you."

"I know. But sometimes I ask myself what in the world we're doing. I wonder if maybe Jimmy's right. He's changed a lot," Susan said with a serious look on her face and closed her eyes.

Ken had never seen this side of Susan. It was true, everyone was changing.

The transparent rays of the sun sliced into the room. Mixed with the cold, they hinted at a wintry dusk.

"What are you doing with the interview tonight?" she asked, opening her eyes.

"I've left it to Jimmy and Bob."

"Can Bob handle it?"

"He's studied this topic a lot.

"Yeah, even I've studied it."

"Where's Jimmy, anyway?"

"He's going to the radio station directly from the hospital."

"The hospital?" Ken looked at Susan.

"Didn't you know? His younger sister's sick."

"I thought she was in Seattle."

"She moved here two years ago. To get proper care."

Ken sighed softly. Two years ago he'd been in and out of hospital, too.

"You must be the only one who didn't know. Only interested in yourself, that's your problem," said Susan sarcastically, before quickly turning serious again. "Jimmy… He's being weird lately. He's always deep in thought. He's looking pale, too."

Ken remembered how Yamada had mentioned a Japanese-American journalist named Jimmy who had asked after Williams and spent two hours staring at his picture at the lab.

"It's December. All us Japanese Americans turn pale. You white people—"

"Stop. How about we go out for dinner tonight? We could go somewhere classy, get something yummy. Ann's not back yet, right?" Susan's voice had turned nasal. She placed a finger on Ken's lips, then trailed it down his neck and across his chest. He could smell her makeup with every move she made.

Ken gently pushed away the arm that Susan had put around his waist. "I'm sorry, but I need to go somewhere."

"I forgot, it's Friday."

Ken nodded silently.

"Well then, I guess I'll just have to find myself another dinner buddy," lamented Susan, her expression dimming slightly. She slapped him lightly on the back and walked out. Her gait showed her exhaustion.

The part-timer returned with dinner. Ken picked up the flute case in the corner of the room and stepped outside. He went down the hill slowly, towards the south of the university campus. He cut across the campus, walking through damp grass. Before he realized, he was in the public park, where the evergreens were thick and lush, filling the air with their leaves' moisture. The place's subdued calm could gently envelop raging flames in contrast with the college campus' youthful sparkle.

This had been the woods where Ken met Ann.

At the time, Ann had been attending grad school in the evenings while working as an elementary school teacher during the day. She was somehow different from the other American women Ken knew. She was strong-willed and uninhibited, but generosity and sensitivity imbued the depths of her heart, evocative of his mother, whose blood ran through his veins, and the land that he'd never seen.

"I want to live together."

It was Ann's idea. She accepted everything about him. At first he was shocked, then hesitant. Within six months they'd moved in together.

She'd been there to wrap her kindness around his tortured soul and played a major part in getting him back on his feet. Even now, just knowing she was out there was the number-one crutch for his spirits. He believed she accepted him for who he was, including his defect. So when exactly did he begin to feel the disconnect? He wondered if she felt the same.

Ann had been back at her natal home in Utah for the past two months, looking after her mother, who'd been diagnosed with lung cancer. It had already been five months since the doctor at the university hospital had given her three months to live. She was an elderly lady, which probably helped slow the disease's progression, but she was on borrowed time.

In the center of the park stood an acoustic stage, on which a small concert was held late in the afternoon every Friday, unorganized, free-spirited jam sessions. People in the park would stop and come over to listen, sitting on nearby benches. There were no loud cheers or applause, but there always seemed to be a real sense of solidarity that blurred the border between performer and listener. The sense of freedom and family had captured Ken's heart. Sometimes he'd miss the concert for a couple of months at a time, but he'd been participating on and off for at least two years now.

There were people already sitting on benches here and there, but there was still half an hour before the performance was scheduled to begin, and the stage was still empty. The setting sun's rays stretched and turned red, casting a lonely light over the park.

Ken sat down on one of the benches that faced the stage. His wound-up nerves relaxed, while the cold air sapped his vigor out of him.

Over and over, he told himself he wasn't in the wrong. Yet at the back of his mind, there was an ominous dark shadow.

He placed the flute case on his laps and took out Dr. Williams' letter. He'd read it several dozen times, so it was beginning to tear at the creases and in some parts the writing was fading away. In a way Dr. Williams' life had been like football, a sport that Ken had played in high school and his first year of college until he joined the Marines. Williams had caught the ball and dashed forward, breaching the opposition's defense along the way. Perhaps he'd rushed right through the defense without even noticing they were there. If they brought him down right before the end zone, that would have been nothing to be ashamed of.

For Ken, who had stumbled down so many detours, Dr. Williams' linear life was very appealing. Ken was spurred on by a desire to help the old man get up and to run alongside him to the end zone. That's why he'd met with him and decided to publish his story. Dr. Williams had been strong and calm throughout, far from seeming like a man on his death-bed. But now, the heart-piercing impact had passed and Ken wondered where that burning passion had gone.

Ken raised his head and looked around. He felt someone's eyes on him. Again he took out his cell phone and dialed Jimmy's number. It was still out of range or shut off. The intermittent sounds of instruments began to emanate from the stage. Ken put the letter in his pocket before he finished reading it yet again and slowly got to his feet.

Because it was December, both performers and audience had diminished in number. The couple dozen players of summer had decreased to less than half of that. Only a few stragglers sat on the benches, the older people huddling together as if suffering from some burden. Ken wondered how many of those elderly he would see again after this winter. They remained immobile with their hands in the pockets of their heavy coats as though they were staring deep into themselves. They looked like a herd awaiting extinction.

Ken couldn't get into the groove that day. He screwed up several times, drawing puzzled glances from the middle-aged woman who was conducting.

That night he called Ann.

"Congratulations," said Ann before he could even speak. Her voice had recovered its tranquility. Initially she'd been devastated by just how much her mother had deteriorated, but the two months spent with her seemed to have given Ann the time to make peace with the inevitable.

"The roundtable was on TV here, too. I saw you."

"Newspaper reporters being posed questions on TV. How weird is that?"

"Well, you guys were pretty good. Although Susan's makeup was maybe a little heavy."

"Actually, that was kind of on the light side for her. We confronted her about it."

Ann gave a faint laugh. "I miss you," she said in a low voice.

Ken thought back to the voice in his nightmare a few days ago. *Stop it!* she'd cried out so sadly. *I know what you're saying. But this isn't about logic. How horrible…*

"I'll be back as soon as I can," came the voice down the phone in answer to his silence.

"It's okay, don't worry. Everyone at the office is like a person of character now. Modestly submitting to interviews, having their pictures taken. Charlie has finally stopped wearing his awful boots and I saw Bob in a suit for the first time ever. Can you believe he knew how to tie a tie? Susan's makeup job is getting heavier each day. I think she's hoping to crash Hollywood after this winds down. Apparently Bob flushed all his marijuana down the toilet. And Jimmy is still opposed to the whole thing. I didn't know he had the guts," Ken said with forced cheerfulness.

"I see…" This time it was Ann's turn to falter. "I can't help feeling as if something bad is about to happen."

"Well, your mother…"

"She's okay. She's coming to terms with it, and she's the one who's giving me courage. One life passes, another begins. That's how God made this world," she said in a choked voice. She remained silent for a while. "Do you…regret it? Our child?"

"We've talked about this at length already. I want you to have a child."

"But I'm worried. I'm worried about you," she said in a reedy, depressed voice. Certainly something ominous seemed to be coming. Ann's muffled shout drew out and writ large the anxiety he felt at heart.

"Don't worry about me. You take care of yourself. You're not just you anymore." As he hung up, Ken knew that sleep wouldn't come to him tonight either.

The fourth installment was set to hit the newsstands in two days. A print run of 300,000 had been ordered. The memoir was at last entering into the postwar period, during which time Dr. Williams remained at the military lab at Los Alamos to work on the development of even more powerful nukes. Rumor had it that this article would feature detailed instructions on how to build the latest type of nuclear bomb.

Each installment of the memoirs featured several photographs and diagrams, actual shots of bombs and experiment sites and blueprints of the main structures. Sometimes they were accompanied by data from experiments.

Ken couldn't comprehend the diagrams, but the eeriness of nukes seeped from between the crisscrossed confusion of lines.

A new diagram had been sent to them. Unlike the previous ones, it was hexagonal and was stamped "S50" in the upper-right-hand corner. It ran with the fourth installment.

Washington Post EIC Bill Whitney read the manuscript in silence and let his eyes linger on it for some time after finishing. Warren had pulled an all-nighter rewriting the article titled "The Enigma of a White House Aide's Demise."

Anderson had brought him straight to Whitney after reading it.

"Everything is backed up by fact?" asked Whitney as he finally looked up and fixed his stare on Warren.

"We have the times and dates of the statements," Anderson answered in Warren's place.

A new anonymous witness has provided a statement to the effect that at 3:30 a.m. (Frank Curley's speculated time of death being 3:00 a.m., according to the police), Curley's shoes and watch were still present. The gun and wallet, however, were missing. The witness heard no gunshot. The shoes and watch are thought to have been taken by someone before the first witness, Chris Horne, arrived at 5:03 a.m. Six days later the wallet was found in a hotel room. If Advisor Curley had committed suicide many contradictions arise. This also holds true if Curley was robbed and murdered at the Mall. Isn't it possible that Curley was murdered in a different location and his body carried to the Mall? Might there be someone who intentionally implicated Curley in the murder of a young woman at a hotel? There are too many mysteries and inconsistencies in this case. Based on these new facts, the MPDC must relaunch their investigation.

Warren had written the article giving the utmost consideration to Horne.

"Sounds like you're accusing the White House of pulling strings as the mastermind. And you call the MPDC utter fools."

"People probably said the same thing to the guys who broke the Watergate story."

"So the gun was missing, and the witness didn't hear a gun shot?" Whitney pressed for clarification.

"That's been confirmed."

"Was it just the gun that was missing from the start? The shoes and watch were still on the body at first. You're saying that the only items taken by a thief were the shoes and the watch?"

"There's no mistake." Warren thought about the expensive shoes sitting on his table at home.

"Who is this anonymous witness?"

"I can't give my source's name, I have a duty to protect him."

"An unknown homeless guy? I don't think that'll fly."

"The public will probably suspect the first witness, but I think the police will ignore it."

Whitney fell silent again. "The statement from the security guard is true?"

"I heard it directly from him."

"And Curley called his wife at eleven?"

"She confirmed it. And I can't say how, but I've seen the phone records."

"We're about to make enemies of the White House and the police. We really can't afford to be wrong on this one."

"I know," Warren replied.

"Then make your source a little more clear."

"That would reveal too much about his identity."

"As it stands, the article lacks credibility. You can't back this up under scrutiny."

"My source is terrified. If his name is made public, he won't give us anything more. Please put yourself in his—"

"Fine," Whitney interrupted. He stared again at the draft, deep in thought. A long moment passed. "Let's run it tomorrow morning," Whitney raised his head and said just when Warren was about to open his mouth. "Below the fold on the front page. But any complaints from our readers are going to be dealt with on your side. Understood?"

Whitney swiveled his chair back towards his desk. Warren and Anderson left his office.

"I'm not so sure about it," confided Anderson. "Especially when I think of what this could trigger."

"Wasn't the First Amendment your credo?"

"When we're stating things rooted in fact, yes. And I believe in life. When dealing with the mafia or the White House, you'd better double your life insurance policy. My predecessor taught me that's the first article of preparedness for a reporter."

"Yeah, a cop told me the same thing. But we're living in the heart of democracy. This is a civilized country. It's not like we're in Iraq or North Korea. Don't be so discouraging."

"A civilized country? Do any journalists really believe that?"

"Newspapers are the greatest weapon we have in that regard."

"All I know for now is that we're scooping *The New York Times*."

"That alone is huge. I get shivers just thinking about it."

"It makes me even more reluctant," Anderson said nonchalantly and sighed. "Anyway, how are Cathy and Teddy?" he inquired, changing the subject.

"They're doing well. And that's a big help."

"Any chance of you guys getting back together soon? What's her problem with you, anyway?"

"Looks, personality, work… Everything. Especially work."

"Sounds like she's looking for the exact opposite of you. Come to think of it, that man would be very charming, but I'm scared to even imagine him. Anyway, you should go home and sleep. Save your energy for tomorrow," Anderson advised as he went back to his office.

Warren heard a voice from far away. A familiar voice that spoke directly into his brain. But whose was it? He looked around to find it. The voice transformed into the sound of the phone ringing.

His eyes searched for the digital clock next to the phone as he reached for the receiver. It was 6:12 a.m.

"Is the article yours?" came John's loud and angry voice.

"Have you forgotten how to read? It's got my name on it."

"Damn it! I told you to be careful when writing anything about the government or the mafia. There are lines you shouldn't cross!"

"Yeah, I know. I heard the same thing only yesterday."

"This article crosses that line. Hell, it completely ignores it."

"I'm prepared," said Warren, sitting up in bed.

"I wouldn't given a damn if you were found bloated with the Potomac's filthy water. A pompous ass who doesn't know good advice when he hears it reaps what he sows. But you've got Cathy and Teddy. Think about your family a little. Or I guess they aren't your family anymore. That's why you were able to do something so stupid," John's rapid-fire speech ended on a sardonic tone.

"All I wrote was that the evidence seems too contradictory to conclude that it was a suicide or aggravated robbery."

"Then what is it? Reads to me like you're hinting that there's something behind it and that the White House is involved."

"That's what I want to find out."

"Plus," John started, paused and continued, "you insinuate that the police are stupid and careless."

"Does it ring a bell?"

"At any rate, don't walk alone in the dark from now on. Check to see if anyone's entered your car or if there's something stuck on the undercarriage before you get in. Don't stand too near the train tracks. Give me a call if you're taking bets on whether you'll survive a month. I want in. My money's on your body being found floating on the Potomac or being blown to bits with your car."

"Don't joke around."

"I wish I was," John continued in a serious tone. "Look, the *Post* is going to have a hard time today. I just hope they don't fire you."

John hung up. Warren sat there dazed with the receiver still in his hand. He got out of bed and came back with the paper, with his bylined article covering a third of the front page. The phone rang again. He thought it was John calling back so he held the receiver silently against his ear.

"Are you asleep or what? Get down to the office now," Anderson's voice struck his eardrum. "You hear me?"

"I'll be there within half an hour." Warren hung up without waiting for a reply.

Warren stopped in his steps when he walked into the office. Phones were ringing off the hook at several times the usual rate and almost everyone clutched a receiver.

"Well, well. The star has graced us with an appearance," a middle-aged reporter remarked wryly.

"Tell the operator to transfer all complaints to one line!" yelled Anderson at his subordinates. "If anyone dials a direct line, give 'em that number and hang up!"

Everywhere the same stock response was being given. "We intend to continue investigating this matter. Your cooperation is of great importance to us. We appreciate your support."

Warren took his seat, feeling everyone's eyes upon him.

They forwarded the complaint calls to him.

"You're getting good at it. I'd like to recommend you for a gig at the complaint desk," quipped a colleague, slapping his shoulder as he walked by with a cup of coffee.

"Be sure to tape it next time," Anderson instructed Warren, who skipped lunch in order to keep repeating the same refrain into the phone.

By a little past three, the calls had finally died down. Warren was called into the editor-in-chief's office. All the section heads turned to him when he entered the room. Their eyes said they were looking at a trouble-making idiot. Warren took a seat in the corner of the room.

"In regards to credibility, 17 percent say they feel there is some truth to the article, 30 percent is undecided, and most of the rest think it needed more investigation," the surveys chief shared the results of the emergency poll his section had conducted that morning. "Indeed its standpoint is weak. I'd say 80 percent of our readers have a negative opinion on our take. Some are even saying that we're flirting with treason in a time of crisis, that we're injuring the dignity of the U.S. government."

"On the other hand, some want us to make the MPDC cry uncle," said the head of the city desk, who'd been poring over the survey results. "But it doesn't change the fact that we haven't got enough stuff for that. At worst, we'll be the ones crying uncle."

"And what does the owner have to say about it?"

"He's in Europe. Won't be back until next week. We need to do something before he gets back."

"Yeah, like do some research into unemployment benefits."

"I haven't seen an uproar like this since the whole Clinton thing. I'm actually kind of surprised that the public is still so interested in a White House scandal. It's a little late now, but I feel sorry for the Clintons."

Everyone spat out their own opinions.

"What about a follow-up article? This can't be the end, can it?" asked the head of international news, turning to Warren.

"Look, there's no need to panic," interceded Anderson before Warren could get a word in. "Everyone's watching us now. We can't make even the smallest mistake or they'll eat us alive."

Whitney took his feet off the desk, stood up and looked slowly around the room. "The readers won't stand for another half-cocked article like this. We've thrown a pebble into a calm lake."

"Whether it was murder or suicide, shouldn't we just sit tight until we have some hard facts?" said one of the section heads. "Leave it to the police. They'll have to respond by stepping up their efforts."

"That's naive. We're up against the White House. They're not gonna pull punches."

"Let's just hope this blows over."

The section heads' comments were laden with sarcasm.

"The paper will continue to support Warren, and I'll take full responsibility," concluded Whitney.

That evening different news programs on TV were filled with talking heads' opinions of the article, most of which were negative. It was proving difficult to wipe clean the image of the case that had already been fashioned.

The death of one top aide was sending out major ripples. The White House remained as silent as before.

By the time Warren returned to his apartment, it was already after one. He entered the quiet room, a cavern of sorts where the air smelled of mold and paint. This was always the most depressing moment of his day. He turned on the living room light and sat on the sofa. Fatigue overcame him, and for a moment his mind went blank. The answering machine light was flickering, showing exponentially more messages than usual. He got up, pressed play, then flopped back down on the sofa.

"So you're the one who wrote that damn article. I don't know if you're brave or stupid. No, I'm sure you must be stupid. Stupid people don't live very long."

"You're a pervert lover. You wanna know how I got this number? Bring 500 dollars to…"

He didn't recognize most of the callers' voices. Over a dozen hadn't bothered to leave a message. His number wasn't listed, but it seemed there were plenty of ways to find out. The eighteenth message was from Cathy.

"It's me. Can you look after Teddy this weekend? I have another rush job." Her voice was followed by Teddy's. "Daddy, let's go to the zoo!" It was a trick she always pulled. She probably hadn't read the papers or watched television all day.

He got through the messages with his eyes closed, then hit "erase all." The phone rang right afterwards.

"Listen to what I have to say. Keep your answers short." It was John's hushed voice. He sounded like he would refuse any and all arguments.

"Okay."

"Turn on your computer. Go to the usual page."

"Wait…" The line had already gone dead.

Warren turned on his computer and opened the chat program he always used.

Words flashed onto the screen: *"Look outside."* He leaned toward the window and peered down at the street.

"Is there a car parked there? One that you've never seen or that seems suspect in some way? Does anything look different from usual? If there are people in both the driver and front passenger seats, they're dangerous."

"I don't see anything," typed Warren.

"Then it's a van. Is there one? A van that's not usually there?"

"Yes."

There was a black van parked about fifty feet away at the corner.

"They're the feds. FBI, maybe CIA."

"This must be a bad dream."

"Yes, your worst nightmare has begun. You'll be under surveillance for 24 hours a day. Your phone's tapped. Your room is probably bugged."

"You're the nightmare. This is the most democratic country in the world. You're being absurd. I'm just a journalist."

"You're an idiot journalist who wrote a foolish article. The whole MPDC is calling you a reckless fool."

"Then tell them who I really am. I've had enough of your nonsense."

"You have to trust me on this. If you don't believe me, take another look at the van. They're watching you. There's not question about it."

Warren looked around the room. Nothing seemed to be out of place.

"Forget it, an amateur like you will never find it. They're utter professionals." It was as if John could see what he was doing.

"Is this computer safe?"

"No guarantees. But Internet tapping is pretty large-scale. They'll need time. I don't think they've gotten that far yet, but I can't be sure."

"What should I do?"

"Don't let on that you know me. Contact me through this site. I want to see you, but can you lose the tail?"

"I'll figure something out."

A moment passed. Warren looked around the room again. A moldy old apartment. He suddenly felt that John was telling the truth.

"I'm getting out of here. I can't stand being in a room that's bugged."

"Wait. I'm thinking. It'll be the same no matter where you go."

"What should I do then?"

"I'll come to you. Don't move. If you screw up I'll be in danger, too. I'll call your cell phone and let it ring twice when I get there. Don't come out. Just buzz me in. I'll be there in an hour."

"Make it half and hour."

"I'll try."

Warren turned off the computer and looked out again. The van was still there. Inside it…

He looked under the table and chair, behind the TV and dresser, but there was nothing. He gave up and turned on the TV. A news segment titled "Challenging the White House" was just starting.

An article in today's Washington Post *threw doubt on the circumstances surrounding the death of Advisor Curley… suggesting several problems with the official police report… The White House has yet to issue a statement…*

Warren's cell phone rang twice, then fell silent. It had only been twenty-five minutes. He buzzed the front door, and in less than a minute there was a knock. Warren saw John through the peephole and opened the door slightly to let him squeeze in. Before Warren could speak, the detective covered his mouth with his hand.

He entered the living room and turned up the TV. He took a device that looked like a small radio from his bag, extended its antenna, held it out and walked around the room. He stopped by the lamp near the front window; the needle on the indicator was at full-tilt. He put down the device and looked at the underside of the lamp. John pointed at a small black object that looked like several coins stacked together.

John wrote "bug" on a memo pad and showed it to Warren.

There were two, in the living room and in the bedroom. With the TV still on, they went to the bathroom. John turned the shower on full-blast.

"Were you out of your mind, writing an article like that? How many years have you been a journalist in D.C.?" John scolded in a stifled voice as he glared at Warren.

"We're living in the greatest democracy on earth. We've fought for freedom and justice since this country was founded. I thought the government's business was to uphold that rule of law."

"How about now? Does it still feel like a democracy?"

"My convictions haven't changed. Now I feel even more sure that there's something strange behind Curley's death."

"Don't be ridiculous. They'd do at least this much either way, just because you dared defy them."

"That just makes me even more determined." Already the steam had fogged up his glasses.

"Why did you put your name to it?"

"It's a scoop. I needed to take responsibility."

"Worth risking your life?"

"I believe so."

"Congrats, you may get exactly what you bargained for. Now you're a key figure, under 24-hour surveillance. People tailing you and listening to all your conversations. G-Men. Don't bother going to the cops, since they'll just brush you off. You know why."

"I'm sick of your sarcasm."

"I'm stating the facts. Let's make a bet. You, in a coffin, in three days. Or, if you're lucky, in the E.R. Maybe they might leave you as a vegetable."

"Stop talking and start helping me. Are we friends or not?"

"You've made a fool of the police. They're taking bets as we speak on how long it'll take for you to turn up in the Potomac."

"What's your money on?"

John looked down and took a deep breath in a bid to suppress his agitation. "They're going easy on you now with just the van and the bugs. Seems like they haven't yet installed a camera. But I can't say what will happen if you take this nonsense further."

"What do you mean?"

"There's no guarantee you'll come out alive. It's a warning to get you to back off." John's voice sounded like it was squeezed out of the back of his throat.

"Aren't the police supposed to protect us citizens?"

"Our job is to maintain public order even if it means making enemies of the citizenry. Right now, the one rocking the boat is an idiot reporter playing the hero."

"What should I do?"

"How would I know? Ask the CEO at your paper."

"And the bugs. Should I take them off?"

"Just leave them. If you take them off, they'll take the next step. Leave them, and at least you know one of their tricks."

"I don't have the nerve to sleep with a bug in the room."

"Then sleep here."

"No problem."

"Like I said before. Don't stand close to the edge on train platforms. Avoid walking down empty streets. Check your car for odd signs before getting in. And don't use your cell phone. If you care about your life, that is," John said, suddenly sounding formal.

"Okay, okay. I got that this morning."

"Thank God Himself that you got to hear it again. Recite it to yourself until it's burned into your skull like holy gospel. Because this is the last time I'm saying it. I don't have a college degree. It took me a long time to get where I am. I love detective work and am proud of it. I'm not going to throw it all away."

"I've gotta thank you for what you've done for me today."

John lifted the leg of his pants, removed a revolver from his ankle holster and held it out for Warren.

"Take this."

"Not for me. I've never used one," refused Warren, pushing it back.

"It's not about you. It's for my peace of mind."

John looked at Warren with a seriousness he'd hardly ever shown before. Warren took the gun, took out the bullets and placed them in John's pocket. John watched disapprovingly, then showed a look of resignation. He repeated the warnings again before leaving.

That night Warren dragged a sleeping bag into the bathroom to sleep. The gun in his jacket felt strange on his belly. The cold touch of the floor tiles seeped through the sleeping bag. He was woken many times during the night by the gurgling pipes whenever people on the upper floors of the building flushed their toilets. Each time he got up and went into the bedroom to check under the lamp and the bed.

The next day his body ached all over thanks to sleeping in a funny position on a cold floor. The office was quieter than it had been the day before, but still about one in every five calls was about Warren's article.

Warren was called into Anderson's office. Anderson pushed *The New York Times* on his desk toward Warren. On the front page was the headline "Advisor Curley's Death" and a rebuttal of Warren's article. It argued that Warren's article was too sentimental and lacking in objectivity and, in so many words, hinted that it was a product of the imagination.

"The *Post* vs. the *Times*. The public will love it."

"Well, there's only one truth."

"So what now? If you write a follow-up you need concrete evidence. This circumstantial stuff won't be up to snuff," he said as Warren finished reading the article.

"I'll head to police HQ. They should be working hard on this now."

"You mean they weren't before? A presidential aide dies unseen at the Mall. Plus, his briefcase has gone missing. Everybody is curious to know what was in it."

"The White House is desperately denying that he had any top-secret documents, but I don't think that's true. The briefcase is definitely missing, yet nobody seems to even be looking for it."

"Do you think somebody's putting pressure on the police?"

"I don't know. I'm not a detective."

"Then become one. Do everything to find out. Not just circumstantial evidence, but hard stuff that would convince even those a few fries short of a happy meal."

Warren gave a quiet sigh. Who was it who'd told him not to play at being Sherlock Holmes?

"Listen to me, Warren," said Anderson, quickly lowering his voice. "The dove Curley is dead. He's suspected of raping and murdering a girl. The doves have lost authority, and the hawks run the show now. Your article may have much larger implications than you imagined." His low voice had gravitas. "Now, go and do your thing. It may not seem like it, but I am rooting for you," he shared, patting Warren on the shoulder before waving him away.

Warren left the office and headed straight for the police station. As he entered a large room on the second floor he could tell that all eyes were upon him. He'd been here countless times, yet today the atmosphere was different. Officers who would usually chat with him were today giving him the cold shoulder.

John spotted Warren and came running over, taking his arm and quickly leading him into the bathroom.

"I told you not to come. You're the guy who criticized the cops, the enemy who's trying to outdo us. One small violation and they'll happily throw you in a cell," John snarled, yet his tone leaned towards supplication.

"I'm not here to pick a fight. I've come for information."

"Then go through the PR office and get the chief's permission. Don't just barge in."

"I'm talking to the chief-in-waiting."

"This is no time to be making jokes."

"I'm dead serious."

A middle-aged officer walked in, looked at them suspiciously, headed toward a urinal, peed loudly, then left.

"Just don't talk to me in public. They'll think I'm siding with you."

"I don't want that either."

John glared at him for a few moments before spreading his arms to show how fed up he was.

"When you talk to me, do it someplace where people aren't watching, I'm begging you."

"Fine."

John grabbed Warren's arm as he was leaving. "We found the briefcase. We had Curley's wife check it out. It's definitely his."

"Where was it?"

"In the bushes at the park. A cop on patrol found it."

"Didn't they search that area countless times before?"

"I guess. All that matters is that it was found."

"And the contents?"

"Documents, newspaper, *Newsweek*... And necessities."

"Necessities?"

"Condoms and stuff. A porno magazine and sex toys. The stub of a ticket for an S&M club. He left the White House at 11:10 and headed to the downtown club. He hooked up with the girl somewhere and booked into a hotel. You know the rest. Handcuffs and heroin, too."

"Shit!" Warren kicked the bathroom door.

"He went too far and the girl died. He got flustered, went to the Mall and shot himself in his chest. That's the final answer."

"And I'm saying I don't believe it." Warren felt a burning anger rising within him. He knew Curley was not the sort of man to do such things. As he listened to John he felt a powerful conviction well up.

"The real perp really wants to make Curley look like a sick fuck."

"Maybe he really was a sick fuck."

Warren glared at John, who glared back.

"Were there any documents in the bag?"

"Some. The president's schedule for the day, a general staff directory, materials regarding foreign policy... But if you're asking about confidential stuff, then the answer is no. They were all documents that any member of the White House staff could get their hands on. We contacted the White House and they confirmed as much. As they said before, taking out confidential material is prohibited."

Warren was deep in thought. "Why did the briefcase materialize only now? Didn't you guys search those bushes a long time ago?"

"I wouldn't know. I'm not on this case. Maybe some homeless guy stole it, then got scared when the case blew up. It was found, that's all that matters now."

"No, it was placed there recently, that's why you only just found it. Obviously, not before someone took out the confidential documents and replaced them with handcuffs, heroin and skin mags."

"What makes you so sure? Can you back that up?"

"It's just a hunch."

"You journalists really have it easy, not needing anything substantial to do your job," chided John.

"All I know is that ten days have passed and now the briefcase suddenly materializes out of thin air, stuffed with all kinds of fun things."

"I'm telling you this out of the kindness of my heart. Thank me."

"I'm beyond grateful you told me."

"I know."

"So when is the official announcement?"

"There's a press conference this afternoon."

The door to the bathroom opened and two uniformed officers walked in. They sneered at the two of them conversing, then headed to the urinals.

"You two lover boys getting to know each other?" said one out loud.

John went to punch them, but Warren pulled him back.

"Look, it's time you got out of here. Just make sure you leave inconspicuously," John sighed.

"Sorry to cause you such trouble."

"Try to think about that in the future before you march in here." John kicked the door.

"Just one more thing," said Warren, turning back. "Did they tell Curley's wife what was in the briefcase?"

John cast his eyes slightly downward and nodded.

Warren went toward the staircase, thinking about Mrs. Curley and her daughter as he walked. How she must have felt on hearing such horrible news. He brushed shoulders with a cop as he stepped into the hallway. The fat cop stopped and glared at him, but Warren ignored him and walked out of the police station.

The police chief's announcement was basically the same as John's. Curley was looking increasingly suspicious. A rumor spread that the White House was renewing its push for the case to be closed summarily as continuing the investigation would only tarnish the late aide's name. It was the president's personal wish, the rumor went.

The atmosphere at the paper was different when Warren got back. He was fast losing support even among his own staff. Warren walked to his seat without looking at anyone.

That night, he called Cathy from a payphone on his way home.

"I want to ask you something."

"Good timing. I've tried you many times but I always get the answering machine. You have your cell phone turned off, too... Did something good happen?" Despite her words, she sounded relieved.

"Don't you watch the news or read the papers?"

"I don't have the time. My job and taking care of Teddy pretty much takes up all the hours of my day. All the TV I watch is Teddy's cartoons."

Warren knew that was a lie. It had been nearly two days since the article was printed. Plus, there'd been all that uproar. There was no way she couldn't have known. Maybe it was her way of showing him some kind of consideration.

"I have a favor to ask."

"I'm not sure I want to hear it, but okay. I have one to ask, too. Can you take care of Teddy next Saturday?"

"I'll do what I can. What I need is—"

"Make it quick. I'm putting Teddy to bed."

"If I wanted to see the computer files in your lab, how would I go about that?"

"You should come to the lab and ask the head of the department. But of course, he won't let you."

"That's why I'm asking you."

"Are you talking about cracking?"

"Something like that."

"If you manage to hack into our lab's computer, you'd win an award. The Pentagon would come ask you to work for them. Our security system is protected by three firewalls. You'd never get past them. Even if some kind of hacker genius managed to, each person's file has a different password once you're in the system. No stranger could guess them."

"Your password is 1125XX, isn't it? November 25, 20XX. Teddy's birthday."

"That's just because you know me. Cracking isn't like you see on TV or in the movies."

It's through innocuous little lapses like yours that information leaks out, Warren thought to himself.

"Besides, the most important files are entirely locked down. They're only accessible on an internal network and not even the best cracker in the world could get into that."

"That's what I was afraid of."

"What do you mean? You're not planning to hack the White House computers, are you? You could be charged with treason and executed for that. Get such crazy thoughts out of your head," Cathy cautioned flatly and hung up.

Warren stood by the phone booth with the receiver still in his hand. A piercing cold wind blew around him. He thought how Curley's wife had been told about what was in her husband's briefcase and felt a sharp anger and sadness surge up inside of him.

Warren replaced the receiver and walked away.

The air was heavy and rain-laden clouds stretched out across the sky. The dark skies made the streetlights seem even more lonely. *Don't walk down lonely streets,* John's warning rang in his ear.

He hurried off toward his apartment. A drop of cold water hit his cheek. A light rain had begun to fall. Warren shivered. A horrible shake started in his brain and took over his entire body.

He stopped in his tracks and stood there for a while watching the cars speeding down the street in front of him. He buried his hands deep in his pockets, hunched over and resumed walking.

Chapter 5
The Blueprint

There was a loud noise in the distance, an unpleasant sound that reverberated through the core of Ken's head. It took a moment for him to realize that it was the sound of someone banging on the front door of his apartment.

Ken glanced at the bedside clock. It was just a little past six. He got out of bed and headed toward the door still in his underwear. There was an unpleasant sensation under his foot. Looking down, he saw a beer can had tipped over, soaking the carpet with a dark stain.

It was probably just Charlie or Bob. He couldn't think of anyone else who would knock so loudly. They came by on the way to an interview on days that he'd slept until noon with a hangover. But then again it was a little too early for either of those guys.

He hadn't put the chain across the door since Ann left for her mom's.

As soon as he unlocked the door, it flew open, knocking him back. Three men burst in. One of them twisted Ken's arm up behind his back, grabbed his head and pushed him into the wall. Ken felt a strong pressure against his windpipe and couldn't breathe for several moments.

He regained his breath and tried to twist free, only to be struck on the throat with a hard object, halting his breath. His arm was pushed further up his back. It was a quick, effective attack meant to force him to lose his desire to put up a struggle, and came from someone who was used to making such moves.

"FBI. We're bringing you in for leaking classified government information," said the agent. His tone was polite, but he didn't weaken his grip. Ken's arm felt like it was going to tear off.

"You have the right to remain silent, you have the right to speak to a lawyer, anything you say can and will be used against you in a court of law... You are entitled to one phone call..."

Ken tried to regain his composure as the agent recited the Miranda warning. He wondered what had gone wrong. He was pretty sure he didn't deserve this.

He somehow turned his neck to see what they were up to behind him. The other two agents were going through his desk drawers and the closet in the living room, while the one holding Ken produced a pair of handcuffs. They went on his twisted arm, and then the other, behind him. The agent yanked the cuffs to make sure they were secure before finally relaxing his grip. Ken tried to move, but the metal bit into his wrists and sent a sharp pain shooting up to his shoulders.

Finally Ken was allowed to stand away from the wall and see his assailant head-on. He was a sleek man with a well-proportioned face in his early thirties in a tailored navy suit and a plain maroon tie. He looked like he might be a banker or an insurance salesman who was putting up good numbers. It seemed odd that the slender, attractive man could exert such physical force.

With his hands firmly cuffed behind him, Ken was ordered to sit down on the sofa by the window. His beaten throat ached every time he swallowed.

An agent sat in front of him and studied him closely with a look of hostility in his eyes.

The sound of empty cans being kicked came from the bedroom.

"So you Japs live in pigsties, huh? I thought you lived in rabbit hutches," observed a heavy-set guy in a gray suit as he walked in from the bedroom.

"What's going on?" asked Ken, pushing out the words through his sore throat. In response, the agent sitting across from him slapped down a newspaper on the table in front of him. Today's morning edition. Ken had picked it up from the printers late last night on his way back from work.

Slapping Ken across the face, the agent pointed at the diagram on the front page. "Where did you get this?" he demanded.

"Our sources are confidential."

The agent delivered a sharp kick to Ken's right leg. Ken groaned reflexively and arched back. He grimaced as the cuffs cut into his wrists even more.

"This diagram is a top-shelf state secret."

"I recall the Justice Department revoked their order to cease publication."

"That was then, this is now. You're leaking government secrets and I think you're even enjoying it. Traitorous Jap."

"So why didn't you arrest me earlier?"

"I told you. This diagram is special," the agent repeated.

"Really? I heard you can buy one just like it for four bucks at the Library of Congress," said Ken, glaring at the agent, who sat there with a look of bold composure. Ken's knee was throbbing in rhythm with his pulse.

The agents who had been tearing the apartment apart came and stood, arms crossed, on either side of Ken.

"Everything else you've been printing up to now with a smirk was just crap. But this is something else," said the first agent, slapping Ken across the face with the newspaper. "It was stolen from The Los Alamos National Lab. It wasn't set to be declassified for a hundred years."

Ken's face stiffened. "That's the government's logic. The mere fact that anything is a government secret is not normal. That's not what citizens pay taxes for."

Ken's cheek sounded with a sharp slap. The agent was sneering. "You're so full of shit. Difficult to believe you're an ex-Marine corporal and a hero of Grenada. Times have changed while you've been wallowing at the bottom of a bottle."

The agent kicked Ken in the knee again. Ken bit his lip and braved the pain.

Still sneering, the agent looked down at Ken's crotch. "Tell me where you got it, you ball-less yellow monkey!"

Ken threw his body at the agent, knocking him onto the sofa, and slammed his head several times into the agent's face. It quickly turned red. Arms grabbed Ken from either side and brought him to his feet. A punch landed square in his stomach. Ken tried to break loose, but his head was thrown back by another punch to the jaw. His mouth filled with something warm. He felt his consciousness fading away.

His knees gave way, but the agents continued to hold him up and pummel his stomach with their fists.

"Don't touch his face," said one of the agents.

"We heard all about your missing balls. You may have a Silver Star, but all your junk got blown off. Now you gotta have hormone injections every couple of weeks. We also heard your wife is six months pregnant. How'd that happen? She really get artificially inseminated?" The agent spat bloody saliva at him.

Ken glared at him furiously, then howled, his face crimson.

"I thought steer were supposed to be docile."

"That's enough, Scott."

The fat agent gripping Ken's left arm held down his cheek. The pain went all the way into his brain.

"We'll just say you resisted arrest," said the agent called Scott before delivering a kick to Ken's knee, sending a jolt of pain to his skull. "Come on, let's take him in."

The fat agent grabbed Ken's slacks that were hanging over the back of a chair and tossed them in his direction, while another took the cuffs off just long enough for Ken to get dressed. After cuffing him again, they marched him out of the house and pushed him into the back seat of a car. Agents sat on either side of him.

As they drove, Scott checked his face in the mirror to see if his face showed any swelling.

"Don't let Scott get to you. His grandfather was an engineer on the USS Arizona at Pearl Harbor. Got burned to a crisp. His corpse is still on the bottom of the harbor. His father became an orphan at six, plus he lost a leg to a Zero fighter's machine gun fire during the attack. So Scott was raised to think of the Japanese as nothing but cowardly murderers. Can you see why he feels that way?" informed the agent on Ken's right.

"Plus, his older brother is a salesman at Ford. Japanese cars are giving him a hard time. In fact, I'd say his whole family wants the Japanese to leave the face of the earth," added the agent on Ken's left with a smirk.

Ken was put in a holding cell in the police station with no explanation. After two hours, he was finally allowed to make one phone call.

When the cuffs were removed, Ken's wrists were bleeding and his muscles were stiff from his shoulders down to his wrists. He'd spent the night here before after bouts of heavy drinking, but on all of those occasions, Ann had been there to rescue him.

He wavered over whom to call, but ended up dialing the office and asking for Charlie. He was transferred before he even finished speaking. In the background he could hear people arguing; he recognized Bob's voice and Susan's higher pitch. Charlie told Ken he would come right away.

Twenty minutes later, Charlie and the paper's lawyer came and bailed Ken out. Charlie said nothing, but kept shaking his head.

"What happened? You know, don't you?" Ken asked once they were safely inside the car in front of the police station. "What's the big deal? What about that diagram is—"

"I've kept my nose clean all this time. I'm this close to retirement," Charlie interrupted. "I've always been a regular guy, a representative petty bourgeois. No shame in that. I've worked steadily and hard for thirty-five years to get where I am. I know you laugh at me behind my back and call me Mr. Silent. Donkey Boots refers to me, too, yeah? But I don't care. All I've got to do is show up to work for the next year and ten months, and then I'm receiving my pension and going fishing for the rest of my days. Yet you jerks are trying to ruin that," Charlie spat.

Suddenly, a motorcycle passed by, nearly hitting the car. Charlie floored the gas and honked a few times and passed the bike. Ken looked back to see the bearded guy on the motorbike yelling and giving them the finger. Ken gave Charlie a shocked look.

The area in front of the newspaper was far from normal. There were more than ten parked cars and a small crowd of people outside. Ken looked at Charlie, but he said nothing, got out of the car and spat on the ground. Leaving the lawyer behind in the car—he said he wanted assess the situation—they made their way through the crowd and into the building.

Austin sat surrounded by a couple dozen reporters. When he saw Ken and Charlie, he stood up. "Well, here are the gentlemen you want. They can answer the rest." He looked momentarily relieved but fixed Ken with a look of raging fury. Next to him, Susan shrugged comically.

A female newscaster stuck a microphone in Ken's face. "Was the blueprint in today's article also given to you by Dr. J.W.?"

"Was the blueprint taken from Los Alamos? Meaning, did he steal it?"

"Did you know the information was classified as a top secret?"

"Is it true that North Korea, Iran and Iraq are already on the move? Rumor has it that Dr. J.W. had contact with North Korean agents."

The TV reporters let off a volley of questions.

"Please wait. I don't have a full grasp of the situation yet," pleaded Ken, pushing away their microphones.

"The blueprint published in this morning's *The Daily Californian* is apparently for a new type of nuclear bomb. And not just any nuke—one our government has been developing under the utmost security. The Fourth Nuke, a cutting-edge uranium bomb," a female newscaster next to Ken explained rapidly. "Since it can be produced using uranium-238, it has the potential to redraw the nuclear world map. You can create a nuclear warhead just by adding a catalyst to the fuel used in nuclear power plants."

"It was safeguarded as top-secret information by the military," added a middle-aged reporter.

"Do you have a more detailed version of the blueprint for the Fourth Nuke, or data from experiments?"

"Are you aware that the DOJ has issued an order to halt the series?"

"I don't know anything about it. I spent all morning locked up in a cell," Ken said warding off the questions and taking a seat at a table. His bad knee was hurting too much for him to continue standing.

"Well, did you know that an arrest warrant has been issued for Dr. J.W., that is, Dr. James Williams?"

"They arrested him?" Ken looked toward the speaker.

"He's gone missing from the San Diego Naval Medical Center. No one knows where he is."

"Did you expect them to order his arrest? There's information that you helped him escape."

Again they began peppering him with questions.

Dr. James Williams. How did they get hold of his name? Ken could hear his blood rushing through his veins.

"Please, just give me some space. I need to think," yelled Ken, raising his arms above his head.

The barrage of questions kept coming for another hour. Realizing that they weren't going to obtain any information to speak of from Ken, they finally left.

A very tired-looking Bob and Susan left for a late lunch, leaving only Ken, Charlie and Jimmy sitting in the office. Jimmy hadn't said a word since Ken had walked in.

"Why don't you say something?" Ken prodded Jimmy.

"I've got nothing left to say. I've already said everything on my mind. The path a newspaper should take is obvious, no?"

"Thanks for the sarcasm."

"We've come this far. May as well let it run its course. But…" Jimmy stopped for a moment in thought. "Have you heard anything from Donald Fraser?"

"I haven't," replied Ken, who turned to see Charlie shaking his head.

"Fraser is trying to use us. When a journalist friend from the East Coast called this morning about the Fourth Nuke, he mentioned Fraser's name."

"Are you saying that Fraser told media across the U.S. about the diagram?"

"He didn't go as far as to say it was actually him. But like I said, my friend knew his name. He said that every single article in this series has had Fraser lurking in the background, trying to leverage the uproar to shore up Green Earth's standing across the country. He's probably thinking of eventually running for public office. Just like our owner."

"Well, that's his choice. We've got nothing left to lose," stated Ken, looking to Charlie for agreement. Charlie remained silent.

"It was all a mistake," Jimmy declared as he got up and left the room.

"What should we do?" Ken asked Charlie now that they were alone.

Charlie had his feet on the desk and his arms folded. He was back to wearing his old boots again.

"I've always been one to avoid conflict. My father always stuck his nose in the wrong places," Charlie let drop. "My father was forty-two, my grandfather was thirty-seven and my great-grandfather was twenty-nine when they died. My father stepped in to stop a fight and got stabbed in the stomach. It was a fight between women, too. My grandfather was trampled to death trying to stop a mad bull. My great-grandfather died fighting with the International Brigade in the Spanish Civil War. All of them died poking their head in other people's business. I don't want to go that way. I want to live out my life." Charlie gazed out the window, speaking as if he were giving a monologue.

Ken stood up and walked to the coffeemaker in the corner. Every move made his beaten body ache. He placed a steaming cup of coffee in front of Charlie, who stared at it without a word.

"Maybe it's time to give up," Ken murmured. His face hurt where he had been struck by the FBI agent. He pushed a finger inside his mouth to find a tooth had also been worked loose.

Charlie sighed. "And yet, I'm a Brown after all."

Ken looked over at Charlie.

"We're just fated to get mixed up in things." Despite his words, Charlie looked fed up and shook his head. "I guess I need to go as far as

I can go. I already have lived longer than my father."

"Don't worry, I won't let you die before your time's up," promised Ken, patting Charlie on his shoulder.

"First we need to find Dr. J.W. Do you have any idea where he might be?"

Ken shook his head. If he wasn't at the hospital in San Diego, then he had no clue. He thought of Dr. Williams and how he had watched the sunset on the ocean from his wheelchair. A lonely old man. Where could he possibly have gone? Where in him was the vigor for an escapade?

Suddenly it occurred to Ken to check Williams' homepage. It still existed but hadn't been updated in the past week.

"I'm going to San Diego," announced Ken, standing up.

Ken sped along the freeway at a hundred miles an hour, reaching San Francisco airport in less than an hour when it normally took two. He made it in time for the first flight in the afternoon for San Diego, where he touched down two hours later.

He called the naval hospital from the airport and asked to speak to Williams' doctor. A female voice on the other end asked him to wait. After a while a middle-aged man came to the phone.

"James Williams went missing on the thirteenth of December," said the man in a formal, almost digital voice.

"I know. I want to talk to his doctor."

"That would be Dr. Wayne. He left yesterday for Europe on business."

"When will he be back?"

"Six months? Maybe a year. It's a publicly funded study trip to France. It's for research, so he's not going to be back anytime soon. Even we don't know when he'll return."

Ken didn't know what to say to that, so he hung up his cell phone. After taking some time to consider what to do next, he decided to go to the naval hospital anyway and got into a cab.

Just as before, the hospital shone elegantly in the sun atop a hill.

He went straight to the fifth floor and found the room at the end of the hall where Williams used to be. There was a new nameplate on the door with a woman's name on it. Just then a Mexican lady passed by pushing a large cart with sacks, collecting the sheets for the laundry. Ken asked her about the new patient in the room and found that she was a lieutenant junior grade who'd fallen down some steps on an aircraft carrier, breaking her leg in the process.

"Do you know anything about the man who occupied that room before the lieutenant? Dr. James Williams. The elderly cancer patient who always wore a yellow cap," said Ken as he took out a ten-dollar bill from his pocket.

"I transferred to this wing just three days ago. I was with the outpatient ward until then."

"Then do you know who used to work here?"

The lady snatched the bill from Ken and suddenly spoke quickly in Spanish.

"Who is it?" a voice from inside the room called out.

Ken, flustered, hurried away and took the elevator down. When he tried the reception desk, the staffer was a 6'4" well-built man with close-cropped hair who was keeping a sharp eye on the lobby. This was obviously not the person Ken had spoken to briefly on the phone earlier. He was indeed at a military hospital.

Ken asked the man about Dr. Williams. The staffer shuffled through a few files before telling Ken that the doctor had been discharged on the thirteenth.

"Discharged? I thought he went missing."

"He probably went missing after that."

"Was his discharge approved?"

"If he was discharged, then it must've been approved." The staffer looked at Ken suspiciously.

"But he was in no state to be discharged. He had terminal lung cancer. He said he would die here at this hospital, staring out at the sea."

"I can't tell you anything more. Mr. Williams was definitely discharged three days go."

Then, just as Ken was about to ask him to check again, the man shut the file and indicated with his eyes for Ken to move down to the end of the counter.

"Who are you with? Police or media?" he asked, leaning closely towards Ken over the counter. His glare made it clear he expected a straightforward answer.

"I'm with a newspaper."

"This place was packed with guys like you this morning, and I told them exactly what I just told you."

"And were they satisfied?"

"No choice. They had to be, 'cause it's the truth," he said, laying both his hands on the counter. One of his thick, sunburnt arms had a tattoo of a mermaid sitting on an anchor.

"Then I guess I'll have to be satisfied, too." Ken put both hands in the air and walked away from the reception desk.

Continuing out to the hospital gardens, he climbed up the hillock he'd first seen from Williams' room and turned around to find his old window. The curtains were open, but Ken couldn't see inside.

When he started making his way towards the main entrance, he suddenly heard someone calling to him. He turned to see a blonde nurse running towards him. It was Emmy.

"You were asking about Dr. Williams?" she said, panting. Her healthy face glistened with sweat.

"Do you know anything?"

"Not really, but something funny's going on."

"Tell me what you know."

"After he met you he did seem to perk up a bit, but there was no way he was healthy enough to be discharged. And there was something else. Two men came to visit him on the day before he was discharged. They were the only visitors he'd ever had, apart from you, that is."

"What did they look like?"

"They were a couple of tall guys in navy blue suits. One probably in his thirties and another in his forties. I didn't talk to them directly but apparently they were polite. My colleague Penny told me. You see, the younger one was her type. Blond hair, blue eyes."

"And the next day Williams was discharged?"

"Yes...or rather, he disappeared," Emmy said, lowering her voice and tilting her head slightly in thought. "That day I was on the night shift. I passed by his room at night and—"

"Emmy!" A man in a white coat was standing at the inpatient ward entryway, waving for her to come over.

Emmy stopped mid-sentence and looked around. "I need to go. We're operating."

"Can I see you after work?"

"Okay. Meet me at nine. There's a downtown bar called Little Honey at the corner of Ninth Avenue and Hall Street. Wait there." She made to leave, then turned back. She took a pen from his breast pocket and wrote a phone number on Ken's hand. "This is my sister's place. We live together." She ran off toward the building.

When Ken turned to the ocean, he saw the sunset just like the one he'd watched with Williams. He gazed at it for a while, then left.

He headed downtown and checked into a motel. He called the office and was told by Bob that everyone was out.

"Austin is whining that the series has to be stopped. He's a total fool and coward. And he's really pissed with you."

"Never mind him. He's laughing on the inside, what with our sales up 1,000 percent, and numbers can't begin to measure the boost to our brand recognition. He's probably busy trying to calculate how much extra tax he's going to have to pay. Anyway, have you heard anything more about Dr. Williams?"

"He's totally vanished. Rumors are flying about, saying the CIA took him out, or he was kidnapped by Iran, Iraq or North Korea. Personally, I think it's the latter."

"What an unimaginative journalist. Can't think of anything juicier?" Ken hung up.

When it was past eight, Ken headed off to Little Honey. He took a seat at the counter where he could see the entrance and ordered a beer. By half past nine, the bar was becoming crowded, but still there was no sign of Emmy. He ordered another beer. This was his fifth. He looked around again for Emmy but didn't see her.

After yet another hour had passed, a dark spot appeared in Ken's heart and proceeded to spread to his entire body like alcohol seeping into his system. He took out his cell phone, but he figured it would be too noisy in the bar for him to hear anything, so instead he stepped over to use the payphone near the entrance.

A child picked up. Before Ken could say anything, the little voice said, "Auntie Emmy has been in an accident so mommy's gone to the hospital."

"Do you know which hospital?"

"San Diego City Hospital. Mommy told me to tell anyone who called."

Ken thanked the child, hung up and walked out and hailed a taxi. He gave the destination to the driver, who floored the gas wordlessly. They were there within ten minutes.

When he told the security guard that he was there for a family member who was in an accident, he was treated to a pitiful look and let through. He passed through the darkened waiting room to the nurse's station, gave Emmy's name and asked after her. The nurse on duty silently pointed down the hall.

Two women and three men were standing in front of a room filled with bright light. One of the men was a police officer and the other was a doctor.

"Emmy passed away ten minutes ago. She stepped off the bus and got hit by a car as she was trying to cross the street. A hit and run," a nurse said with a grimace.

One of the women was crying in the arms of the other, who spoke comfort to her. Ken turned and began walking away, dragging his bad leg.

"Aren't you a relative?" the nurse called out from behind him. Ken ignored him and kept on walking.

In a daze, he walked out of the hospital.

Could it really have been an accident? Or... Emmy must have known something about Dr. Williams' disappearance. That was why she had told him to meet her at the bar. Which meant that... Ken halted his steps, squeezed his eyes shut and tried to erase the thought from his mind.

The sound of traffic from the nearby freeway reverberated loudly. Ken opened his eyes and started walking again. When he faced up, he could see the naval hospital glowing softly against the backdrop of the darkened San Diego hills. He gazed at it for a while, then went back to his motel.

As he did the first time out, he took the first flight back to San Francisco in the morning. He arrived back in Barton at a little after noon. The number of reporters hanging around the front of the building was about a fifth of yesterday's crowd. On seeing him, one asked where he'd gone to, but Ken ignored him and walked straight past them into the second floor office. On his way up the stairs he nearly ran right into Susan.

"We've decided to run the series to the end," she told him with a grave expression. "Charlie convinced Steve by promising to take all responsibility. It's the usual story. Steve never takes responsibility himself, but he's always ready to take the credit when things work out well. The only thing on that man's mind is money. We've sold 300,000 copies. No way would he cancel the series with sales like that."

"And Charlie?"

"He went to the printers. He'll be back in half an hour or so."

"Any news?"

"Nothing's changed since you called from the airport. The FBI and the media are all looking for Williams."

"The hospital said he was discharged three days ago."

"And you believe them?"

"That's what the scary man told me. But Williams was in no shape to be discharged," mused Ken, recalling Emmy's words. "Besides—"

"Listen carefully, Ken. You need to be more careful from here on. You're under FBI surveillance. They're tapping your calls and tailing you wherever you go. Keep that in mind."

"So I'm getting the VIP treatment."

"It was Steve who told me to tell you. I didn't realize he was a fan of detective novels. Turns out the financial papers aren't the only things he reads," Susan remarked with a shrug.

When Charlie returned, Ken told him all about San Diego. Charlie nodded and told him to continue the search for Williams. Ken sensed something different about Charlie's expression, but couldn't be sure. He called all the journalists he knew at other papers. They'd all been unsuccessful in finding Williams' whereabouts. He left the office at just after eight.

When he got home, the door was unlocked. It was just as the FBI agents had left it yesterday. In the bedroom there was a newspaper-size stain by the night table. He kicked a crushed beer can towards the wastebasket, sat down on the bed and stared into space for a while.

The contents of his closet and letter desk were ransacked. The books and picture frames were all toppled over. He didn't feel like tidying up, but decided to pick up a picture frame from the carpet. The glass had a diagonal crack running through it. It was a shot of himself and Ann, shoulder to shoulder and smiling, taken by Yamada back when they were in school. Ken tried to remember when it had been taken, but his head was confused and jumbled with thoughts. Eventually he gave up and put the frame back in its spot on the nightstand.

The phone rang. He didn't want to answer, but it kept on ringing. It eventually stopped, but it soon started again. He started counting partway, and when he reached twenty he picked up the phone.

"Kenji Brian?"

"This phone is tapped," said Ken quickly before hanging up.

His heart was racing. It had been less than a second, but the voice was carved into his mind. That was Dr. James Williams.

He began to regret hanging up, but fortunately it rang again and he picked up after three rings.

"It's Yellow Cap. Yellow Cap, Kenji Brian," said the voice before hanging up.

Yellow Cap... Ken quietly repeated the words. The voice had definitely sounded like Dr. Williams. Ken reached for his computer but then stopped. The phones were bugged. His cell phone probably wasn't secure, either. He thought it was likely they'd rigged his computer, too. He paced the apartment, unable to calm down. After half an hour he left.

He jumped on a bus going downtown. It was ten at night, but seven other people had gotten on at the same stop. A young couple in their twenties, an elderly man, a middle-aged man reeking of alcohol, two construction workers and a priest. Ken watched them closely but couldn't imagine an FBI agent among them. Or perhaps there was no one following him? No, he corrected himself. Someone was certain to be following him. He stared out the window at the passing traffic and Christmas lights and decorations adorning the stores.

Seven blocks from the office, Ken got off the bus and walked into a nearby bar, where he sat down and ordered a beer. On finishing it, he went to the bathroom. Next to the bathroom was a side door connecting to an alley.

Ken slipped out and ran as fast as he could for a good five minutes. His heart was screaming and his knee felt ready to snap off. He looked behind but couldn't see anyone following. He crouched behind a trash-can and steadied his breathing. After ten minutes he made his way to the back entrance of his office using only side streets.

He opened the door to the office and snuck in. He got down on his hands and knees and crawled along to the editorial department and stopped in front of Charlie's desk. This spot wasn't visible from the street. He took off his coat, placed it over the computer monitor and switched it on. Once it had booted, the screen filled with light and a menu appeared. Dr. Williams' words had to be a reference to a file on his homepage. The password: yellow_cap.

"This is it," whispered Ken to himself as he keyed the words in.

About twenty different documents opened up, one of which had an address with the heading "JW, Turtle City." It was a place near Yosemite Park. There was also a map, which Ken printed before deleting the file.

The Washington Post published the second part of Warren's article: "The Enigma of a White House Aide's Demise." In it, Warren once again wrote how Frank Curley was a well-respected man and pointed out the delay in police action as well as the media's unidirectional take on the incident.

The article concluded by stating, "A man's reputation is being destroyed. He left behind a loving family. We are duty-bound to consider his wife and child and to handle this incident more rationally and with greater care and compassion." At first, Anderson had deleted that last bit, but he'd put it back in after Warren promised to take full responsibility for the article.

7:30 a.m. Warren left his apartment but couldn't decide whether to go by car or Metro.

He was meeting with John after work so he eventually decided on the Metro and started walking towards the station, glancing at the van through the corner of his eye as he passed by. He had turned the corner and walked about fifty yards when he saw several men unloading the trashcans from in front of an apartment complex into a garbage truck.

A car came flying around the corner, its tires screeching. Coming to an abrupt stop in front of Warren, the car's rear doors burst open and two men jumped out.

Warren turned around to see yet another car approaching. He tried to run, but one of the men grabbed his arm. When he tried to break free of the man's grip, he felt a sharp pain shoot up to his shoulder.

"Come quietly if you don't want to get hurt," a voice spoke quietly into his ear.

The back seats of the car were empty. Two men grabbed his neck and shoulders, trying to push him in. Warren tried to straighten up, but a strong punch hit him square in the face. A middle-aged woman walked out of the apartment building, but on seeing Warren and the men, she hurried back inside.

He remembered John's warning that his life was in danger. Suddenly Warren felt a surge of fear. They were going to kill him.

Warren bent his knee and kicked the groin of the man on his right as hard as he could, making him crumple on the spot, moaning. When he head-butted the other man, there was a groan, and Warren had wrenched himself free.

The arm he'd flung off tried to grab him again, but he slipped past and started to run. A man's hand touched his shoulder. Warren braced himself and hunched over, and the force that was slamming into him went tumbling across his upper back.

When Warren made it to the corner and glanced back, he saw two men being supported by their arms into the back of the first car.

The second car was speeding towards him in reverse.

144

Warren ran as fast as he could. He raced into the street and jumped into a taxi.

"Go as fast as you can. For every turn you make I'll give you an extra dollar. If you run a red light you'll earn an extra three," offered Warren, looking out the back.

The taxi sped off. "One, two…" the young African-American driver counted out as he turned the steering wheel. After he counted to seven, Warren told him to head downtown. Then, on spotting a crowded area, he got out and lost himself among the masses. He walked briskly, continuously checking over his shoulder.

He spotted a red brick apartment building on a corner. He'd been to this place many times, but the grand building always had an intimidating air. It was hard to believe it was only fifty years old.

He got into its old-style elevator with its accordion doors.

Within seconds of ringing the doorbell, the door opened and an arm dragged him in. John had lived in this antique of an apartment for over ten years.

John looked through the peephole to make sure the hallway was empty before turning back to Warren.

"What happened to your face?" asked John, staring.

The skin under Warren's eyes was burning. When he touched it a stinging pain reached into his head. He must've gotten scraped up in the struggle, too, because when his hand brushed against his chin it came away with blood.

"All I know is that they weren't robbers." Warren explained what had happened.

John, sitting Warren in a chair, applied antibiotic ointment to his cuts with a practiced hand. When he was done, he snuck over to the side of the window and peered out the curtain. "Did anyone follow you?" he asked.

"It's fine. I did as you told me. Had the taxi let me out four blocks away."

"Did you see their faces?"

"The one who attacked me was a white man in his thirties. The driver was black. Everyone was in good shape."

"Did they have their faces covered?"

"No."

John frowned and fell silent.

"Don't worry, they were just giving me a scare," soothed Warren. He remembered the man telling him that if he kept quiet no harm would come to him. Warren sipped from the mug on the table. The inside of his mouth stung.

"If they were just trying to scare you they would have covered their faces. They were going to kill you."

John said this casually, but it sent a shiver through Warren.

"Where did it happen?"

"Just around the corner from my apartment. The car was a black sedan. I don't remember the license plate. Didn't have time."

"How many were there?"

"There were two cars and each one had at least three people. Maybe the second car had more. The windows were smoked so I couldn't see."

"How were they dressed? And their ages?" John asked rapidly.

"They wore suits. Plain ones. They were all around thirty. I don't know about the guys in the second car. But I think they've all had special training." Warren remembered the sharp pain he'd felt when the man grabbed his arm. It was a miracle he'd gotten away.

"If that's the case, how stupid are they? Letting an amateur like you get away."

"They probably didn't expect me to fight back."

"Not an egghead reporter like you," John nodded. "Do you want to call the cops?"

"What would I say? I wrote a stupid article and now I'm being hunted by a bunch of hit men? Would the police believe me and provide protection?"

John didn't answer.

"I'm convinced more than ever that Frank Curley didn't kill himself. He was framed for the girl's murder, too. What the hell really happened?" Warren paced around the room, practically talking to himself. He felt like something was caught in his throat, but he didn't know what.

"He was a policy advisor, right? What exactly did he do?" John asked, eyeing Warren.

"He advised the president on policymaking."

"And the president's top issues right now are what?"

"Re-election. Then the Iraq war, rebuilding the economy, the new stealth bombers… There are so many."

"Any hints at all?"

"I think Curley's briefcase must have contained something. A memo pad, a CD-ROM, a flash drive. Someone went after it."

"His laptop?"

"He had it on him. It was in the briefcase."

"No one at the station told me that."

"Have the police found anything suspicious at pawnbrokers or on the black market?"

"Nothing."

Warren pressed on the bridge of his nose. "How about the watch? Horne said he had a friend in New York sell it for him."

"I'll look into it today, but I would imagine it'll be difficult. They should have looked thoroughly already."

"Is there anything else? There must be something we're overlooking."

"I can't think of anything."

"Do you know anyone at the White House?"

"That's your domain. I've done the best out of all my classmates. I know a few who're fed thanks to tax dollars, but they're all behind bars."

Warren nodded.

"Have you seen Curley's family?"

"Once, after the incident. I don't really want to talk to them about it, I feel too sorry. The police would have already gotten the details from them. They would have taken Curley's documents too."

"All the evidence was sent to the FBI."

"Are we forgetting to ask something?" Warren placed a hand on his forehead and mumbled to himself. There was still a dull pain in his cheek.

"What do you want to know? I can get information if it's at the police station."

"I want to know what work Curley was involved in. As specifically as possible. I want to know about his reputation among other White House staff. His personal life. Everything about Curley. I would have looked into these things if I was a cop."

John nodded, looking a little fed up. "Go see Curley's wife. It's about her husband's character, after all. She might be willing to help if you explain."

Warren looked at his watch. It was already nine. "My boss is gonna yell at me. Again." He called the office and told the reporter who answered to tell Anderson that he was visiting Mrs. Curley.

"I'll go with you," said John, picking up his cell phone. He called the station and told them he'd be running an errand before coming in.

The two of them headed to Curley's house in Georgetown in John's car. It was just fifteen minutes away from Cathy's.

"The press might be there," Warren said.

"It's been three weeks already. I thought you media guys were quick to overheat and just as quick to lose interest."

They parked the car a block from the house and watched. There were a few police cars parked in front of the house, and a small crowd was forming. Warren and John walked over.

"Wait here," John told Warren as he flashed his police badge to step inside the cordoned-off area.

"What's going on?" Warren asked the middle-aged woman standing beside him.

"There was a robbery. This area has become so dangerous. It's so different from how it used to be. Poor Mrs. Curley. She's already having a hard time with what happened to her husband." Her eyebrows lifted in a look of pity, but her eyes shone with curiosity.

"How's the family?" Warren asked.

"They got back from her parents' and found the house ransacked. At least they didn't run into whoever did this. She has a young daughter, too." Suddenly her expression changed. "Who are you, anyway?"

"Our kids go to the same kindergarten. My son is a big fan of Cindy."

"Cindy… She's a strong girl." The woman smiled for a second, then quickly frowned again.

John returned after a moment and pulled Warren away toward the car. "Apparently it was the work of real professionals. The house was alarmed, but they disengaged it. They didn't break the lock but opened it using tools. The security company didn't even know about it until the police rang them. These were true pros."

"What was taken?"

"Jewelry, but nothing too valuable. They were all imitations. Other than that, they took cameras and video tapes."

"Did they look in the study?"

"Mrs. Curley isn't familiar with the CD-ROMs and such. Apparently she hasn't entered the study since the incident. They've probably been taken."

"Wasn't there a computer?"

"I didn't get a chance to look."

"Can't I go in?" Warren looked toward the door where police officers were coming and going.

"Don't be ridiculous. Even I got the odd looks. They wanted to know why an unrelated officer was on the scene. There were a few people I didn't recognize. They're probably FBI agents."

"FBI agents at a scene of a domestic robbery?"

"They're overseeing the investigation. The FBI has authority over all Curley-related matters. They think the FBI will probably take over the investigation."

"What does that mean?"

"Just what it sounds like. The FBI will take charge. But it's not like they're interested in cracking the case."

"So all evidence will be taken by the FBI?"

"I expect."

"And the MPDC will just stand by and watch?"

"Presidential orders. What can we do?" John shrugged.

"I guess this means we have to go through the FBI or White House to learn anything. Should we crack their computers?"

"Is that even possible?"

"Apparently their security is up there with that of the Department of Defense," Warren replied remembering Cathy's assessment.

"I'm going back to the station. My partner's waiting." John took a key from his pocket and slid it in Warren's. "It's the key to my apartment. I've made a copy and you should stay the night."

"I was planning on it."

"Take this too." John pulled his hand out of his pocket and showed Warren his palm, and six bullets. Warren pushed the hand back, leaving John looking slightly annoyed. Warren kept a tight grip on the key and gun in his pocket.

"The chief was looking for you," informed a political reporter, tapping Warren on the shoulder as soon as he got to the editorial floor. No sooner had he said that than Anderson stepped into view.

"Where have you been wandering around?" he practically yelled. "You should keep your cell phone on."

Warren took out his phone. "Battery's dead. It's three years old so it dies fast."

"Then get a new one," Anderson said expressionlessly.

Spotting Warren, a newbie reporter's eyes nearly bulged out of their sockets.

Anderson indicated with a look to follow.

"Things are heating up out west," said Anderson. "*The Daily Californian*."

"I heard about it on the radio in the cab."

"Don't you read the papers?"

"It was reported simultaneously nationwide. Is the information from a reliable source this time, too?"

"It's from a wire service. It was sent around the globe. The wire service probably has a reliable source. North Korea, Iraq, Iran and a number of other countries are acting on the information. The government is in a panic. There'll be an emergency cabinet meeting this afternoon. Hey, aren't you interested?" demanded Anderson, peering into Warren's face as he walked.

"The Fourth Nuke? Is a nuclear bomb blueprint really so important in this day and age? It all just seems so unreal to me."

Warren wanted to tell Anderson that he could think about nothing but the Curley case, but instead he swallowed his words. After all, a Washington political journalist should be showing exponentially more interest in leaked classified information.

"Did you know that there was a robbery at Frank Curley's house?" Warren blurted out as soon as they entered Anderson's office.

"That's why I tried your cell phone. How many times do I have to tell you? Keep your phone charged and switched on at all times. If this happens again—"

"The FBI was there," Warren cut in. Anderson's expression changed. "A police officer on the scene I knew told me. Unfortunately, I wasn't allowed in."

"So the White House is on the move."

"The FBI seized everything worth taking. Apparently anything linked to Advisor Curley will be handled by the FBI from now on."

"Are they onto something concrete?"

"I don't know. But if the FBI showed up, we know it wasn't just your everyday burglary."

"What was stolen?"

"Jewelry. Imitation stuff, though. Probably all his CD-ROMs, flash drives and his computer as well."

Anderson knit his brows.

"I want to know what Curley was working on in the White House. How can I get that information?" Warren asked Anderson.

"A friend of mine from college is a secretary to the attorney general."

"But not actually in the White House?"

"Not good enough for you?"

"It would just really help if I can talk to someone inside it."

"Do you know the name Donald Fraser?" Anderson asked out of the blue.

"I know he's an activist in some San Francisco environmental organization. But other than that…"

"Remember that name. Apparently there's some link between him and the source for *The Daily Californian*. His name seems to come up a lot these days. I hear he's got connections with the Justice Department, too." Anderson picked up the phone and started dialing. "Go back to your desk. Do your work. I'll get in touch with you later."

That afternoon Warren headed to a restaurant near the Justice Department that Anderson had told him to visit. Ms. Collins was flaxen-haired and 5'9". She wore sunglasses, a white blazer and slacks, and gave off an unapproachable aura. If she were in Anderson's class at Yale, she would be forty-seven. Anderson had arranged for them to have lunch.

Collins pushed up her sunglasses slightly and sized up Warren.

"So you're the talented journalist writing those articles. Elmore told me."

"Elmore?"

"Your boss' first name," Collins chucked. Her intimidating aura vanished as a friendly smile took its place. "He was such a studious guy. He wasn't interested in girls at all."

"I thought he would have been the biggest playboy at Yale."

"What did he say about me?"

"He said you were a lady so don't be rude. You were Miss Yale?"

"Such sarcasm. He hasn't changed." The waiter came by the table and Collins ordered a coffee, yogurt and a low-fat cake.

"You're trying to get even skinnier?"

"The loftier the ideal, the more sublime it is. Now then," she said, sitting up properly. "What did you want to ask me, Mr. Smartypants Reporter?"

"Is my article correct?"

"Well, you're very direct." She looked momentarily surprised but recovered quickly. "You wrote it because it was the truth, didn't you? Or was it all a lie?" She watched Warren closely.

Warren looked away. "The public wants to believe whatever sounds more interesting, regardless of what the truth really is."

"I have to tell you up front. Just because I came here doesn't mean

I'll be able to help."

"I understand. In your position—"

"You don't understand anything." She placed her sunglasses on the table. Her light blue eyes made her look a lot younger than her years. "The White House is very insular and conservative. To put it nicely, it's like a family, very human. Normally they try to climb over one another, but when there's danger they stick together. The Cuban Crisis, the Gulf War, 9/11…every time." She placed her hands on the table, keeping her eyes on Warren's. With some feeling she added, "The only exception was Vietnam, but even then everybody was united at first, to stop the spread of communism. It just took too long. They were exhausted. The whole place was in tatters towards the end and everyone ran to save themselves."

"What about now?"

"Anyone who's against the White House is their enemy. They'll unite and fight them."

"So the U.S. is in a crisis?"

"Has been ever since 9/11. The aftermath of that is still dragging on. The U.S. military is still in and around Afghanistan. Same with Iraq. You shouldn't be surprised to see war break out again at some point."

"And without full public support."

"As time passes, tempers will die down and people will come to their senses and want peace. But if another terrorist attack happens, then they'll step up the war again, no matter how small the incident."

"Do you think there's an attack coming?"

"I don't know. But unfortunately there are people out there who desire war. There are businesses that cannot survive without it. War is about so much more than allies and enemies. There are many elements tangled together. It's not uncommon for allies to make weapons together, then turn and kill each other with those same weapons. Afghanistan doused the flames a little, but those people will soon be getting desperate."

"The military and defense contractors. Demand and supply."

"You see, peace is maintained under very dangerous conditions that the average person knows nothing about. There are negotiations taking place behind closed doors that are just as tense as during the Cold War. Actually, it's probably worse now. Then at such a time the policy advisor dies. It can turn into a major scandal. The White House is really on edge," she continued, skirting Warren's question. "It's the same as Watergate. I was in high school at the time, but my uncle was in the Justice Department and told me all about it. The battle between the government and courts was unimaginably fierce. I think neither won in that case."

"Then who did?"

"The media. You guys. Be that as it may," she said with a change of tone, "there's that next-gen stealth bomber plan. I don't understand why the president suddenly became so enthusiastic about it. Congress is against it and the people favor military cuts. Next year is re-election..." She paused and glanced at her watch. 12:38.

"If what I'm about to say is wrong then shake your head. Otherwise, just listen," said Warren.

"No, I won't. I'm not going to betray our government. Besides, I don't know anything."

"Secretary of State Robin Dayton and V.P. Gerard Hopkins are for reducing military spending. Chief of Staff Simon Schmidt and Stewart Jones, the Secretary of Defense, are for increasing the military budget. The White House is basically split in half. So the president is caught in the middle," Warren started in, ignoring Collins.

Collins placed her elbows on the table and rested her chin in her hands, as if she had given up.

Warren continued. "Of course, Frank Curley was for arms reduction. He had an especially close relationship with President Jefferson but was outranked by the others. His opinion wouldn't affect policy directly."

Collins stared at Warren but didn't move. This was apparently correct.

"After Curley's death, the president rapidly leaned toward military expansion. In other words, Curley's death was damaging to the dove faction after all." Collins remained silent and Warren breathed out. "Now," he resumed, "the work Frank Curley was involved in..."

"No comment. Even if I'm here by Elmore's request, I can't betray the government."

"How would you be betraying the government if you answered my question?"

"We're not allowed to talk about what goes on inside the White House without permission. Not even if it was about the food served there. You're a skilled journalist, you should know that."

Warren nodded. He remembered a report he'd read about how the number of pizzas they ordered there hinted at frequent and serious security council meetings. The next day the U.S. bombed Kosovo.

"Besides, I wouldn't know. The advisor was presidential staff. I'm just a secretary to the attorney general. I've only been to the White House twice on tours and once for a dinner party."

"So only the president knew what Curley was working on?"

"And those around the president. There was the chief of staff ranked above Curley and five advisors at the same rank. Each administration has a different balance of power and different relationships among aides. With the current administration, the chief of staff has quite a lot of power."

"Are there any books or articles that nail the power balance in the White House?"

"I can tell you that the titles aren't that important. The atmosphere of the White House depends on the president. On whether the president is outgoing or quiet, full of vitality, or ambitious... It depends on the president's character and the era. That's what changes the balance."

"And what about the current president?"

"What do you think?"

"Full of vitality with a touch of ambition. Frank Curley kept him in check," Warren blurted out his own take. Judging from Collins' reaction he wasn't too far off.

Collins looked at her watch and picked up her sunglasses from the table.

"What was the relationship between Curley and the Justice Department?"

"I told you. That's classified information. I don't want to lose my job, and I definitely don't want to go to jail. You do realize leaking government information is a crime?"

"Then why did you come here?"

"I owed it to Elmore for looking after me. Now and in the past. I wouldn't turn down a chance to do him a favor." She gave Warren a meaningful look and shrugged.

"That's all I want to ask about the White House. Now..." Though Collins was looking at Warren with a fed-up look, he sensed a budding interest. "Do you know a man named Donald Fraser?"

"He's the head of Green Earth, a rather powerful environmental organization on the West Coast. He lives in San Francisco. He's not too well known on the East Coast but he's plenty ambitious. He'll probably run for office one day. What about him?"

"I just wanted to know more."

"He's not just the manager of an environmental organization. Be very careful if you're getting involved with him." Her expression changed.

She looked again at her watch.

"You look prettier without your sunglasses," flattered Warren as Collins rose from her seat.

"Elmore said he looks forward to your future. Among all your peers at the *Post*, it seems he has the greatest expectations for you."

Collins left a ten-dollar bill on the table and headed for the exit. Warren watched her from the table. When he looked down, he noticed that she'd left a small envelope behind as well. Opening it, he found a photocopy. Agitated, he looked up again, but she'd already disappeared.

It was a document request, as stated on the top. It was made by the White House and submitted to the Justice Department. At the bottom was a signature. Frank Curley.

Chapter 6
Reunion

After more than two hours of driving in the mountains, Ken had only seen one other car—a forest ranger's jeep. Soon he'd reach snowy territory, so he'd have to get out and walk. As soon as he reached Turtle City, his cell phone rang. He let it go to voicemail.

He pulled over and listened to the message.

"We need to talk. Can you make time?"

It was a voicemail from Jimmy. He deleted the message and turned off his phone. He looked at the map he'd printed out from Dr. Williams' website. He was almost there, but he didn't see any people.

Thick clouds were forming in the sky, looking ready to snow at any moment. Snow was already on either side of the road, and the road itself was slippery with ice. It was too dangerous to keep driving. He carefully pulled the car onto the shoulder and got out. The cold was piercing. Ken shivered.

He moved away from the road into a valley between the mountains. The snow reached his knees. He walked for ten minutes until sweat formed on his cheeks. He bent to retie his shoelaces, and when he looked up again he noticed a small cabin down among the trees a few hundred yards ahead. He quickened his pace.

The cabin blended in with the surrounding nature and looked very calm. He stood in front of the door and lifted his hand to knock, when the door flung open from the inside. A tall, skinny man stood directly in front of him. As Ken hesitated, the man gestured and asked politely for him to step inside.

The interior of the cabin was dim and quiet, yet warm and comfortable. A fireplace straight ahead was blazing red. In front of the fireplace sat a man in a wheelchair. Ken narrowed his eyes and looked at the man, who was wearing a yellow hat with the brim pulled down over his eyes but also dark sunglasses.

"You…"

The man took off his sunglasses, turned to face Ken, then put his sunglasses back on. "You'll have to excuse the dark glasses. I can't handle even the softest light. My retinas have become rather fragile from the cancer treatments."

The man spoke in a voice so soft that Ken had to concentrate on it to make out the words, but he had no doubt about it—it was Dr. Williams. He seemed healthier than the last time Ken had seen him in the hospital about a month before. Gone was the foreboding sense of death and deep suffering. Ken wouldn't have been surprised if the doctor got up out of the chair.

Manipulating the controls on that chair, the doctor slowly moved over to Ken.

"What a pleasant surprise. You look very well."

Ken shook the hand that was held out to him. He tried to remember their first handshake, but all he could recall was that there had been a lack of strength in his grip.

"I was surprised myself. Modern medicine failed me, yet I am finding myself healing here in the bosom of Nature. Perhaps this is the power of God," he said quietly as the other man nodded. "But for me, the best wonder drug was you publishing my notes. Through that, you confirmed my existence. I was able to leave behind my footprints. Knowing that made me feel so liberated." His voice grew louder as he spoke.

"Please don't get too excited," said the other man, leaning in to the doctor.

"Sorry, how rude of me. Let me introduce you to Campbell. He used to work for me as my assistant. Then he came to visit me after a seven-year absence, and I felt inspired to leave the hospital. This is his cabin. He took me here in his private jet and helicopter from San Diego."

"I work with semiconductors in Silicon Valley. Dr. Williams' tutelage at Los Alamos was helpful beyond words. It's no exaggeration to say I wouldn't be where I am now without him. I plan on caring for him from here on out," Campbell said gently, his hand on the doctor's shoulder.

Campbell was wearing a smart pair of glasses with a shiny metal frame. His suit looked expensive, making him look every inch the successful businessman. He was a man who had achieved the American Dream.

"Are you aware of the trouble occurring in this country right now?" asked Ken after a moment's hesitation.

"Didn't you notice the antennae on the roof? We've got satellite TV, you see. And the internet brings us the world's news all the way up here. Amazing how connected we are."

"It all started because of the final diagram you sent me. I'm sure you were well aware of the potential consequences," probed Ken in a tone that was a little too strong.

"I'm sorry about that. I should have told you beforehand what it signified. But, if I had, I don't think you would have printed it."

"I don't know about that."

"There's no way you would have. You are more of a patriot than you realize. Or rather, you are a man who understands the responsibilities of a human being."

"Which means I wouldn't have published it?"

"Correct. The problems that arise from that diagram are serious. You would not have willingly shouldered such responsibility."

Williams stared at Ken with a force the younger man had not witnessed before.

Ken had no reply. Suddenly, the room lit up as the clouds that had been looming over the eastern sky cleared, bringing the sun into view. The wheelchair-bound man stood out in stark relief to the dark background. Quickly, Campbell rushed to the window and pulled the curtains closed, and the old man disappeared again into the shadows. Pinpoints of light found their way in through tiny gaps in the curtains, lighting up the floorboards.

"That...was a part of my very last theoretical research. Please think of it as the protest of one foolish scientist who was shut out of awards and honor, whose existence itself had been denied," said Williams, his low voice filling the room. "I made a revolutionary discovery, that a nuclear reaction could be generated from uranium-238. Uranium-238 makes up 99.3 percent of natural uranium, and I found that by adding a certain catalyst it becomes fissile." His voice grew ever so slightly louder. "It was a discovery with the potential to completely rewrite the world's relationship with energy. You see, my discovery meant a nuclear reaction using natural uranium could be generated without having to enrich the uranium, a process that requires advanced scientific technology." Williams spoke slowly, chewing every word. "My discovery had the power to significantly aid Europe, Japan… Countries lacking in natural resources.

"But," he said, his face darkening momentarily, "my discovery also had the potential to rewrite the rules for nuclear power. Nuclear warheads could be made without enriched uranium. So, naturally, the government did not wish for my discovery to be revealed to the world. They buried it, research and all, behind heavy doors." Williams removed his sunglasses and sighed heavily, but his eyes were sparkling with contentment.

"So you used me to reveal your secret to the world?"

"No…" the old man objected. "Please don't talk like that. I was truly moved by your reportage. The feelings I shared with you in San Diego were not lies. I just didn't want the record of the discovery I left in the field of science to be left buried like that."

The old man stared at Ken with such sadness. A quiet moment passed.

"Now, let me introduce you to one more problem," said Williams, gesturing to Campbell, who pulled a CD-ROM from a desk drawer.

"This details the technology and formula for the catalyst needed to transmute uranium-238. It also includes detailed data that complements that diagram. In other words, these are the specifications and experimental data for the so-called Fourth Nuclear Bomb. It has the potential to provide mankind with an unlimited energy source. It's priceless." The light that crept in from the gaps in the curtains faded, sending the room into darkness. "I will give this to you," he said quietly.

"Why me?"

"I told you before. I am intrigued by your attitude towards the truth. The diagram was not enough. It only suggested the possibility of a new type of nuclear bomb. But it would not be an exaggeration to say that the content of this CD-ROM is capable of changing the world. You're free to use its contents as you see fit."

"And if I said I didn't need it?"

"Then I will send it to a different newspaper."

Ken looked at Williams, who took in his glance briefly before turning his gaze to the curtains.

"Will you be okay with that?" the doctor asked, his eyes still on the streams of sunlight filtering through the curtains.

Ken stood staring at Williams. "I don't know. What if I were to just throw it away?"

"Fine. I will leave all decisions up to you." With this, Williams turned to Ken, stretching out his arm to pass him the disc, and Ken accepted it unconsciously. "I am heading to Europe tomorrow. Campbell will be taking me," Williams said, grabbing hold of Campbell's arm. Campbell kindly patted the old man's bony hand. "I'd like to see the mountains…" Williams murmured, signaling for Campbell to open the curtains.

Campbell seemed to hesitate for a moment, then made his way to the window. After making sure that the clouds had once again covered the sun, he opened the curtains slightly and a weak stream of light poured in. Williams gazed out at the mountains capped in snow.

"You should stay the night. The mountain roads are dangerous, and it looks like it's going to snow."

"Thank you, but I need some time to think alone," Ken turned down the old man's offer. He left the cabin.

The surrounding areas had grown dusky. Within thirty minutes the mountains were shrouded in darkness. Ken drove carefully. He had spent most of the day driving, but he didn't feel tired. Instead his head was awash with thoughts of the CD-ROM and Williams' words. He felt flushed, like he had a fever, yet he also felt chilled to the bone.

Just as Williams had foretold, it began to snow. White specks floated madly in his headlights. It took Ken four hours to make his descent to Turtle City. By then the snow had stopped and the city was deathly quiet. He drove through the city and headed straight on to Barton.

By the time he reached Barton, it was after three in the morning. The streets were empty and the Christmas decorations were switched off, looking like dangling skeletons in the moonlight.

He went into his room, feeling dizzy. The threads of tension snapped audibly. He fell into bed and lost consciousness.

The next morning when Ken woke up, the sun was shining high. He rushed out of bed and checked inside the pocket of his jacket hanging on the chair. The CD-ROM was there, in its plastic case. He stared at it for a moment, then put it back. He thought back on everything that had happened the day before. It all seemed like a dream. Dr. Williams' figure, his voice… He'd actually seen and heard him. There'd been a man named Campbell, too.

At a little past five in the afternoon, he left for the office. All the articles for the next day's edition had been written and the office was quiet.

He looked for Jimmy but couldn't find him. Only Charlie sat at his desk, doing some proofreading. Ken pulled up a seat next to him and sat down. The two sat in silence for a while.

"You met Williams, didn't you?" asked Charlie, slowly dragging his eyes towards Ken.

Ken nodded his head in silence.

"And?" Charlie asked.

Ken shrugged his shoulders and looked back at Charlie. They looked at each other for a moment, then Charlie went back to his proofreading.

When Warren walked into the office, there was a crowd around the TV.

It has come to light that the bomb specifications in the series, "A Scientist's Confession," printed in Barton's local newspaper, The Daily Californian, did actually divulge defense secrets of the highest order. The government, through the Department of Justice, will be immediately ordering a halt to all subsequent articles in the series. FBI agents are now investigating how this top-secret information made it to the newspaper and will question Dr. James Williams. They are currently attempting to recover all copies of this edition of the paper. Also...

A photograph of an old man came up on the screen. It was Dr. James Williams, a nuclear scientist who'd worked at Los Alamos. He looked thin and frail like he really was suffering from terminal cancer. He wore a yellow knitted cap.

Just as Warren leaned over to try and get a better look, the shot changed to a photo of a middle-aged man with black hair and black eyes. Warren stared at the screen. The face was round and he had stubble. Japanese... There was something defiant about the man's expression that struck a chord in Warren's heart.

Someone tapped him on the shoulder, making him jump in surprise.

"Can't help feeling sorry for the guy, can you? Could have been you." Anderson was standing behind him. "Overnight, the country's champion of justice and a leader in the search for truth turns into a criminal, with the FBI hot on his heels. Take heed."

Anderson stared back at the TV screen.

It's obvious that the article has made highly sensitive and dangerous informa-tion available to "Axis of Evil" nations North Korea, Iran and Iraq. The U.S.

and other countries that honor anti-nuclear proliferation treaties… Well, we're now faced with a new kind of threat with regards to nuclear development. This will have a major impact on our nuclear policy. In fact, we may be entering a new kind of Cold War.

A female newscaster was interviewing Secretary of Defense Stewart Jones.

Warren could hear the others in the office talking about it.

"We may be entering into a situation similar to what we had in the eighties. Maybe worse."

"That local newspaper really stepped in it. This gives a lot of ammo to hawks in both the Democratic and Republican parties."

"I hear they might up the military budget. I hope we aren't entering another era of runaway military spending."

The room filled with reporters' comments.

Anderson stood up, gesturing for Warren to follow him.

"Did you meet Ms. Collins?" he asked as they arrived at his office.

Warren pulled out the envelope from his pocket and handed it to Anderson.

"This is a request for classified documents. Where'd you get this?"

"She left it at the table for me. It's Advisor Curley's."

"What does it mean?"

"Frank Curley was interested in the Justice Department's stance towards protecting classified information."

"I mean, what was he actually up to?"

"I don't know."

"Then find out. That's your job. Anything else?" Anderson put the envelope in Warren's pocket.

"It means the White House isn't a monolith."

Anderson thought this over for a moment, then strode over to open the door. Thomas Harris, another political reporter, in his late fifties, was sitting in front of his desk. He gave Warren a casual wave.

"This has gone beyond Advisor Curley," Anderson told Warren. "There's going to be a press conference at the White House in two hours. I want you to go with Thomas."

The balding man was a veteran reporter who had spent many years covering the White House. He would have been on the front lines during the reporting on Watergate.

"Is it about *The Daily Californian*?"

"Most likely. It's an emergency press conference."

Warren and Thomas left the newspaper and headed to the West Wing of the White House.

The press room was filled with people. The two sat in the very front row.

"A big crowd, isn't it?" Warren murmured to Thomas. "It'll be Chief Spokesman Stock Gerald, eh?"

"Probably somebody higher than that."

"Someone from the Justice Department?"

Thomas didn't reply.

The door opened and the crowd began to clamor as a group of about ten people walked in along with Chief of Staff Simon Schmidt.

"I thought the president himself might come," said Thomas in a low voice.

The conference was indeed about the Fourth Nuke that had been written about in *The Daily Californian*. After a brief explanation of the situation from the staff, Schmidt walked up to the podium.

"The administration is devoting itself to identifying the person who leaked the information on the Fourth Nuke. At the earliest, we expect to identify the source of the leak in a week. In the meantime, a special team has been set up to prevent any further breaches of security. We have also ordered all nuclear-related facilities, research organizations, universities and power plants nationwide to implement thorough security measures," said Schmidt slowly, looking around at the gathered journalists.

"Wayne. *New York Times*. How do you presume this leakage incident will influence foreign policy?" asked a journalist sitting next to Warren.

"Of course, there will be some effect. That's inevitable. We are currently evaluating the extent of such effects. The leaked information was under the highest level of classification. Now it's possible for any country to begin manufacturing nuclear weapons, possibly drastically redrawing the world's nuclear map. Fortunately, the leak concerns only a small percentage of the info," Schmidt replied, but it sounded like an excuse.

"How will the government take responsibility for this?"

"We will conduct a thorough investigation. At the same time, it may be necessary to reorganize the administration to prevent any such incident from taking place again."

"Does that mean that from now on the government will be taking a hawkish line?"

"If necessary," replied Schmidt, staring at the questioner with a willful expression. "No concrete decisions have been made yet. But there is no denying that we will be reexamining our policies."

"We would like to know about specific policy changes."

"Like I said, they are still under review. I cannot say anything more on that."

"Ford. *Los Angeles Times*. Will the government effect tighter controls on the media?"

"Not directly."

"By 'not directly,' you mean…"

"The First Amendment should be protected. Within its scope."

"What the…" Thomas mumbled to himself.

"And what does that mean?"

"Just as it sounds."

"So, the administration will be deciding its scope?"

"It will depend on the situation. In this case, there was a clear error."

"Do you think the government should have reacted more severely?"

"That's right," answered Schmidt decisively, casting his gaze across the room. Tension coursed through the air. The chief of staff's nonchalant remark was nothing other than a threat against the media.

"What measures will be taken against Dr. James Williams and the reporter Kenji Brian, as well as *The Daily Californian*?"

"The FBI is currently looking for Dr. Williams on grounds of leaking classified information, and the Justice Department is presently examining charges against Brian. I believe it's impossible to bring charges against *The Daily Californian*," Schmidt replied, matter-of-factly.

"This incident has made us think more deeply about the role of journalism. As a fellow reporter, I hope you will be lenient when dealing with Brian." The *Los Angeles Times* reporter took his seat.

"I'm Cameron, from *The Boston Tribune*. Dr. Williams is a terminal cancer patient. How does the government plan to treat him after taking him into custody?"

"We have heard that his condition is very severe, but currently, his whereabouts are unknown. The local police and the FBI are doing everything they can to find him, so I believe it is only a matter of time. There is a strong possibility he'll be needing treatment while in custody. However, the government will do everything it can to obtain the truth."

"What are the charges against him specifically?" a follow-up question came without an introduction.

"Breach of national security. And it's possible that charges of grand larceny will be added. There may be additional charges depending on how he stole the reports and data."

"Chief of Staff." Thomas raised his hand and all eyes turned on him. "How might the president's thinking change regarding the so-called Axis of Evil countries Iran, Iraq and North Korea?" he asked without identifying himself.

Schmidt glanced quickly at the other aides.

"The president…"

One of the aides walked up to the chief of staff and whispered something to him. Schmidt listened while nodding his head.

"That is all for today. We will keep you updated on any progress in a timely manner."

A commotion rose up in the room.

"Wait. Please at least respond to that last question," a reporter's voice followed Schmidt. Instead of answering, Schmidt waved his hand and headed for the door. The other staff members unceremoniously wedged themselves between him and the crowd of journalists. The momentary commotion died down.

"That con artist got away with that one," spat Thomas.

"What did that aide say to him?"

"Probably something about what they were going to have for lunch. Just a signal to escape. They'd planned it from the beginning." Thomas was thinking hard. "Looks like the White House doesn't want the president to come to the fore on this."

"What do you mean?"

"I thought the president would be coming to the conference today. This matter is that big."

"This West-Coast-small-town scandal of dubious veracity?"

"It'll likely develop into a much bigger issue. No, actually, it already has. The impact on foreign policy is massive, and every dove in the White House faces disgrace."

"It's still not clear what kind of secret information was leaked."

"That's why it can be blown out of proportion as much as people please. You'd be surprised…" Thomas said vaguely.

Warren split from Thomas after they left the White House, heading to Georgetown in his car. He stood in front of Curley's house. The street in front of the house was mostly empty; quiet had returned. It was difficult to imagine it swarming with police, FBI agents and rubberneckers as it had been that morning.

Warren rang the doorbell, but there was no answer. He stepped back to the street and looked at the windows. He could sense that there was somebody inside. Once more, he stood in front of the door, exclaimed his name and explained how they had met at the Smithsonian Museum before.

After a while the door opened, and he saw Mrs. Curley's face behind the chain, which was still on. She looked extremely tired and haggard.

"Have you read my article? It was about your husband's incident."

"I haven't read any newspapers or watched any news."

"Please read the article. I'm confident it will show that I am not your husband's enemy."

"I want to forget everything. I plan to let go of this house next week and move back to my parents' place in Boston." She looked away and closed the door. He could hear the lock turning.

"Please, wait," Warren called out earnestly. "I'm very sorry. I shouldn't have used my child to approach you. I am a political reporter, not on the culture desk. But I want to restore your husband's honor. Mr. Curley was not the man that people are saying he was. I know it. I feel that he is watching over you and your daughter. Please, read my article."

The silence behind the door stayed unbroken. Warren waited, holding his breath. After a while, he heard the lock and chain being released, and the door opened. Cindy appeared at her mother's side and waved her hand.

"You're Teddy's dad."

"You remembered." Warren bent down and shook Cindy's hand.

"Please, come in," Mrs. Curley said, after showing a moment's hesitation.

Sitting down on the sofa, Warren spread out a newspaper in front of Mrs. Curley.

"This is the article I wrote."

Without a word, she picked it up and read through it.

There was a small Christmas tree in the corner of the room and several presents lay underneath it. This house was far removed from any holiday spirit, but the lady must have wanted to cheer up her daughter.

"What do you want to know?" she asked, looking up from the paper.

"When your husband was killed..." Warren stopped. It was too soon for such words. "Could you please tell me about how your husband was acting before he passed away? Anything would help. Anything unusual? Even something very subtle is fine."

"Not really… He was very serious, and quiet. He was never a talkative man." She let her eyes wander to the photo frame sitting on the cabinet. The familiar face was laughing.

"It's just…like I told you the last time we met. He first started bringing home his work about six months ago, and he shut himself up in his study for hours."

"Work he couldn't do at the White House?"

"I don't know. It seemed that most of the time he was on his computer, writing something."

"Can I see his computer?"

"There isn't a single flash drive or CD-ROM left. Everything was taken by the police."

"Can you think of anything else, even something really minor?"

Mrs. Curley stood up and asked Warren to follow. Cindy was facing the television in silence. She was conscious that the two were talking about her father. This was probably her child-like approach to politeness.

"In her own way, she understands her father's death and what people are saying," Mrs. Curley said quietly as they walked into the study.

It had an air of authority. One wall was taken up by a bookshelf that started at the floor and ended at the ceiling and was filled with titles relating to politics and economics, as well as culture and art. It was exactly the kind of room you would expect of a scholarly policy advisor. A big desk was set before the window, upon which sat both a desktop and a laptop computer. Warren's eyes settled on the computers.

"Why didn't the police take those?"

"I don't know."

Warren walked over to the computers.

"Was my husband involved in something illegal?"

"No, that's not what happened. I don't believe that your husband died because of the reasons raised by the press. There has to be something else."

"I also don't think he'd be capable of such…"

Warren turned on the computer, but as he expected, no files were left. "No wonder the police didn't find this interesting. All the files have been deleted."

The same applied to the laptop. Rather than take it, the burglars had erased everything.

"I guess it was too bulky to take."

Everything in the room was organized in a way that revealed Curley's personality. As his wife had said, there was not a single CD or flash drive left.

"Sometimes, he used to work in the living room or kitchen, where Cindy would be playing. He would use his laptop then," Mrs. Curley said, going over the surface of the laptop with her fingertips, as though cherishing the memory.

"Can I borrow the hard drive and the laptop?"

"But…"

"I'm on your side. Please trust me."

"Everyone says that. But there is no one we can trust."

"You want it to end this way? It's not just for your own sake. Later in life, Cindy will ask you why her father had to go through what he did. How are you going to answer?"

Tears were welling up in Mrs. Curley's eyes.

"Mr. McCarthy…" Cindy had suddenly appeared behind her mother. "Take this," she said, holding out a pink laptop. "Daddy gave it to me for my birthday."

"But you're using that, aren't you? It would make your daddy happy if you kept it."

"But you need a laptop for daddy's sake, right?" Cindy was looking at him with a serious expression. Mrs. Curley nodded at Warren.

"Well then, why don't I hold on to it for a while? I'll take good care of it, okay?"

Warren took the laptop. It had a cartoon drawing of Einstein on it, and the words "To a future scientist" written next to it.

Warren placed the hard drive and laptops into a supermarket bag and left the house. He pulled out his cell phone, but after thinking for a moment, he turned on the engine instead. He stopped at the first payphone he could find and dialed. After the tenth ring, the answering machine clicked on, and he hung up without saying anything. He tried dialing again. This time he got through after the fifth ring.

"It's you, isn't it?" the voice said before Warren could speak. "Only you would be so persistent. I was just giving Teddy a bath and he said it was probably you. He—"

"It's daddy, right?" Warren heard Teddy pipe up in the background.

"Well? Don't keep me waiting. I'm leaving him standing naked."

"I have a favor to ask."

"Your favors are usually indecent. I'll listen, but it depends on what you're gonna ask."

"Is it all right if I come over now?"

"You've got some nerve. Of course it's not all right. What time do you think it is?"

"It's barely evening to you."

"Teddy's here. We're separated, you know…"

"It's really important. And there's no one else I can ask."

Silence.

"Come on, I'll do anything in return."

"Really? Even become my slave?"

"If that's what you want."

"No, you just can't come over. I'm about to read Teddy his bedtime story."

"I just saw Patty and Cindy."

"How long will you be?"

"I'll be there in thirty, no, twenty minutes."

Warren put down the receiver and headed back to his car. He took several fake turns to throw off anyone who might be tailing him and parked a few blocks away from Cathy's house. He took the alley and knocked on the back door.

Cathy opened the door, looking annoyed.

"Daddy, did you come to babysit me?" asked Teddy, who'd been hiding behind his mother.

"Aren't you in bed yet?"

"He's at kindergarten during the day, then with the babysitter. I think it's important for there to be some mother-and-son time."

Warren went to the living room and peeked out from behind the window curtains. There was nothing but the sleepy residential street.

"What is it this time?" Cathy said, her arms crossed as she studied Warren suspiciously.

"I'm just looking out at the road."

"You'd better not bring any trouble here. Remember, we have Teddy."

"That's why I'm being careful."

"How horrid to have to spend your whole life peering at the road. It's because you're in a thuggish occupation like newspaper reporting."

Warren ignored Cathy's words and placed the shopping bag on the table, pulling out the laptops and hard drive.

"You did this for me once before. You recovered a draft I erased by mistake."

"You were so grateful. Said you'd never forget it," Cathy recalled. "Well, that time, it wasn't actually erased. Only the file name was, which meant the actual contents still existed somewhere. So it was just like finding a child that got lost because its stupid parents were careless."

"So the erased data should be left inside this laptop and hard drive, right?"

"You're saying you want me to find a lost child again?"

"Only a great mathematician like you could catch on so quickly."

"I got lucky the last time, that's all. Only God can revive a dead man."

"You're my God." Warren looked at Cathy, whose eyes were fixed on the laptop.

"So this was Frank Curley's?"

Warren nodded.

"You didn't steal it…"

"I wouldn't have that much courage. I met his wife and borrowed it." He explained how burglars stole all the CD-ROMs and erased the data from the computers. Cathy listened quietly.

"And what's this?" asked Cathy, picking up the pink laptop.

"That's Cindy's."

Teddy reached out for it.

"She insisted that I take it. I couldn't say no. They're both desperate. We may not be able to bring Frank Curley back to life, but we can at least help restore his reputation."

"Keep an eye on Teddy," said Cathy and sat down, plugged in Curley's laptop and switched it on. She hit a key and the start-up screen appeared. She adjusted her posture, moved the mouse around and clicked several times.

"It takes some time to completely wipe data from a hard drive. Normally, when deleting, the file is flagged as deleted, but actually the data is still on the drive. That's why if you use recovery software, it's possible to bring data back. But if a new file is made that writes over the flagged files, then there's no way you can bring that data back. The only reason I could recover your files was that they hadn't been overwritten." As she spoke, Cathy kept typing and moving the mouse, but nothing appeared on the screen. "It's been completely initialized."

"Nothing left at all?"

Cathy ignored him and kept typing. The screen remained stubbornly silent.

"The burglars knew how to use a computer, all right. They used data deletion software. Random codes have been written over the deleted files. Recovery software won't be of any use to us here. We'd only recover the random codes. That's why they didn't take it."

"No wonder the FBI left it behind. Isn't there anything that can be done?"

"You always ask for the impossible," complained Cathy, placing her fingers on her temples and closing her eyes.

"With your brains, it must be no problem."

"It's not only a technical issue. It's a legal issue. Isn't this illegal?"

"You just happened across some data while fooling around with a second-hand laptop. How is that theft?"

"Either way, it won't work. This was done by a professional," said Cathy, turning off the power.

"The key to saving a poor widow and her child is in your head. Don't you feel any obligation?"

Cathy removed the power cord from the laptop.

"For the rest of their lives they'll have to discredit him altogether. What if you and Teddy were in the same position? Think of their father in heaven."

Cathy replaced the hard drive and laptops into the shopping bag without replying.

"Please, Cathy. Only you—"

"Come on, Teddy. We're going out now," she said, lifting the bag and getting up. "Even if you're expecting a miracle, I can't do it here. I need equipment. I have to go to the lab."

"I'll follow you anywhere. You are truly my goddess."

"So you've finally come to appreciate me?"

"I always have. You just didn't notice."

Cathy helped Teddy put a sweater on over his pajamas, then told him to go get his jacket.

The three of them headed to the Strategic Mathematics Research Lab at Georgetown University, a think tank that made the most of its proximity to D.C. by conducting research and analyses on politics, the economy and the military through collaboration with governmental organizations. The lab was world-renowned especially for simulations conducted in various fields using supercomputers, and most of its funding came from the government. Cathy had said she was doing research on coding there.

It was already past 11 p.m.

"Hey there, Teddy," said the older one of two security guards as they drove in. Teddy nodded in reply.

"This is Teddy's father. My husband, Warren McCarthy. He'll be my bodyguard tonight. It's all right if he comes into the lab, yes? I don't want to make him wait in the car."

"That's fine," said the older guard, giving Warren a friendly smile. "You might as well move in here with your family."

"Do you always work so late?" muttered Warren.

Cathy ignored him and signed the check-in sheet, and the security guard handed a visitor's name tag to Warren. Both guards wore guns in hip holsters.

They walked along a quiet corridor. A few rooms still had lights on and voices could be heard.

Cathy stopped at the very end of the hall, where a plate that read "Strategic Mathematics - Code Deciphering Lab" hung on the door.

The room was about 900 square feet, with desks lined up against the wall and alien equipment everywhere. There was a white board at the end of the room that was covered with formulae and codes.

"More than just paper and pencil here, huh?" conceded Warren, looking around the room.

"Be careful. These are all precision instruments. If anything breaks, it's going to cost you at least half your annual salary."

Cathy placed the PC on the side of the desk and started plugging in cords with practiced hands.

"Our lab is currently doing research on hard drives. It's a revolution-ary technology actually related to recovering files that have been over-written several times."

"So that revolutionary technology is what's going to help us now?"

"It's still a little like Teddy, though. You can't rely on it, and it's fragile enough it could break. But the potential is unlimited."

Cathy lifted her right hand while looking at the screen. It was a sign for Warren not to talk to her.

Teddy sat on the sofa by the window side and opened Cindy's laptop.

"You know how to use a computer?"

"Cindy taught me."

Warren sat next to him and looked at the screen that had icons for a few games and some half-finished cartoon drawings. On the side of the desk, there was a framed photo of Teddy and Cathy smiling. It had been taken about a year ago at an amusement park on their last outing as a family. A third of the picture had been folded back so that Warren wouldn't be visible.

Teddy started snoring quietly. He was clearly used to this.

An hour passed.

Warren went out into the hall. The lights of the long hallway had been switched off, and only the red emergency lamps shone. He got a coffee in a paper cup at the vending machine in the corner of the hallway and came back and handed it to Cathy, who took it without a word and without taking her eyes off the screen.

Another thirty minutes passed.

Cathy raised her head. "Here we go, what you wanted. But it's only a fraction of it."

Warren peeked at the screen, which was filled with random letters and numbers.

"What is this?"

"This was what was in the first file. It's something that's been coded. Decoding this is going to be pretty difficult. And I haven't got any clues."

"But it's not impossible?"

"Theoretically speaking, no, it isn't. Codes are a science of probability and statistics."

"How long will it take?"

"Using a supercomputer? Approximately ten thousand years."

Warren felt all the strength leave his body.

"Is this some secret document from the government or some corporation?"

"If it's either one, it's probably the government."

"I hope you're not trying to make me an accomplice in a crime."

"If the government is guilty of a crime, then trying to uncover it is different."

"So it belongs to the government," she whispered, facing the screen again and letting out a small sigh. She began typing again.

"If it does, can you decode it?"

"Well, there's a pattern. For the administration, Congress, the CIA, the FBI… There are slight differences in the codes they use. It must be a world full of people who don't trust each other."

"And you can decode that?"

"I'm not some super genius. It's a matter of probability. There's always the chance I can."

Even as she spoke, she continued to type, her gaze pinned on the screen.

"Nope, I can't do it," she said, looking up. Her eyes were bloodshot.

"So how did Curley read his own documents?"

"He would have had to run it through decoding software. It's like a translation device."

"And that software's not on the computer?"

"Probably not. It's usually kept on a separate CD-ROM or flash drive and installed only when needed."

"It's something special?"

"Like I said, there are government-specific, military-specific, and corporate-specific programs. Even within the government, the programs may differ according to rank, office and organization."

"And if you don't have that software?"

"Then it will take me until the next ice age," she estimated, pointing at the screen.

"You mean global warming."

Teddy turned in his sleep with a moan. The two of them looked at him.

"Okay," sighed Warren. "Let's wrap it up for tonight."

"Hold on," insisted Cathy, her fingers working the keys.

"Come on, you have work tomorrow."

Warren placed his hands on her shoulders. Cathy stared at the screen for a few seconds before nodding and switching off the power.

The three of them headed back to Cathy's place. Warren looked around the area carefully after getting out of the car, but nothing seemed amiss. He picked up a sleeping Teddy and carried him inside.

"Listen, this is very important."

After putting Teddy to bed, Warren explained how his room had been bugged and how there was a surveillance van parked outside his apartment 24 hours a day. He neglected to mention that he was nearly abducted. It would only scare her.

"I didn't tell anyone that I was coming here. It should be fine, but I want you to be extra careful," cautioned Warren.

Cathy listened quietly. After a long moment she asked, "And what we're doing, it's for Patty and Cindy, right?"

"Yes. It's for all three of the Curleys. It's so Cindy can grow up feeling proud of who her father was and proud of who she is as his daughter."

Warren placed his hands on Cathy's shoulders and pulled her to him. He could smell the faint fragrance of her shampoo, and he pressed his lips to hers. Cathy, offering no resistance, closed her eyes.

"Daddy! You made up with Mommy?" Teddy was looking at them, eyes open wide.

"We were never fighting," asserted Warren.

"I'm going to sleep, so you guys can continue," Teddy offered, closing his eyes and going right back to sleep.

"Please take care of him tomorrow morning," Cathy requested, pulling herself away.

"That's the least I can do. You go get some rest."

"You've gotten much better with words, at least. Wait," she called out to Warren as he walked towards the door. "You'd want to hold on to this, right?"

She held out a piece of paper with letters and numbers printed on it, before giving him a gentle kiss and a push towards the door.

It was past three by the time Warren reached his apartment. He'd wondered briefly if he should stay with John, but ultimately decided to go home. The van was still there. He was so exhausted he couldn't even think properly. He remembered to check the piece of tape he'd left across the bottom of the door and frame. It was still intact. He'd set it up on John's advice.

Even so, he found himself gripping the gun in his pocket as he slowly opened the door. He still hadn't put any bullets in it, but it made him feel tougher. There was no hint of anyone inside. He put the gun on the table and felt all the energy drain from his body. The muscles along his neck and shoulders were stiff from anxiety and from doing and carrying things outside of his daily routine.

There were eleven messages on the phone, but seven of them were just the sounds of someone hanging up. Of the remaining four, one was a magazine salesman, and the last three were Anderson.

"So did you make any progress?" Anderson asked on the first message. "I told you to give me frequent updates. And keep your cell phone on! There was a call for you from Ms. Collins. She said you were very amicable. Though I don't see at all what's so amicable about you." He said this in a more-or-less kind tone.

The second message had come in ten minutes later. "You probably haven't even read your own newspaper."

And in the final message, Anderson was ranting: "Where the hell are you?"

Warren pulled out milk from the fridge, smelled it and made a face.

He poured it down the sink, making the air reek with an acrid smell. He had no idea when it was from and hadn't gone to the supermarket for a week. Instead he pulled out a bottle of water and drank it. He turned on the television and saw the same Asian man he'd seen during the day.

The reporter, Kenji Brian, who was taken into custody by the local police, has been released... The whereabouts of Dr. Williams is still unknown. The Daily Californian will continue to publish the series of articles... Specialists will advise on content going forward... The Justice Department was planning to order a halt to the publication... President Jefferson, who had been planning to start his vacation from tomorrow, has made an abrupt change of plans... Congress will take this issue to the administration's...

Behind the quick-talking newscaster, an honest-looking face stared back. Japanese... It was impossible to discern his thoughts behind his poker face. Sixty years prior, America had hated such faces, marching them out to internment camps in the desert.

Warren moved closer to the screen and stared at the man's stubble-covered face. He had intense eyes and a rounded nose. His melancholic gaze weighed on Warren's mind.

He stepped away from the TV and switched on his PC, finding an email from John.

How did the date go? I might be able to help.

Warren typed his reply into the chat window:

I've gotten a hold of the bear's love letter, but its written in bear language. The rabbit is translating it, but it might take some time.

Then he lay down on the sofa. He took out the printout of the data from Curley's computer and stared at the row of numbers and letters.

What had Curley gotten himself involved in? He was a policy advisor. A lot of his work must have had far-reaching implications. But could it really have gotten him killed? His family, left behind...

Warren went back to staring at the jumble of numbers and letters for a while. He closed his eyes, letting exhaustion pull him into sleep. Just as he was drifting off, the phone rang.

"You remember the journalist Kenji Brian?" asked Anderson as soon as Warren picked up the phone.

"Yeah, the reporter at *The Daily Californian* responsible for those articles. What did—"

"His source is confidential, but it looks like he's gotten his hands on something big. Everyone is scrambling to back it up. I figured you didn't know yet."

"About that source—"

Anderson ignored Warren and hung up. The chief had spoken with an odd air of importance. Warren hadn't been to the office since yesterday afternoon. The fact that Anderson hadn't told him to go into the office immediately most likely meant that the article was already out. When he was on the phone with Anderson, he had gotten the sense that a lot of people were still at the office.

Warren considered making some calls but gave up. He would find out all about it in the morning, anyway. He lay back down on the sofa and closed his eyes.

Chapter 7
The Fourth Nuke

4:50 a.m.

The street below the office window was dark. The Christmas decorations had been turned off and only the streetlights remained to illuminate the night.

Ken had been typing on his computer in the editorial department since arriving at the office an hour earlier. He wasn't getting any sleep that night. Two days had passed and he still couldn't get the image of Dr. Williams out of his mind. By 3 a.m. he had given up trying to fall asleep and had come into the office.

Two fax sheets dropped in front of his keyboard. He looked up to see Austin standing there, his handsome features slightly reddened and lips trembling.

"'*Daily Californian* Acquires Fourth Nuke Secret'? What's this all about?" he demanded in a strained voice.

Glancing away from the computer screen but keeping his fingers on the keys, Ken glanced at the sheets. They were the front pages of the morning editions of *The Washington Post* and *The New York Times*.

Daily Californian *Reporter Kenji Brian Suspected of Contacting Dr. Williams*

Japanese-American Journalist May Hold Key to Secret of Fourth Nuke

"A friend on the East Coast called me at 4:00 a.m.," said Austin. "He sent me these by fax. Apparently a morning TV show in New York ran the same story."

Ken looked at his watch. It was 5:05 a.m., which meant it was already 8:05 in New York.

"What's going on?" Ken turned in his seat to face Austin.

"That's what I'm asking you."

Right then, the door flung open and Charlie came rushing in.

"Ken, you..." he began, but immediately swallowed his words as he noticed Austin in the room.

"*The Chicago Tribune* is running with a similar story, and I expect the *LA Times* will go with the same thing, too. It's caused an uproar on the East Coast already, and it'll be all over the country in a few hours. The only paper not running with this news is us!" Austin gave Charlie a brief glance and continued. "Do they have a real source?"

"I don't know," said Ken, handing back the faxed articles to Austin.

"So, what, it's all bullshit?"

"No comment."

"Where were you the day before yesterday?"

"Again, no comment."

"Williams sent you that blueprint. You're the one with the best access to him."

"Look, you own a newspaper. You should understand the relationship between a journalist and his source."

"I'm sick of this. I'm not getting my hands dirty anymore. From now on, you're going to put your name to every article you write on this topic. That way, we'll be clear on where the responsibility lies," Austin laid down as he slammed the articles on Ken's desk. "You will do exactly as Charlie says from here on," he added, glaring at Charlie on his way out.

"Austin called me in saying he couldn't get a hold of you at home. I told him that I wasn't your babysitter," said Charlie, picking the fax up from the desk. "But I can see why he's upset. Where'd these guys get this info?"

"I wish I knew."

At just past seven, Jimmy arrived. He cast dubious glances at Ken and Charlie but didn't say anything. When Charlie slid the fax sheets over to him, he read them without saying a word.

"Aren't you surprised?" asked Ken.

"I got a call from a friend in New York. He said the intel was from a government source but he wanted to confirm with me."

"And what did you say?"

"That I didn't know anything. I called you after that but it went to voicemail. I was going to talk to you about it first thing this morning, but I guess it's too late now. The info was only disseminated to the big boys. *The Barton Journal* got passed over on this one, too."

Charlie let out a sigh. Ken glanced at his watch and got to his feet. It was time for him to head off to San Francisco airport. Just as he was about to walk out the door, he turned around and walked back to his desk. He pulled a few sheets of paper from his desk drawer and placed them on Jimmy's desk.

"Here. This is the draft for the last article."

Ken waited for more than two hours on a plastic bench at the airport. He leafed through a copy of the *LA Times* he bought at an airport newsstand. The content was the same. He quietly reached into his pocket to confirm that the CD-ROM was still there in its plastic case, then continued reading. In his mind, the image of Dr. Williams at the cabin kept coming and going. An announcement blared out of the speakers that flights from Salt Lake City were delayed. Apparently there was a bad snowstorm in Utah.

The plane finally arrived, three hours late.

"Ken!" A woman rushed through the gates and into his arms. He shot a casual glance at her belly, but he couldn't detect any change. "Sorry you had to wait so long," she said.

"I was going to give it another minute before leaving."

"We had a terrible flight. I thought we were going to crash." Ann sounded so cheerful, he could barely recall how depressed she'd sounded on the phone recently.

"How's your mother?" he asked as he shoved her large suitcase into the trunk.

"At first I cried when I saw how thin she was, but this morning she actually got out of bed on her own to see me off."

"I hope your family wasn't upset that I didn't come with you."

"Not at all. They understood. They both apologized. You may think they were against you when we got married, but they were just being overprotective. And people change. Especially when they're nearing the end."

"It's all right. I understand. Nobody would be happy about their daughter marrying a guy like me."

"Don't talk like that."

Life could be merciless. He'd learned that on a battlefield near the equator. Even if you were a good person, even if you prayed to God, it didn't matter, bad things could still happen to you. Perhaps that was why he could deeply identify with the doctor's need to leave something behind to prove his existence in the world. A soul crying out.

Ken wanted to ask about the baby, but held back. He had expected to be over this by now, but clearly that wasn't the case, even though it had been his idea in the first place.

"You should have stayed until Christmas," he said.

"I did consider it," replied Ann, her voice trailing off. "Why don't we both spend Christmas at my parents' place next year?"

Instead of answering, Ken hit the gas. Cool air rushed through the slightly opened window.

"California's so warm. Utah was covered in snow." Ann's voice trilled in the wind. "Mom and dad want to see you."

Ken stepped harder on the gas, drowning out her voice with the noise of the engine.

His parents had been killed in a car accident seven years earlier. Their car was flung into a guardrail on the freeway by a large truck that suddenly changed lanes. They both died instantly. At the time, Ken had been working at the paper for a few years and had constantly been in and out of rehab for alcohol abuse. He didn't know they'd died until after the funeral. That they'd died on the way back from visiting him in the hospital, he didn't learn until half a year later. He was the reason the two people who loved him the most had died. It was still a raw wound in his heart. It was probably why he didn't want to get to know Ann's parents now.

"It's okay, Ken. There's still time."

Time—something Ann's mother didn't have a lot of.

Ann leaned her head on his shoulder. Ken had to stiffen his arm to keep the car from drifting.

"You know," she whispered into his ear, her breath warming his neck, "I want you to see where I grew up. I'd like us to live there someday."

Ken still hadn't come to terms with it. He thought he'd given it careful consideration, but he still couldn't see himself as a family man.

"What's up with that case? With Dr. J.W.?" asked Ann suddenly, sitting up straight.

"It's going well."

"I'm a little scared of it."

"I thought you were happy for me."

"Well, actually…" her voice trembled. "I was opposed. Nuclear weapons… But I hadn't seen you so excited in such a long time. Maybe I should have said something sooner."

Ken had never heard Ann talk like a scared woman before. He changed the subject. "How's your body holding up?"

"I'm well. I should start showing soon." Her expression softened, and she placed a hand on her stomach and smiled happily. She was an intuitive woman who no doubt understood the thoughts going through Ken's mind and was acting cheerful on purpose.

At home, Ken stopped in front of the door. "Please don't be surprised."

"I'm ready," Ann nodded with a meek expression.

Ken opened the door and Ann sighed quietly. There were several trash bags piled up inside the door.

"I was just about done."

Ann locked the door behind them, ignoring him. "So the bedroom's all clean, right?" She took his arm and led him off to bed.

Ken walked out of the office after sending a new article to layout.

He'd spent the rest of yesterday cleaning up. Today too he stayed until noon helping Ann, then went to the office in the afternoon.

When he turned a corner, he saw two men in dark suits coming out of a nearby restaurant and walking directly towards him. Just as Ken stepped towards the curb, the doors of a parked Ford opened up. The two men rushed up and shoved him inside.

It all happened in a flash. By the time Ken realized what was going on, the car had rounded the corner and was speeding off towards the suburbs.

One of the men kept a tight grip on his neck, pushing him down into the seat and out of view. When he struggled, a sharp pain ran up his back. The man had elbowed him, hard.

Ken thought he recognized the voices that spoke in brief conversation in the front seats. He tried to remember, but he couldn't focus.

For twenty minutes or so they traveled westward until they arrived at a port. Warehouses lined a dark, dusky street.

The car stopped in an alley behind the warehouses. The ocean was right across the street. They told Ken to get out of the car.

Three of the four men were the same FBI agents who had busted into his apartment.

"I'm going to be honest with you. I hate Asians. Especially the Japanese," said the agent called Scott.

"So you said. But if you'd read up on me, you'd know I'm American. Born and raised here. I could even become president if I wanted."

"I don't care what the government says. A Jap is still a Jap." Scott slightly furrowed his brows and spoke in the same cool tone he'd used five days prior.

"You're a government agent, right? Have you ever stopped to think who you're really serving?"

"I serve justice, and America. Never had any doubts on that front. And you're an enemy of the U.S.A."

"What do you want from me?"

"You know what we want. Hand over what you got from that Jewish traitor."

"I don't know what you're talking about."

"Step aside," the fat agent ordered Scott, pushing his shoulder. Scott glared at him for a moment but complied and lit a cigarette.

"The powers that be are willing to strike a deal with you. If you quietly give them what they want, there's a good chance they'll reduce your sentence. They're getting impatient. We can just say you didn't realize the importance of the materials in your possession, so you decided to hand them back to the government. Already, countless countries and organizations are making a move. Screw this up, and you're looking at more than twenty years for leaking classified information. If your judge hates the Japanese or has family in the military, you'll get a life sentence. There are intelligence agencies all over the world who know that you met with Williams. You could easily be found dead in an alley or face down in the ocean. You ought to settle this, and soon," the hefty agent said with a sympathetic look.

"So the DOJ wants to make a deal?"

"Normally we prefer to beat this stuff out of Japs and Jews," spat Scott, kicking a stone that hit Ken in the leg with a dry snap.

Ken felt something hot slowly rising in his body—anger, which he hadn't felt with such intensity in a long time. Before, his hatred of Scott had been purely personal, but this time it was different. He was surprised to discover he still had it in him.

Scott flicked his lit cigarette at Ken, hitting him on the cheek, scattering ashes on his shoulder. Before he realized what he was doing, Ken's fist connected with Scott's jaw. Bone struck bone with a loud crack. The shock went up Ken's arm. He hadn't even planned the attack.

Scott lurched toward the ocean. The next moment, Ken felt a sharp pain in his side. Scott had kicked him in the waist.

Ken fell to his knees. His jaw received a forceful uppercut. He tasted something bitter. Before he had time to get to his feet again, another and another blow rained down on his face. Something warm began to leak from his nose.

Ken curled up on the ground and Scott delivered another heavy kick to his stomach. And a third. A fourth. A fifth. Then, when the agent tried to land yet another kick, Ken grabbed a hold of his foot. He gripped it with all his might and stood up and lunged forward.

"Jap!" Scott groaned, falling to the ground. The fat agent twisted Ken's arm and pulled him away.

"Let him go!" shouted Scott. Blood dripped from his mouth from where he'd fallen on the concrete. His shoulders shook as he panted, and his eyes were bloodshot. He managed to land another forceful punch square in Ken's face. With each punch, Ken's mind went hazy.

Ken's face burned. He couldn't feel the pain anymore. His body wasn't cooperating, as if it didn't belong to him. Sheer will kept him on his feet. *I can't lose to this guy. I refuse to be brought down by a guy like this*, he thought to himself as he struggled to hold onto consciousness.

He tucked his head in low and launched himself at Scott with a yell, catching him by the waist and slamming him into the wall of a warehouse.

Ken slammed him into it again and again, until the agent let out a strange sound and his arms went limp. When Ken finally released his hold, Scott's arm sprang to life, hitting him in the face and sending him crashing over a nearby handrail. The agent came walking over with his hand gripping the right side of his waist.

"Listen to me, you Jap. This is our country, built with the blood and sweat of our forefathers. The most powerful country in the world. And people like you do nothing but contaminate this sacred land. I'll never let you assholes get away with doing what you want," shouted Scott, his shoulders heaving.

"Let us know when you're ready to talk," said the fat agent, leaning over the rail to stuff a piece of paper with his number on it into Ken's breast pocket.

Ken closed his eyes and listened to the voices. Eventually the agents got back into their car and drove away. *They're leaving?* he thought to himself in his flickering consciousness. *Why didn't they just kill me?*

When he walked back into the apartment, Ann gasped and covered her mouth with her hand to stifle a scream. He placed his fingertips over hers to tell her not to say anything.

"But your face..." she murmured, tears already welling in her eyes. "You're going to be a father this spring."

Ken couldn't help looking away when he saw his own reflection in the bathroom mirror. His face was bruised and swollen, and blood from his nose was spattered all over his jacket. He ached all over and it took all his strength just to stay on his feet. Yet his injuries weren't as bad as they looked. He didn't have any broken bones.

Ignoring Ann's pleas for him to visit a hospital, Ken got into bed. She disinfected his wounds and packed ice into plastic bags to bring down the swelling.

By the next day, the pain had largely subsided, but the swelling on his face was much worse.

Ann tried to stop him, but he eased her worries and left for the office at around noon. Several acquaintances in the parking lot called out to him, but he ignored them and walked straight into the editorial department. All eyes went to him when he walked in, but once they saw it was him, they looked away. After all, it hadn't been unusual for him to come into work in such a state as recently as a month ago.

"A bit special this time, isn't it?" Susan asked as she passed by. She touched a bandage on his forehead with a red lacquered nail. He grit his teeth and shut his eyes.

"What happened?" asked Bob curiously, nearly bumping into Susan.

"The usual."

"You haven't been drinking recently," he said, leaning closer. "Some drunk pick a fight with you?"

"It's December. People remembering Pearl Harbor," Ken shrugged. In an instant, pain raced through his body and he gave a low moan.

Jimmy was watching him from a distance. There was a tenderness in his gaze that Ken had never seen before.

"Perhaps you were right." Ken said as he settled into his seat.

"Don't back out now. You can't run away now. You've come too far."

"I don't have the strength to run away."

"I feel a little better after reading your last article. I understand what Dr. Williams wanted now. Not that I approve of everything, mind you."

"I'm not his spokesman, you know. I don't worship him."

"The old man is on his deathbed looking back at his eighty-plus years of life, realizing it's all been covered up by History and Government. To face death and look back and think there was no purpose to your life would be unbearable. A repudiation of your very existence. Yet his actions could also be seen as a challenge to society. Maybe not 100 percent, but I'm sure he felt that way in part. I guess revealing his life story to the world was a form of penance."

"I don't think so. All lives have meaning. He lived the best he could. I wouldn't have been able to do what he did. No one has the right to criticize his life."

"Let's stop this. It's done now," said Jimmy as he leaned over to answer the phone.

Later that afternoon, Fraser came to pay Ken a visit. As usual, he smelled of pipe tobacco. Ken couldn't help but wince as he imagined the aroma seeping into his wounds and inflaming them further. Fraser looked at Ken and furrowed his brows.

"I suffered a fall," shrugged Ken, as if nothing was amiss.

"America has a lot of slippery roads. Be careful. Sometimes people fall down stairs and break their necks." Fraser took out his pipe and lit it. "By the way, is it true that you received information from Dr. J.W. about a Fourth Nuke?" Fraser elegantly exhaled smoke and placed the remaining tobacco in its deerskin pouch.

"I wonder how that rumor got started." Ken followed the tip of the pipe with his eyes. A thin line of smoke rose up.

"What if it's not a rumor, but truth?" Fraser pulled the pipe away from his mouth and looked at Ken.

Ken took in his glance. "And if it is?"

"North Korea, Iran, Iraq, Libya… Many countries want nukes. Add in terrorist groups and there are countless interested parties. If they were to get their hands on that info… I really think you ought to show it to me."

"I don't have anything. The media made it all up," Ken said flatly. He touched the skin under his eye and a sharp pain shot into his brain. "It's the job of the media to provide stories the public wants to hear. We're just trying to sell papers, that's all. Those are your own words."

"What about this last article in the series?" asked Fraser in a calmer voice.

"It's going ahead according to plan."

Ken stood up. Every injured every inch of his body revolted and for a while, he couldn't move.

Ken left the proofreading to Bob and left the office at around six. His head felt stuffed with a heavy clump and his joints creaked as if they needed oiling. The beating he got from Scott made his month-long exhaustion pour out all at once.

He turned the key in his apartment door, but the lock offered no resistance. Something dark and viscous wrapped itself around him. Carefully, he stepped inside and immediately froze. Destruction. A scene of total destruction.

"Ann," he called out, but there was no answer. "Are you there?"

The sofa had been ripped open and the springs were showing. All the drawers had been opened and their contents scattered across the floor. Even the electrical sockets had been torn out of the wall and the wallpaper partially ripped off.

Stepping over the mess of books and broken vases on the floor, he hurried to the bedroom. It was in a similar state, with the contents of the desk and closet dumped on the floor. The bed was shredded, the mattress springs exposed, and pillow feathers littered the room.

The kitchen was no different. A milk carton was left, crumpled, on the floor. Milk had been thrown all over the walls. The freezer had been left open to melt. Someone had been looking for the CD. Someone who was clearly dead-set on that goal.

Fraser's words came to Ken's mind. *North Korea, Iran, Iraq, Libya… Many countries want nukes. Add in terrorist groups and there are countless interested parties.*

The FBI agent had said, *Already, countless countries and organizations are making a move.*

Ken returned to the living room and walked over to the table by the window that he used when working at home. A dozen or so CDs he kept there were missing. He started up his computer and checked the history on his files. Every single one of them had been opened.

Ken looked around the room in a daze. Random thoughts came and went. The only thing he felt sure about was the fact that they'd taken Ann. He reached for the phone to call the police but stopped himself. The face of Scott, the FBI agent, sprang to his mind. It was possible that he was the one who took her. If so, there was no point in calling the cops.

He thought for a while more, but he couldn't organize his thoughts.

His computer speakers chimed. It had been set to automatically alert him of incoming email. Hastily, he tapped the keyboard, trying to retrieve the email. He tried to type his password, but in his panic couldn't quite remember it. No, he knew it, but his head was so confused that his fingers weren't doing what his mind was telling them to. He decided to speak the password out loud, typing each character carefully as he did.

"We have your woman and your future bundle of joy. Come to the Saint More Wharf at 11:00 p.m. Don't forget Dr. J.W.'s little present."

"Ann…" Ken moaned. The little willpower he had left started to fade. Suddenly he felt ten times heavier and sat there like stone. His mind was shutting down. He couldn't think at all.

After several dozen minutes, or perhaps just a few, he felt he had to do something, even though he was totally devoid of will. He read the words on the screen again. He read them aloud the third time. When he was sure he'd memorized it, he hit delete.

He returned to the office. Charlie and Bob were still there. They eyed him dubiously as he sprang in. He sat down at his desk, started up his computer and accessed a file. The data from Dr. Williams' CD was in a folder on his computer. The original disc had gone through the shredder. He dug around in his desk looking for a blank CD. Usually he had several, but now he couldn't find even one.

"Here, use mine," said Bob, throwing a blank disc to him. "Isn't this what you want?"

Ken thanked him and inserted the CD into his drive.

Ken was about 200 yards ahead of the bridge. The moored yachts had Christmas illuminations tied about their masts. Red, blue and yellow wavered on the water's surface for a fantastical atmosphere. There was not a soul in sight.

Ken shivered in the icy wind. But that wasn't the only thing that sent a chill through his body. He couldn't stop thinking about what might unfold. He tightened his grip on the CD case in his pocket.

He heard the faint sound of waves lapping. He checked his watch, which read 11:10. Ann's captors could be watching him from a distance, waiting until they thought it was safe to come forward.

He heard the sound of an engine from behind. He turned to see a gray van approaching slowly, then stopping thirty feet away. When the door opened, three men in dark gray construction overalls appeared. Was it the FBI? No. Ken had never seen these men before.

"Where's Ann?" Ken yelled.

"Hand over the CD first," called back a short man in the middle.

"Ann first!" Ken shouted.

Shorty signaled to the van and the door opened. Another man came into view as he dragged a woman out roughly. She was wearing a white down jacket, and they'd handcuffed her hands behind her back and duct-taped her mouth shut. The man shone a flashlight in her face to prove that it was Ann. Her eyes were wide open and she was shaking her head fiercely. It was definitely her.

"Take off the handcuffs and tape," said Ken, taking a step forward.

The man behind Ann held a gun. He looked over to Shorty for confirmation. When he nodded, the man ripped off the tape.

"Don't give it to them!" cried Ann. As soon as she did, the man punched her.

"Stop!" shouted Ken, unconsciously stepping closer. The man with the gun raised his arm.

"I heard she's pregnant," said Shorty with a smirk. "Hand over the CD."

"Let her go."

The man with the gun took off the handcuffs but kept a firm grip on her arm.

Ken slowly took out the plastic case.

Shorty took a few steps towards him. Ken responded by holding his arm out to dangle the case over the edge of the wharf, right above the water. Shorty stopped in his tracks.

"I have to get her somewhere safe first."

"Don't do it!" cried Ann again.

"Come any closer and it's going into the ocean."

Ann tried to wriggle free of the man's grip. There was a loud crack as the man's fist hit her jaw. Ken's head grew hot.

"Doesn't that contain information on how to make that new type of nuclear bomb? It's the devil's key. It's worth far more than my life!" yelled Ann.

"Hurry up and let her go," demanded Ken.

Ann suddenly managed to break free and made a dash for the ocean. The man followed her with the sight of his gun.

"Don't shoot!" he shouted, throwing the CD case towards the man with the gun. Everyone's eyes followed the plastic case. Ken launched himself at the man with the gun. A gunshot rang out in the silence. Then, from the corner of his eye, Ken saw someone come forward, grab the case and run towards the ocean. Something splashed off the wharf.

"Ann!" yelled Ken at the dark sea. People began to appear on the decks of the yachts, talking amongst themselves. He slipped over the rail and splashed down into icy water that froze his whole body. He quickly surfaced and looked around. It was too dark to see anything. The seawater was weighing down his clothes and making it difficult to swim. He struggled out of his jacket.

"Ann! Where are you?" he spluttered, seawater getting into his mouth as he spoke.

He coughed. He couldn't breathe. *Calm down,* he told himself over and over, *Ann is a good swimmer.* Then again, this was the ocean in December and she was six months pregnant. *Hurry!*

The freezing water soon robbed him of his body heat, but he was unable to feel the cold.

Up above, he heard voices, but soon they disappeared. Ken and Ann were no longer of interest. All they cared about was the CD. Ken heard splashing behind him and turned to see a black mass moving in the darkness. He swam towards it. Lights from the yachts danced on the water. A police car's siren began to sound in the distance.

"It's over. Let's put it behind us." Ann reached out and put her hand on Ken's shoulder. Ken gently took her hand and gave it a squeeze.

"You were so brave. You put your life in danger to protect something that matters a whole lot to the world."

"I'm just glad. But Dr. Williams wanted you to put that info to good use. That's why he trusted you with it."

With the CD sunk in the sea, maybe it was time to put the whole thing behind them. He tried to convince himself that it was for the best. But… The file for the Fourth Nuke was still on his work computer. His finger had hovered over the delete key many times, but for some reason he couldn't bring himself to do it. It held information for a brand-new source of energy via uranium-238. Williams' dream-like words and Ken's own will had made him hesitate.

Ken sat down on the living room sofa and gazed at the Christmas tree next to the window. Charlie, Susan, Bob and Jimmy had kindly managed to clear up the apartment in just one day. To Ken's surprise, Steve Austin had sent him a new sofa, bed and television.

"There's no need to be grateful. I'm sure he made a lot of money from all this. The cheapskate," Susan said dismissively, yet even she couldn't hide her surprise.

Ann had returned after a half-day stint at the hospital. Luckily, both her and the baby were fine. People from nearby yachts had pulled them from the water. On the way to the hospital in the ambulance Ken had prayed for the first time in his life. He promised to never touch alcohol again and to live for Ann and the child if God would save their lives.

"Mom and baby are both safe, thanks to some miracle. The down jacket she'd been wearing had kept in her body heat while also helping her to stay afloat. Just don't let her take a dip like that again until the baby's safely delivered," the doctor who'd examined Ann had said.

The moment had brought tears to Ken's eyes, to his own surprise.

"We've got a strong little one here," boasted Ann, taking his hand and placing it over her abdomen. He could feel the breath of life moving.

On December 23rd, the last in the series of articles appeared as planned, with no new blueprints or diagrams: just the words of a dying man. It was a kind of penance, as Jimmy had called it.

All over the city, people were preparing for Christmas. Just as Fraser had predicted, all the anti-nuke activists had disappeared from the streets. Everyone was off enjoying the holiday season. Most people were skiing, fishing in rivers or scattered to warmer places like Hawaii and Miami. Hardly anyone touched on Dr. Williams' new type of nuclear bomb, the Fourth. Major media outlets broke no new stories on the issue.

Ken felt as if a taut thread had snapped and a chasm had opened up inside him. Yet he still felt the eerie shadow of the Fourth Nuke in his mind.

The plan for the next-gen stealth bombers had made it through the House of Representatives just before the holidays. Many had thought the margin would be razor-thin, but it had been a landslide with 303 votes for it and 132 against. This signaled that America was headed towards expanding its military. Conservatives hailed the bill, saying that it would bring an end to the reckless reduction in defense spending, but the majority of the media and intellectual community cautioned that it could herald a slip back into the days of mindless military build-up. Yet somehow such commentary failed to gain much traction and the press coverage quickly fizzled out.

"Fits you just right," said Ann, placing her hand on his sweater. Her mother had taught her how to knit while she was in Salt Lake City.

"I didn't have time to buy a present for you," Ken apologized. He actually had bought her silver earrings, but they'd been lost when the apartment was turned upside down. Either they were mistaken for trash and thrown out, or the men who ransacked the apartment stole them. In any case it was too depressing to think about. The most important thing now was to start afresh. Ken took Ann's hand and tugged it to her belly.

A vibration drove into his head like a stake. It spread through Warren's skull, into his spine and churned up his whole body before transforming into his cell phone's ringtone. He reached out to pick it up.

"Tell me about your date. Tonight. How about the cafeteria from last time?" John asked right away.

"It was very fruitful. Same time as before. I've got to get to work," replied Warren simply and hung up.

He glanced at his watch. It was a little after seven.

Most of the media had wall-to-wall coverage of the Fourth Nuke. Warren was the only one still chasing down the Curley story. Recently he'd been taking care of Teddy for Cathy. Last night, after retuning from Cathy's, he'd continued working on his article and gone to bed at around four, which meant he'd only slept for three hours.

He stumbled toward the window and looked out. A man emerged from the parked van, looked cautiously around and slipped into the alley. Clearly aware from eavesdropping on the phone conversation that Warren was about to leave, the snoop was heading for the back entrance of the apartment.

Warren went down to the first floor and stepped out of the front entrance. When he casually glanced at the van, the guy in the driver's seat who held a wireless device hurriedly ducked down out of view. Warren got in his car and headed for Georgetown. He turned on the radio. They were rehashing points about the Fourth Nuke. It seemed to be the only news story these days.

Dr. Williams is still missing and the FBI is working closely with local authorities to... the information on the so-called Fourth Nuclear Weapon. Kenji Brian is thought to be in possession of classified information that was stored at Los Alamos Research Center... Mr. Brian is refusing to give a clear answer. With regards to this info, the government is...

Warren turned off the radio. He found it hard to believe that such

192

a bomb existed, but from the way the government had been reacting recently, he was starting to wonder if it might be true after all.

As usual, Teddy was sitting on the front steps.

"Where's mom?"

"She's still sleeping."

She'd worked on the decryption for several days. Once something piqued her interest, she dove headlong into it. She was that kind of person.

Warren dropped Teddy off at kindergarten and returned to his apartment to park the car. The van apparently hadn't moved.

He headed straight to work. He kept looking over his shoulder along the way but didn't notice anyone tailing him. Either he didn't notice the tail, or they were only interested in bugging his conversations.

Everyone in the editorial department was talking about the Fourth Nuke. *The Washington Post, The New York Times, The Chicago Tribune...* All of them had run a story on the front page covering *The Daily Californian*'s article and the government's reaction. They all agreed that the issue would have an impact on the presidential election next year. Each paper's interest had shifted from Frank Curley's death to the presidential election and the West Coast.

Warren remembered something Editor-in-Chief Whitney had said: *The world is like a baby. It'll stop crying in no time.*

A TV reporter was talking about the ongoing search for Dr. Williams. They also reported on the Senate's deliberation regarding the new stealth bomber plan. Previously strong opposition in the Senate was now more muted. Wall Street was reacting to the news from the West Coast, with the stocks of military contractors on the rise.

The world is changing. The events of the past month have forced the government to take rapid measures... The president will be asked for a decision as early as New Year's... The decision has great implications for the security of our nation... need to keep a close watch on the state of international affairs...

Stewart Jones, the hawkish Defense Secretary, was speaking with a peaceful expression that directly contradicted his extreme pronouncements. He seemed to be popping up on channels everywhere all of a sudden. As ever, there were protesters against a military build-up outside the White House. Yet their numbers were clearly in decline, even though just a month ago opposition to the plan had been the mainstream opinion.

Warren quickly typed up his article and gave a summary to Anderson, who sat there in silence, giving neither positive nor negative feedback. He simply told Warren to continue with the investigation.

At exactly 6:00, Warren left the office. The city was animated by Christmas decorations. All of the shop windows were lavishly decorated in preparation for the biggest sales season of the year. Once he got off the avenue, the streets were darker, with only the lamps lighting up the people passing by. Snow had fallen the night before and still lined the street.

Picking up his pace, Warren headed for the Metro. He boarded a train and got off at the first stop just as the doors were closing and made his way back up to ground level. It was another trick he'd learned from John. He got into a taxi, gave the driver instructions and slid deeply into his seat. Two blocks away, he got out of the cab and made his way through the crowd and into the cafeteria. John was already sitting at a table at the back.

"Was anyone following you?" asked John, keeping an eye on the door.

"No. I'm as difficult to tail as one of you guys now."

John leaned forward over the table. "Bear language. Rabbit. What does that mean?"

Those were the words Warren had sent via chat last night.

"That they were professionals, all right. They hadn't simply deleted the data. They'd used a special deletion software that wrote junk code over the files. Fortunately, Cathy's a genius. She's using a program they're developing—"

"And you let such a woman go. Anyway, did you find Curley's file?"

"I told you. She's a genius. But..." paused Warren as he took a piece of paper from his pocket. It was the sheet she'd given him. "It's encrypted. It could be an encryption system used by the White House, some branch of government or Curley's own proprietary system."

"Can Cathy decode it?"

"She's working on it now."

"So the reason for his death might lie somewhere in here?"

"Curley had some kind of secret. Or he sniffed out a secret. Someone killed him to silence him, taking the laptop in his briefcase. Furthermore, they staged a burglary, took all the CDs and flash drives and deleted everything on his home computers," Warren conveyed quickly.

"Who would go to so much trouble?"

"People who don't want anyone else to know what he was working on."

"His work… You mean it was something to do with the White House?"

"What else could it be?"

"Wait a minute," John leaned over and whispered. "Are you telling me that Curiey was killed by someone in the White House?"

"Not directly, of course. They wouldn't dare get their hands dirty. These are elites among elites that brag about carrying the whole country on their shoulders. They'd never dream of killing anyone themselves." Warren organized his thoughts as he spoke. He himself didn't have a clear answer yet; all he had were fragments. "It's the same as with the mafia. The kingpin never kills anyone. It's the guys on the bottom of the food chain that do the killing. They're the ones who get locked up. All the higher-ups do is lift a finger. But I guess a D.C. cop born and bred downtown doesn't need me to know this," Warren provoked, but John stayed silent. "A top-ranking government official would have connections. It wouldn't have been difficult for them to hire a pro. Or maybe they used the CIA. Or even some ex-military mercenary."

"But why?"

"If I knew that, it would already be published in the paper."

"So let's look into it," said John, steeped in thought.

"Where to start?"

"After the incident, did any mercs go missing? Did some thug suddenly come into a conspicuous amount of money? Anything totally out of the ordinary? Anything at all. They staged it as a suicide, which is not something an amateur could do. Professionals are definitely involved. Someone must have a clue."

"Should I send a questionnaire to the White House?"

"Do whatever you need to. You have dime-droppers in your line of work, too. Anyways," said John, handing a paper bag to Warren, "here, Christmas presents for Teddy and Cathy."

"I'd forgotten. It's Christmas Eve tomorrow, isn't it?"

"Tell them they're from you."

"I got busted doing that last year. Giving Cathy that piece of underwear was in poor taste."

"Don't tell me that's why you separated."

"I still have one more shopping day, anyway."

"Wanna take a turn before God heads out?"

On John's invitation, they left the cafeteria. The detective led Warren down an alleyway. A flight of stairs led to a basement. They started down the steps together, but John suddenly pushed back Warren's shoulder.

"Wait here. I don't care what happens to you, but I don't want Cathy and Teddy to hate me. They'd ask why I didn't stop you," John said reprovingly.

"I feel like a drink," countered Warren, pushing John aside.

"Do what you want. Just don't lose those presents."

A thumping beat reverberated from beyond the heavy doors. They stepped inside. The place was illuminated red and completely packed. The music was ear-splitting and the lights bore into their brains. Young people writhed to the music. In the center was a dance floor where a few half-naked girls were shaking their hips. The sweat glimmering against their dark skin was erotic.

John and Warren could barely hear each other speak. The detective proceeded to the bar without hesitation, but all eyes were on Warren. He was the only white guy in the place.

John spoke directly into the bartender's ear. Warren stood to one side and looked around. There were people with all kinds of hairstyles ranging from massive curls, shaved heads, to Mohawks, and all sorts of outfits; leather jackets on bare skin, T-shirts with skulls, shiny lamé suits. Sweat-soaked shirts clung to dark skin. Warren did his best to look cool, but even he knew his face betrayed how out of place he felt.

John slid a twenty-dollar bill to the bartender and signaled for Warren to follow.

"He says it's been the quietest month in D.C. in a long while. But he looked very uncomfortable. Very unusual. Like he was afraid to talk to me. Some big shots are involved in this," John noted as he walked.

"So have we hit a wall?"

"It depends on how we look at it. At least we know that a big shot is involved."

The two of them headed off to another bar where the clientele was a bit more diverse. John called over the bartender.

"Cops get paid really well, eh?"

"I was just about to ask for funds. I'm almost bankrupt."

Warren tucked a few twenty-dollar bills into John's pocket. After that, they went off to another three bars. At 11:00 p.m., they still hadn't dug up anything useful. The temperature had dropped sharply and there were only a handful of people on the streets.

"Let's call it a day," said John, and the two of them headed toward an avenue.

John's pace suddenly slowed. Warren looked around to see that they were sandwiched by several men—three in front and two behind.

"I hear you two are poking your noses into the Mall incident," said one of the guys, stepping to their side. He had long hair that touched his shoulders and wore a skull earring. He seemed to be the boss. The others had shaved heads or mohawks and were all young African-American males around twenty years old.

"I was just wondering if you knew who did it," John said without taking his hands out of his coat pockets.

"That hot shot did it himself. He was a junkie and a pervert. That's what the TV said."

"We cops are obliged to investigate anyway, you know."

"Whatta waste of taxpayers' money. Don't you have more important things to do?"

"You're one to talk. Have you ever filed a return?" laughed John.

The man's expression changed slightly.

"Well, here's a twenty for you if you can tell me something," John said, waving the money with his right hand.

"Supposing someone had done it, they'd be on the other side of the planet by now."

"So it was someone rich enough to buy a long-distance plane ticket. Or the payoff was that big. It wasn't some random thug or homeless guy."

"I said, 'supposing someone had done it.' It's got nothing to do with you. Stop snooping around like this."

"But they say whoever did it ran off with his shoes and watch. Not the sort of thing someone with enough money to buy a plane ticket would do."

"That's a big, fat lie. Besides, there wasn't anyone."

"But your face is telling me otherwise."

The man's voice was getting agitated. He was regretting sticking his nose in. A guy with a mohawk elbowed the boss and whispered they should just kill them already.

"Anyways, he's not here. Give it up."

Warren broke his silence. "How about the people who ordered the hit? Are they watching us from a car parked nearby? Or are they waiting at a hotel for you to get back? They must still be in D.C. Whoever it was that asked you to kill Curley and bring them his briefcase."

John shot Warren a glance, warning him to stay out of it.

"You don't know what you're talking about, man. If you keep hanging around here I can't guarantee your safety. They say the Potomac is especially cold and filthy this year."

John's expression and tone changed. "Are you threatening a cop? You do realize I'm with the MPDC, don't you?"

Warren's grip tightened on the paper bag containing the presents.

"Everyone's the same floating in the river. The fish don't care whether you've got a badge or not. Though I'm sure cop flesh tastes like shit."

"Thank you for the warning. We'll go on home and think on our actions."

"You know what the biggest problem is you cops have? You can't act on impulse. Gotta check with your superior first. Us? We don't hesitate."

The boss had stepped in closer and placed his hand on John's shoulder. Right then, he doubled over as a muffled sound burst out. He screamed and crouched down, clasping his foot with both hands. The other men simply looked at him, dumbfounded. John pulled his hand from his pocket. He was holding a gun. At first the man had no idea what hit him.

"You fucking asshole! You shot me! You shot me!" screamed the man, still clutching his foot.

"Step away!" John yelled sharply to the others, pointing the gun at them. Keeping their eyes on John, they did as they were told. "Stay right there, you useless trash. Don't move."

He then grabbed a skinhead to his right by the collar, turned him to face his buddies and pressed the barrel of the gun to the thug's temple.

"Show me your hands, slowly. Show me what you've got. If you try anything stupid I'll put a hole in your head," John ordered.

The skinhead, his face stiff with fear, pulled out his gun.

"Hurry up. Everyone show me what you're holding."

John signaled to Warren to pick up the two guns and knives.

"Now when I give the word, I want you to back away slowly," whispered John to Warren. The men looked like they were frozen in place. "Now, you guys," he turned to them and continued. "You're going to run off down this road and if you so much as turn your head, I'll shoot it off. Don't forget to take this asshole with you. Go!"

The boss was sitting clutching his foot. They hauled him up and ran away. "Keep running!" John yelled.

When they were about fifty yards away, John snatched the bag of presents from Warren and ran into a side street. Warren followed.

They ran like hell for their car.

"Why did you shoot him? They were just kids," asked Warren as soon as they got into the car.

"It won't kill him. Besides, that one was just dressed young."

"You didn't have to shoot him."

"Would you rather they killed us? Those weren't some Catholic school kids. It's a point of pride for guys like them to kill a man." John held the steering wheel with one hand and adjusted the mirror with the other.

"They wouldn't have. They were bluffing."

"Are you blind, Mr. Reporter? They all had weapons. You don't get them at all, do you? They knew I'm with the MPDC and didn't hesitate to threaten a cop. One false step and we wouldn't be here right now. Did you see the kind of guns they had on them? Those weren't back-street purchases. They were brand-new pieces, still slick with grease. Someone's backing them, the ones who ordered the hit. We can't show any weakness. They obey only money and power," John's agitated reply came in a torrent.

"I didn't want to make you use your gun."

"I just grazed him. But he won't be wearing shoes for a while. Somehow I don't think he's going to sue. If anything, I should sue them." John poked his finger through a 3-inch hole in his pocket. They stopped at a light. John kept glancing to the sides and at the rear-view mirror. He turned to Warren. "But that was a hell of a reaction. We may have hit on something. They were on edge. There's definitely a big shot behind this whole thing." The lights turned green and John floored it.

"From now on—"

"They're out to get us. We have no choice. It's kill or be killed."

John said this in his usual calm tone. He glanced at Warren's profile, took his hand out of his pocket and spread his palm open. Six bullets rested on it. Warren took them without a word and put them in his own pocket.

John offered to put Warren up for the night, but the reporter declined and returned to his own apartment instead. He followed the same steps as before and carefully entered the room. He couldn't see any signs of forced entry, but he couldn't be sure. He was totally exhausted.

There were twelve messages on his answering machine, but he didn't feel like listening to them. He sat on the sofa and looked out of the window. The black van was still there. He wondered which agency it belonged to. The Department of Defense? The FBI? The CIA? Or even some other secret organ? In any case, they seemed different from the thugs he'd encountered that night. Or were they there to protect him? And if so, by whose orders?

All kinds of thoughts crossed his mind. A gray mass had formed in his head. It grew darker and larger and spread through his body. What was the purpose of all the running around and thinking? He dragged a chair to the window and watched the street from between the curtains.

Standing up, he picked out the bugs from the two spots, smashed them and flushed the remains down the toilet. He started to pack his bag while listening to the answering machine. He had a strong urge to see Cathy. He wanted to at least hear her voice. He reached for the phone a few times but, remembering John's words, gave up on the idea. He turned off the light, picked up his bag and left the apartment. He exited the building from the back door, approached the van from behind and made a note of the license plate before leaving.

But where was he going? He couldn't think of a destination. He pictured John's face, but suddenly exhaustion washed over him. It wasn't physical. His nerves felt swollen. Strings pulled taut over so many days had abruptly snapped. He didn't want to see anyone. All he wanted to do was think of nothing and go to sleep.

He took a taxi downtown and checked into a hotel. It was a cheap place that smelled of fresh paint. Warren sat on the bed and turned on the television.

The "Scientist's Confession" series has ended and The Daily Californian... *The large repercussions the series has... The government will draft a new bill concerning classified information... Public opinion, however, remains positive toward* The Daily Californian *and Dr. James Williams...*

Warren changed the channel and saw President Jefferson heading back to his hometown in Massachusetts, with the Congressional session concluded. Apparently the next-gen stealth bomber plan had made it through the House by a huge margin. It looked like the president would be really enjoying his Christmas break.

Warren reached into his pocket and retrieved the printout from Curley's laptop. It featured a jumble of random numbers and letters. He turned off the television and walked to the window. Peering between the curtains, he could see the obelisk in the distance: the Washington Monument that stood in the center of the Mall.

He took a hot shower and got into bed, but couldn't sleep. When he closed his eyes he kept seeing Curley with a hole in his chest and a line of letters and numbers. But exhaustion overpowered him and eventually he drifted off.

The next morning he called Cathy from the hotel.

It was Teddy who answered.

"Where's mom?"

"She's working."

"She's left already?"

"No. She's not going to her company today. She's working at home." Teddy always referred to the research lab as a company.

"Can you call her to the phone?"

Warren heard Teddy calling for his mother.

"Keep it down. I've got a headache," yelled Cathy from a distance.

"What happened?" Warren called into the phone.

"Stop shouting. I have a headache." It was Cathy. She'd taken the phone from Teddy.

"You haven't slept?"

"I might be on the verge of solving it…or not. No, actually, it might be impossible."

Warren could hear her typing as she spoke. It reminded him of how, even back in her student days, she used to type while holding the phone between her shoulder and neck.

"Can I come over?"

"Bring something to eat. Pizza is fine."

"Don't work too hard."

"I could slap you. Don't talk nonsense. Who do you think is making me work hard?"

The phone went dead.

Warren bought a pizza and soft drinks before finding a taxi. Along the way he remembered it was Christmas Eve. He stopped by the supermarket and purchased a turkey, a cake and Champagne. The Mickey Mouse alarm clock was still sitting on his desk at work, so he bought the $7.50 Superman watch by the checkout and had it wrapped. Then he used the usual techniques to make sure he wasn't being followed and headed toward Cathy's house.

It was quiet there. The low sound of the television came from the living room. When Warren approached Teddy, the boy raised his hand in greeting without taking his eyes off the screen. Warren gently placed John's presents and the watch he bought at the supermarket under the Christmas tree in a place where Teddy couldn't see.

He went to the bedroom, where he found Cathy working at the computer in her pyjamas. He walked behind her.

"I had a thought last night."

"You've been working on this nonstop?"

"I'm used to it."

Cathy had been this way for as long as he'd known her. She even kept a notepad by the bed. *The god of math loves the night. He comes to visit suddenly when it's late*, she'd say, grabbing the notepad whenever she woke up in the middle of the night.

"Don't you need to go to the lab?"

"I told them I have a fever."

"You had Teddy take a day off kindergarten, too? Aren't they having a Christmas party?"

"His mother is sick at home. Who would take him?"

"You should have asked me."

"I always get your answering machine. This morning too…" Cathy's eyes were glued to the screen and her fingers were continuously tapping the keyboard. Warren leaned in to see. The numbers had been transformed to letters and some spots had complete words. Some stretches were even readable sentences.

"James Williams. His name appears many times. Is he a doctor?" Cathy stopped typing and leaned back in her seat.

"You're kidding me," said Warren, without thinking.

"Somebody you know?"

"Don't you watch television or read the newspaper?"

"Sometimes. I watch television with Teddy sometimes. Mostly cartoons."

"He's the scientist the whole country's looking for. He stole classified information concerning a new nuclear bomb."

"You're right. This was his name. People were talking about him in my lab. But what he 'stole' were his own research results, right? He probably has all the numbers and details from the blueprints drilled into his head. If you think about it, I'm a walking lump of classified information.

My contract is loaded with non-disclosure agreements." Cathy sighed. "There's a journalist with his teeth in this case, isn't there? This profession of yours is so unseemly…"

"Dr. Williams disappeared from the Naval Medical Center San Diego," said Warren, leaning over her and reading out where she was pointing on the screen. "Gerard Hopkins… Veep. Stewart Jones… SecDef."

"Even I know that."

"There's Simon Schmidt as well. Chief of Staff. Frank Curley's boss."

"How about this person?" Cathy pointed at another name.

"Thomas Dotwell. He's the president of United Industries. A leading military aviation supplier."

"Nuclear bomb…plutonium…classified information… It can be taken that way. Perhaps it's a scientific paper. But from here on…." She leaned toward the screen. "I can't tell. This file looks like a blueprint. Wait…" Cathy knitted her brow and her fingers moved on the keyboard like a pianist's, the display changing from second to second. Then she stopped. "No, I can't make it out."

"Wait a minute," said Warren, pointing at the number at the top right-hand corner.

"It's a date. November 12th. Probably the date it was written."

Warren sank deep into thought.

"What's the matter?"

"*The Daily Californian* published Dr. Williams' paper and the bomb blueprint at the end of November."

"Is that odd?"

"Why does his name appear in Frank Curley's computer at that date?" he asked as though talking to himself.

"How should I know?"

"Please carry on decoding. If we can decode what used to be on his hard drive and laptop…"

"Then Patty and Cindy can get on with their lives," Cathy finished. Warren nodded.

"Well, I'll do what I can. But even if I had ten Einsteins helping, it would still be tough. Remember, this is basically impossible without the decryption software."

"You got this far on your own."

"This part wasn't encrypted. I just collected what wasn't properly deleted. It's just one or two parts out of tens of thousands."

"Is there any way of getting the decoding software?"

"We're talking about the White House. They probably use Department of Defense or CIA-level encryption. Mere individuals like us have no chance."

"Don't you have any friends working on government encryption? Isn't half the work at your lab for the government?"

"They wouldn't outsource such important tasks. Since 9/11, the government has tightened its grip on confidential information. I heard they encrypt even the most trivial of reports."

"Which means decoding software must be widely circulated, too."

This made Cathy think. "Maybe Curley had several."

"Would it have been on the hard drive?"

"There is a good chance of that. It would be a lot safer than carrying it on a CD."

"Maybe the thieves tried to delete the decoding software in addition to all the documents."

"That's definitely a possibility."

"Then one of the files you retrieved could be the decoding software."

Cathy turned to face the display and began typing intensely. After one hour had passed, her eyes were still glued to the screen. Teddy was still in the living room watching TV, eating cold pizza.

Warren got Teddy to brush his teeth and told him to read his picture books while Warren prepared tomorrow's lunch for him in the kitchen. After checking in on Teddy to make sure he was reading, Warren slipped out of the house.

He had to go to the office. There was a meeting coming up he had to attend. Just as the chief had said, it didn't look like he'd have a chance to celebrate Christmas.

The heads of each department plus Warren were gathered in the editor-in-chief's room. There was tension in the air. Editor-in-Chief Whitney placed the manuscript he was reading on the desk. Everyone's eyes followed him. He looked around the room, finally settling on Warren.

"This…" He stopped to choose his words carefully. "You understand what you have written, Mr. Warren McCarthy?"

"I understand completely."

"Then you are either stupid or very courageous."

"I'm neither. I just followed my journalistic instincts."

"The burglars entered Curley's house with the goal of deleting files from his computer. All his CDs and flash drives were taken… What was in those files? A bag of heroin was removed from his body, only to be replaced... What was in Curley's bag? Dark shadows lurking in the background. This article has much more concrete detail than the previous one. But you do realize what you are doing here?"

"Making an enemy of the White House," said the head of the city desk, taking over from Whitney.

"I'm just stating plausible facts."

"More than half of it is circumstantial evidence, and your conclusion is nothing but conjecture."

"The chances are that I'm right."

"You seem to be confused about the role of newspapers. We're here to convey the truth. Not what you imagine happened or what might have happened. There's no room for chance—"

"Stop," interrupted Whitney. He drummed his fingers on the table. The sound echoed through the room.

The city desk chief looked at Whitney and cleared his throat. He opened his mouth to speak but closed it instead.

"What we need now is not an emotional debate, but a calm, level-headed decision. This is a democratic society and I believe newspapers play a major role in protecting democracy. So let's have everyone share their opinion." Whitney looked around at everyone in the room.

"I think it's too dangerous to print this article as it is. The most important points are still unknown. The message is the same as the last article, but this time it's more extreme."

"The story is still full of holes. All this article does is connect the dots of convenient facts to force a picture to come into view."

"Curley was doing something important, so that's why he ended up dead? That's not enough to convince the readers."

"We all agree that the MPDC's investigations were not thorough enough. Was it negligence or pressure from a higher-up? We don't know enough to be able to convey anything to the readers. If we go down this road, then the cops will consider us an enemy, too. Considering what might happen, I believe it might be best to postpone the publication of this article."

Each of the department heads wildly tossed out their opinions. Whitney silently listened for ten minutes or so. Though they all spoke against publishing the story, they didn't sound completely convinced.

"I would like to take a vote," said Whitney, somewhat authoritatively. The air in the room was filled with tension. It was rare for all the department heads to debate so much over the fate of a single article.

"Who's for publishing the article?"

Not a single hand went up.

"And who is against it?"

After a moment's hesitation, all five department heads except for Anderson raised their hands.

"What about you?" Whitney asked Anderson.

"Warren is on my team, so I don't think I can be objective about it."

"Well then," said Whitney as he gathered up the manuscript from his desk. "It's true that the article is full of holes. It will probably produce more problems for us. So I agree with everyone's opinion."

The nervous tension subsided. Warren felt his shoulders droop.

"But," said Whitney, looking around the room and catching the eyes of each person. "Let's think what will happen if this article isn't published. Curley won't be redeemed. If the police close the case as is, then his reputation will be tarnished forever and his family will bear that burden. The truth…" he paused. "The truth, too, will vanish. This is nothing more than my own assessment of the situation, but the truth may be far more enormous than we think."

He rested his gaze on Warren. "I'm going to publish this article. I will take responsibility for all the problems it may lead to."

Everyone had fallen silent.

"Over. You can all go back to work now."

The department heads stood for a moment without saying a word before turning and leaving the room. They all looked relieved.

"That's the boss' idea of democracy," said Anderson on the way back to his desk, stifling a laugh. "He thinks his vote is worth more than everyone else's combined."

"Did you expect that outcome?" asked Warren.

"Everyone did. He listens to everyone's opinions. That's why everyone was free from the burden of responsibility and could freely offer their views. He could hear them simply as opinions. Same for their conclusions. Then he deliberates and makes the decision on his own."

"I'm grateful to him and to you."

"This is the beginning of a new war." Anderson patted Warren on the back.

Warren felt his body heat up. In several hours his article would go to print, then be distributed across D.C. and the rest of the country.

Warren remained at the office until just after midnight making a few preparations in response to possible reactions. Before leaving, he hesitated, then decided to give Cathy a call. She was still awake. He asked if he could stop by, and she immediately said it was okay. Perhaps John had told her he was living in a hotel.

By the time he reached the house, all the lights were out. It was completely silent, illuminated only by the blinking lights of the Christmas tree. Warren went into the kitchen and saw that a place setting for dinner was on the table. Cold turkey, flat champagne and a half-eaten cake.

He returned to the living room to where a blanket had been tossed onto the sofa. He walked to the door of Cathy's room and stood there for a moment but gave up and returned to the sofa. He lay down and wrapped himself in the blanket without even taking off his coat.

Outside, the night was so quiet that he could nearly hear the snow falling, and when he closed his eyes he imagined himself dissolving into the darkness.

He felt a warm breath on his cheek. He opened his eyes. In the corner of his field of vision the Christmas tree flickered. A darkened figure blackened out part of the lights. The figure climbed in under the blanket.

"Merry Christmas," whispered Cathy. "This is my present to you." She slid a folded piece of paper into his breast pocket before caressing Warren and taking off his jacket. The smell of her shampoo and perfume enveloped him.

"I've always loved Christmas."

"I'm such a sweet Santa. I'm adding a little special something to that present."

"I love special somethings."

"Me too…"

Santa pulled the blanket over her head and removed her pyjamas. Her warm body entwined with his. He held her soft body close. Soft moans mixed in with their breathing.

When he woke up, Warren didn't know where he was for a moment. Then he quickly remembered and looked around him, but Cathy was gone. At first, he wondered if it had all been a dream, but then his body remembered it all.

You should get back with her soon. Anderson's words echoed in his mind. Wrapping himself tighter in the blanket, he turned to look out of the window.

It was a quiet Christmas morning. A garbage truck turned the corner.

A black sedan was parked outside the house. It seemed out of place for the neighborhood.

Suddenly, Warren heard Cathy's voice from the garden. "Let's go. Hurry up."

Teddy, in his uniform, was running along behind her clutching his present. The black sedan outside started up and moved out of view. In a split second, the scene from ten days ago flashed through Warren's mind.

"Wait!" yelled Warren out of the window. Cathy turned around, looking bewildered. "Stay right where you are!"

Warren dashed out onto the lawn, still barefoot. Cathy gave him a fed-up look.

"We're late. I can't play along with your spy game anymore," she said as she reached for her car door.

"Don't touch the car!" yelled Warren. Cathy ignored him, so he grabbed her arm and tried to drag her out.

"Stop it!" A sharp noise rang off his cheek. She'd slapped him across the face.

"Please don't turn on the engine. I'm begging you." He got down on the ground to check under the car. He broke out into a cold sweat. There was a metal box about four inches across attached underneath. He reached out to touch it, but thought better of it and drew in his hand before crawling away. There was a four-inch antenna on it, too. Since it hadn't exploded, maybe it wasn't remotely activated. Perhaps it was set to go off when the ignition fired. He got up slowly.

"Please. Get out of the car," he told Cathy, who was still in the driver's seat, holding the wheel.

"Don't be silly. We're late for church. It's Christmas day, and I'd like to go pray. I'm not a heathen like you!" she shouted, but one look at his pale face made her expression change. She slowly removed her hand from the wheel.

"Stop!" Warren shouted at Cathy, who was about to pull the key from the ignition. She froze. It hadn't gone off yet, and it was better not to alter any details.

"What's wrong, mommy?" asked Teddy, who was standing behind Warren.

"Be a good boy and go into the house. Mommy and daddy will be right behind you," Warren told him gently.

A woman next door who had stepped out to toss the garbage gave them a funny look.

Teddy went back into the house, glancing back at them countless times. Once the boy was inside, Warren turned to Cathy. She was sitting there with her eyes closed, with both hands on her knees.

"Get out of the car without touching anything. There's a bomb underneath it."

She obeyed without protest this time and Warren wrapped his arms around her shoulders and guided her to the house. He could feel her shivering slightly.

He decided to call John.

"Don't let anyone touch the car. Keep an eye on it from a distance. I imagine turning on the engine is the trigger, but it might have a timer. I'll notify a cruiser nearby. I'll be right there."

Warren told Cathy and Teddy to stay in the house, while he stepped outside to tell people to stay away from the car. Less than ten minutes after hanging up with John, three cruisers approached with sirens blaring. Ten uniformed officers surrounded the car and told the gathered rubberneckers to keep away.

"The bomb squad is on its way," one of the policemen told him. After a while, an undercover police car with flashing red lights and a blaring siren stopped in front of the house. John jumped out.

"Are you safe?"

"Cathy's scared."

The two of them entered the house. Cathy was in the second-floor bedroom with Teddy. When the two men entered, she looked at Warren as if ready to bite his head off.

"You know this is because of your article this morning," John whispered to Warren.

"It's Christmas, Warren! Is this your present to us? Do we ever get to have a normal Christmas? No. Last year you slept at the office thanks to unrest in the Mideast. The year before that you were running around the city, chasing a story about a terrorist attack in the District. You don't seem to notice, but this is not normal!" Cathy fumed.

"You should pack your bags and go to your sister's."

"I can't. I have work!" she shouted, glaring at him.

"Just until they catch the guy and it's safe again."

"And when will that be? You got us into this mess. If something happens to Teddy it's all your fault!" she screamed, hysterically.

"Calm down. Teddy's watching."

Warren placed a hand on Cathy's shoulder but she brushed it away.

She went over to Teddy and held him, who in turn held up his arm to show off his new Superman watch. John shrugged at Warren, wished him good luck with his eyes and left the room.

"Please, pack your bags."

"Why do *I* have to leave? You always do this. You only seem to care about your plans."

"When this is over I'll do whatever you like."

"I'm sick of hearing that. You say that, but you always end up doing just as you please once I'm on board. You make it look like you're asking for help, but really it's just your way of getting what you want. You're really just forcing the responsibility on to me…" Her voice cracked and tears began to flow down her cheeks. "Why can't we ever get through these things together?"

"Because I already ask too much of you."

"Are you talking about how we came here instead of California? Don't bring that up now. We both agreed on that decision."

When Cathy had received a job offer from Cal Tech, they had con-sidered living apart. On the day Warren said he'd quit the *Post*, she found a position at Georgetown University. He had a feeling things would work out that way, which was why he'd offered to quit.

"I feel bad."

"I don't care how you feel. You always say that then end up doing whatever you want."

"Can I come in?" John had returned and was standing by the door, hesitant. "We've removed the bomb. It was a plastic explosive. If the en-gine had been turned on, the car would've been blown to bits. It was professionally made. We're sending it to forensics to be checked out."

Warren suddenly crumpled to the floor. He felt like his chest was being squeezed. An oppressive weight was spread over his body, and he couldn't breathe.

"Are you okay, Warren?"

John's voice sounded far away. He saw Cathy's face before him. She was loosening his tie.

"Ca…thy…."

He tried to speak but his throat could only let out a puff of air. He gradually lost consciousness.

When he came to, he was on the sofa. He felt heavy like he had dead space inside his brain, and his body was sluggish. When he tried to sit up,

John pushed him down.

"It's okay. I'm all right." Warren brushed away John's hand and sat up.

"Should I call an ambulance?"

"No. It's okay. How long was I out for?"

"About ten minutes," said John, looking at his watch.

"You've been thinking about your father, have you?" said Cathy as she handed Warren a glass of water. Teddy was standing behind her.

"No!"

"Yes. I thought it was odd, you taking Mr. Curley's incident so personally. You saw your father in the case," she continued, ignoring him.

Warren drank some water and coughed violently. Cathy rubbed his back.

"Their work may have been different, but they both died with their reputations in tatters. Patty and Cindy are sunk in despair. That's why you want to make sure this time it's different." Cathy looked at Warren and John. "You want to put an end to your nightmare."

"That's not it," denied Warren, his voice hoarse.

"You have to let go. It's been over fifteen years. Yet it's still writhing inside you." Cathy's eyes, wide open, swayed slightly. Teddy was clinging around her waist, trying his best not to cry. "Your father's death wasn't your fault. It was no one's fault. It was just that your father was weak."

"No, we were the weak ones. We should have believed him."

"I…have to go back to the station," John said with an uneasy look and left the room.

"I want to be alone," Cathy said turning her back on Warren.

He instinctively tried to reach out to her shoulder. Instead, he pushed Teddy in her direction and left the room. At times like this, she wouldn't listen to anyone. It was better to let her be.

Outside, John was giving instructions to a uniformed officer. A tow truck had arrived and parked across the street.

"Sorry, but we need to take the car to the station to check it out."

"Here's the plate of the van that was parked in front of my apartment," Warren said as he slipped a piece of paper into John's breast pocket. "Please look after Cathy and Teddy," he muttered and walked away.

He could hear John saying something but couldn't parse the words' meaning. He let them pass as noise through his head.

Warren went in to the office. Even though it was Christmas day, the place was abuzz. Like the other time, the entire editorial department was on the phones. But this time, each of the reporters spoke calmly and methodically, clearly drawing on their recent experience.

"Are you okay?" Anderson called to Warren, who was still standing in the doorway. Warren had called him earlier to tell him about the bomb on the car.

"I guess so."

"Go home and be with Cathy and Teddy. We'll handle the rest. Next year we'll try to choose a better timing for the release of sensitive articles."

"Cathy's much stronger than me."

"But she still needs to be consoled. I wouldn't want things to get worse between you two because of me. But before you go, write up something about the car bomb. I'm going to run the story in tomorrow's morning edition," Anderson said, patting him on the shoulder.

Warren walked over to his desk. What was he to do now? He closed his eyes and tried to calm down, rearranging the random pieces of the puzzle in his mind to try and make sense of everything. The puzzle was beginning to take shape, but some core pieces were still missing. He shook his head violently in frustration.

He wrote up the article about the car bomb and spent two hours or so on the phone before leaving the office.

Once he stepped outside, he noticed a piece of paper protruding from his pocket. He remembered Cathy telling him it was a Christmas present. He unfolded it and found more names and sentence fragments decoded among the randomly scattered numbers and letters. Pushing the paper back in his pocket, he looked for a public phone.

He called John at the police station but he wasn't there. He hesitated, then decided to try the detective's cell.

"John Morse," a blunt voice came on before the second ring ended.

"Meet me at the usual place in an hour."

"Okay," came the reply after a few seconds. It was clear he had to force himself to speak. Warren knew how he felt.

When Warren reached the cafeteria, John was already there, surveying the area with sharp glances and looking unsettled.

"I have two men with Cathy for protection. They'll be at your house all day."

"Thank you."

"The bomb was Semtex, a military-grade plastic explosive. The trigger was professionally made with loads of IC chips. Starting the engine would have triggered the explosion. It was good that you didn't touch it since any unnecessary movement might have turned you into mincemeat. It seems like a bigger organization is behind this than we expected. You know who they were targeting. You're in a lot of danger," John said quietly.

"Now we know for certain that Curley was murdered."

"I can't believe you're still going on about that. Cathy and Teddy nearly died."

"That's why we need to end this for good," groaned Warren, to which John sighed and gently shook his head. The reported continued: "As far as I can tell, people who were against Curley include Chief of Staff Simon Schmidt and Stewart Jones, the Secretary of Defense."

"Wasn't Curley a neutral figure?"

"That's the tricky part." Warren said, almost to himself. He took out the paper from his pocket and spread it on the table. "This came from Cathy. A kind of Christmas present."

"A letter written in bear language by a rabbit. Or was it the other way around?"

"Chief of Staff, Secretary of State, Secretary of Defense, Vice President... A list of key White House players. It even names Dr. Williams, who's been getting press recently. Thomas Dotwell. Do you know that name?" asked Warren, pointing at the disconnected words.

"He's a regular name in articles in the *Wall Street Journal*. His face was also on *Time*'s cover."

"He's the CEO of United Industries. The don of America's defense industry. He was also central in gathering campaign funding for the mid-term elections." Warren leaned closer to John.

"So he's rich and powerful. What else?"

"His name appears in Curley's file alongside high-ranking White House officials. This isn't your typical exclusive interview in a financial paper. Take these characters and put together a story with the president as the lead. No, actually, he's just a bit player."

"'All the President's Men's Conspiracy'? All I know is the title. But sounds familiar."

"And that suffices."

"Are you saying that they took Curley to the Mall because he got in their way?" John pointed his index finger to his chest and pretended to pull the trigger.

"I can't be sure if the president himself was involved. It could just as easily have been a power struggle amongst his entourage. The White House going amok. Or…" Warren mumbled and gazed into the distance trying to find the words to finish the sentence.

"Either way, Curley was murdered," John finished the thought for him and they fell silent for a while.

"But…it can't just be a power struggle." Warren's fingers came to a stop by one of the names on the list. "Dr. Williams…" he said in a low voice.

"What is it?"

"Nothing."

"You look as if you've seen a ghost."

"Maybe I have."

They fell into silence. John gave an uneasy glance around the cafeteria.

"What's wrong?" inquired Warren.

"Nothing."

"Just tell me what it is."

"At any rate," John fixed his eyes on Warren and, changing the subject, asked, "What was Cathy talking about?"

Warren didn't answer.

"She was crying. She won't tell me anything, but I can tell she's suffering because of you. I can't forgive a guy who makes his lady cry."

Warren stood up without answering and walked toward a window. Cars and people bustled by. The city still looked glamorous with its Christmas decorations everywhere. It was a typical winter scene.

He returned to the table and looked around. It was the same old cafeteria.

"John, where were you in 1987?"

"I was born and raised in D.C. I don't love or hate this city. It's just my home. I don't feel like leaving and I don't want to."

"I was born and raised in a town called Dazey, North Carolina. Like you, I loved my hometown. But something happened there." Warren took a sip of his coffee and the cold, bitter liquid spread through his mouth. "There was a scandal in local government. The state's water quality surveyors overlooked some serious pollution in return for a hefty kickback. A whistle-blower exposed the fact that the local wells were polluted. Prosecutors came to investigate and found the culprit to be a major chemical company, which was pretty much the town's source of funds. The chemical company had illegally dumped industrial waste, tainting the town's drinking water. The local newspaper was all over the story. It kept tongues wagging among the population of a mere 30,000 for more than half a year."

"So what happened?"

"The investigation fingered a lot of big names, from the mayor on down, since they were connected to the company. The police force was in a panic, too, since all the senior officers were named as suspects in the kickback scheme. Even a hot-shot prosecutor ended up implicated. The prosecutor's office was desperate to put out the fire. It was then that a certain city employee's name came to the forefront of the investigation. Then..." Warren trailed off and sat in silence for a while.

"That city employee killed himself, and suddenly everyone had their scapegoat. At least they say it was a suicide. Nobody could be sure. The man crashed his car into one of the contaminated lakes. Judging from his station and the fact that there was no sign he hit the brakes before the crash, they ruled it a suicide. The autopsy showed high levels of alcohol in his blood. There was a rumor that the brake fluid had been drained. But no one knew anything for sure. In the end, the case was closed as the main suspect had died. No more investigation. No more complaints."

"It's a pretty common tale. At least among African Americans."

"He was a white guy, 45 years old. He was straight-laced and never touched a drop of alcohol."

"Did you know him?"

"He was my father."

John gave a jolt and sighed deeply.

"The case was officially closed but it remained open forever for our family. People stared at us oddly when we walked through town. Our tires were slashed. Sometimes the windows in our house were broken... Instead of being sad about dad's death we hated him for what he'd brought upon us. He alone had escaped. My sister left town as soon as she graduated high school and moved to Los Angeles. I escaped northward. Only my mother stayed behind." Warren stared at the coffee cup in his hands. "I regret having left. If I believed his innocence I should have stayed. Should have proven them wrong. Instead, by running, I had admitted his guilt."

"But what if he was actually guilty?"

"I still should have exposed the truth. At the very least our family wouldn't have fallen apart."

"Is that why you became a journalist?"

"I tell myself that's not the reason. From Cathy's point of view, I'm carrying the burden of never fully believing in him and running away from my hometown."

"And your mother?"

"She died four years after we left town. I haven't been back there since the funeral. That was seventeen years ago," Warren said deliberately as he moved his fingers over a crack on his plate.

"And your sister?"

"She's living in San Francisco. We exchange Christmas cards."

"It's no one's fault. We black people call it fate. We have to accept that before we dare rebel. But times are changing," John remarked in a low voice.

"Cathy thinks I'm seeing parallels between the Curley case and what happened to my father. That's why I'm stubbornly trying to find the truth this time."

"Is she right?"

"No…" denied Warren, but he couldn't find words to back it up.

John took a piece of paper from his pocket. "The van in front of your apartment."

"FBI?"

"I don't know, but it's definitely a vehicle registered by the U.S. government," John mumbled, his eyes darting about restlessly.

"I feel like you're hiding something. Please, just say what it is. You're not very good at hiding your emotions. It's a real Achilles heel for a detective."

John's expression darkened and he looked away. He finally looked straight at Warren as if he had made up his mind.

"I was called in by the chief on the way back from Cathy's. This is someone a guy like me rarely sees."

"Doesn't sound good."

"I was asked if I wanted to join the FBI. The chief said he'd write a recommendation for me. Isn't that amazing?"

"It's Christmas after all. Better thank God. When?"

"Next week. The deal is that I move to the training school in Quantico, Virginia in three days. They want me to be there for New Year's," he said, naming the training grounds for the FBI.

"So they want you to leave this case."

"That's not it. I'm not even on this case. They listened to my request. You knew about it. It just happened to go through now. I never went to college, and as for my police academy grades, you'll find me faster if you count from the bottom. This is a once-in-a-lifetime chance," he said quickly, staring at his coffee cup.

"So go for it. Becoming an FBI agent has been your dream. Anyone would take such a chance. Even I…" Warren's job had changed the course of Cathy's future. He'd wanted to work at the *Post*.

John glanced at his watch and stood up. "Cathy and Teddy will be in the care of two officers, 24 hours a day. They're both good men. I selected them myself. They'll do fine even after I'm gone."

"I won't forget your help. Thank you."

John patted Warren on the shoulder and headed for the door.

"John," Warren called out. "Congratulations."

John lifted his hand in acknowledgment and left the shop without turning back.

As soon as Warren returned to the newspaper, Anderson walked over briskly. As Warren was reaching out to answer the phone, Anderson motioned for him to follow. Warren asked the reporter next to him to answer the phone and followed his boss. Together they went into his office and Anderson lowered the blinds. He turned to Warren.

"I thought I told you to go home. If you want to stick around, fine. But has there been any progress?"

"Nothing so far."

"The CEO called in Whitney."

"What are you trying to say? Out with it."

"He was called in regarding your article. I doubt it was to congratulate him."

"Might have been. You never know, look at the things happening in the world these days. Anything can," said Warren half-desperately.

"I didn't know you were an optimist. Here I am worried about getting axed," moped Anderson, slashing at his neck with his hand. Then, as if to find his own will, he nodded deeply several times. "If there's no progress in the next few days, then we have three ways to proceed. We bring in help, we take you off the case or you write a retraction and we close the issue."

"Or option four: I continue to handle it myself," Warren rebutted, his voice unexpectedly loud.

"Fine. Then do something about it. But remember that you're going up against the White House, the pinnacle of world power."

"I'm going to take down the White House."

"A cub reporter can talk big, but a veteran needs to produce hard facts."

Warren walked out of Anderson's office.

Despite his declaration, he had no idea what to do. He walked over to one of the walled-off segments at the end of the news floor used for meetings. He fought to quiet his agitated nerves and closed his eyes.

He spread the piece of paper Cathy had given him on the table, picked out the names of White House staff and jotted them down in a notebook. All the president's men.

He knew that Curley enjoyed a special relationship with the president as an advisor who served him directly. Warren also knew that, recently, the president tended to take Curley's input over that of Schmidt, the chief of staff. If this trusted person was to turn out to be a drug addict and a pervert, the effect on the president, let alone the populace, would be unfathomable. After Curley's death, the president's approval rating had dropped a full ten points. It was a miracle it hadn't been worse. Perhaps his anti-terrorism measures and proactive stance toward Iraq had propped him up.

Unwittingly, Warren had split the names into two groups, with the president in the middle. Vice President Gerard Hopkins, Secretary of State Robin Dayton and Senior Policy Advisor Frank Curley were against expanding the military. Chief of Staff Simon Schmidt and Secretary of Defense Stewart Jones were for it. In between was President Richard Jefferson.

Next to these groups were three more names: James Williams, Donald Fraser and Thomas Dotwell. These three didn't work for the White House.

Warren sat and stared at the pyramid for a long while. "A faction eager to build up the armed forces, and another that urged caution. The White House was divided," he mumbled.

Curley was gone from this world. The three men outside the White House all lived in…California. Why were their names there? Especially Williams—

He picked up the phone and asked to be connected to Dulles International Airport.

Chapter 8
Meeting

Ken stretched out his arm, felt around for the phone and picked up the receiver. The cold air snuck into his pyjama sleeve, making him stiffen. They were keeping the room several degrees cooler now that Ann, who got hot easily, was back from Utah.

"Who is it..." croaked Ken. He looked at the clock on the nightstand. It was 4:50 a.m.

"Is this Kenji Brian?"

The voice sounded calm. Though it had a mature tint, the speaker seemed to be a man in his thirties.

"My name is Warren McCarthy. I'm a reporter with *The Washington Post.*"

Ann rolled away from him in her sleep. Ken cupped the receiver with his hands and moved to the edge of the bed. The nightlight faintly lit up the room.

"No comment. It might be daytime where you are, but it's the middle of the night here." He moved to hang up. He was sick of rude people trying to get an interview with no concern for his circumstances.

"Don't hang up!" pleaded Warren. "I want to talk to you about Dr. James Williams."

"I have nothing to say. Something is very wrong when a reporter becomes the subject of a story. You're a reporter, you should know that."

"I would really like to meet with you." The man was practically supplicating. Ken could hear a female voice announcing a departure in the background. Apparently he was calling from an airport. "Your involvement in the case—"

Ken silently hung up. The phone immediately began ringing again. He picked up the receiver and put it down straight away. Ann opened her sleepy eyes and watched Ken get out of bed to pull the phone line out of the socket. He went straight back into bed, but it was no use—he couldn't fall asleep. The light from the street-lamps spilled through the gaps in the curtains. Though Ann had her eyes closed and wasn't moving, Ken could tell she was awake.

He had an illusion of something inchoate lurking in his mind revealing itself and tearing his body to pieces.

He pulled his wife towards him. She curled up with her face against his chest. Her warmth spread through his body.

Ken left for the office having barely touched his breakfast. When he arrived, Susan slowly moved her eyes from the top of his head to his feet and back again, then shrugged her shoulders.

"You're like an empty shell. Like you've left your soul somewhere."

"I don't remember ever having one."

"We're all shell-shocked, but at least we're brushing ourselves off and trying to move on. We've squeezed ten years of work into the past month. Why don't you take some time off? We won't be busy again for a bit. Take a breather, then think about hitting home runs again," advised Susan, trying to sound cheerful, but the strain was obvious.

"I'm too worried about losing my job. Especially now that I'm about to become a father."

"You've no worries there. I bet Steve is privately jumping with joy. Why else would he have sent you a new sofa, bed and television? We sold ten years' worth of papers in the past month alone. Plus, our subscription base has more than doubled, though I don't know how long that will last. Most importantly, Steve got his name and photo in the national papers, and he got on TV and radio shows. He'll never live through such a moment again. Rumor has it that he's got photos from the papers framed on his living room wall and that he's sent all his relatives tapes of his TV appearances. He was able to fulfill his dream of becoming famous, even if only for a short time. This past month has been the time of his life."

"All I'm hearing is sarcasm."

"I'm just saying he's grateful to you. So are we. You let us dream of making it to the big leagues. *The Washington Post* and *The New York Times* featured us. We even dreamed of winning the Pulitzer for a while there." Susan's face had a heretofore unseen gentleness and her tone was sincere, but at that moment, there were no words that could console Ken.

He walked over to his desk, catching sight of two large envelopes mixed in with mail from readers. One bore the seal of the reference division of the International Atomic Energy Agency. The other was from an anti-nuclear group. Both were addressed to Editorial. He reached unconsciously for the envelope from the IAEA first. Inside was a polite letter accompanied by a document titled *Iraq Nuclear Weapons Inspection Data*. In the envelope from the anti-nuclear group, he found an expert's opinion on "The Fourth Nuclear Weapon." Both title letters were addressed to Jimmy.

Ken overheard Susan talking on the phone.

"Jimmy Tokida hasn't come in yet... No, I don't know when he will be in... I will let him know... Yes, we will have him call... I told you, he's not here!"

"I'll take that," said Ken.

"It's the Oak Ridge Institute. They're being really persistent," informed Susan, raising three fingers to indicate line three. They were calling to say they couldn't comply with Jimmy's request for information.

Ken slammed the phone down before reaching for his mobile phone. He wanted to scream out for everyone to stop bothering them. Susan was staring at him with saucer-like eyes.

As he started to dial, he heard Susan say, "If you're thinking of calling Jimmy, he's out of range. Probably has it turned off."

"Where is he?" demanded Ken, standing up.

"At the hospital, probably," replied Susan while typing.

"You mean with his sister?"

"I don't know," she said indifferently without taking her eyes off of the computer screen.

Ken left the office and headed for the hospital up in the hills on the outskirts of the city. It wasn't as large as the naval hospital in San Diego, but it was a quiet and tidy general hospital. The grounds had a view of the ocean. It had one of the best psychiatry departments in California and patients went there for help with mental as well as physical ailments. Ken had stayed in the hospital for about a month a few years back, and he'd returned for outpatient services for several months after being discharged.

Ken gave Jimmy Tokida's name at the reception.

"Here to see your sister?" said the receptionist, who gave him the ward and room number. His edgy fighting spirit suddenly drooped.

Taking the elevator to the fifth floor, Ken stepped out and found the door with Elizabeth Tokida's name. He raised his hand to knock but hesitated for some reason. The next moment, the door opened and a middle-aged nurse walked out.

"Go ahead. She seems to be doing well today," smiled the nurse as she walked past towards the elevator. Ken stayed by the doorway and stared into the room. Jimmy was sitting on the bed. At first, he seemed surprised to see Ken, but his face reverted to its typically calm expression.

"Come in. No need to be shy, Kenji Brian," ushered Jimmy. Ken just stood there, unable to move. "Don't worry. She won't bite."

As if pulled in by Jimmy's words, Ken entered the room. "Susan told me where you were. I—"

"It's all right. It's not a secret or anything."

The room was filled with sunlight. There were several IV stands and equipment including an aspirator lined up around the bed. In the bed was Jimmy's sister, a hag with blank eyes that stared out into space. Oxygen tubes were inserted in her nostrils and IV drips ran into her dried twig-like arms.

Ken turned his gaze away.

"Big...brother..." the hag croaked. She was shivering. Panic spread across her expressionless face.

"Don't worry... He's a...colleague...from work." Jimmy leaned close to her and spoke slowly and clearly, putting his arms around her until she regained her calm. Ken remained standing behind them in silence.

"This is my sister Elizabeth," said Jimmy, quietly. "She turned twenty-eight on Christmas Eve."

Ken felt a shiver through his body and looked away. He looked back towards the bed, taking in the woman's mostly white hair, the sunken eyes that had lost their sparkle and her pale, wrinkled skin. Her fleshless arm rested across her breast. Her frilly pink nightgown only served to emphasize how miserable she looked.

"Please sit down and talk with her. She gets scared when people are quiet. Just speak slowly and clearly. She can't understand you if you speak too fast."

Jimmy brought a chair over from the corner of the room and placed it in front of Ken.

"I'm...Kenji...Brian. I work...at the same...newspaper...as your brother... Jimmy," Ken uttered, pausing many times.

Elizabeth strained to say something in a tremulous voice, but he couldn't make out what. He looked to Jimmy.

"She knows who you are. I read to her from the papers. 'The Last American' is a favorite of hers. And also, 'A Scientist's Confession.'"

"Thank you."

Ken put his hand out slowly, but there was no reaction from Elizabeth. Jimmy took her hand and placed it on Ken's. There was no strength in her hand, which felt like dry tree bark. It reminded him of when he'd touched Dr. Williams' hand.

"Elizabeth is blind. And her health is...well, as you can see. She was born disabled. She used to be able to get around using a wheelchair, but seven years ago she fell from her wheelchair and broke a leg. She's been like this ever since."

Ken tried to say something, but only a croak came out of his throat.

"She's a smart girl, though, which makes it all the more tragic."

Elizabeth tried to say something, but all that came out was a wheezing sound. Jimmy leaned in closer to hear.

"Beautiful mountains, beautiful rivers, the beautiful ocean. I've never...seen them...with my...own eyes. But...your writing...helps me imagine...what they are like... Makes me feel happy to be alive... I love your writing," Jimmy repeated her words haltingly.

"You're the...first person...who has said that...about my writing." Ken himself was still struggling to find words.

"I'm sure...everyone...feels the same...even if...they don't...say so."

"Thank you." Ken felt something hot welling up inside his chest.

"I...want to...hear your articles...again."

Jimmy leaned back away from Elizabeth and said to Ken, "I hadn't visited for a while because I was busy."

There was a knock and the door opened. The nurse from before walked in.

"Could you both step out? It's time for the lady to take her bath."

Another younger nurse walked in. Ken said goodbye to Elizabeth and walked out of the room with Jimmy.

The two of them went to the garden on the hospital grounds. Grassy hills stretched into the distance. A cold winter wind blew in from the ocean. Several patients were taking a walk with their nurses by their side.

"I'm—"

"Don't feel sorry for us. There are people who are much worse off,"

223

Jimmy cut Ken off.

A nurse pushing a patient in a wheelchair with an IV and an oxygen tank attached passed in front of them. The patient remained motionless, his head flopped to the side.

"They have a rehabilitation program here. But how effective it is, I can't say," remarked Jimmy, his eyes following the patient.

"I know. I was here for a while, too. For a different reason, though."

The two of them sat down on a bench. The tall hospital building stretched out in front, and Ken unconsciously searched for Elizabeth's window.

"So why did you come here? It wasn't to see my sister. Did you follow me?"

"I didn't follow you. I just wondered about these," said Ken, placing the two envelopes in Jimmy's lap. "What are you up to, and how long do you plan to keep it up?"

Jimmy ran his fingers over the envelopes but said nothing.

"I took a call from the Oak Ridge Institute. They wanted me to tell you that they can't release the documents you requested. That they were classified."

"I asked for the research that Dr. Williams was involved in. I wonder how long they plan to keep it classified. It's thirty years old."

"You also looked up Williams' work at the University of California research facility, didn't you? Why are you still pursuing this? It's over."

Jimmy turned around slowly and fixed his eyes on Ken. The sun gave his face a whitish glow but deepened the shadows, making him seem almost ghost-like.

"Kenji Brian. Your grandparents were from Hiroshima, weren't they?" Jimmy asked quietly, then looked away. "Well, my grandparents were also from Hiroshima," he continued, saying "Hiroshima" as gently as if it were the name of his lover. "The first city in the word to be devastated by a nuclear weapon. Two hundred thousand Japanese died in that city. But…"

Jimmy fell silent for a moment.

"It wasn't only Japanese in Hiroshima who died. My father was also from Hiroshima and came to America with his parents when he was two. My grandparents worked on an orange farm, and after twenty years, they bought one for themselves. My father chose to study instead and went to med school at Berkeley to become a doctor. As soon as he graduated, he volunteered for the army. It was what people were expected to do at the time, for the honor and safety of Japanese Americans across the country. At the time, the world was split into two opposing camps. He did what he did in the hope that his parents, who'd been detained in an internment camp in the desert, would be treated better. Because he could speak Japanese, he was sent to Hiroshima."

Jimmy let out a sigh.

"My father returned to his hometown thinking that he'd be treating the victims of the atomic bomb. But that wasn't the task he was assigned. Instead he walked through the ruins of Hiroshima examining dead bodies and rounding up bomb victims to measure the effect of an atomic blast on the human body. He bought thousands of bodies for next to nothing, peeled off the burned skin, pulled out the irradiated organs and preserved them in formalin. He even had to cut open the dead body of a pregnant woman and pull out a deformed baby. He continued to make specimens of radiation-ravaged body parts. Did you know about any of this?"

Ken was at a loss for words. His neck was damp with sweat.

"My father hated the atomic bomb," Jimmy continued. "But he couldn't say that to anyone. The Americans had Pearl Harbor ingrained in their minds. The general feeling was that all Japanese should be killed. My father suffered alone, in silence," Jimmy said in a faltering voice, his fists gripped tightly.

"The specimens were taken home to the U.S. a year later, and the experiments continued in the name of research. But those weren't the only things he brought home from Hiroshima. He came home with two illnesses. One physical, the other mental. My father carried these two illnesses inside him for over thirty years. They gradually ate him alive."

Ken remembered Dr. Williams with his empty eyes at the naval hospital. His mind must have also been suffering. None of that was a lie.

"Almost twenty years after the war, my father met my mother, who was also of Japanese descent. They eventually got married and my mother became pregnant with me. Apparently they even considered abortion because my father was worried about the effects of radiation. But my mother was determined to have me. So I was born, and luckily I was healthy. They were happy for a while. But my sister, she…"

Jimmy stopped himself and sighed.

"The year my father turned fifty-five, his white blood cell levels suddenly dropped and he started vomiting blood. It was due to his long-term stay and frequent walks through a city steeped in radioactive fallout.

He suffered from nightmares every night and he could hardly sleep. His dreams were plagued with maggot-covered people suffering from terrible burns and bodies floating in murky liquid. My father turned to alcohol and then eventually to drugs."

Ken thought back to when he'd become an alcoholic, eventually going through rehab. If it hadn't been for Ann…

"In the end, he couldn't escape the nightmares. He began seeing the same horrific sights during the day. He would be sitting alone on a chair in his dim study talking to someone. 'Please forgive me,' he'd say, apologizing over and over again. In my second year of college, he took a pistol and put a bullet through his head. He managed to stay alive for two whole days. He looked more at peace than ever, lying there in bed on the brink of death. That's when he told me he was being punished…"

Jimmy went silent again and stared at the hospital building for a while.

"My father wasn't the only one who was punished. Look at my sister…"

Jimmy squeezed shut his eyes, as if trying to block it all out.

"I've been living in constant fear of an invisible disease. Wondering when I'm going to end up like my father. When the fear will become too much and drive me to alcohol, to drugs. That's why I couldn't forgive someone who would publish the blueprint of an atomic bomb, no matter what reason they might have to do so."

Jimmy's fists were trembling on his knees and Ken glanced away.

"We did something that humans have no right to do. And for that, God will punish us all for eternity. I've come into my father's words. I'm against making such a terrible thing public, no matter what the justification. One day, when mankind becomes smarter, I am sure we will calmly rid the earth of such weapons," Jimmy said in a strained voice, his face twisted.

Suddenly the light grew faint. Clouds had gathered around the sun, and Jimmy's face looked even paler.

His voice had taken on an odd tone when he'd said "Hiroshima." It still rang in Ken's ears. The echo overlapped with the figure and voice of Dr. Williams as Ken saw him in Yosemite. The cold sea breeze sapped the warmth from the air, turning it cold. The number of patients walking the grounds had halved.

"'My God, what have we done?' Those were the words of the co-pilot of the Enola Gay, the B29 that bombed Hiroshima. What on earth have we done?" The wind carried Jimmy's voice. "Anyway, we're done here. I'm going back to my sister."

He stood up, started walking, then stopped.

"Please don't make anything of this. I won't cause the paper or you any trouble," he called out, lifting up the envelopes.

Ken nodded in silence and sat back, watching Jimmy walk towards the hospital.

After leaving the hospital, Ken wondered whether he should return to the office or just go home, but he found himself drawn back to the office. Once he arrived and walked into Editorial, Susan immediately came rushing towards him.

"Where were you? You wouldn't even answer your phone."

"At a hospital. I had my phone off."

"A reporter from *The Washington Post* is here," said Susan, leaning in and signaling towards the reception room with her eyes.

Bob was staring at Ken from his seat. "I told him I had no idea when you'd be back, but he insisted on waiting."

Ken remembered the phone call he'd received early that morning. He thought he'd refused to be interviewed.

"How long has he been here?"

"Since soon after you left." Susan looked at her watch. "Almost two hours now."

Ken walked into the reception room. The guy was in his coat sitting with his head bowed. He was asleep. He wore thick glasses, the stubble on his baby face barely giving him an air of maturity. His mouth hung partly open, exposing white teeth, and he was drooling. He certainly didn't look like a hotshot reporter from a prestigious paper.

Standing in front of him, Ken wondered whether he should wake him or not. He could barely connect this man with the person who'd called him on the phone that morning. Ken sat down on the sofa facing the guy and watched the defenseless sleeping figure occasionally draw his brows together in a worried look. Ken thought he appeared more like a rural schoolteacher than a newspaper reporter.

The man eventually let out a slight groan and opened his eyes. Still sunk deep into the sofa, he stared at Ken in befuddlement for a moment.

"So tell me, what does a reporter from *The Washington Post* want with me?"

The man stood up hurriedly and put out his hand. Moved by the simple, frank gesture Ken shook it without thinking.

"Wow, it's really warm here in California. I must have dozed off. I didn't get much sleep last night," the guy apologized with a forced smile.

Ken, who realized that the man must have gotten on a plane immediately after calling him, stared back silently. The man stood there, looking awkward, yet Ken sensed sincerity in his eyes.

"I was moved by the view of the Pacific Ocean from the plane. Especially the way the waves glisten in the sunlight. In Washington, we're expecting snow next week—"

"Have a seat. I'm sure you haven't come all this way to chat about the weather," Ken interrupted bluntly, wishing he had decided to go home after all. His whole body was seized with exhaustion.

"I'm Warren McCarthy. I've been reporting on the Curley case."

Ken tried to recall the story he was referring to. He usually followed what they were doing over at the *Post*, but it felt like a film was plastered on his brain. Maybe the impressions from the hospital visit were too strong. "You mean the policy advisor who killed a girl and committed suicide? That White House scandal?" At last the story had come into focus.

"That's what they say."

Ken took another look at Warren. The man's expression had changed. Gone was the sleepy rural schoolteacher, replaced by a serious reporter. "And…you think the media coverage is wrong?"

"I do. At least, that's what my journalistic instincts tell me."

"You're saying media all across America have been making false reports? But even *The Washington Post*, and our paper—"

Ken searched his memory again. Warren McCarthy. Advisor Curley. There had been an article that displayed an unusual amount of emotion that was out of place in *The Washington Post*. It had carefully avoided making any definitive claims and only served to stir doubt in readers' minds. It probably would have piqued Ken's interest if he hadn't been preoccupied with Dr. Williams' case. But it had nothing to do with him.

"So what is it you want to tell me?"

Ken sat back down and Warren took a folded piece of paper from his pocket and spread it out on the table. It was a list of names. James Williams and Donald Fraser were on it. So were President Richard Jefferson, Vice President Gerard Hopkins, Secretary of State Robin Dayton, Defense Secretary Stewart Jones, and Chief of Staff Simon Schmidt.

Ken felt blood rush through his veins on seeing the first two names, but he was quick to regain his calm.

"Of course you know Williams. How about Donald Fraser?" asked Warren, pointing to the list.

"The head of Green Earth. We were getting advice from him on how to deal with the political fallout of the series we recently carried. He has a lot of experience in that area. But why is his name—"

"That's what I want to know."

Ken looked down at the sheet and pointed to one of the names. "Thomas Dotwell…"

"United Industries. The second largest military contractor in the world. Dotwell made the front cover of *Time* magazine last year," Warren said, placing another sheet on the table.

"Capital of 5.2 billion dollars. Orders totaling 11.3 billion dollars this year. Has an aircraft division, a missiles division, and a missile defense development division. They're also coordinating the government's next-gen stealth plan. If they win contracts for the F118A stealth fighters and the B3A stealth bombers, they'll surpass Lytton Dynamics and become the world's largest military contractor."

Ken pushed the list back towards Warren. Warren looked surprised, but picked up the sheets.

"Aren't you interested in this?"

"It's all in the past."

"This list was on Frank Curley's personal computer."

"What are you trying to tell me?" Ken looked Warren straight in the eyes.

The visitor shifted his glance and let out a small sigh. "I don't know myself. I've been looking into Curley's death to try and make sense of it. In the process I stumbled upon this list." He put it down in front of Ken again. "Just take a look at the date."

Ken looked at the *Post* reporter again. Something stirred inside him, his curiosity aroused more by this modest man from the East Coast than by his list of names.

"It's the day that Curley created this list on his computer. What do you notice about it?"

Ken took a closer look. "November 12th… That's more than a week before I received the letter from Dr. Williams."

"Did you have any contact with him prior to that?"

"I didn't even know the old man existed." Ken thought back to that rainy late November day. He'd returned to the office from covering an event and opened a first-class envelope on his desk. That was how it had all started.

"Curley knew Dr. Williams' name before you made his existence public. Donald Fraser's name, too."

"That's impossible."

"The impossible has become possible." Warren looked hard at Ken.

Ken could only sigh. In an instant, the fire that burned within him died like rain disappearing into dry sand. "At any rate, it's all over as far as I'm concerned," he said, looking away from the list and standing up from the sofa as if to brush everything aside.

Warren reached into his bag and pulled out several photocopied sheets. "These are the articles about Curley that I wrote for our paper. Will you read them?"

"What does it have to do with me?"

"I don't know. It's just…" Warren's voice went up in pitch and his gaze grew more intense. "James Williams… Donald Fraser… You should make these names your responsibility."

Ken couldn't respond.

"Curley had a wife and a five-year-old daughter. They are good, honest people and they were a happy family. It pains me to think of the burden they'll have to carry for the rest of their lives. I want to do what I can to help them."

"That's the police's domain, not a reporter's."

"No, it's in the human domain," Warren said with such conviction that it took Ken's breath away. "I'm staying downtown at the Ocean Hotel. I'll be taking the last plane home tomorrow. Please call me, at any hour."

Warren took out his business card and handed it to Ken together with the materials. Ken took them despite himself.

"My cell number is on there. I trust in your conscience as a reporter…and as a person."

Warren looked at Ken one more time, then walked out of the reception room with his shoulders slumped forward. All eyes in the office were fixed on Warren as he headed for the exit. Ken placed a finger to his lips, the materials still in hand, to indicate to the others who were starting to gather around him that he had nothing to share.

Ken left the office right on time and went straight home and sat down on the sofa. He switched on the TV to see a game-show host whipping the audience into a frenzy. He didn't want to think of anything troublesome. He wanted to just forget everything.

Faces kept coming to mind. Dr. Williams, Jimmy, Elizabeth…and Warren McCarthy. What did he want?

"Is something the matter?" asked Ann as she leaned over to look into his face.

"No."

"I don't believe you," she said, sitting next to him.

"It's all over now. You said so yourself." Warren's words echoed in his ears: *You should make these names your responsibility.*

"We have to put this behind us. Though I realize it's impossible to do so right away."

With this, Ann took Ken's hand and placed it on her stomach. Every so often he could feel a gentle kick that was getting stronger day by day.

"Something new is about to begin. The most important part of our lives."

"I know," said Ken, pulling Ann closer.

In his sleep, Ken dreamed that a large dark entity was squeezing his body. It hurt, and he couldn't breathe. It grew stronger, compressing his flesh, shattering his bones—

He rolled over and opened his eyes in the darkness. He couldn't shake the image of Jimmy's sister or the memory of his conversation with Jimmy. *That's why I couldn't forgive someone who would publish the blueprint of an atomic bomb, no matter what reason they might have to do so.* He thought back on what the *Post* reporter had said: *I want to do what I can to help them.* He pictured Curley's wife and daughter, even though he'd never met them. Their faceless shadows seemed to plead with him.

He quietly got out of bed and went to the kitchen.

Sitting down at the table, he pulled the files from his briefcase and the photocopies of the articles written by Warren. He had skimmed these latter before, but they hadn't left much of an impression. He'd been too preoccupied with Dr. Williams.

The names on the list were still fresh in his mind. The president, his top cabinet members. Williams and Fraser. Why did Curley have their names? Ken wondered what the connection was between two incidents that had occurred 2,200 miles apart, one on the East Coast, the other on the West. All kinds of thoughts flashed through his head.

His heart started beating faster. But why? What they had in common were—Williams and Fraser. Plus the mission of the media.

The digital clock on the table read 3:02 a.m. He no longer had any reason to hesitate. He picked up the phone and dialed. In less than two rings, it was answered.

Ann didn't say anything the next morning, but there was a hint of supplication in her behavior. Ken knew she must have noticed how he'd gotten up in the night and made a phone call. For now, it was easier for them both to say nothing.

After leaving the house, Ken called the office to say he would be taking the day off. Then he drove downtown to the Ocean Hotel. Warren was sitting on a sofa in front of reception with his eyes trained on the entrance. As soon as he caught sight of Ken, he got up, walked towards him, silently took him by the arm and led him into the elevator.

They went into his room.

"I knew you'd call," he said as soon as they had entered.

"Were you waiting up for it?"

"I have trouble falling asleep. Especially when I'm away from home and there's something on my mind."

"I read your articles again last night. They're biased, risky."

"That's what everyone says."

"But it's what made me call you. There's something oddly convincing about them. It felt like they came from the heart. They're also full of compassion for the ostracized wife and daughter. That's what the media's mission should be about."

"I felt something similar in your articles. Your strong will to save a lonely old man." A smile crossed Warren's face. It was a nice, friendly one that made Ken want to reciprocate.

"Anyway, we've got to consider some points of fact."

Warren nodded at Ken's words. "Why were the names of Dr. Williams and Fraser found on Curley's computer? And before you published your article, too."

"I didn't even meet Fraser until much later."

The two of them sat in silence for a while. Neither of them seemed to know what to say next.

"I need to revisit Naval Medical Center San Diego, where I first met Dr. Williams," said Ken, breaking the silence.

Warren looked at his watch. "We only have two and a half hours. I actually booked two seats on a flight from San Francisco to San Diego after seeing you yesterday."

Warren stood up.

The two of them headed for San Francisco in Ken's car. The Pacific Ocean stretched out to their right, glistening in the sun. Warren sat squinting in the passenger seat. He turned to Ken.

"Why did you decide to go to the Naval Medical Center?"

"Why did you book the flights to San Diego?"

"Dr. Williams was told that he was going to die there and that's where he was supposed to spend his last days. That's also where he was last seen before he disappeared. It's the place he had the deepest connection with. If anyone on Curley's list made contact with him it would probably be there."

"The president, the veep, the chief of staff, the defense secretary... I can't imagine any of them making direct contact with him."

"But there has to be a connection somewhere. Curley knew of Williams before you did. Fraser as well. It's hard to believe it's just a coincidence."

The conversation died down. Ken gripped the steering wheel, staring straight ahead. Warren narrowed his eyes and looked at the ocean.

By the time they arrived in San Diego, it was already afternoon. They took a taxi from the airport to the hospital. They'd hardly exchanged any words on the plane and remained silent in the cab. There were a million things to talk about, but neither could find the words to begin.

Once inside the hospital lobby, Ken stopped in his tracks.

"Something the matter?" Warren asked Ken, who stood staring at the reception desk. Ken started walking again without replying.

There was a short man leaning against the middle of the desk, talking with the receptionist. He had black hair, oddly shaped ears and a blue knapsack by his feet. Ken tapped him on the shoulder. The man turned around and his face shifted.

It was Jimmy, looking stunned to see Ken right there before him.

"So you were drawn in by Dr. Williams' spell as well, huh?"

"You, too, want to find out the truth, don't you?"

Jimmy turned his gaze to Warren. Ken introduced them. Jimmy didn't seem at all surprised to hear that he was a reporter from *The Washington Post*. Perhaps he'd heard about Warren from Susan or Bob.

"Did you find anything?" asked Ken.

"No. There's nothing of note here."

The security guard standing next to reception was sizing up the three of them. He had a walkie-talkie in his left hand; his right rested on a holster. They went to sit down in the corner of the waiting room.

"So what were you trying to find here?" Ken asked Jimmy. "Williams' attending physician is in France and they don't know when he'll be coming back. And Williams' nurse, Emmy Jones, is dead."

"Yeah, I heard about the nurse when I called last night. Traffic accident."

Jimmy reached into his bag and retrieved a couple of photocopies of articles from the local paper.

"I got these from the paper before I came here."

One article was about Emmy's death. The other was about the discovery of the vehicle that had hit her.

"She was hit at a bus stop near her house. She had gotten off the bus and was crossing the road when she was hit by a truck at full speed. The truck never even stopped," he said.

"And the driver?"

"Apparently it was a middle-aged man, but nobody got a proper look at him. It was already dark. The vehicle was found on the Mexican border, about ten miles from the scene of the accident. It was a stolen '87 pick-up truck."

"How did they know it was the truck that hit Emmy?"

"They found hair and blood on the tires and front bumper. The truck matched the description of the one that hit her, so they ran a DNA test. But they found nothing else. No fingerprints or anybody else's hair. Not even footprints around the vehicle. No witnesses, either. I learned all this from the local police this morning."

"So what do the police think?"

"Their theory is that an illegal immigrant stole the truck and got into an accident as he was making his escape. They think he got scared, tried to run back home to Mexico and crashed into the border fence."

"So they think the driver is in Mexico."

"Yeah. But who would steal a battered truck well over a decade old? And why had he driven twenty miles from the scene of the theft towards Mexico before getting into the accident? Surely he would have stolen it to go anywhere but back towards the border."

"So you think someone tried to kill her?"

"I don't know."

Ken recalled the nurse with her big, bright smile. That night she had wanted to tell him something. In a sense, he had been responsible for her death.

"Have you talked to her family?"

"I called them from the airport as soon as I arrived, but they refused to meet me. Said they didn't want to think about the accident ever again. I understand how they feel. But still… You know, the police have practically closed their investigation. They want to call it just another hit and run. Makes me wonder if they're getting orders to cover it up. Orders from somewhere high up."

"How high?" asked Warren.

Jimmy knit his brows and shook his head. "The only people I can think of are the governor or the mayor. Though I have no reason to suspect them."

Ken looked at Warren.

"How about the District gang?" asked Warren. "The White House?"

Two patients walked over to the nearby vending machine to buy colas.

"Why do you think it's the White House?" asked Jimmy, trying to keep his voice down. He looked nervous.

"I don't have much of a reason. But…" Warren hesitated, watching the two patients take their sodas back to their table. "It does remind me of the Curley case. A whole bunch of convenient evidence showing up all neat and tidy."

Ken thought about the people on the list. Not one of them was your ordinary citizen.

"Since we came all this way, I want to get a look at Dr. Williams' charts, if possible. They must still have them," said Jimmy, focusing on the present.

"We probably couldn't make heads or tails of it."

"That won't be a problem. I'm used to looking at my sister's."

"So, what to do?"

"Charts for deceased and discharged patients should be kept in one place."

"But we can't just ask for them, can we?"

"We can try meeting directly with the head of his ward. If I remember correctly, Dr. Williams was in the care of the Radiation Department, Internal Medicine Ward," said Warren, looking over the hospital guide he had picked up at reception.

"There's no way the head would meet with us."

"I'm the type that'll try anything once," said Warren, getting to his feet.

The three stood outside the office of the ward director. Warren knocked and a voice called out.

"Who is it? The door's open."

They walked in to find a plump doctor in a white coat sitting at his desk writing something.

"Dr. Strone?" asked Warren. The man gave a small, puzzled nod. "I'm a reporter from *The Washington Post*. I have a favor to ask," Warren announced in a polite but firm tone as he handed over his business card.

"Is there a problem?"

"There's a chart we would like to see. We're not here to bother you."

"That's not possible. We have regulations about these things. Especially since this is a naval hospital."

"I do understand the regulations make it technically difficult, doctor. But it makes no difference whether you're a naval or private hospital when it comes to issues concerning malpractice."

The doctor's face was growing increasingly stiff. "If that's the case, please take it up with the hospital's legal department, not me."

"We're not here to dig up evidence of malpractice. We just need to identify a patient's condition. It may not even progress to a malpractice suit. But there's no knowing what this will escalate into if you're unwilling to cooperate."

"But there's no such precedent—"

"One creates precedent. Our nation is at its best when we respect tradition while welcoming innovation. There's strength in novelty. That's why we love America," declared Warren, his tone different now.

The doctor stared back at him in shock. The plain-looking man in front of him hardly seemed capable of such forceful words.

"The patient's name is Dr. Williams. You must've heard of him. I'm sure you've had all kinds of questions about him from the police and the media. Tell me, did the police ask for his chart?"

"They did, but they weren't so insistent… So we…" the doctor mumbled ambivalently. He was clearly flustered.

"So you still have it, then. Let's see it. Hurry up."

"All right. Come with me." The doctor stood up and took the three of them out into the hallway. He led them into the elevator.

"He doesn't work for a major paper for nothing. So unlike us. Just steamroll, and it works," Jimmy muttered to Ken, his voice dripping with sarcasm.

They were led to the director's office. A large desk stood in front of a window that took over one wall. Several elegant vases adorned the shelves. It was a tastefully appointed room.

A petite woman sat behind the desk. She had gray hair and refined features and was wearing a modest blue blazer. The doctor whispered something in her ear.

"I'm Dr. Howard, director of this hospital," said the woman, standing up and putting out her hand. She was indeed petite, only standing as tall as Ken's shoulders, but a strong presence.

She sat down on the couch facing her guests and appeared ready to hear whatever they had to say. She must have been familiar with the case and been hounded by the media, but she showed no indication of it.

"We're here to find out the specifics of Dr. Williams' medical condition at the time of his disappearance," said Warren. "We've been told that his attending physician is currently on study leave in France. If we can't talk to him, we'd like to see the charts."

The director listened with a pleasant look on her face. "Yes, Dr. Wayne was Dr. Williams' physician. But as you mentioned, he transferred to the Institute Pasteur. That's been his dream for a while. There's nothing odd about—"

"So why is a clinician going back into research?" interrupted Jimmy.

"He was interested in genetic treatments for cancer. He put in a request to be transferred to the institute a while back," she said, looking at Jimmy.

"But he left rather suddenly, didn't he?"

"Well," she said, retrieving documents from her desk, "there was a corporation that sponsored a special fellowship. It was a very generous offer and they chose him. But the condition was that he had to get to the Institute within a week."

"Can you tell us which corporation this was?"

Dr. Howard smiled gently. "If you really want to know that, you've come to the wrong place. You should try a court."

"Fill out a ton of paperwork and wait several months just to have our request turned down?"

"Don't ask me. You never know until you try."

"Is it really so common for doctors with patients to suddenly leave for research trips?" asked Ken, leaning forward.

"I can't say there are many, but it's not unheard of," replied Dr. Howard, pointing at some documents. She then pressed a finger against her temple as if she was trying to recall something.

Ken was about to speak, but Warren stopped him.

Dr. Howard stood up, walked over to her desk and pressed the intercom. "Bring me Dr. James Williams' charts. He was *discharged* about two weeks ago." Turning to her guests, she added, "Just because I asked for the charts doesn't mean I'm going to show them to you. It's for me, personally."

There was a knock at the door and Dr. Howard said to enter.

The middle-aged man who came in shot a suspicious glance at the three strangers before walking over to the director and whispering something in her ear. Dr. Howard sat down at her desk and turned on her computer, stared at her screen and clicked the mouse several times with her brows furrowed.

She called the man over and pointed at the screen while whispering to him. Ken couldn't make out what she was saying. The man reached over and typed something on the keyboard. The two of them resumed their discussion. Eventually Dr. Howard slowly turned her seat to face the three of them.

"The charts are missing. Moreover, all data on James Williams in our database have been deleted," she said with a look of disbelief.

"You mean, any evidence that he was even here has been erased?" asked Jimmy.

The director nodded.

"And do you have any idea who did it?"

The director looked at the middle-aged man, who shook his head. "It's unimaginable," she maintained. "The computer system is managed by the Department of the Navy. Outside access is out of the question."

"But someone on the inside could have done it?"

"It wouldn't be impossible. But only a limited number of people can access the mainframe. We have their background information, and entry into the room with the computer is monitored. They wouldn't do anything like that," claimed Dr. Howard.

Then she lowered her voice and started discussing something with the man again before turning back to her three guests.

"Our computer system is protected with a double firewall. It's simply not possible for someone to hack into the system. But..." She let out a small sigh. "Apparently, it would have been possible for someone in the Department of the Navy. They're the ones who supervise all our facilities. They have administrator access."

"Wait a second," said Warren, pulling a piece of paper from his pocket. It was the sheet with letters and numbers, from among the materials he'd shared with Ken the day before. "The company that supplies the computer systems for the U.S. Navy is United Electronics. It's a subsidiary of United Industries."

"Meaning..." Ken muttered.

Leaving Dr. Howard's office, the three men took the elevator down to the first floor and went to the cafeteria. It was bright, thanks to a large window that faced the garden. There were several groups of patients and their families.

"So we're back to square one," lamented Jimmy.

"That's not true," Warren objected. The others looked at him. "Emmy's death, the disappearance of Dr. Williams' charts and computer records... What's clear is that whoever is behind all this is far more powerful than we imagined."

Ken recalled the list Warren had shown him.

"Isn't it possible that Dr. Williams erased his own records from the hospital's database? To make sure he wouldn't be found? He did know a lot about computers," wondered Jimmy, looking from Warren to Ken.

"I doubt it would have been possible for him to steal his charts. He could barely walk. Besides," Ken added with emphasis, "he didn't want to disappear. He wanted to confirm his existence, for the world to know who he was. That's why he sent me the blueprints. Such a man wouldn't—"

"Then who did it?"

The trio fell silent. They didn't dare say it, but they were all thinking the same thing. The people who held the keys to the greatest concentration of power in the nation, or rather the world.

"What should we do now?" prodded Jimmy, breaking the silence. No one had an answer.

Several nurses walked into the waiting room, all of them appearing to be Hispanic. They were probably from Mexico.

One nurse, a man, kept looking over at Ken, and when he caught Ken's eyes, he walked over to where the three of them were. "You're the guy who was talking to Emmy, am I right? You're a newspaper reporter.

I saw you on TV."

"And you are…"

"A friend of Emmy's. Such a shame. She was so sunny. Everybody liked her. Especially the patients."

"Is there anything you can tell me about her patient, Dr. Williams? He was an old man with terminal cancer."

"The guy who went missing, right? It was on TV. The hospital was in an uproar, crawling with police and the press. You were here too, right?"

"Did you notice anything out of the ordinary? Like someone paying him a visit before he went missing? Or did he make a phone call? Anything you can think of."

The man leaned in closer. "I don't think anybody ever visited that old man. Emmy told me about a month ago that he got his first-ever visitor after being here a whole year. That was you. But now that you mention it…"

The nurse carried over an empty chair from a neighboring table. He put his head in his hands and sank into thought. Once in a while he'd peer up at Ken.

Warren placed a twenty-dollar bill on the table in front of the nurse. He glanced at it, then looked away. Ken and Jimmy added more bills on top of Warren's.

"There was one time I saw him speaking to someone through his computer. I could see the other guy's face on the screen. How amazing is that? It was like a video phone, but through the computer."

The money had disappeared from the table.

"Anyone you recognized?"

"I couldn't butt in. He was a terminal patient, so maybe he was dictating his will or something. That's the rules here."

"Was it a man or a woman?"

"A man."

"Age?"

"There was a guy who looked to be in his late forties and there was an old man. I don't remember the others."

"Please, try to remember. Anything at all."

The nurse lightly drummed his fingers on the table, sinking again into thought. "I came from Mexico to work here. I have three kids back home. And I have to support my wife's mother, too. She likes to spend lots of money," he confessed.

The trio exchanged glances. Ken lay down two more twenties. The man nodded and sat back.

"My friend Gomez tells me that he saw several guys carrying something on a stretcher in the middle of the night the day before Williams disappeared. Apparently they got into the freight elevator. They weren't from this hospital. They were all big Navy guys. Probably some special unit like the SEALS."

"How could he tell? Were they in uniform?"

"Live here long enough, you learn to recognize the type." The man glanced around, stood up and walked back to the other nurses.

"So you think the guy who got carried out on the stretcher was Dr. Williams?" asked Jimmy, keeping his voice down.

"No, he wouldn't need a stretcher," Ken pointed out. "He could use a wheelchair. He was in one in the cabin in Yosemite."

"So…he hid in a stretcher to escape from the hospital," Warren speculated.

"He wouldn't have to do that. He could've just gone out the main entrance."

"Sometimes you just don't feel like dealing with paperwork. Or maybe something urgent came up and he had to leave in a hurry."

Ken didn't know what to say. Apparently, neither did the other two. They just stared at the now-cold coffee in their paper cups.

A dozen or so patients bustled in with several nurses. One nurse carried a cake. It was a patient's birthday.

The three left the hospital and went into a nearby restaurant.

"So Dr. Williams was in Yosemite National Park five days after he left San Diego. How did he make the 370-mile trip?"

"He said he traveled on a private jet. With the help of a Silicon Valley millionaire friend."

"So they flew to a nearby airport, then took a helicopter to the cabin in Yosemite. I guess it's not impossible—"

"Wait," Ken blurted out in an unexpectedly loud voice against his will, "that can't be right!"

The other customers at the restaurant stopped eating and looked at them.

"He…" Ken was at a loss for words. He recalled the image of Dr. Williams in the evening sun at the cabin in Yosemite. Ken began to remember his face, his voice, his figure… A film covering his mind was slowly peeling back. But he still couldn't put his finger on it.

"What's the matter? Are you sick? You really don't look good."

"I'm just going to go get some fresh air."

Ken stepped out of the restaurant. Jimmy and Warren watched him with worried eyes. The cold ocean breeze enveloped his body and flowed into his lungs. As he took a deep breath he felt a little better. He looked up towards the towering naval hospital on the hill across the freeway.

Later, on the plane ride back, Ken sat next to Jimmy. The plane reached cruising altitude, and as the seatbelt sign turned off, Jimmy leaned in to say, "What on earth is going on?"

His gaze was on Warren, sitting diagonally across from them. They could feel the vibrations from the plane's engine.

"A man who couldn't walk across a room leaves the hospital and re-appears 370 miles away in the mountains of Yosemite."

"Someone was carried out in the middle of the night on a stretcher. If that was Dr. Williams, maybe they got him out disguised as a corpse, then had him flown to an airport near the cabin on a private jet. From there he could have traveled to the cabin by helicopter."

"But no matter how annoying discharge paperwork is, he still could have left by the main entrance in his wheelchair. Then, out of nowhere, a reporter from *The Washington Post* flies all the way across the country to see a reporter at a local paper in Barton, California. I'm guessing we must be dealing with a pretty huge organization."

Ken casually turned his head to look across the aisle at Warren, who was sitting with his eyes closed. The man looked as if he was sleeping, but he'd said he had insomnia.

After a moment's hesitation, he decided to tell Jimmy more about the list Warren had shown him the day before that he'd found on Curley's computer. Jimmy listened without a word. Even after Ken had finished talking, Jimmy didn't say anything. He remained silent for the rest of the flight.

Once they touched down in San Francisco, Jimmy told the other two that he'd be taking his own car back to town. Warren and Ken drove back to Barton in Ken's car. The neon lights faded away and the dark California night spread out on either side of the freeway.

"The trail's gone cold, hasn't it. What'll you do next?" Ken asked gently.

"I disagree," replied Warren, sounding unexpectedly optimistic. "I mean, you did meet Mr. Disappearing Act himself. In Yosemite, right?"

Warren asked back, looking into the darkness ahead of them.

"In a cabin about three hours from Turtle City at the foot of the mountain."

"How far is it to Turtle City from here?"

"About a four-hour drive. Less if we drive fast."

"Would you be interested in going there again? I'm planning to go myself either way."

Ken glanced at his digital watch. "Why don't we meet at six o'clock tomorrow morning in front of your hotel."

"Fine with me. Like I said, I have trouble sleeping."

Ken glanced at Warren's face, but the dim freeway lights made it difficult to discern his expression.

It was already past eleven by the time they got to Barton. Ken dropped Warren off at his hotel before heading home. He opened the door, took one step in and stopped in his tracks, immediately sensing that there was someone in the living room. He looked towards the sofa, felt around for the switch and flicked it.

"What are you doing in the dark?" asked Ken.

"And you?" said Ann, looking up at Ken from the sofa. "What are you doing? I thought this was over."

"I can't explain right now. Please be patient. Just a little while longer."

"I don't want to know anything. All I want to do is live in peace. Just you, me and…" Ann placed both hands affectionately on her stomach. "It will all be over soon, won't it? And you'll come back to me when it is."

"I promise."

Ken took Ann by the arm and helped her to the bedroom. He tried to organize the day's events in his mind, arranging disparate bits into ordered shapes. He still couldn't see the whole picture. He could feel Ann breathing next to him.

He closed his eyes. He was tired but couldn't fall asleep. Ann rolled over. She was awake, too.

He gently draped his arm over her shoulders.

It was still dark in Barton. People and cars were still sporadic on the streets, giving the city an eerie feel. Ken and Warren left before sunrise.

They arrived at Turtle City before ten. Warren had kept one eye on the rear-view mirror all the way from Barton.

"Worried? Think we're being followed?" asked Ken.

"Not really. Just a habit of mine. I won't be able to get back into my normal lifestyle for a while."

"What happened?"

"I was attacked three times in D.C. An attempted kidnapping, thugs with guns, and on Christmas morning someone put a bomb under my car."

"You should have told me earlier."

"You never asked."

"I have a wife. And a child on the way too."

"I didn't know that."

"So you think the same guys may have followed you here?"

"I don't know, but they're capable of anything."

"Speak plainly."

"We seem to be okay so far," said Warren, glancing again at the rear-view mirror.

They filled up at a gas station on the outskirts of Turtle City and put chains on the tires. Up in the mountains, it was snowing quite heavily. Already the snow was much heavier than when Ken had been there ten days earlier, so he drove with extra caution. About an hour later, his phone rang.

"So I got to the office and found out you'd taken the day off." It was Jimmy.

"I'm headed for the cabin where I saw Dr. Williams."

"I see. I came across something interesting, too."

"What?"

"I'll tell you when I know more."

"Well, sounds like we've got a lot to look forward to when we talk next."

"When will you be back?"

"Some time tonight."

"I'll be waiting at the office."

"Okay. Take care."

As Ken hung up, he remembered Susan's words: *Steve told me to tell you that you're under FBI surveillance.* He decided to switch his cell phone off to be sure.

For another two hours, they drove up a mountain road, the snow slowing them down more than they had expected. It was a lonely landscape and they hadn't seen a soul out since an older couple way back at a farm near the gas station.

"Have you noticed them?" asked Warren, who'd been constantly worrying about their rear.

"Been there about twenty minutes."

"It's the car that was at the edge of the gas station where we put chains on the tires. Now that I think about it, I also noticed a black sedan when we left Barton. It's probably the same vehicle." A black car was visible in the rear-view mirror, about 500 yards behind them.

"I missed that. Guess that's why you're with *The Washington Post*."

"I've got a friend who's with the D.C. police. He taught me a thing or two about survival."

"Where I live, all you need to do to enjoy peace and quiet is to be an upstanding citizen. I guess I need to change my habits from now on."

"What should we do?"

"This road isn't wide enough to turn around on."

The woods became thicker and rows of snow-covered trees endlessly stretched down both sides of the road. They continued along their white path. Ken glanced at the rear-view mirror again, noticing the vehicle had moved up to only about 300 yards away.

"Is there a house or a store up ahead?"

"Who'd go shopping around here?"

"I guess the bears and deer don't carry cash." Warren let out a small sigh and pulled out a gun from his pocket.

"Do you *Post* reporters always walk around with one of those?"

"It's a gift from my detective friend."

"The TSA needs to get their eyes checked."

"I only remembered I had it in my pocket when I was filling out an application for a ticket. I mailed it from the airport post office along with a toy I bought there. I couldn't just toss it into a trash can. It had arrived at my hotel by the time I got back from Barton last night. I felt too uneasy just leaving it there."

"How fortunate, but if they're professionals and they mean business, one measly gun isn't going to stop them."

"It's better than none at all."

Ken stepped on the gas, the engine roared and the car sped forward. They continued on for ten minutes, but the car behind maintained the distance, neither falling back nor approaching closer.

"What are they up to?" asked Warren, looking back.

"You want to stop and ask them?"

Ken stepped harder on the gas. Their field of vision suddenly opened up as a bottomless ravine spread out on their right and a tall cliff jutted upwards to their left. The car behind them sped up, closing the gap with urgency. Ken also sped up. Glancing in the rear-view mirror, he could see a man's face leaning out the window.

Gunshots rang out.

"They're shooting! They're gonna kill us!" screamed Warren.

"You brought killers along with you from D.C. I thought I was done with this kinda thing after Christmas."

A cliff face loomed before them. Ken grappled with the steering wheel. The back tires skidded, causing the back half of the car to swerve.

"Slow down!" shouted Warren.

Suddenly, with a loud, piercing noise, a crack stretched across the rear window.

"You've got the gun. Didn't your cop friend teach you how to use it?"

Warren frantically rolled the window down and pointed the gun behind them. Ken braced himself for the shot, but it never came. More bullets struck the car with metallic rings.

"Hurry up and fire the damn thing! Let them know we're armed, too!" yelled Ken, looking into the rear-view mirror.

"I've never shot a gun before. Have you?"

"Marines. Decorated."

"Then you'd better let me drive on the way back."

"If there is a way back."

Another bullet hit the car.

"Come on! Speed up!"

"Do you want me to drive us into the ravine? It's 3,000 feet to the bottom."

"Gunshot or car crash, we're dead either way!"

Warren ducked down in his seat. By now they could make out the face of the driver in the car behind.

Tires screeched. A heavier sound came from elsewhere, too. Warren searched the skies.

A volley of shots was fired from the sedan, now just a hundred yards behind them.

"This must be the end."

Ken followed Warren's gaze to spy a tiny dot in the sky that was gradually growing in size.

"A helicopter! They sent a helicopter!" Warren cried in panic. Again he leaned out of the window, and again, he couldn't fire the gun.

"Please, just fire. All you have to do is pull the trigger."

"I'm trying. But it won't."

"Calm down. Unlock the safety. The thing by your thumb. Aim a little lower than your target and pull the—"

The gun went off before Ken could finish. A crack stretched out across the windshield of the car behind and it swerved erratically.

"Beginner's luck. Now keep shooting!"

The car soon righted itself and closed the gap between them once more.

"Watch out for the sky. If they swoop down and start shooting…"

Before Ken could finish, the helicopter zoomed low over their heads. Reflexively, both of them ducked down into their seats. A man was leaning out of the helicopter with a rifle in his arms.

A report came, then another loud noise.

Ken checked the rear-view mirror. The black sedan was smashing through a mound of snow and careening toward the ravine edge.

"Yes!"

The sedan crashed through some bushes, then abruptly dropped out of sight.

The sound of rotor blades grew louder, the helicopter swinging back over their heads before slowing down in front of them. Ken floored the accelerator.

"Wait!" Warren shouted, leaning out of the window and looking up at the sky. The man in the helicopter was leaning out, waving and yelling something. "Stop the car!"

"You want to die?"

"The guy in the chopper is my friend from the MPDC!"

Ken stepped on the brakes and the car ground to a halt. The two of them got out of the car and peered down into the ravine. From the in-ward-banking bend, they could see the sedan stuck diagonally on a slope. It was caught in a large tree.

From the helicopter hovering above, Warren's friend was shouting and pointing to a flat clearing about a hundred yards ahead of them. The chopper headed towards the spot and began to descend.

A man hopped off the helicopter, an African American with an M16 slung on his shoulder.

"I thought you were in Quantico," greeted Warren.

"Teddy asked me to help his daddy, and Cathy begged me to bring her stupid husband back alive or she'd never let me darken her doorstep again. As a lieutenant with the MPDC, I couldn't say no. It's my duty to protect the citizenry."

"Where are they?"

"I told you, two trustworthy officers are with them."

"Why didn't you tell me you were coming?"

"I wanted to make a dramatic entrance. But I was hesitant, even when I was already on a plane."

"There was something about the FBI."

"I realized I'm not cut out to be an FBI agent. Taking on street thugs suits me better. You should have seen the chief's expression when I told him I wouldn't leave the city. He thought I'd lost my mind."

"Now you can go after big shots that even the FBI can't touch."

"The car that was watching your apartment…" John said after a pause.

"Government, right?"

"FBI. I'm no voyeur, no matter what the objective," John maintained as if trying to convince himself.

Warren introduced Ken to the detective. A second man wearing sunglasses stepped out of the helicopter. He was wearing a San Francisco police uniform.

"This is Sam Jones, my cousin. He's a captain with the SFPD. I trust him like I trust myself."

"So it would seem."

"How did you know where we were?"

"It's a long story. First I heard from Cathy that you'd gone to San Francisco. She said you called from the airport saying this time you were going to get to the bottom of it. I knew right away that you'd gone to see the reporter from *The Daily Californian*. You'd mentioned Dr. James Williams before." John looked at Ken. "Then things got tough. I found the name of the journalist who wrote the Williams series. You'd been on TV, right? Kenji Brian. Then I called your house and said I was a friend of the reporter from *The Washington Post*. Your wife sounds very nice."

"Everyone says so."

"She said you had gone to Yosemite National Park. I had a bad feeling about that. My detective's instincts, you see. Then I discovered that neither of your cell phones were working."

"The battery on mine is dead. But I'm definitely getting a new one now," promised Warren. Ken took out his cell phone and turned it on.

John spread his arms out and sighed dramatically. "You're not going to a concert. Leave your cell phone on. Have you never even heard of 'crisis management'? Don't you know that your car has a GPS tracking system on it anyway?"

"I'd forgotten about that."

He'd purchased a new car when Ann became pregnant. The addition of a theft recovery system had been part of the reason.

"We called the security company and had them search for you using the GPS tracker. At first they refused, but they were impressed when I told them I was from the MPDC. I told them I needed their help in cracking a major case."

"And the helicopter?"

"Sam calls some shots at the Traffic Department. It's not difficult for him to gain access to a helicopter."

Indeed, SFPD was painted across its body.

All of them got into the car and drove over to take a look at where the sedan had gone off the road. It was still lodged in a tree 300 feet down. White smoke was rising from its hood. Sam leaned out from the edge to get a better look, then went back to the others.

"Can you tell me what on earth is going on? I mean, what am I supposed to tell my boss? That I invited my cousin to join me on a helicopter ride and was patrolling around Yosemite National Park and just happened to come across a car chase involving gunfire? That a warning shot my cousin fired sent one of the vehicles skidding into the ravine? You think my boss is going to buy that?" demanded Sam, glaring at all three of them in turn.

"I actually don't know what's going on," surrendered Ken.

John looked to Warren, who just shook his head.

Suddenly, there was a large explosion followed by what sounded like screams. The four of them ran back to the edge of the road and looked over.

"He's still alive!" Sam yelled.

One man was struggling to climb away from the sedan, which looked like it was about to fall. Flames were now leaping from the hood. The car wobbled with the man's efforts.

"Don't move!" warned Ken. "It'll fall!"

The man looked up in a panic and started firing.

"We're the police!" Sam called out. "Throw away your gun. We'll come get you."

A gunshot rang out as if to interrupt Sam.

"Damn it! Is he insane?"

"Leave him. He's a goner anyway," John shrugged.

"This isn't D.C. I gotta report this to my boss. I can't tell him I just left them to die."

"He's probably already radioed or called for help."

"Are they CIA? FBI?" asked Warren.

"They're probably not with the government. Otherwise, he wouldn't be stupid enough to shoot at us. He would ask us for help."

"Then..."

"There were only two cars on this mountain," nodded Sam. "Help would take three hours to arrive. That is, if anyone felt like coming."

"There's nothing we can do," John agreed, looking down at the car.

The sedan, stuck on the root of the tree, teetered. The man screamed. His coat was hooked on a side mirror, which held him suspended over the ravine.

There was a sound of snapping wood. The car slid and fell, leaving only the echo of a loud rumble.

"See ya," muttered Sam.

"Think he's dead?" John asked.

"Be a miracle if he isn't. Wanna take a bet?"

John and Sam leaned in close, talking, occasionally glancing at the bottom of the ravine and at Ken and Warren. After ten minutes or so they approached the journalists.

"I'm joining you for the rest of your journey. There's no knowing who might show up," John stated as a matter of fact, looking at both Ken and Warren.

"I need to return to the station and file a report," announced Sam. "I'll just say I found a car in the bottom of the ravine. We'll come retrieve it, but not for at least two days. It's going to snow tonight. You guys should leave as soon as possible."

"Will this get you in trouble?"

"They'll find the gun, but it'll be written off as another gang war incident. Thugs shooting each other in Yosemite in the middle of winter. The brass will be happy with that story, since nobody will come complaining," Sam quipped, looking down into the ravine once more as if in confirmation.

John, Ken and Warren watched the helicopter take off. Ken started the car. After an hour or so, they arrived at the spot where Ken had parked on his previous visit. But he couldn't see the chimney of the cabin that had been visible through the trees. Ken double-checked, but this was definitely the place.

The three of them got out and walked down into the valley. Even when they reached the bottom, the cabin refused to come into view. Ken kept glancing around. There was no mistake. They were in the right place. Yet...

Ken stopped. He stood there in a daze.

"Is that it?" Warren stared ahead and groaned. "You didn't know?"

"I would have told you if I knew."

At the base of the valley was a slightly elevated pile of snow. Several charred wooden beams stuck out of the snow and the stones used for the foundation were visible.

"It's been burned to a crisp."

They went to take a closer look. The part of the cabin made of wood had burned down completely and was buried in snow. The fireplace was now nothing more than a black pile of stones. Dr. Williams had sat in his wheelchair before that fireplace. Ken picked his way carefully through the layers of rubble.

"This was recent," Ken whispered. He pushed on a charred pillar. It crumbled.

"Looks like there's no corpse here," mumbled Warren.

John crouched in the middle of where the cabin used to stand and waved the other two over. Between the layers of fallen wood coated with snow was a riot of footprints that had not been covered up with snow.

"There were a lot of people here."

"The ones who burned the cabin down?"

"No, it was after the fire. These bootprints belong to the forest rangers and police. If there was a body they would have collected it then. We just need to ask the town sheriff."

"It was just the cabin that burned down. The surrounding trees are mostly untouched," observed Ken.

Some branches were burned along the edges, but the damaged stretch was slender. The snow had probably extinguished the fire.

"I think the cabin went up in flames quickly. They must have used some sort of accelerant."

They walked around the cabin ruins in silence but found nothing of importance. Just when they noticed that their shadows had grown longer, the sun dipped behind the mountains and they were surrounded by darkness. The temperature dropped rapidly and the cold seeped into their bodies.

Two hours later they returned to the car. They had found nothing.

The cold air felt heavy with moisture. Sam was right—it felt like it would snow that night.

By the time they arrived back at Turtle City, it was already six o'clock. They borrowed duct tape at the gas station to cover the bullet holes in the rear window. John, sitting in the back, had spent most of the ride complaining about the cold air seeping through the holes. One taillight had been shattered and there was another hole in the trunk. There were a few other marks left by the bullets, too. It didn't affect the way the car drove, but Ken was worried about how Ann would react when she saw the state it was in.

Stopping in at a branch office for the *San Francisco Times*, they inquired about the fire. A twenty-something kid brought over a bundle of newspapers and placed them on the counter.

"We hadn't had an incident that big in a while. The whole town was buzzing. A lot of people went to volunteer with the firefighting, but it was basically dead by the time they got there. It had snowed. The snow stopped it from becoming a forest fire."

"But the cabin itself totally burned down."

"The sheriff said they must have had a lot of kerosene or gasoline in there. They also found a home electric generator."

"Who found it burning?"

"The military."

"The military?"

"The armed forces contacted our fire department. Even a small fire can develop into a major forest fire. So the military keeps a lookout using reconnaissance satellites. They can spot even a small fire like this one. Here's an article about it."

He pointed to a ten-line article under the heading, "Cabin Burns Down; Unidentified Charred Remains," and proceeded to read it out loud.

Turtle City. A cabin burned down on the 19th. A burned body was recovered from the ruins. The condition of the body was such that police were unable to determine its gender. The town fire department and sheriff's office announced that it was most likely caused by a homeless person who used the cabin as shelter and knocked over an oil lamp.

"That's the day after I met Dr. Williams," Ken pointed out.

"It was a big deal for the town, but that's all the newspaper coverage it elicited," the young man stated.

"Was there only one body?"

"Yes."

"Where did they find it? It didn't say in the article."

"I heard it was in the bedroom. Burned to death in his or her sleep."

"Where's the body now?"

"Dunno. The sheriff's office took it away. It was probably buried in the town cemetery," replied the young man, clearly uninterested.

They thanked him before leaving.

"But there were two people in there, right? Williams and the Silicon Valley businessman."

"I guess the businessman escaped into the forest. Only the cabin burned," said Ken, though he thought it highly unlikely.

The sheriff's office was in the center of town. The sheriff, who was in his fifties, looked at them with open distrust as they walked in. Once they introduced themselves he became even more unsociable. He obviously wasn't the type to be impressed by *Washington Post* reporters or D.C. cops. Even so, he agreed to tell them about the incident.

"It was a horrible sight. Most of the body was reduced to ashes. We buried it the next day. There was no way we could have determined who it was from the remains. But we did take an X-ray of the teeth," the sheriff said slowly as if he was dragging the information from the pit of his memory.

"And the cause of death?" John asked.

"Fire."

"But a fire can kill a person in many ways. Suffocation from smoke inhalation, carbon monoxide poisoning. Didn't you look into the cause of death?"

"How do you examine a chunk of coal? Anyone could see that the person had died in the fire. No one had any questions. If you're not satisfied with that, go dig up his grave. I won't stop you, but I certainly won't help. Some of his internal organs were only partly roasted," said the sheriff, glaring at John with frank displeasure.

John frowned in response. Warren slapped his shoulder as a reminder to keep his temper.

"So were you able to determine anything from the teeth?"

"How do you ID a homeless guy from his teeth? 'Course, we could always compare 'em with dental records from missing people—"

"And did you?"

"Unfortunately, there's nobody missing from this town. It must have been an outsider." The sheriff shrugged, and his expression shifted. "Why are you so interested in this guy anyway?"

"It may have been someone privy to classified government information. We came from Washington, D.C. looking for him," John leaned over to the sheriff and whispered.

The trio then made their way towards the door.

"Wait a minute," said the sheriff. The three stopped and looked back. "You're that journalist from *The Daily Californian*. I've seen you on television. Kenji Brian, right?"

"The camera really doesn't do me justice."

"I read your series, 'A Scientist's Confession.' It was good. And that other one, 'The Last American.' It was something a major paper wouldn't dare to publish."

"I'm happy to hear you say it."

"My father was in the war, too. He fought in Europe. He loved to talk, but he never spoke about that. Probably saw a lot of terrible things." The sheriff wrote something on a sheet of memo paper and handed it to them. "Go here. We've kept some materials from the body, just in case. The DNA test results should be in by now. Recent DNA testing makes it easier to ID people. It's got nothing to do with a small-town sheriff like me, though. I'll call ahead for you." The memo had the name of a hospital and an address on it.

"Shit! That rotten old hick of a sheriff. I want to teach him some manners," John spat and kicked the ground.

The street lamps dimly lit up the road. Only a few cars and people passed by. The three of them sped along to the hospital named by the sheriff.

"I think someone killed Williams and carried him to the bedroom," said John slowly, thinking aloud. "Then they covered the living room and bedroom with an accelerant and lit it. Those were the places most badly burned. Whoever did it was determined not to leave any evidence behind."

"So you think Williams was killed."

"Obviously he didn't commit suicide. He was filled with hope."

"But why did they kill him?"

"They didn't need him anymore," said John, casually.

The hospital was a private facility located across from a supermarket. An older woman greeted them. When they showed her the note the sheriff had written, she ushered them wordlessly to a meeting room. Almost immediately, a young female doctor came out carrying an envelope. She had well-defined features, a kind of intellectual beauty.

"The sheriff called me. I did the autopsy. Though the body was in such terrible condition…"

"Are those the results of the DNA test?"

"I thought it might be difficult, since so much of the tissue was destroyed by the heat. But fortunately we were able to get some results from an internal organ that wasn't too badly damaged." The doctor handed Ken an envelope. There was a CD inside.

"This is…"

"The DNA data for the deceased."

"This is all?"

"The tissue we recovered is frozen. Would you like to take it?"

"Can we?"

"Of course. The sheriff told me to do everything we can to help. But if you don't have the right equipment it'll rot quickly."

"Can we determine identity just through DNA analysis?"

"It shouldn't be a problem. You'll just need a sample to match it to."

They thanked the doctor and headed towards the door.

"Mr. Kenji Brian," the doctor called. "May I shake your hand? My father told me to. He said you were the journalist responsible for 'A Scientist's Confession' and 'The Last American.'"

"The sheriff?"

"He's my father. He's a big fan. He was too shy to ask, but he really wanted to shake your hand. He keeps all your articles in a scrapbook. He shows them to anyone who goes to our house. He says you're the leading American journalist. I've read your articles as well, since I was in my teens. I hope you continue to write more great articles."

Ken shook the hand that was extended to him. Warren and John looked on with tense expressions.

They left the hospital carrying the envelope with them.

"Are you…" Warren started to utter to Ken. It looked like there were tears in his eyes.

"Let's hurry. We don't have much time," cut off Ken, hurrying back to the car, pulling his collar close.

Something grazed his cheek. He lifted his face as sleet rained down.

"Do we have a DNA sample of Dr. Williams to match this to?" asked John, pulling his collar shut.

"His hospital files have been erased and all his belongings are gone as well."

John suggested that they spend the night there, but he was ignored. They kept an eye out for any vehicles that might be following them, but there were none.

It was already past midnight when they got back to Barton. They headed directly to *The Daily Californian*. A light was still on in the editorial department.

Jimmy was at his desk when they walked in. His face showed exhaustion but he was otherwise in good spirits.

"Did you find anything more?" Ken asked Jimmy after telling John and Warren to find chairs.

"I want to hear what you found first," Jimmy urged.

Ken explained how a badly burnt corpse was found in the ruins of the cabin where he'd met with Dr. Williams, then placed the envelope the doctor had given them in front of Jimmy.

"And the body belonged to Dr. Williams?"

"We don't know. These are the results of the DNA analysis on the corpse. I want them tested for a match. Okay, now it's your turn," pressed Ken, knowing that Jimmy wouldn't still be in the office if he hadn't come across something important.

"Wait. If you can test Williams' DNA that would be perfect."

"But is there anything left of him? Anything that would yield DNA?"

Jimmy stared at the envelope. "There might be something left at a lab even if there's nothing at the hospital. Blood tests, cell tests... They must have done all sorts of tests on him. He had terminal cancer, after all. I doubt that all the tests were conducted at the naval hospital."

"What if they've already gotten to it?"

"Then we'll just have to find another way."

"But the lab wouldn't give out that kind of information. That's probably impossible."

Ken looked at Warren, who in turn was looking at John.

"All of this is beyond me. You guys think of a solution," John recused himself, waving his hand in front of his face.

Jimmy stared at the floor in thought and Ken sighed quietly. It was getting difficult to ignore the pain in his knee, which had been bothering him all day.

"What if the naval hospital were to request an outside lab to do a sample comparison?" suggested Jimmy, looking up.

"The medical data and charts for Dr. Williams were erased. I really don't think the hospital would willingly help us out."

"Then we'll be the naval hospital."

"You mean, we should pretend to be from the hospital? Isn't that a crime?"

"Fraud, forgery, with a dash of telecommunications law-breaking."

"Not as bad as murder. At least, no one'll get executed over it."

"Crimes are only called crimes when they do real harm. Try to think of it as a victimless crime. At any rate, if no one notices, we should be fine. The fact that the data was erased works in our favor, since there's nothing to check against."

Jimmy accessed the Naval Medical Center San Diego's website and clicked away. "From spending time with my sister, I've gotten used to tests at hospitals and medical facilities. I know a lot about what tests are performed for what reasons. I'm looking for anything related to genetic illnesses. Here. Genetics laboratory. The naval hospital sends most of their tests to them," he said, eyes still on the screen. "We'll say we're from the newly-established branch of the medical center located in Barton. We're so new we're not yet in the system. We'll tell them we need an urgent crosscheck with the attached DNA test sample and the DNA from the patient James Williams. We'll have them send us the results directly. For the attention of Dr. Jimmy Tokida."

"Do you really think this will work?"

"We'll say there was an accident during top-secret training. This requires urgent attention and should be treated confidentially. Currently the ID number is unknown. I'm asking them to search for it," Jimmy said as he typed, then took out the CD from the envelope and inserted it into the drive.

"What if the laboratory comes calling?"

"They must be suckers for the word 'confidential.' It's the Pentagon they deal with. The folks on the bottom rungs just do as they're told without thinking. Worst-case scenario, they contact the hospital and the police get called in. If that happens, apologizing won't save our asses. So we just pray they're too busy to inquire."

"This could mean big trouble for the paper."

"I used my personal email address. If it all goes smoothly, we should have the results by tomorrow evening," said Jimmy, switching off the computer.

"Okay, you've kept us waiting long enough. So what is this amazing discovery of yours?" Ken fixed Jimmy with a look.

"I did a search on the list of people that was on Curley's computer." Jimmy took a folded printout from his pocket and spread it out on the desk. There were detailed profiles of all eight persons including the president. "This was easy. A simple internet search. They're all important characters involved in running this country. There were tens of thousands of hits for each of them, but that's beside the point. There are other ways to search for information. Stuff that isn't out in the open. These are all people who have worked their way to the top. They all have some skeletons in their closets they'd rather keep hidden."

Jimmy placed another sheet of paper on the desk. There were only two people listed on this one.

"I'll cut to the chase. These are the two we'll focus on. Donald Fraser and Thomas Dotwell."

"Well, get on with it, will you? I'm getting hungry," coaxed John, visibly irritated.

"First, Thomas Dotwell. His father, Benton Dotwell, was a Texas oil baron. Net worth of 2.7 billion dollars. His wide array of holdings included oil companies, hotels, other real estate. He had political power, too. Thomas, his eldest son, was raised in Texas to be a purebred businessman. He attended Harvard and majored in politics and economics. He's got a good brain and a cautious personality, but he's a touch temperamental. After graduating, he joined his father's company where he was groomed in management, to get to where he is now."

"He's got a finer pedigree than me. Rich, too."

"As for Fraser, he was born and raised in California by his mother. He is bold and a bit of a loose cannon. He's got a sharp mind. His mother, Diane Fraser, was a budding actress when she had him. She must have been a looker when she was young. But she never succeeded as an actress and ended up running a high-end boutique in Beverley Hills instead. She died twelve years ago."

"So the only connection is that they're both rich."

"And they both graduated from Harvard."

"So what?"

John looked at Warren, another Harvard man, but Warren ignored him.

"There's one more thing."

"Do you West Coasters always give everything such a tedious build-up?"

Jimmy scowled broadly at John. "Benton Dotwell provided Diane with the seed money for starting her boutique. Diane was Benton's lover. Thomas and Donald are half-brothers."

John whistled.

"Thomas Dotwell is the older brother. Donald Fraser is three years younger."

They all looked at one another.

"So what? What does that mean?" John asked after a while.

"Do you think that's just a coincidence?" Jimmy shot John a fed-up look. "Think about their positions. Fraser is the leader of an environmental organization. He protests against the military. Dotwell is top dog in military contracting. They are the complete opposites of each other. And yet…" Jimmy paused, gauging the others' reaction. "The funny thing is that they get along surprisingly well. They're only three years apart so they overlapped at Harvard for a year."

"Well, even if they had different mothers, they're brothers. I don't see why they shouldn't be."

"Charmed by their story, are you? I spoke to a friend of Fraser's from Harvard and apparently Fraser visited Dotwell's room frequently to attend a certain kind of party. I also have evidence that they meet in Las Vegas from time to time even now. Dotwell's family owns a hotel there."

John raised his eyebrows and shrugged.

"I'm not saying we should drive these brothers apart, but it does sound a little unusual."

"My God…" Ken mumbled.

"That isn't the only surprising thing I found out. United Industries donated 1.2 million dollars to President Jefferson's re-election campaign."

"How extravagant."

"It's not a surprising amount. Depending on the president's plans, the company's sales can jump by a few billion dollars. Plus," Jimmy sighed, "Dotwell and the Secretary of Defense, Stewart Jones, were classmates at Harvard Law."

"But they were more than just classmates, right?" urged John, tired of the reporter putting on airs.

"That's right." Jimmy smiled slightly. "Jones' younger sister is married to Dotwell."

"So what does that have to do with anything? There's no link to Williams or Curley," spat John, losing interest and walking over to the windows.

"No. I still don't get it, myself," Jimmy gently conceded.

"What if we thought about it this way?" Ken said, picking up a red pencil and drawing a line between the eight names on the sheet. "On the top are the doves, on the bottom are the hawks. They're having a bitter political struggle."

All three pairs of eyes concentrated on the two groups of names.

"Only the president tried to maintain a neutral position," said Warren, reaching over from Ken's side and circling President Richard Jefferson's name with a blue pen. "At least that's my opinion as a reporter covering the White House. The two factions were at loggerheads, so they needed some kind of way to break the deadlock."

Ken felt a surge of heat building at the core of his body. The pieces of the puzzle were beginning to come together to form a picture. "If these two forces went up against one another, Curley would…"

Tension built up in the room.

"Thought to have a strong influence on the president, Curley had to get discredited as a person."

Everyone stared at the eight names on the desk, the dignitaries in whose hands lay the future of the United States. They were divided by a red line.

Time elapsed.

"Let's think about this again tomorrow. I'm as worn out as a hundred-year-old dishrag."

It was John who broke the silence and brought everyone back to reality. It was already three in the morning.

Ken drove Warren and John to their hotel before going home.

Seeing Ann resting in bed, Ken immediately felt all the tension drain from his body. He wanted to take a shower but didn't have the energy for even that. His knee was cold and numb and his leg felt like a club. Dragging it behind him he crawled into bed in just his underwear. Ann turned in her sleep and wrapped her arm around him.

The next day, past noon, Ken went to Warren's hotel room. Warren and John were seated at a table poring over a list of people at the White House and the information Jimmy had given them. There was a mountain of fried chicken bones, empty donut boxes, and close to a dozen empty coke bottles and coffee cups. There was a toy truck and a teddy bear on the bed—presents Warren had sent from the airport.

The two of them had looked as full of life as dried parsley sprigs when Ken had last seen them the night before, but they had regained their vitality. Ken placed an apple pie on the table in front of them. "Present from Ann," he said. The two men cheered.

"Sam called about an hour ago. They went via helicopter to the crash site yesterday," John said while pinching a crumb of apple pie to his mouth. "I asked him to let me know as soon as possible about the guys in the car." He spread out a piece of notepad paper in front of Ken. "Turns out there were four of them, three of whom died inside the car almost instantly. The other one was found crushed underneath it. That was probably the shooter. They also found two submachine guns and four hand grenades, one of which went off inside the car. The rest had rolled out. There were also a couple of pairs of night-vision goggles."

"That's some equipment. Whoever hired them must be someone worth shitting our pants about."

"The guy who shot at us was Thomas Franklin, some thug from Los Angeles. He had a Californian driver's license on him."

"Was it real?"

"It was. The local police wrote it up as a fight between gang members."

"And nobody objected?"

"Different police divisions are always hostile to one another, but there is one policy they all abide by. Avoid messy business at all costs," said John, sinking deep into thought.

"Is there some connection with this list? Could the government have hired them?" Ken asked.

"How many years have you been a journalist? Why would the government do such a risky thing? That guy was such an idiot, still trying to shoot at us while hanging by a thread. There's no knowing what he'd say if he was taken in. The government would have access to top-flight professionals, not morons like that."

"So some other organization. Thomas Dotwell is the CEO of United Industries," said Ken, pointing at the name on the list.

"What's he got to do with any of this?"

"If we only knew…" Ken fell silent. He felt like something was coming into view but was still shrouded in mist. Even so, he thought the fog was slowly lifting.

"What's wrong?" asked Warren, peering down at the list.

"No, it's nothing."

"We're going back to D.C. tomorrow," announced John as he set his paper cup on the table. "We have three days left of this year including today. Time for the MPDC to step up security for New Year's celebrations. This year, even those who are supposed to be off duty have been called up. Part of some new anti-terrorism measures. I'll be fired if they find me taking a vacation on the West Coast."

He looked to Warren for confirmation, but he was sunk in silence.

Suddenly, there was a knock at the door. Jimmy's voice sounded from the hall. As soon as they let him in, he strode across the room, moved the cups and empty boxes to the bed and put his computer on the table. He started accessing the hotel's internet.

"What is it?" asked John, but Jimmy didn't reply.

"You said there was a body carried out on a stretcher from the hospital the night before Dr. Williams disappeared," said Jimmy, almost to himself as he typed. "If that was a corpse…"

The words "San Diego Press" appeared on screen. It was the name of the main local paper in that city. Jimmy searched for the December 14th issue, the day after Williams was spirited away.

"For that day, there were no suspicious deaths. At least according to police reports," reported Jimmy.

"Do papers here report all deaths?" John asked, looking surprised.

"Some local papers do. But probably not in large cities like Los Angeles or San Francisco, just like D.C.," replied Jimmy, typing. "Let's take a look at funeral parlors in San Diego. There can't be that many." The screen displayed the names of several.

"Isn't it a bit early to be booking a funeral parlor? Don't tell me this is the way you do things here out west."

"If it was a real corpse, they wouldn't be able to just keep it in a car trunk."

"They could toss it in the ocean. Or bury it in a mountain or in the desert. Wouldn't take too much effort either way."

"But a body dumped at sea might wash up on a beach somewhere. A wild dog might dig up a buried body. Haven't you seen cases like that as a cop? If they were sloppy with getting rid of the body, they'd definitely pay for it later. It'd be safest to get rid of it legally, especially if White House big shots seem to be connected," Jimmy retorted without looking away from the screen.

"There are ways of totally destroying a body. A corpse is just—"

"If you've got the time to criticize, pick up the phone and start calling funeral parlors. See if anyone saw any suspicious remains."

Warren picked up a cell phone from the table. Ken had taken his out from his pocket and placed it there.

"My battery's dead," Warren explained. Ken just shrugged and picked up the hotel room phone.

The four of them divvied up the list and spent two hours calling every single funeral parlor in the San Diego area. Unfortunately, they turned up nothing.

"This is the last one," said Ken, sounding fed up as he punched the digits on the phone. "Hello. I'm trying to locate a grave for a person who died on the thirteenth of December. Name of Williams."

"I'm sorry. We don't have anything listed for that name," said the courteous middle-aged woman on the other end of the line.

"Well, to be honest, that's his true name. It's my uncle, you see. He's been missing for some time. We were told he had died and was buried in San Diego. There's a chance he might have been living under an assumed name. We just want to know if he's dead or alive."

"Is it a legal issue?"

"That's right. The price on a house under my grandfather's name has appreciated."

"This is the second time this month we've had such an inquiry. These inheritance issues are thorny." Suddenly the woman's tone became much more friendly. "But you really do need to get them cleared up, even if it's an unpleasant process."

Ken gave the woman a description of Dr. Williams and the possible dates for his burial.

"Let me see. We keep data on everyone's height, weight, physical characteristics and such for use when prepping a coffin," came the woman's voice accompanied by the sound of her fingertips on a keyboard. "No... We don't seem to have dealt with anyone matching that description," she said apologetically. "Oh, hold on..." she muttered as Ken prepared to hang up. There was silence. She was probably typing. "There were five cremations in December. Three of them had their ashes scattered at sea. One of them was a woman, 47 years old. Another one… Hmm. Now that's odd."

"Please take your time. I'm not in any rush. I want accurate facts."

"There's a Tony Crauts, 58 years old. That's not him, is it?"

"No, my uncle was over eighty. He looked much older."

"I have an 82 year old. December 14th. The family attended just the cremation but had to leave due to urgent business. We took care of scattering the ashes at sea."

"That's probably it. Are there any ashes left? Even in a small nook in the urn?"

"It wouldn't be of any help to you if there were. You wouldn't be able to extract DNA from the ashes, since the heat destroys it."

"Is that right…" Ken thanked her and was about to put down the phone when the woman chided him for his impatience. Ken gripped the receiver. The other three, who had stopped calling, stared at him.

"We always keep samples of the hair and fingernails, just for cases like this. Saves an awful lot of trouble, even if the deceased was buried. Saves people from having to exhume their bodies, you see."

"Can you send that express to a genetics lab immediately? I'll contact them and let them know to expect it."

After sorting out the payment details for the funeral parlor and giving the name and address of the lab, Ken thanked her again, hung up and briefed the others.

"So you think the ashes scattered at sea belonged to Dr. Williams?" asked Warren.

"That's what we're testing for," responded Jimmy.

"What about the man you met at the cabin?"

Ken's heartbeat quickened. His leg was beginning to hurt again and he placed his hand over it protectively. Jimmy and Warren looked at him.

"I have no idea what's going on," exclaimed John, spreading his arms wide.

They contacted the genetics testing lab and were told that it would take a little while to identify the DNA from the corpse found burned in the cabin. They also said it would take half a day to extract the DNA from the sample being sent from San Diego.

Warren and John resigned themselves to extending their stay another day. They remained at the hotel while Ken and Jimmy went to their newspaper's offices.

A young part-timer was manning the phones in Editorial. He looked relieved as their arrival meant he could go home. Now that the series had ended, all the staff in the department was back to business as usual. Unless there was some major incident, everyone was finished by late afternoon.

Susan and Bob had gone on vacation from the day before until after New Year's, and Charlie was the only remaining person who seemed to be keeping regular hours, using freelance journalists and student part-timers to get the work done. Yet even he had already left an hour before they'd arrived, leaving a message that he was to be contacted only in the event of an emergency.

"I didn't want to say anything in front of the other two," confided Jimmy, "but something smells fishy. I mean, if Williams was dead on the thirteenth, then who sent you the blueprint of the Fourth Nuke? Or do you think he posted it right before he died?"

Ken ignored Jimmy's words and turned on his computer at his desk. There was a low hum and the screen lit up. Ken hit some keys and then froze, staring hard at his screen.

"What's wrong?" Jimmy walked over and looked at the screen.

"The file… Williams' website is…gone," Ken mumbled.

The website he'd accessed only days ago had disappeared. In a panic, he tried pulling up different links, but none were working. He typed quickly, making countless typos.

"My backup of the blueprint of the Fourth Nuke is gone too." Ken sat there in a daze looking at the screen. He started typing again. All of the files related to Williams were gone. It wasn't that they were missing; it was if they'd never been there to begin with. "What the hell is going on?"

The two sat in silence, gazing at the white screen.

"If this is real, then there are a few possibilities that come to mind," Jimmy sighed. "The first: Donald Fraser. I have a friend in D.C., a journalist, very well-informed. When I told him we were getting advice from Fraser of Green Earth, he told me to be careful. This friend of mine has a relative who's a top-ranking member of the administration. I helped him out a lot way back when and he felt obligated to warn me."

"What about Fraser?" Ken could hear nervousness in his own voice.

"Don't get so excited. Remember, this is all in the past," said Jimmy, oddly calm. "I didn't say this at the hotel, but Fraser is not only half-brothers with Dotwell. He's got connections with the CIA as well. Perhaps it's more accurate to say Fraser is some kind of operative."

"What does that mean?"

"It's not just the CIA. He has close connections with the military and the defense industry. He's a lobbyist of sorts who uses very peculiar methods."

Ken could almost smell Fraser's expensive pipe smoke.

"Besides, he also has the ear of some top government people. It makes sense, if he's Dotwell's younger brother."

"I still don't see what you're getting at."

"Hold your horses." Jimmy held up a hand to get Ken to settle, sighed, walked over to the coffee maker and poured himself a cup. "Want one?" he offered. Ken shook his head. "Fraser, or the CIA, or perhaps we should say some potent force in the government—what on earth do they want with us, anyway? Didn't you feel that there was something strange about the mass media's coverage?"

"Other people did seem to know a lot about what we were up to."

"That's right. Someone on the outside had info on what we were doing even before we announced it. Anytime we considered calling it quits, it was as if there was something urging us onward. First the media backed us up, then the order to stop the series was revoked… Everything was working in our favor so we didn't think about it too much at the time. We were riding the wave, moving onwards. But I don't know if it should have been possible." Jimmy looked away from Ken and breathed with his shoulders. He stood up and walked towards the windows, leaned his arm on the windowsill and looked out to the street as if he were searching for something.

"Apparently info was sent to *The Washington Post* detailing our every movement. They thought it was coming from us for promotional purposes."

"I asked one of my friends in New York who works for a paper there how they knew so soon that we received the manuscript. How did they know the government was going to revoke the order to stop the series, and about the CD that Dr. Williams sent you? What do you think?" Jimmy turned to Ken, his small body looking frighteningly large for a second. "My friend said there was an informant, someone high up in the government. But he didn't give me a name. It was a leak. The informant knew what the manuscript contained and even the planned dates for publication. This information was sent to all the major newspapers in the country. Same for everything that followed."

"So the man I met at Yosemite…" Ken eked out and glanced away from Jimmy. The winter's darkness spread outside the windows. Within the darkness, the pale image of an old man stared back and spoke in a suppressed growl, and Ken had to squeeze his eyes shut against the hallucination.

They left the office around midnight.

Ann was already in bed.

Ken showered and crawled into bed quietly. He could hear her steady breathing, but he knew she wasn't asleep. He lay there thinking of Jimmy's words, tense.

He got out of bed and headed for the kitchen. He drank a glass of milk and picked up the phone.

"It's Ken, isn't it?" Yamada's husky voice came through the receiver.

"What time is it?"

"That's my line. It's twelve minutes past two."

"Please wake up, there's something I want to ask."

"I was already awake. In fact, I was actually waiting for you to call," Yamada replied, sounding levelheaded now.

When they were rooming together, Yamada would often stay up with Ken, who functioned better at night. Amazingly, Yamada would be half asleep listening as Ken talked but always wake up the next morning and make it to class on time.

Just like in the old days, they talked for a good thirty minutes. Ken actually wanted to talk longer, but Yamada's voice was growing fainter and harder to catch, so he thanked him and hung up. Ken sat down at the kitchen table and tried to organize his thoughts.

He slipped into bed again, managing to catch a few hours of sleep just as dawn approached. As soon as he got up, he called Warren. John answered the phone, and Ken told him that he was heading over to the hotel with Jimmy.

The table at the hotel was littered with new chicken bones and empty donut boxes. Jimmy wordlessly moved them all to the bed.

Ken told them about the deleted files and his conversation with Jimmy at the office the night before.

"The file containing the blueprint for the Fourth Nuke has been deleted, too. It was as if it was never there to begin with…"

"Who had access to your computer?"

"Only people who knew the password."

"Any other protection?" asked John.

"What do you mean?"

"Like firewalls to keep out hackers."

"We don't have anything like that. It's a computer belonging to a local paper in the sticks."

John sighed dramatically. "Then it would be like walking into an unlocked villa for a professional."

Right then, the phone started to ring.

"It's Cathy," said Warren, covering the receiver.

"Where are you calling from?" John jumped over the sofa and ran over to Warren, yelling at the phone.

"From a payphone."

"Looks like you took my lessons to heart. There shouldn't be any bugs on a payphone or in this hotel room."

At first, Warren tried covering the receiver with his hand but quickly gave up and turned it partway towards John, who waved over Ken and Jimmy.

"Is John there?" asked Cathy.

"John and two other guys."

"Is it okay for you to talk in front of them?"

"They're fine."

"Okay. Well, I was able to open Mr. Curley's file. It was very interest-ing." she said, suddenly sounding excited.

"You were able to decode it?"

"That's impossible. Like I said, even if I had access to a supercomput-er, decoding it would take until the next ice age. No, what happened was I found the decoding software. Guess where it was." It had been a while since Warren had heard Cathy's bright voice.

"Inside Teddy's head?"

"Actually, you're not a world away with that answer. It was on Cindy's laptop. It's made for kids, but only a generation ago even the Pentagon used computers of a comparable power. Of course, the file had been de-leted once. Teddy came to ask me how to play a game on it, and that's when I tried out some retrieval software. Mr. Curley must have used the laptop at some point. Either that or he guessed that this might happen. In any case, we have to thank Cindy."

"So what was in it?"

"You just might get what you wanted."

"The Pulitzer Prize?" asked John. Warren elbowed him away.

"What else is there? When you pick up the prize, I expect to be the first one you thank."

"My very dream."

"Where's the file?" John butted in again.

"I just sent it via email."

Warren pointed at the computer and motioned for someone to turn it on. "How's Teddy?"

"Daddy, come home," came Teddy's little voice. "I haven't been to kindergarten for three days. Not that I care."

"I'll be home tomorrow or the day after. Look after mommy for me."

"We're fine. John told me the bomb was for you. So mommy and me are safe. But mommy got really mad at John and asked him to go help you right away."

"The truck and bear got lost but they're right here with me."

"Bring them back, okay?"

"I already put them in their boxes so they can take the trip back. Can you give the phone back to mommy?"

"Okay! The watch you gave me is working fine."

"He likes it more than the one I got him, because Superman's stronger than Mickey Mouse," Cathy said, doing her best to sound nonchalant, but her voice sounded a pitch higher than usual. Perhaps she was fighting back tears.

Warren's eyes were moist, too. "I'm really grateful."

"Considering what happened, we're doing all night. Kids don't really understand. He thinks it's kind of fun."

"Are the security guards with you?" John chimed in.

"They're standing next to me right now," said Cathy, sounding fed up.

Warren told her again that he'd do his best to return as soon as possible, then hung up. He hurried over to the computer, typed in his password and accessed his email, finding the message from Cathy. For the next hour, all four of them pored over the document.

Chapter 9
The Truth

Ken and Warren looked up at the edifice. The thirty-seven-story smart building gave no hint that it housed the headquarters of the world's second largest military contractor. Its glass walls shimmered in the sunlight, looking bright and clean, an epitome of modern America.

"Business as usual, even on New Year's Eve," observed Warren, watching people entering and leaving through the main entrance.

"Journalists are hardly different. Or does *The Washington Post* let its reporters take off all the way from Christmas?"

"I think one of the reasons my wife separated from me is news breaking at Christmas and New Year's."

"This year is no exception. In the new year, the Senate is going to pass the next-generation stealth bomber plan. That's why no one's taking time off. It's apparently going to be worth a total of 5.4 billion dollars."

There were security guards in uniform on either side of the main entrance, each with a gun and a radio attached to their belts.

Ken stopped walking and held his handkerchief over his nose. He felt like sneezing. He took several deep breaths until it passed.

"Nervous? So am I," said Warren.

"I just have a cold. These past few days have been a bit tough on my middle-aged body." His nose had become stuffy, which made it itch.

Warren swung the blue backpack he'd borrowed from Jimmy off his shoulder and held it in his hand.

The two of them walked through one of the three metal detectors at the entrance, but not before Ken had spent ten minutes explaining the metal pins in his knee. Warren had stood off to the side, a meek look on his face, but it was when he passed through the metal detector that the alarm went off. The security guard's hand hovered over the handle of his gun as Warren pulled his keyring from his pocket, deposited them in a nearby tray and then walked through again, the alarm silent this time.

"The security here is tighter than the White House," Warren whispered to Ken.

"I thought you had a gun."

"I gave it back to John."

"That was a smart move."

They entered a lobby with a high ceiling and polished marble floor. A one-tenth scale model of a B3A stealth bomber was on display in the center of the hall like a monument. The smart, mysterious 230-billion-dollar aircraft symbolized the future of this corporation, yet there was something ominous about it.

They walked up to the two receptionists, one blonde and one brunette. They both looked like they'd walked right out of a fashion magazine. They wore uniforms that accentuated their cleavage.

"We would like to see Thomas Dotwell, the CEO," requested Ken, taking out his press ID and showing it to the blonde receptionist.

"Do you have an appointment?"

"This is our first time here."

"The CEO won't see anyone without an appointment."

"Just tell him that Kenji Brian from *The Daily Californian* is here to discuss Dr. James Williams and Donald Fraser."

"And if he still doesn't want to meet us, tell him that Warren McCarthy from *The Washington Post* is also here to discuss Frank Curley," added Warren.

"As I said, to meet with the CEO you need an appoint—"

"You just need to relay what we said to the CEO."

"Do you really think I can speak directly to the CEO? Besides he has guests right—"

"Tell his assistant. As long as it reaches him in the end," said Ken, leaning forward. Fear ran across the blonde's face.

"Sir, I'm going to have to call security," she said, looking over to the group of three security guards, one of whom was walking towards them.

"All you need to do is give him the message. If you turn us away and the CEO hears about it, you'll be racing to find another job. But hey, maybe that's what you want."

The blonde glared at them as she lifted the phone. An assistant answered, and she spoke quietly while masking her mouth with her hand. From time to time she glanced up at Ken, and a security guard came and stood behind them, ready to pounce if needed.

"Tell him the ghosts of Dr. Williams and Frank Curley are here to see him," Ken urged the blonde. She hurriedly looked away, nodding as she listened.

"All right," she said. "He will meet with you. Take the first elevator on the right and go to the thirty-seventh floor. The assistant will be waiting for you," she instructed, looking surprised as she replaced the phone.

They walked towards the elevator. When they coolly glanced back, the receptionist and the security guard had their heads together conferring and looking over at them.

On the thirty-seventh floor they stepped out into a clean, bright hallway. The whole space felt as if it were artificially controlled. A man came out of a room at the end of the hallway and walked toward them.

"Mr. Kenji Brian and Mr. Warren McCarthy."

Ken nodded slightly.

"Please follow me."

The man headed back to where he had come from—a spacious room with floor-to-ceiling glass that had a fantastic view over San Francisco and the Golden Gate Bridge, beyond which lay the Pacific Ocean sparkling in the sunlight. A man was standing facing the window with his hands clasped behind his back. A 40" screen was built into the wall on one side. On the other wall were built-in shelves showcasing a lineup of expensive-looking porcelain pieces. Next to those were models of an F17 and an F18, like the replica in the lobby but just three feet long. Above those was an elaborate model of a fighter plane that Ken had never seen before. It had a smooth, flat body—a stealth fighter. Perhaps it was a prototype currently being developed.

As the two entered, the assistant bobbed his head slightly and left the room.

The man facing the window turned around slowly. It was Thomas Dotwell, the CEO of United Industries. Standing six foot two, he was reminiscent of a Hollywood star. His brown hair was half grayed and he had refined features. His eyes had a sharpness that could pierce anyone they settled on. He certainly looked like Donald Fraser.

"So how can I help journalists from *The Daily Californian* and *The*

Washington Post?" his calm voice echoed in the room.

"Your assistant must have told you. We want to ask you about two people," Ken answered.

"You each seem to be very involved with those two people. I should think you would know more about them than I do," said Dotwell, walking gracefully towards them.

"You probably haven't met them in person. Yet I'm sure you know all about what happened to them. You should know, since you're the one who orchestrated it."

"I don't know what you're talking about."

Ken glanced at the fighter-plane replica visible above Dotwell's shoulder. Its slick form matched both the man and his office.

"I understand that you are an ex-Marine," Dotwell said to Ken. "You were awarded the Silver Star. How do you like our Air Force?" Dotwell asked, following Ken's gaze.

There was a bar in the corner of the room that held a dozen liquor bottles and glasses. Dotwell walked over and began pouring himself a brandy. "Would you like one? I've heard you like the occasional drink," he offered with a faint smile.

"I'll pass. I don't think you have my brand."

"So, Mr. McCarthy. You've been writing about Curley's suicide," Dotwell remarked, turning to Warren.

"That's right. I'm claiming back his honor for the sake of his wife and daughter."

"So two journalists from our two coasts, 2,200 miles apart, have come to see me about re-establishing the honor of two men. But no matter what you might say, I know nothing."

"Maybe you'd prefer to talk about Donald Fraser? Your half-brother?"

Dotwell's calm expression wavered and his eyes darted away. It was only momentary, though, and he soon regained his composure.

"Excuse me taking a seat," Ken said. "I'm a bit of a coward. I can't sleep when something's bothering me. I only slept for two hours last night."

His right knee was heavy with a tingling pain, but sitting on the sofa relieved it, making his whole body feel lighter.

"At the end of November, I met Dr. Williams in San Diego. Then I met Donald Fraser some days later. The story begins there," Ken began as Dotwell, with typical grace, lifted his glass to his lips. "With regards to the series, just as with *Knowledgment* and *The Daily Washington,* the public and the media overlooked the heart of the issue. Instead of discussing the validity of the thesis we presented, the focus shifted to the freedom of press, freedom of speech and how classified government information should be handled. In the end, the government made large concessions. We thought the government had relented in the face of public opinion. But was this really true? Would the government have let actual top-secret information be made public so easily? They could have taken a number of measures, but they didn't. In the end, the existence of the Fourth Nuclear Weapon was made public. Or rather, the possibility of its existence was revealed. The key to this new bomb was that it could be made without using enriched uranium. What a sensational story. The military had already been applying this theory and conducting experiments. A majorly significant discovery not only for America, but for the whole world. If it were true, then just as the media reported, the number of countries with nuclear capabilities would increase exponentially. Such weaponry would no longer be the province of a select few countries. North Korea, Iran and Iraq could easily develop them because they could now be made from the same fuel used in nuclear power plants. In the face of such danger, there's no way anyone in this country could argue in favor of arms reduction. Do you understand where I'm headed with this?" Ken adjusted himself in the chair and breathed deeply.

"I don't know what any of this has to do with me. But are you trying to suggest that I'm trying to destroy the world?" Dotwell inquired.

"George Washington said, 'To be prepared for war is one of the most effectual means of preserving peace.' Although I don't agree, a surprising number of people do, especially among politicians. The Soviet Union greatly expanded their military for the dozen or so years before its demise. The Department of Defense and the CIA released reports stating that in the few years prior to its collapse, the Soviet Union's military power exceeded that of the United Sates. The world at that time had entered an unlimited arms race. I'm sure you know the details better than I do. After all, you were in the thick of it," offered Ken, looking to Dotwell for affirmation.

Dotwell held Ken's gaze with a calm expression.

"But the world changed after that," Ken continued. "The Soviet Union collapsed, the Berlin Wall came down and many Eastern European countries gained independence. For a time, the world reveled in the end of the Cold War. But then came the Gulf War and the wars in

Afghanistan and Iraq after 9/11. The United States is continually prioritizing the military in its policies, but its citizens are sick of war. America had to adopt a new way of thinking in order to move forward, just as Curley had suggested. The president nearly decided to change America's path. But after having his mind changed in cabinet meetings he's tried to get the next-generation stealth bomber passed by Congress. Just look at how Congress has behaved in the past few weeks. The plan, which had widely been expected to be shot down, was instead passed by a healthy margin in the House and will probably soon pass in the Senate. Furthermore, there are voices calling for an expansion of the defense budget to allow development for previously rejected proposals of modern weaponry, including neutron bombs, satellite-guided missiles and new recon satellites. Some are even saying that the halted Star Wars plan might be resurrected. Plus, bills relating to classified government information and reinforcing intelligence operations, which had been repeatedly rejected by Congress, were the subject of major debate for the first time since Watergate.

"Isn't that right, Mr. Donald Fraser?" Ken asked towards the door next to the bookcase. There was a clatter. "I know you're there. Why don't you come out and join the conversation?"

The air in the room, despite being perfectly air-conditioned, was hot and heavy, making it difficult to breathe. The three of them waited with their eyes fixed on the door.

At last the knob turned and the door opened. Donald Fraser walked in slowly, holding his pipe in his right hand.

"You are indeed quite sharp."

"I told you, I'm pretty dim." Ken touched the tip of his nose with his finger.

Fraser looked at the pipe in his right hand and smiled faintly.

"To return to our narrative," reprised Ken, "when the existence of the Fourth Nuke was made public, all talk of downsizing the military went out the window. The next-generation stealth bomber plan that was bound to be rejected was suddenly approved, redirecting the U.S.—no, the world—toward continued military expansion. Your times aren't over. You'll only grow bigger."

Scorching flames that had been concealed deep inside of Ken were flaring up.

"You spurred Congress into action by planting an implicit sense of crisis. Classified government information was leaked to a local newspaper and published. That's deeply embarrassing to the administration.

Nuclear bombs, which we Americans had all believed to be the ultimate weapon, could now be built by any country with nuclear power plants. Instilled with that sense of national crisis, members of Congress accordingly pushed for beefing up our military. Then the government decided to withdraw its order to suspend the series, pretending to show compassion and understanding."

"This is all just conjecture. You have no evidence to back any of this up," said Fraser in a calm voice.

"But before the news of the Fourth Nuke came out, several parties, including your brother's firm, bought up huge amounts of military industry stock. Their value, which had been hovering around historic lows, skyrocketed once rumors of the new bomb came out. You know who these people are. It even includes Northrop, the Republican Senator who supported defense cuts."

Ken turned his gaze to Dotwell. Though the CEO kept his mouth shut, he was sticking out his chest and staring off at a fixed point to mask his visible agitation.

"The presidential elections are coming up next year. United Industries, Aerocraft, Utiligent, Able Industry and Lytton Dynamics are all companies dependent on Pentagon contracts. They all made major donations during the previous election. They're powerful enough to influence presidential elections. Basically, top-level government officials are involved in this huge conspiracy."

Ken's knee started hurting again. He rubbed it until it relaxed.

"But there is another sad truth to this story. I believe this *Washington Post* reporter is far more knowledgeable about it than I am." Ken looked to Warren.

Warren nodded and stepped forward. "The late Senior Policy Advisor Frank Curley's daughter goes to the same kindergarten as my son. He was a kind and fair man who loved his family." He paused, staring at the sky for a few seconds as if to reaffirm his intent. He began speaking again, slowly. "The world has changed drastically in the past twenty years. The U.S. has changed, too. Since the ice melted between the Eastern and Western blocs, we've engaged in new wars. Every one uses vast amounts of arms, which leads to the production of new weapons. A never-ending cycle of meaningless, mindless consumption."

Warren carefully enunciated each word. "Now the U.S. is faced with a quandary: Revive a flagging economy or expand the military. The president arrived at a decision, but his decision was certain to incur the wrath of a group of firms. There was also fierce opposition from within his own administration, and the White House was split in two to the point of crisis. In this rift over whether to build up or build down the military, the president was in the middle, torn between the factions. It was Frank Curley who entertained the closest relationship to the president. They were friends and enjoyed a deep level of trust, the president seeking the relatively young advisor's opinion on many occasions. Curley was an excellent and fair man who loved his country and its people. He loved his family. That's why he made a proposal. He suggested to the president that the U.S. should prioritize peace instead of waging war."

Dotwell, glass still in hand, turned his back on Warren to look out of the window.

"This was obviously going to create enemies among those who stood to profit from the vast attritions of war. It was then that Dr. Williams' thesis became news. Classified information about a nuclear bomb was going to be published in a newspaper..." Warren glanced at Ken for confirmation, and Ken nodded. "But who was behind it? Whoever it was succeeded in sowing indelible fear in the minds of peoples around the world. This is exactly as the reporter from *The Daily Californian* said."

Warren paused and took a deep breath. Then he proceeded with care, choosing his words carefully. "By chance, Curley came to know about the conspiracy. It could be the biggest scandal the White House had faced since its inception. He knew that if the media were to get their hands on this information, the president would be forced out of office. But if Curley remained silent, the whole world would be left fearing the outbreak of a world war. I'm sure he suffered over his decision: Should he tell the truth to the people or protect the president? In the end, he came to a conclusion he deemed best. He tried to negotiate with you. I don't know if that decision was wise."

Warren fell silent and watched for Dotwell and Fraser's reactions. Ken coughed lightly, encouraging Warren to continue.

"Either way, he didn't report it to the president. Instead, he proposed an idea to you. Curley was ready to forget about the planned conspiracy if you would give up pushing for an arms race. This matches the White House's shift in policy around that time. Isn't that right, Mr. Fraser? Mr. Dotwell?" Warren prodded, watching them steadily. "Curley was holding all the chips. That's why he..."

Inordinate tension filled the room when Warren fell silent. Beads of sweat began to form on his brow.

"So you believe Frank Curley was murdered?" Fraser asked in a cold voice, breaking the silence.

"I don't know who actually did it or how. But it wasn't just murder. You even used his death." Warren raised his voice. "The reputation of Advisor Curley shifted 180 degrees. The media, which had supported him as a progressive young leader in the past, savagely turned on him. Public opinion was swayed by the media, and the White House power map was completely redrawn. As a result, the president leaned heavily toward expanding the military."

Isn't that right, asked Warren's eyes as he looked at Dotwell, who stubbornly maintained his silence.

"I knew Frank Curley. And I know he could never have done what he was accused of. He was murdered by—"

"That's enough," said Fraser, raising his right hand to cut Warren off. "You both seem to have quite fertile imaginations. But that's not necessarily suitable for journalists."

Fraser fixed his gaze on Ken. The strong smell of his tobacco permeated the room.

"Mr. Kenji Brian. You received the blueprint of the Fourth Nuke from Williams and published it. You received detailed information about it as well. The responsibility entirely lies with you. It was you who plunged the world into fear."

"This is where the issue gets complicated," Ken parried calmly. He looked down for a while, seemingly lost in thought. "Dr. Williams was dying from cancer. That is a fact. In his email he said he would probably never leave that bed. When I met him at the Naval Medical Center in San Diego, the nurse confirmed this fact. He wasn't well enough even to walk. And yet three weeks later I met him in a cabin in Yosemite. Or at least, I believed I did." A smile formed on Ken's lips. "But what if Dr. Williams had already died at the naval hospital? We found out that he died on the thirteenth of December, two weeks after I first visited him."

"Absurd…"

"That was the day before the blueprint for the Fourth Nuke was sent to me. His body was cremated and the ashes scattered from a helicopter over the Pacific Ocean. However, the funeral home kept a sample of his hair and nails. DNA analysis matched them with the DNA of Dr. James Williams. There was still a sample of his DNA in a lab used by the Naval Medical Center for testing."

Ken admired again the functional beauty of the fighter plane. It looked like a symbol of American might and projected a mysterious allure that calmed jangled nerves.

"The elderly man I met in the cabin in Yosemite was definitely not Williams. All one had to do was find someone who looked like him. A little plastic surgery made it perfect. The face of a man on his deathbed would change, anyway, so it's not really a surprise that I didn't make much of slight differences. In any case, it was easy for an organization like yours to fool me, since I'd only met the real Williams once. When I met the fake Williams, I was given the CD with detailed information about the Fourth Nuke. At least, that's what the world believed."

Ken sighed before continuing. "A scientist was suffering doubts over the meaning of his life. A journalist sympathized with the man. I don't know how you found out, but you learned of our existence. A local paper far away from the capital, with no major organization and unfamiliar with federal politics, was easy prey and made the news all the more sensational. You waited for Williams' death. Or perhaps you sped it up. You then created a new Dr. Williams and sent me a new blueprint. The Fourth Nuclear Weapon. But..."

Ken stood up slowly. A pain shot through his knee, but it was tolerable.

"The Fourth Nuke doesn't exist."

He looked up and glared at Fraser and Dotwell. Warren, standing to his side, silently gazed at the three men.

"Dr. Williams was certainly a bright scientist, but he wasn't a genius. I asked a friend of mine, a specialist who is also an excellent nuclear scientist, and he was very suspicious. He wondered where this information was from. According to him, with present technology it would be nearly impossible to cause nuclear fission in uranium-238 anywhere near the level of uranium-235. Of course, he couldn't be 100 percent certain. After all, scientists have realized feats that just ten years ago were considered impossible."

Dotwell was growing pale, as if he were being dragged into a dark, bottomless abyss.

"But that's beside the point," continued Ken. "All you had to do was hint at the possibility, to give the impression that such a nuclear bomb existed. The potential for a Fourth Nuke. That a large number of countries could now make nukes with ease."

Dotwell was standing completely still.

"Now you need to fix what you've done as any further confusion could very likely damage the United States and hurt the president, whom Curley sought to protect."

"No one will believe such an outlandish story," rasped Dotwell, at long last breaking his silence. His face was twisted in pain.

"Whether people believe it or not is up to them, but I'm going public with this."

Such are politics, Fraser's voice echoed in Ken's mind.

"Can I ask you something?" Ken put to Dotwell, who raised his head as if being pulled back to reality. "Was Dr. Williams part of this plan? Did he send me the email knowing all this?"

Dotwell didn't answer, instead settling himself slowly into a chair. He placed his hands on the desk and stared at them as long moments passed. Then he looked up at Ken and Warren.

"Do you have evidence?" he breathed out. "Do you have anything to back up this extravagant story?"

Ken looked at Warren, who took out a laptop from his backpack and placed it on the desk. The display flickered, lighting up to the startup screen. Warren moused the cursor around and clicked through. He finally entered a password and turned the display to face Fraser and Dotwell, who stared at it in silence.

"We found this on Frank Curley's computer. You had it deleted, but we managed to recover the file. He'd put together this document to negotiate with you. He was asking you to drop the idea of the next-generation stealth bomber in exchange for his keeping this document away from the media. So that the economy and peace, rather than expanding our military, would be our priority. But you declined his offer. Then…"

With each of Warren's clicks, a new image appeared on screen.

"There's no proof that Frank Curley wrote that."

"With this much information, the FBI or the D.C. police, pros, can uncover the truth. There was also a phone call for me the day before Curley was killed. Unfortunately I was out. He wanted to meet me and talk, to tell me what was about to happen on the West Coast. He was nervous and probably wanted to leave the document in my keeping."

"Is that all, then?" Fraser took several steps away from the computer and straightened up. He was holding a gun.

Warren turned off the laptop and shifted it ever so slightly.

"Come on, this isn't like you," Ken said, stepping toward Fraser with a glare.

"I'll simply say I shot two unlawful intruders who tried to blackmail the CEO with a trumped-up scandal. That's not incorrect."

"No one would believe you," Warren asserted, calmly tapping a key on the laptop. Suddenly, the display lit up showing Fraser on the screen holding the gun. "Video conference software. Just like the ones you probably use for teleconferences at this firm. Dr. Williams used it, too." When Warren tapped another key, an African American with a nervous expression appeared. "This video is being sent to my friend's computer. Of course, it's being recorded and can be played back, too. What a world."

The black man coughed and sat up straight. "This is MPDC lieutenant John Morse." Jimmy was standing behind him. "We've been listening to your conversation. I'm waiting for my two friends to return. If they're not back in an hour, I'm sending this video to the station. And these, too," said John, waving a few CDs. "They contain the files Curley was using to negotiate with you. You've already seen them. After all, you ransacked his house looking for the originals. These also contain records written by the two journalists there, this other journalist here, and myself. We have enough evidence to prove that Curley was murdered. Don't forget it. This is also going to serve as insurance for those two. I predict a long, bitter winter for you and the White House."

"Three people have died already. I certainly hope there will be no further casualties," Ken said, turning off the laptop.

Fraser stayed frozen to the spot, gazing at the darkened display. He looked as pale as if he'd seen a ghost. Dotwell walked over, gently took the gun from his grip and placed it down on the desk. He stared in a daze at his brother.

"We'll be going now. We have a lot to do. You probably need to call your lawyers, too."

Ken tapped Warren on the shoulder. Warren turned to him as if snapping out of a daydream.

They walked to the door. When Ken looked back with his hand on the doorknob, Dotwell was just sitting there with his eyes closed and his head in his hands.

The two reporters started making their way back to the elevator.

The office door shut, then opened again immediately. Fraser burst out.

The assistant opened his own door but closed it in a panic when Fraser yelled at him to step back inside.

"How about a million dollars? Each. For both of your friends too," Fraser, catching up with Ken, offered.

Ken ignored him and kept on walking.

"I'll make it two million."

Ken stopped and looked at Fraser. "I thought you had more pride than that. At least your brother does."

"Then how about you two run a newspaper together? I'll buy *The Daily Californian*. Grow it into the largest paper in the country. It'll be worth the effort."

Ken sighed, shook his head and hastened his steps toward the elevator. As the doors opened, he paused before stepping in.

Ken and Warren looked at each other. Fraser looked stricken.

A high-pitched sound and muffled echo had come from the room at the end of the corridor. The assistant stepped out of his office next door and looked at Fraser for a cue.

Fraser ran toward the room, the sound of his steps echoing through the hallway. The elevator doors silently slid shut.

When the elevator opened onto the lobby, frantic security personnel were hustling to and fro. One guard shouted into the phone, "We need an ambulance, quick!"

Ken and Warren stepped out of the United Industries building.

The sun had already set, and cold air wrapped around them. Ken clutched his collar close.

They walked the streets of San Francisco. A throng of teenagers wearing jeans with combs stuck in their back pockets rushed past, shouting and hollering. New Year's fireworks crackled in the distance though there were still seven hours until midnight.

"I'm impressed you knew Fraser was there. The pipe. I didn't notice."

"I have a cold, remember? The receptionist had said he had a guest, but we didn't pass anyone in the hall and no one was in the office. So I knew he must have been in the adjacent room. I thought it was probably someone we knew, and someone close to Dotwell. But it was mostly a guess."

"Can I ask you something?" Warren requested meekly.

"If it's something I can answer."

"When did you realize Curley's death was connected to Dotwell and Fraser?"

"Just last night. But it was all still a theory. I had to see them in person to confirm it."

"And your conjecture was dead-on."

"Seeing as they didn't deny it, it's probably true. But you knew it, too."

"When did you realize Dotwell was the mastermind?"

"I had a gut feeling when Jimmy said Dotwell and Fraser were half-brothers. I didn't know for sure. Besides, I didn't say Dotwell had planned everything."

"Then who did?"

"Ask them." Ken frowned slightly.

"What do you think will happen now?"

"I don't know…" Ken fell silent for a while. "But we can be sure they'll put together one hell of a legal team. They've got the money and the connections. I don't know how much of Curley's files can be considered evidence. If we can set the record straight about the non-existent Fourth Nuclear Weapon, that's all I ask for. It's not like the government ever announced it in a press release. It was just a media-created frenzy. Such a bomb never existed. But it'll still make people feel nervous. What if such a weapon really existed… And that's all those guys needed, darkness in our hearts. That fear is the real Fourth Nuke. No one will simply take us at our words. It's all just my conjecture, after all."

"It's the truth," said Warren, his voice filled with confidence.

"We're going up against a monster," chuckled Ken. "We're too small and weak."

"This is just the beginning. Time to test the power of journalism."

The letter from Williams, his voice on the phone and the words of Fraser and Yamada all passed through Ken's mind.

A dark stain spread on his shoulder. He stopped and looked up at the sky. It was starting to rain San Francisco's wintry rain.

As they passed a restaurant, Ken saw their faces reflected in the window. The face he was used to seeing looked pale and ghostly.

When he closed his eyes, he could see flames burning. The entire world was burning with crimson flames, the oceans turned red with lava. The word Yamada had uttered came to mind: a meltdown. The heavy stress of the past month coursed through Ken's body like a bout of drunkenness tinged with nausea.

He closed his eyes and remembered what Jimmy had said to him at his sister's hospital.

My God, what have we done? Those were the words of the co-pilot of the Enola Gay, the B29 that bombed Hiroshima. *What on Earth have we done?*

When he opened his eyes again, he saw Warren staring at him with a worried expression.

"What's wrong?" asked the *Post* reporter.

"Nothing."

As if spewing out everything there was to, Ken let out a deep sigh and started walking again.

The sky over San Francisco was clear. The azure winter sky and the chilly breeze bearing the ocean's humidity were refreshing enough to be bracing.

On the first day of the new year, the airport was bustling with people both returning from and departing to vacations. Fully armed anti-terrorism personnel could be spotted all over the place. Both the CIA and the FBI had announced new terror threats around New Year's.

Ken and Ann were there to see off Warren and John.

"The District's experiencing a cold front," Warren noted. "My son told me over the phone this morning that it snowed almost eight inches last night."

Ann smiled. "Teddy, right? He's so cute. He sounds smart, too."

Warren had shown them a photo of Teddy when they were having dinner together the night before.

"You sure you don't want to come to—"

"No thanks," said Ken. "I'm not cut out for big cities."

After dinner, Warren had asked Ken if he'd be interested in working in D.C.

"But you could easily get a job with the *Post*."

"I like Barton," said Ken, smiling at John.

"Well, I guess I like D.C., and I'll take the MPDC over the FBI any day," John chimed in, slapping Ken on the shoulder.

"Then you should at least visit. I want to introduce you to Cathy and Teddy."

"When we meet next time, we'll be a family of three, too."

Ken was able to get the words out honestly. Ann silently wrapped her arm around his.

The child would be Caucasian. A child who didn't share his blood... It would have been a lie to say that he'd entirely come to terms with his fate, but he was able to accept the reality.

"Ann, your apple pies are truly amazing. I'll come again just for another taste. Reason enough," John thanked with a serious expression as he shook Ann's hand.

"We should write a book together," suggested Warren, his face tense. "We could call it *The Fourth Nuclear Weapon: A White House Conspiracy* —shoot for a Pulitzer."

"You're on."

"There'd better be mention of the super cop in the MPDC."

"I'd like Jimmy on board, too."

"Of course."

"How about if we go with *The Fourth Nuclear Weapon: A Scientist's Confession* instead?"

"We'll talk about that."

"Who's the main character? Not the two of you, I hope," cajoled Ann as she placed her hand on her stomach. She was just starting to show.

"A lonely old man. Plus another man who loved his country and family."

Dr. Williams. He had probably been totally unaware of the conspiracy, just an old scientist who sought confirmation for his life but ended up being used instead. And Frank Curley, an aide who'd sacrificed his life to safeguard nation and family. They were the ones who really deserved a Pulitzer.

"Just don't write about me, or our child'll hate me. I took a dip in the ocean in the middle of winter while six months pregnant." Ann stopped walking and a smile spread across her face. "I just felt a kick."

She took Ken's hand and placed it on her belly. He felt the baby's movement.

They looked up and saw a jet describing a wide arc, heading out over the Pacific.

About the Author

Tetsuo Takashima was born in 1949. After working for Japan Atomic Energy Research Institute, he moved to California, where he studied at the University of California. Upon his return to Japan, he began writing while managing a private preparatory school. *Fallout* won the 1994 Shosetsu Gendai Mystery Newcomer Award. Other novels include the action thriller *Intruder*, which won the 1999 Suntory Mystery Award. He has written more than twenty novels in the action/thriller/suspense/mystery genres.